Praise for The Alliance: Book One of the Faeltheon

Reminiscent of George R.R. Martin in style and originality, this complex and creative inspirational fantasy is sure to engage, intrigue and delight readers. *The Alliance: Book One of the Faeltheon* is a timeless tale of duty, faith and trust in our Creator.

—Vicki Hinze, award-winning author

Read just a few pages and you'll understand why I recommend this book so enthusiastically. *The Alliance* is simply magnificent.

—James BeauSeigneur, author of *The Christ Clone* trilogy

This fantasy novel offers adventure, mystery, and romance while staying true to its Christian themes. I especially recommend it to young adults who may find parallels in their own lives to the struggles of the youthful faeries and elves who are searching for the right path while being tested in their faith. I highly recommend this book and am already anxiously awaiting the others."

—Virginia Loman, lawyer

I truly and deeply enjoyed reading *The Alliance*. It is the beginning of an epic journey that touches the reader in a meaningful and enjoyable way—teaching as it entertains. The values expressed by these three young authors and their former teacher are wholesome, giving a well-rounded worldview that will inspire both the young and the old. I recommend it highly to anyone who loves the worlds of Lewis and Tolkien, and to anyone looking for an alternative to the darker literature so popular with young people today. Parents, teachers, students: add this to your libraries—you won't be sorry.

—Polly Thorpe, former middle school teacher

My kids and I have absolutely LOVED reading *The Alliance*. It is masterful storytelling and keeps you on the edge of your seat the whole way through. If you enjoy fantasy, you will LOVE the first book of the Faeltheon!

—Mary Henry, author, business owner, and mother of two

The art in this book was wonderful! The story keeps a great pace and has a wonderful message that occurs in undertones throughout the story. The fact that the authors are teacher and students is another plus to reading this book.

—Jason Rodarte, high school teacher

Run Before The Wind

Book Two of the Faeltheon

Run Before The Wind

Book Two of the Faeltheon

Rachel DiDomenico
Chrystine Kern
Samantha Ward
Michele Yardumian

Tate Publishing & *Enterprises*

Published by Tate Publishing & Enterprises, LLC
127 E. Trade Center Terrace | Mustang, Oklahoma 73064 USA
1.888.361.9473 | www.tatepublishing.com

Tate Publishing is committed to excellence in the publishing industry. The company reflects the philosophy established by the founders, based on Psalm 68:11,
"The Lord gave the word and great was the company of those who published it."

Cover design by Kandi Evans
Interior design by Nathan Harmony
Cover art and interior illustrations by Michele Yardumian

Published in the United States of America

ISBN: 978-1-60696-626-6
1. Fiction: Fantasy: General
2. Fiction: Christian: Fantasy
09.03.19

This book is lovingly dedicated to our parents:
Debbie and Eric DiDomenico
Cathy and David Kern
Mary and Brad Ward
Jean and Joe Yardumian
and
Evelyn Durgarian.
Thank you for always believing in us, thus giving
us the freedom to believe in ourselves.

We also dedicate this book with reverent love
to the Creator Who chose to be our Father.
May our work bless You, bring You glory,
and further the work of Your Kingdom.

Ea randal
Ai yeonder
Cyb ear ren
Ende yori randia

ACKNOWLEDGMENTS

The authors would like to thank the many people who have helped us make this series a reality. We cannot name you all, but we would like to make special note of a few whose help was above and beyond the call of friendship.

Thanks to our families and friends who helped edit this work, including, but not limited to: Rachel & Alex Nagy, Jean & Joe Yardumian, Judy Schaab, Deborah Newren, Sarah Rehberg, Molly Weber, James & Geri BeauSeigneur, Carolee Brown, and Roz Leyba. Thanks, "Grandma Y," for making the publication process possible for us.

Thank you to Randy Stonehill and Ray Ware for permission to use Randy's outstanding lyrics.

Thanks to Ruth Searle at University of Wales, Swansea, for information about dolphins and the Sargasso Sea.

Appreciation and thanks go to the wonderful team at Tate Publishing. We really value your love and enthusiasm!

Most of all, and beyond all others, we would like to thank the Lord for His sovereign grace and mercy, and for the gift of creativity. Thanks, Lord, for allowing us to be a part of Your work.

Contents

Icon Index

 Chassidy

 Marliondolen

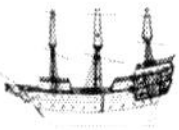 the Land

 Elves at sea

 Corot

 Pirates

 Egauswas

Prologue

She was surrounded by beauty that was stunning in its awesome power. As if captured in a kaleidoscope of a rainbow, color and light shimmered and refracted on every side, until she knew not where to look. Even as her eyes opened to their widest to soak in all possible delight, her soul warned her to turn away her gaze before her heart was utterly broken.

Before her stood the forms of the most beautiful people she had ever seen, the almost alien perfection of their faces and features dimmed by the light that radiated from their pure souls. The living flame that was Theomanus stood wavering not ten paces from her own feet, and, one by one, her dearest friends and companions were passing through the heart of him and disappearing into the unknown that was Marliondolen. The light that flickered from the Master's body cast dancing refractions over faces solemn and joyful, over clothing spun of dragon silk, over the sun-drenched grass that seemed so dull by comparison to those who stood so lightly upon it for the last time.

Tears coursed down Chassidy's face, yet did not blur her sight, as one beloved face after another passed before her and departed the world forever.

The beauty would choke her.

The loss would kill her.

How would she survive when these noble beings were gone?

Though many Faeltheon still held the line behind her, only Elwyn and Elrad, standing on either side of Theomanus and facing the approaching Faeries, were faces she knew now. Still the parade of beauty marched slowly past her. Face after face, tall form after graceful figure, the Faeries were leaving the world.

Because of her.

Her tears turned to fire and burned her throat, pouring like liquid grief down her face. She wanted to cry out, to scream her anguish, to protest their leaving, to fight the utter desolation she sensed would surround her when they were no more. Elwyn, the last Queen of Faerie, turned her eyes to Chassidy's, a world of compassion and understanding in their violet depths.

Chassidy felt her heart break and wondered if she would be forced to live with the tearing pain, or if, mercifully, it would someday heal over. Despite her lack of years, she was wise enough to know that one didn't die of a broken heart; one merely wished escape could be so easy. Still, acknowledging herself culpable, Chassidy knew she did not deserve such a quick and merciful end to her torment.

She watched the faces of the Fair Folk as they passed her, many with a smile for her and a sympathetic look, and wondered in her heart that they could be so composed, so peaceful, embarking on this unprecedented journey into the unknown. She knew their faith in the Creator was deep and broad and sustaining, but she had never before seen such faith in action. Some of the Faeltheon were singing as they passed, and Chassidy knew that their tune would haunt her heart forever, even when she could no longer remember it. She had a fleeting wish that she could know the meaning of the words they were singing in their ethereally lovely voices.

Another swelling of the tempest within her brought a fierce longing: if only she might have been granted more than just the past few weeks with this wise, ancient people. Oh, what she could have learned from them! They, who still spoke the original tongue and could talk with the animals and even some of the trees, could have taught her so much about communication! They, who took centuries to weave a tapestry or the branches of a living house, could have taught her so much about artistry beyond mere craft or skill! They, who willingly gave up near-immortality to obey the Creator, and did so without rancor toward her or her kind, could have taught her so much about how she was to live the barren, short, unbearably dreary life that now faced her!

How was she to bear it? With the passing of these Folk, all that was potentially beautiful in herself seemed to be drawn out of her, the way a parchment draws dye, sucked from her soul like marrow from her bones. *How was she to bear it?*

Dashing the scalding tears from her eyes once more, Chassidy saw that there were only one or two more Faeries left to pass through that bright, living portal. In another breath, only Elrad and Elwyn remained.

Then, *oh too soon—too soon*, Elwyn stood before her, frail to the point of transparency, yet strong as the strongest sunlight, holding out to her a last gift. This parting, surely the hardest of them all, nearly undid Chassidy. How could she find the words to tell the Faerie queen what the brief time of their friendship had meant to her? How could she tell her how the mere knowledge that the Faeltheon existed had changed her? How could she begin to convey to Elwyn how the wisdom, beauty, goodness, and compassion of her people had shaped Chassidy's faith and her understanding of life and the world? How could she speak at all, choked as she was by the tears of a deep and fathomless grief?

In the end, no words came forth, yet a measure of Elwyn's peace was granted Chassidy. Her heart breaking with love and grief, she accepted her necklace, and stood watching, holding little Chloe, as the last Faerie stepped through her husband's soul, drawing him with her into the unknown, leaving the two sisters alone at the end of the world.

The meadow remained innocently green and lush in the winter sunlight, unaware of the miracle that had transpired in its midst. The absence of the Faeries from the land left a deep, hollow feeling in Chassidy's heart. For a time, it was as though all beauty and color had fled, leaving the world painted in drab, uninspired mediocrity. Her strength spent in grief, Chassidy sank down to the cool grass, holding Chloe in her lap. After a few minutes, the baby grew bored and wandered off to inspect the small bundles of possessions left behind by the departing Faeries. Chassidy simply sat, motionless, unseeing.

©M. YARDUMIAN

After a very long time, Chassidy became aware that the grass had gone from cool to cold and there was a chill in the darkening air. Night approached and she had not moved all afternoon. Gradually, awareness of her surroundings penetrated her numb mind. Not far away, she could hear the chuckling sound of water over rocks and the solemn song of the wind in the trees of the nearby Western Wood.

Gathering herself, she rose stiffly, ignoring the pain of her back and legs. Looking around, she spied Chloe, curled up asleep in the deep grass of the meadow. When Chassidy reached her, she saw with compassion the tear streaks on the child's face and knew she had cried herself to sleep. Wearily, Chassidy began to collect the discarded packs of the Faeries. When she had them all, she found a sufficient amount of food to keep herself and Chloe for two or three days, as well as a carved bowl and spoon, a few horn cups, a serviceable knife, and a few garments. Taking the bowl, the knife, and two of the larger carry-sacks, she set off toward the sound of the water.

Not far away, she found the small stream, cold and clear and bracing. There were a few trees along its banks and sufficient twigs and small branches on the ground to make a comfortable fire. She gathered the debris, using the knife on some of the longer pieces, and stuffed it in the packs, then stooped and filled the bowl with water. She returned to the meadow and started a small fire burning in a circle of stones. A short time later Chassidy had her little sister awakened and washed with cool water from the bowl, and Chloe sat nearby, messily consuming a fig cake and a wedge of soft cheese. When their meal was done and the baby was bedded down in the folds of a goose down-lined cloak, Chassidy prepared to face the long, dark night.

Sleep must have caught her unaware, for she was wakened abruptly by Chloe's sobs. Rousing groggily, Chassidy realized the toddler was crying in her sleep. Listening, the older sister recognized a familiar mantra.

"Nauska!" the baby wept pathetically. "Want Nauska!"

Despairing, wrenched afresh with grief in the lonely night, Chassidy gathered up her sister's small, sturdy form and rocked her till she quieted once more. Though she held the child for the rest of the night, Chassidy had never felt so alone.

For Chassidy, the next day was a weary trial of chilly wind, fussy baby, and empty heart. Knowing the party of men that searched for them would likely find them within a day or two, she set about clearing away all evidence of the Faeltheon. The food she kept, in the plainest of the carry-sacks, as well as the simplest cloaks she could find to protect herself and Chloe from the wind. The rest, even the beautifully carved bowl and spoon, she burned as fuel on their makeshift hearth. It broke her heart afresh to do so, but the ground was too hard and cold for her, with the one small knife, to dig deeply enough to bury the beautiful things. It hurt her to destroy such beauty and craftsmanship, but she didn't want the men to ask too many questions she knew she wouldn't be able to answer.

It didn't occur to her until late afternoon that the search party might have tracked them through the castle itself and have already seen the beautiful work of the Faeltheon before they ever reached the meadow. When this thought came to her, she bowed her head and wept for the things she had destroyed, perhaps without need.

Several times during that long day Chloe cried for Nausika, refusing to be comforted. Finally, Chassidy sat down with her and cried too for loss of those bright beings, those true friends. She wondered, in the calm after their storm of weeping, if anyone else in all the world would have the wit or wisdom to sense how the world itself was changed, skewed, by the departure of this unfallen people. Chassidy felt so clearly how the very fabric of the world she had always known was now warped, because of the absence of those beings it had never acknowledged. It seemed obvious to her that it must be so: that the world, twisted by sin into its present tortured shape, must itself be further changed by the removal of the few sinless folk that had shared its exile from the Creator. Surely, with the departure of these pure ones, whatever forces exulted in the fall of the once-perfect creation must be strengthened and must rejoice.

With a heartfelt sigh, Chassidy wondered if the Elves, the Kindred of the Faeries who remained in their great City by the sea, would indeed survive to take their ships southward in the spring. Would the families of Laslorn and Theomanus and of the other Elves who had entered into Marliondolen escape discovery by the Goblins and Humans? Would they succeed in finding the island of their birth, as Chassidy had been told was their goal, and would they ever know what fate had befallen their Faerie Kin?

As the sun was setting, slanting dark golden beams across the meadow and washing the world with departing light, Chassidy looked up from tending the fire to see what Chloe was doing. Finding the child safely occupied with a handful of orange wildflowers, Chassidy was just turning back to her task when she spied movement out of the corner of her eye. She was on her feet in an instant, straining to see through the gloaming. In another moment she was sure: it was a flame she saw—a torch most likely, and it was moving toward their fire, coming up from the south. Remembering the Map of the Realm in Elwyn's office, Chassidy realized with quick relief that the search party must have found their way to the higher curve of the River Fleet and followed it north to the meadow, bypassing the castle altogether.

Soon, she could hear the sounds of men on the wind and recognized her father's voice. She was surprised at the warm squeeze she felt in her heart when she heard the familiar tones. Her old life was coming to claim her again. Though her spirit was weighed down, somehow she knew that her future, even devoid of the liveliness of the light and love that was embodied in the Faeries, would still be worth living for having known them. When she saw the tall figure in the front of the cluster of men break away from the others and start a shambling run toward them, she picked up Chloe and went to meet her father's embrace.

The next day, the party left the meadows and headed south, following the River Fleet, which eventually would lead them back to their own territory. At the last possible moment, Chassidy turned back for a final glimpse of the meadow. Under the fitful light of an overcast sky, it didn't seem a place out of the ordinary. Looking at it now, one would never guess at the supernatural events that had taken place there only days before. Knowing her life had been forever and irrevocably changed by the amazing events of the past few weeks, culminating in the spectacular display of the passage into Marliondolen, Chassidy found it hard to believe that everything was now so . . . prosaic, so ordinary and unremarkable. No one would ever believe her story, if she told them the truth of it, but in her heart, Chassidy cherished the changes made in her by her association with the Faeltheon. As her father's voice summoned her, Chassidy turned away from the meadow and the invisible site of the departure of the Faeries from the world.

Coming suddenly awake in the pale dawn light, with the chill of tears on her cheeks, Chassidy realized that all the rich experiences she had just relived had been but a dream. Again.

The memories were so vivid and realistic in this dream that no matter how often it recurred, she never knew it for a dream, but thought she was living the events for the first time. Though the dream had haunted her sleep for months now since her return home, the tangled and juxtaposed emotions wrenched her heart afresh.

Knowing there would be no return to peaceful sleep that morning, Chassidy arose as silently as possible, so as not to wake the little sister huddled under their colorful quilts. With fingers shaking from the intensity of the dream, Chassidy pulled her dress over her shift and fastened the simple wooden buttons all the way up to her neck. Shivering, she crossed to the one window their attic room boasted. Kneeling upon the planed wood floorboards, she crossed her arms on the rough wooden sill. Resting her chin on her forearms, unmindful of the gradual coloring of the gray sky, the girl struggled to lift a morning prayer, seeking solace for her aching heart.

The transition to home life after that great and sad adventure had been difficult, to say the least. She and her family had been overjoyed to be reunited once more, and Chassidy and Chloe had enjoyed the open cherishing their parents had lavished upon them through the long winter months. Yet Chassidy, a little wiser and more mature for her exposure to the Faeltheon, had also realized the awful toll losing both of them had placed upon her parents' hearts. Though it had turned out all right in the end, Chassidy was less heedless in her actions now, mindful of her mother, who was still thinner and frailer than she had been before all the trouble began. No one spoke of their exploit, nor even referred to it obliquely in her mother's hearing. Chassidy knew talk had gone round the village after the men had returned with them, and she was pretty sure the story had grown in its retelling around the hearthfire in the pub.

Even now, months later, there were mothers who pulled their children away if Chassidy walked by. Of her old friends, only Clara still spoke to her naturally, though the others were coming around. After all, a whole season had passed, and Chassidy was no different for being "lost in the Forest," except perhaps for a little added maturity in her outlook, but that could be put down to her age. With spring approaching, all the young maidens were thinking about possible matrimonial arrangements, and Chassidy was no exception, so things were getting back to normal.

Still, with the awful silence that Chassidy felt she could not break came the necessity to bear her grief alone. Though she had known the Faeltheon for less than a month, the impact of their personalities and culture had been so powerful that losing them, especially knowing the part she'd been forced to play in their destruction, had brought an equally intense emptiness and grief to the girl.

My life is different—richer—thanks to you, she mused, her thoughts on her lost friends, as the rising sun bathed the new day in gold. *But what about you? My actions destroyed your way of life and drove you from your home into the unknown realm of Marliondolen. Are you happy there? What will your lives be like? Will we ever meet again? I wish I could know that you're all well and happy. I wish I could know it for sure ...*

Laslorn and Theomanus sat leisurely under a large birch tree in Marliondolen, waiting for their wives to join them. Though the Faeries and Elves who had escaped into Marliondolen had been there for some time now, they did not know exactly how long, for there seemed to be no sense of the passage of time. There was a dreamlike quality to their existence here; the days drifted by in wonder, one much like the others. They were still amazed by the tranquil beauty of the haven the Creator had provided for them. There were broad, rolling meadows, lushly carpeted in wildflowers of every hue. The music of streams and waterfalls wafted on the gentle breezes, as did the exotic and luscious scents of the many flowers and herbs that grew in wild profusion all around. The Faeltheon were comforted by thick forests whose familiar trees recalled their lost home. They also felt much closer to the Creator in this place, because it was free from Humans and Goblins.

In the aftermath of the thirty-day scourge of the *Finnal Izhodan*, the relentless pursuit of the Goblin army, and the invasion of the Land by Men, those who had found sanctuary in this cool green land were more than grateful for its peaceful bounty. Many had been lost to the fading curse or had fallen in those last defensive battles. The remnant who had escaped was small. When those beleaguered survivors had finally reached the legendary haven, their rejoicing was doubled. Not only had they found safety, but here waiting for them were the loved ones they thought they had lost forever, for the dead had been gathered into Marliondolen just before them.

Laslorn and Nausika had spent much of their time getting acquainted and reacquainted with his mother, Elamani, who had died when Laslorn was a boy. Both Theomanus and Elwyn had found their parents shortly after they had entered Marliondolen, and Elwyn had rejoiced further in finding her dear Captain Tal alive and well and awaiting her with open arms. Lucina and Davin had been reunited with their good friend Kier. Others had experienced similar joyful meetings.

In the rich peace of Marliondolen, Laslorn and Theomanus had ample time to court the wives they had married so hastily. It had been a very happy interlude, and the four friends spent nearly every hour together, learning one another's ways and discovering new depths in each other's characters. Now, hearing mirth upon the breeze, the brothers turned in unison to see Elwyn and Nausika approaching, talking and laughing, as always. Theo was grateful anew to see the sparkling health that shone from Elwyn now. It was a vibrant contrast to the pale wraith she had become just before the end of their time in the Land.

"It's about time you two finally showed up!" Laslorn teased. Nausika tried her hardest to glare at him but was unable to maintain her mock severity when he pretended to look hurt. She burst out laughing and rumpled his hair, darting quickly out of his reach. During this byplay, Theomanus was stealing a kiss from the willing Elwyn, which Laslorn caught out of the corner of his eye.

"All right, that's enough, you two!" he cried with a laugh, securing his airborne wife by one slim ankle and hauling her down into his arms. Laughing from sheer good spirits, the four companions settled under the tree.

A gradual shimmering built in the air nearby, arresting their attention. The Elves immediately stood to investigate, their wives but a step behind. Even as they reached the spot, the shimmering wavered and solidified into a window of sorts; at least, they could look through a gap into something that was not the meadow before them.

They had been presented with one of these portals before, soon after their entry into Marliondolen. Similar windows had appeared to various small groups of the Faeltheon, and they had been shown their relatives in the Elven City and in the outlying homes in mountain valleys and coastal villages. In each passing picture, a family was struggling with the disappearance of their kin. The viewers had not known what to make of the scenes they were shown. A sense of unease for the grief of the Kindred left behind had come over them, and they had separated to private places to pray for their loved ones.

Theomanus was still uncertain as to the purpose behind these glimpses the Creator had granted them of their former world. Now it seemed they were to receive another. A strong urge to look came over them, and Theo recognized the touch of the Creator's Spirit. Exchanging curious glances, the four drew near and peered in.

As their eyes searched the view before them, they recognized the faraway landscape as that of their former home; the fields north of the castle, extending to the Western Wood. The Land was greening with early spring growth, but it could not compare to the lovely, lively beauty of Marliondolen.

No sooner had they recognized the familiar landmarks then they noticed a pair of Elven scouts waiting near the orchard behind the castle. The watchers searched farther and saw the scouts were waiting for another pair, who were coming up from the direction of the Great Birch Forest. Elwyn was reminded of the Map of the Land, that enchanted tapestry that could allow the user to see things hidden in the depths of the map, for as they focused on the meeting of the two pairs of scouts, they could suddenly hear and see them very clearly. It was obvious from their conversation that they had been sent out by King Beregos to see if any Faeries remained in the Land and were now on their way back to the Court of the Elven King.

"We searched all the way down to the Southern Border and found nothing but abandoned homes and the ravaged castle. We could find no sign of the Faeries. The signs of war were old enough to have been from before the winter," one of the scouts from the second pair reported to the others.

"After you had been gone a few weeks, King Beregos sent us to see what had become of you. We got as far as the castle, where we discovered these items." The leader of the other pair gestured to the sack on his back. "We saw your signs and waited here for you to catch up."

"What did you find to take?" asked the other scout. "We didn't stop to look beyond the first glance, for we had a long journey ahead."

"We found a few personal items in the rooms of the towers, things the Goblins overlooked. We did not remove any beyond those we deemed necessary, but their presence suggests the Faeries and those of our Kin who dwelt among them must have left suddenly, not even pausing to take treasured heirlooms!"

"What clues did these items give you?" asked the younger scout.

"Clues to who might have been at the palace in the end. For example, we found a hair ornament in the Queen's Tower. It was a silver and platinum comb, inlaid with brilliant indigo, deep green, and glorious aqua stones of exquisite workmanship. It had to have been fashioned by Tiros himself! From the look of the carved birch branches and the colors of the stones, I would guess it belonged to someone in the Brithoniel Family, someone who had to leave without it."

"Nausika!" exclaimed Elwyn. "That must have been the hair comb your mother gave you."

"I loved that comb!" mourned Nausika. "It was so beautiful the way the birch branches intertwined. Mother gave it to me for my sixteenth birthday."

Elwyn looked down and smoothed her wedding band, one of the few things from before that had survived their passage into Marliondolen. "Tiros always did such lovely work."

"Still does," remarked Laslorn. "Now, listen!"

The guards had gathered around the one who bore the pack as he removed it and revealed the contents.

"We are reasonably sure that Theomanus and Laslorn were there at the palace, because we found Theomanus's family ring in the Even' Tower." He displayed the bright circle, the gem flashing in the sun.

"Good," murmured Theo. "I was hoping they would find that. I left it there so they could know we had been there to the last and would perhaps realize what happened."

"That was good thinking, Theo. Father and Robse are clever enough to put our absence together with your prophecy and that note I sent them and guess that you had become the Master of Marliondolen and led us to safety."

The scout reverently pulled out a larger object swathed in white linen, carefully unwrapping it for his companions to see.

"We believe the Seer Elrad was also with them, as we found these Ancient Scrolls in his suite at the Even' Tower." The others sucked in their breaths at this narrow escape, one voicing their common thought.

"It's a good thing the Goblins didn't take or desecrate those!"

"True. They destroyed almost everything of beauty or value. If they had known how precious these Scrolls were, I'm sure they would have taken them too," the leader replied, carefully repacking the items in his bag.

His companion shared out some waybread among them all, and, munching, they set out in a ground-eating jog through the Western Woods toward the coastal City of the Elven king, eager to show Beregos what they had found.

"Laslorn, do you know any of those scouts?" Nausika asked.

"I'm not sure. Let me get a closer look at their faces. Do you recognize them, Theo?"

"I don't think so. Wait! The picture is pulling away, getting wider! We can see almost the whole Land of Faerie. I wonder what the Creator wants us to see this way." They all drew nearer to the window, peering all about, searching. Laslorn squinted, striving to focus on something that caught his eye.

"There's some sort of movement in the south," he alerted the others. They watched for a time, until they could get a clearer glimpse of what they were seeing. A look of horror came over the normally jovial countenance of Laslorn.

"Are those—" Elwyn's words stopped short, as the tiny black forms became clear.

"Goblins," Nausika finished for her.

They watched intently as the unbelievably huge mass of the enemy army marched northward, toward the Court of the Elven King.

Part I

The Land

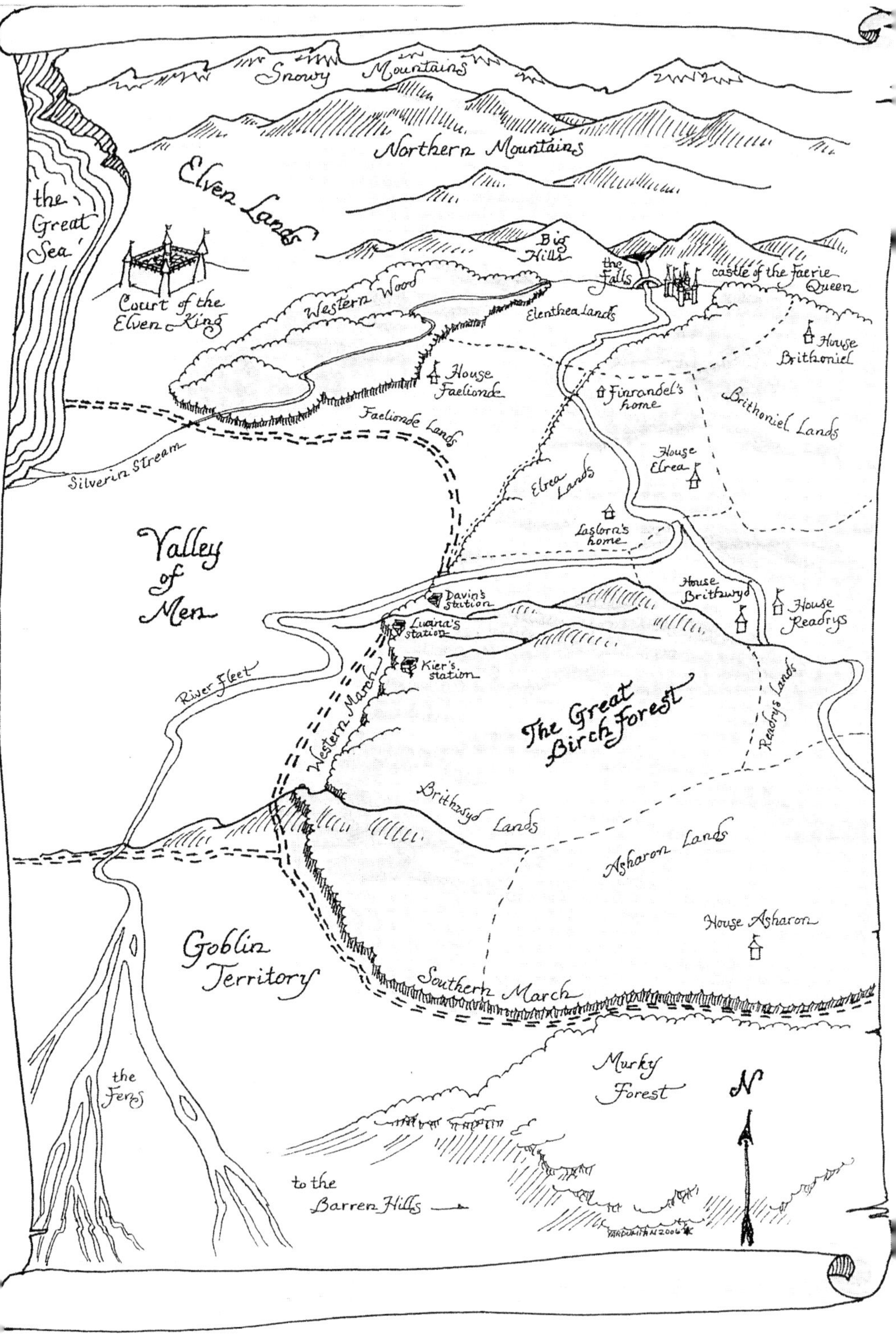
Snowy Mountains
Northern Mountains
Elven Lands
the Great Sea
Court of the Elven King
Big Hills
the Falls
castle of the Faerie Queen
Western Wood
Elenthea Lands
House Faelionde
House Brithoniel
Finrandel's home
Brithoniel Lands
Faelionde Lands
Silverin Stream
House Elrea
Elrea Lands
Laslorn's home
Valley of Men
Davin's station
Luaina's station
Kier's station
House Brithwyd
House Readrys
River Fleet
Western March
The Great Birch Forest
Readrys Lands
Brithwyd Lands
Asharon Lands
House Asharon
Goblin Territory
Southern March
Murky Forest
N
the Fens
to the Barren Hills

Chapter One

The screams and clashing, the hoarsely shouted orders and hideously gurgled cries of the mortally wounded washed forward and back over Robse, even as did the tide of battle. He dodged a blow, fought for breath through the stitch in his side, and raised his bow yet again, smoothly nocking and releasing his next arrow with arms that trembled and burned with fatigue.

This battle had begun in the darkest hours of the preceding night. Robse and his friends had arrived out of the mountains, at their best speed, in time to join it three hours past dawn. He had seen two of his friends go down in those first hours but had been unable to pause and ascertain if they yet lived. The battle was fierce and ugly; the malice of their ancient enemy clear in those baleful, red eyes. By the angle of the sun, the weary youth figured it was now nearing noon.

Glancing around him, Robse saw Prince Aelric not far away to his left. Before he could move to join forces with his young leader, Robse caught a telltale glimpse of movement: a Goblin sword arcing toward the royal head. His next arrow was sped upon its way before Robse was consciously aware he had sent it. It struck the hideous creature in the throat, flinging it off its feet and away from the prince.

Robse sucked in another breath down a throat too raw and dry to swallow. He flung the sweat out of his eyes and turned sharply to avoid a pike blow. This attacker was too near to shoot, so Robse plunged the arrow he held through its eye, dodging the spray of blood and gore, finishing the move by nocking and releasing the weapon into the Goblin behind the one just vanquished.

A sudden sinking sensation checked Robse's smooth movements, as though he had been encased in ice. Heavier than the weight of losing his adored older brothers, the dark premonition nearly crushed Robse to his knees. The sounds, sights, smells of the battle were suddenly far from him, as though he existed in some other dimension from the massacre raging around him. Frantically slewing around, Robse used his position atop a small rise to scan his surroundings. He felt as if he moved in slow motion, a hapless insect trapped in deadly amber. His eyes searched through the masses of Elves and Goblins, as if the pain and fear in his heart could sear away all that blocked his view. When his sight found its goal, his heart, despairing in the foreknowledge of its dread prescience, rose up in futile protest.

"*NO!*" he shouted, but it came out a tortured whisper of denial.

As he watched the three arrows strike his father in the same moment, a great rage and sorrow swelled within him, and he was sure he would die from the pain of it. The mortal agony broke from him in a great cry, and his aspect as he came down off that rise like a lightning bolt from a stormy sky sent more than one Goblin shrieking in terror. Elven comrades turned to see him and drew back out of his way. Unaware, he clove through them all like a blade, intent on reaching his father's body.

Robse regained his focus to realize he held his father's head cradled in his lap. The ravages of battle continued about them, but to the devastated young Elf, there was no one else in the world besides his father, Riende, the one who had always been there for him throughout his life. He had been father, mother, teacher, and guide in childhood and, for the past six months, all the family Robse had left.

His father's chest labored to bring air to the starved lungs, and the three arrows quivered grotesquely with each desperate gasp, flooding Robse with fresh anguish. The older Elf's eyes opened and searched till they found the waiting eyes of his remaining son. Some of the tension in them eased, and he nodded to Robse, taking one of the young Elf's hands in his strong grasp.

"Robse, my son, my gift." The beloved voice was broken, gasping;

the strong face already taking on a grayish cast. The young warrior was unaware of the hot tears that rained down upon the upturned face.

"Robse." The voice was firm now, by an act of the strong will that had sustained their wounded family for so many years. Hearing the note of command, Robse wrenched his attention to his father's words. The older Elf's pupils were expanded nearly round with the shock of the mortal wound to his body. The dark green irises were narrow rims burning with the import of his message. The youth bent his head close to hear the words.

"Guard the prince!" came the command. The old warrior tightened his grip to forestall his son's protest. "Do it, my son. Fulfill my commission."

"Father!" Robse bit back the rest of his protest, but the father saw it there in his gray eyes, so like the eyes of the young mother who had died bearing him more than sixty years before. *Don't leave me alone!*

The green eyes darkened and clouded with pain and sorrow. The labored breathing caught raggedly once more, and the strong young arms tightened, drawing the beloved father closer. The tortured gray eyes searched the drawn face of the dying warrior Elf. The father's eyes opened once more upon the world and lingered lovingly on the face of his second son, the gift so few Faeltheon were given.

"Remember," he gasped out, "all I have ... taught you."

"I will, Father," Robse promised, holding back the tide of his grief by sheer willpower. The deep green eyes focused just beyond Robse and widened with surprised joy.

"Elamani!" the weakened voice cried out. Robse gasped at the sound of his mother's name and turned to see what his father's eyes beheld, but nothing met his gaze save the massacre of battle. He knew even before he finished turning back that the body he cradled in his arms was empty of his father, gone now to join the beloved wife.

The grief, the loss, the loneliness seemed to grow heavier with each accounting in his mind. First, his mother, whom he had never known, had died birthing him. Then, his older brothers, one blood kin, the other adopted, but both adored by the younger boy, had been lost last autumn, either killed by Goblins or escaped into the hidden realm of Marliondolen. Now, the loss of his father, with whom Robse was particularly close, laid upon him the final crushing weight. The fierce will with which he had been holding the storm of his grief at bay suddenly gave way beneath the onslaught.

Rage from loss and grief, and anger at these creatures who lived only to destroy and sully every good thing the Creator had made, erupted in Robse like the spewing of a volcano. Red mist descended before his eyes, and he grabbed up his father's sword. Of the bloodcurdling yell he gave or the grim silence that followed it, Robse had no knowledge. He was equally unaware of the devastating destruction he wrought among his foes, though he slew hundreds of Goblins that day. Those who saw him and lived said afterwards that he was like an avenging spirit, hewing down the enemies of the Creator as though the thirst of his sword could not be quenched. Many fell before him, but the wounds he took seemed to matter nothing to him. His visage was like that of a stern, holy angel carved in unyielding marble.

To Robse, it was as though he saw, heard, and moved vaguely through a red mist of unclear activity, until he returned to find himself alone on a small rise above the battlefield, a breeze blowing over him from the sea. Dazed, he gazed upon the carnage of the plain before him, stretching nearly a mile from the Elven City on his left to the Great Sea on his right. Strewn across this broad plain were the bodies of the dead; Elves and Goblins scattered where they had fallen. The sun was setting over the water, its late light flooding the plain with redness that washed all, even the walls of the City, as with blood.

In the unnatural stillness, Robse could hear only the keening of the wind and the eternal breathing of the sea upon the nape of the shore. The utter desolation of the scene and the absence of noise flooded Robse's wounded spirit with the deep truth he had tried in vain to keep from realizing: he was alone. The aching weariness of his abused body rose up to join the pain in his spirit, and he was near to collapse when there came to him on the wind a most welcome sound of Elven voices.

"Look, sire, up there! There is another of our own yet living! He is even left standing!"

Robse's eyes picked them out then, the only figures moving upon that fell field. It was a small party of Elven warriors, among them, the prince. His father's last command rose up in Robse's memory, even as the small party reached the foot of the rise upon which Robse was standing. In their wide eyes he read the knowledge of what his own eyes had seen, but his mind had not acknowledged. He stood not upon some natural hill in the plain, but upon the mounded bodies of the Goblins he had slain that afternoon. Hundreds of them clustered about and below him in an otherwise clear part of the field. Prince Aelric raised golden eyes, wide with shock, to meet Robse's own. Robse drew a breath to speak but was denied the chance, as the terrible toll taken on body and soul that day rose up like a giant fist and smote him into darkness.

When Robse next surfaced, he found himself in a chamber whose light and beauty soothed his soul. It took but a moment's incautious, restless movements to draw his attention to his wounds. In body, he was clean and robed in gentle linen, though his left thigh throbbed beneath wide swaths of snowy bandage, as did his left shoulder. He could not draw a deep breath for the tightness of the strips bound about his ribs, but an unexpected sneeze sent a shaft of white-hot pain searing through his torso and wrung a low groan from between his clenched teeth.

Black spots danced before his eyes, and when they cleared, Robse saw the familiar form of the prince standing beside his bed, looking down at him. The long-fingered hand with the carved hematite band proclaiming the prince's rank laid itself firmly on Robse's chest, kindly forestalling the habit of ages to rise and bow before royalty.

"My thanks, Robse, for all your efforts yesterday. Several have told me of your heroic actions, and the tremendous damage you counted upon our enemy was obvious where we found you. The Healer assures me you will mend with no permanent damage. This news brings me joy, as not much else can this day. Not many of our Folk were saved alive from this past week of battles. Those who are able to travel will be dispatched soon to round up any who yet hide in the hills and bring them here to the City. So many fell in battle, Robse... so many." Aelric paused for a moment, his face shuttered as he fought for composure. In a moment he turned his golden eyes back to Robse. A faint smile pulled at the edges of his mobile mouth.

"I am doubly grateful to have you still with me. We were raised together in these courts for many decades, and I count you friend as well as vassal. Come, I am minded to grant you a boon, if it may be mine to give. What will you have of me?"

Robse turned over his thoughts in his mind before he replied, warring within himself to maintain his composure in his grief.

"My outside will heal, my lord, but I fear the wounds within will not. There is but one thing I would ask of you: allow me to place my bow, myself, and the sword of my father in your service as your Guardian."

The prince's face turned pale, and he sank down upon the chair hastily provided by the servant.

"Riende is dead, then? I can scarcely credit it, yet his absence from my side has alarmed me much. We have lost so many! Oh, Robse, my friend, I grieve for your loss more deeply than you can know. Riende was in many ways like a father to me, too, shadowing my steps from the first." The prince bowed his face into his hand for a time. When he raised it, it was to find Robse's steady gray eyes waiting for his answer. Aelric's face became like stone as he grappled once again with the dreadful losses of the past weeks of war. His *amios* cousin, Gaelcar, the youngest member to serve on the Royal Council and its only survivor, came to stand behind him to show support. The prince turned his golden eyes to Robse once again.

"No, my friend, though I thank you for the thought and the loyalty that prompted it. But I am not a child any longer to need a Guardian."

"Nay, my lord," put in Gaelcar, in a voice almost stern. "You are not a child any longer. You are the king now. To you will all the remnant of the Faeltheon now turn for guidance and for refuge. You do not need a Guardian, my lord, but as every Elven king since Amadthalos the First, you need a Champion. Amadthalos had his best friend, Ethalion. Your own father had Rearys, who fell defending him on yesterday's field of battle. Given this one's performance against that same enemy, you could hardly do better than to ask Robse Lyserea to be your Champion!"

The objection on Aelric's face succumbed to his cousin's persuasion, and he turned back to Robse, amber eyes bright.

"Will you do it, Robse? Gaelcar is right: an Elven king should have a Champion."

"Aye, he should," agreed Robse reluctantly, wishing his father had laid some other task upon him. "But the Champion is supposed to be a fell warrior, one who can defend and represent the king! Surely there are many more suited to the honor than I? I don't even have my first century yet. What of those warriors who have been trained to protect you and have served you faithfully for so many more decades than I?"

"Robse, my friend, we have taken grievous losses in these past weeks. I know you and your friends came to us as soon as you quelled the Goblin raiders in the mountains, but you have not seen the battles that have raged here over the past seven days! From what I saw on the field yesterday, you are the most fell warrior we have left. Will you do it?" the prince repeated.

After a silent struggle, Robse replied. "Aye, I will, if you are sure there's none better."

"It is settled then. When you and the other wounded are strong enough to be on your feet and out of danger, I shall be made king. At the Summoning, I will appoint you my Champion."

As the prince and his *amios* cousin quit the chamber, Robse obediently swallowed the bitter dose that would help him rest and heal. The Healer left to tend to others of the wounded, and Robse drifted toward sleep. As his heavy eyes closed, he murmured, "I hope this is what you wanted, Father."

Bright green eyes gazed lovingly upon him, and from the hidden place beyond the youth's reach the beloved voice replied. "Yes, my son, this will do very well." Riende turned toward the beautiful gray-eyed Elven woman who watched beside him. "Come, my dear, let us go tell Laslorn and Theo what we have been permitted to see."

A few days later, Prince Aelric walked down the echoing stone hallway after visiting the wounded. The desolation of the nearly empty castle and City was a constant reminder of the devastating losses they had taken, but there was something in Aelric that refused to give up.

His Champion, Robse, was healing quickly, much to the prince's delight. There were a few who had advised him that perhaps young Robse was not the best choice for a king's Champion. They claimed that he was not old enough, nor strong enough, that he had not yet achieved the maturity that time and experience would bring. Aelric acknowledged the truth in their protests, but time was a luxury he did not possess. There were so few of his people left, and none of the fell warriors of legend. He needed a Champion, for the morale of the survivors, if for no other reason, and he had seen the havoc Robse had wreaked against the Goblin army. The fact that the young Elf was recovering so rapidly from such great injuries showed that there was true strength in him. Given the circumstances, Aelric was satisfied with his decision. In the absence of a Royal Council, Aelric considered that his companions had his best interests at heart but really didn't know any better than he did how to run what was left of the kingdom.

A tall figure, somewhat broader than the prince, turned the corner at the opposite end of the hallway, his pale hair lifting slightly with the swiftness of his passage. He moved with the long strides of a confident Elf. As he reached Aelric, he bowed deferentially.

"My prince," the quiet voice began.

"Gaelcar, I was just about to come find you," Aelric greeted the Elf, forestalling him. Sometimes it bothered Aelric that this *amios* cousin, whom he had known familiarly all his life, still treated him with a touch of formality. "We need to use our time wisely, so that we can leave on the remaining ships as soon as possible. While the injured are recovering, I would like you and the few healthy among us to gather up all of the survivors in the City, including the women and children who stayed in their homes, and bring them here inside the castle walls. Send out messages to the outlying areas that they also must gather their belongings and come to the Court as quickly as they possibly can. We need all of the Elves who remain to be here in the City if we are to leave as soon as the wounded are healed. Now that our honored dead are buried, we must focus our efforts on keeping alive those yet living. The stores must be gathered and counted. I need to know what is lacking to supply our need."

"I will see it done, my prince. May I ask, are you planning on having a council with your advisors anytime soon to discuss your plans?" Gaelcar's tone was slightly reproving. While he would never be disrespectful, he candidly wondered if his somewhat erratic cousin would be able to assume the reigns of leadership and rule as well and wisely as his father, Beregos, had.

Aelric took a deep breath, groping for control. Once again, Gaelcar had remembered something that he himself had overlooked.

"Yes," he replied in an even tone, determined not to show his feelings of impatience with his own inadequacy. "I will summon a select few when they are healed."

Gaelcar nodded his head slightly, both in custom and agreement, before leaving to do the tasks he had been given.

As the weary band reached the summit of the last hill before the long plain that stretched to the sea, Caerdrys halted within the cover of the edge of the forest. Minlienda, Caerdrys's *amia* sister and faithful shadow, stumbled into Caerdrys's back, so tired she had failed to note the halt. Automatically, Caerdrys reached back to steady the slighter Elf, her sharp ears strained for any sounds ahead. For quite some time, she had heard nothing beyond the soft, shuffling footsteps of her ragged little band and the sea breeze in the trees. The absence of all noises was ominous.

Min stepped level with her, looking around and taking note of how far they had traveled. She lifted her face and scented the breeze, her nose crinkling with distaste at the charnel reek under the salt smell. Her deep violet eyes met Caerdrys's pale gray ones, and they exchanged a concerned look. For the past hour, Caerdrys had been smelling that taint in the breeze that warned of recent battle and the burning of bodies. Only three days before, when they had set out upon this journey, they had left a similar stench behind them with the remains of their homes.

Turning her eyes forward once more, Caerdrys grimaced. She would have liked to prevail upon one of the multitude of small birds that typically made their homes in these mountain forests to fly ahead to the Elven City with a message to ascertain if it was safe for them to complete their trek, or if they should remain hidden at the forest's edge. Unfortunately, with the depth of the silence surrounding them came the knowledge that their feathered friends had fled the area. Nonetheless, they needed to know if it was safe to continue onward, and like so many other unfamiliar tasks in the past two weeks, this one would fall to her as well.

She caught Min's attention and motioned her hand downward, palm toward the ground, in the signal to stop and wait. Even as Min turned to gesture to those behind her, adding the signal for silence, Caerdrys shrugged out of her heavy pack and crept to the edge of the tree shadows. In a moment, she was gone from sight, and her followers waited tensely for her return.

Without notice, she was among them again, making several start nervously. Min, knowing her best, was the only one to notice the chalky cast to Caerdrys's face, a stark contrast to her ebony hair. Min raised her eyebrows in query and received a negative headshake. While that didn't tell her much, the fine tremors in the strong hands of her sister as she resettled the pack across her shoulders and took up her ash bow once more betrayed how shaken Caerdrys was by what she'd glimpsed over the hilltop. Still, she was motioning them forward and leading them out into the open, so there could be no threat for them there.

Caerdrys's shock prepared Min somewhat for the sight that met her eyes, but her heart echoed the desolate cries of those following as they beheld the ruins of the once beautiful stone City by the sea.

The gently sloping plain was barren of green, gouged and criss-crossed with trenches of dried mud and blood. The mellow golden stone walls of the City were breached in places; the east wall looked like the battered jaw of a wolf, with many teeth missing. The fishing port had received equally harsh treatment; many of the vessels broached and burned, floating like charred storm debris against the forlorn docks. From various untidy mounds scattered over the plain came wisps of gagging smoke, showing where piles of Goblins had been burned. Closer to the sea, figures were working wearily, filling in a huge communal grave, for there were obviously neither the time nor the hands to bury their own dead properly.

As the small, ragtag band straggled down the plain toward the dubious sanctuary of the City, others saw them approaching and called out alerts to those within. Before they reached their goal, a party of three Elves exited the walls, coming to greet them. As they drew near, the fair-haired one in the center called to her, relief strong in his tone.

"Caerdrys! The Lord be thanked! We had begun to despair of you, as we had not heard from your holdings. Who is with you and are there more following?"

Caerdrys drew to a halt opposite the tall Elf with the spring green eyes, noting the lines of strain on his face and the slightly disheveled appearance, which, in this Elf, signaled grave distress. With as much strength of will as she could muster, Caerdrys tossed her long black braid back over her shoulder and slid the arrow she'd been carrying back into her quiver. With one hand she gestured to the group straggling in behind and around her.

"Greetings to you, Gaelcar. These are all that remain of the Houses of Gaelathnalienn and Quaeliom. We number seventy-three, of which..." She faltered here, but continued determinedly. "I am the eldest." She watched as the shock of her news widened the eyes of the three before her. All present knew that it was the role of the elders of their people, the ablest and eternally strong, to fight to defend the younger, frailer precious children. Gaelcar's fair skin turned a shade paler as his eyes roved over her small band. As his eyes darkened, she knew he was reckoning up the thousands of souls who had fallen in their mountain home, many of them dear friends, many of them wise and ripe in years. As his dazed eyes came back around to her, they seemed to focus by an act of will. He bowed then to Min, as usual at Caerdrys's shoulder.

"Welcome, Minlienda Elashar," he murmured, the habit of courtesy overriding his shock. Min inclined her head to him, responding with the questions that nagged at Caerdrys.

"Thank you, Gaelcar. The battle was as fierce here, I take it? Did we lose many? What of the royal family and the Council?"

Gaelcar shook his head sadly, speaking aloud what they had all feared since they had set eyes upon the plain and the ravaged City.

"Alas, good King Beregos and his wife are fallen in battle, as are most of our defenders. Prince Aelric lives, as do a handful more, but I, like you, am one of the eldest remaining." The dire news passed back through Caerdrys's little group, eliciting sorrowful cries and frightened murmurs. Many bowed their heads, and some of the youngest began to weep, though it was uncertain if they truly understood the gravity of the words or were simply too hungry and tired to be brave any longer. Gaelcar gestured toward the City.

"Bring your folk within the walls. We will find places for them to bed down and the wounded to be treated. There are so few of us left, all those able-bodied will be conscripted to whatever tasks they can accomplish. But there is time enough for that tomorrow. Let's get you fed and quartered first, and, if you will, I will need a list of all your survivors as soon as possible."

Caerdrys nodded and motioned for the gaggle of youngsters to follow as they wended their way down to the City's shattered gates. Within the City's walls, homes and shops were battered and burned, and blackened cobbles were slippery with soot underfoot. Many of the structures, including the palace, were reasonably intact. For all the devastation around them, the few whole structures were more than enough to house the handful of survivors that remained.

Caerdrys and Min concentrated on getting their charges fed and bedded down for the night in the wing of the palace that had been assigned to them by Gaelcar. Too weary and heartsick to do more than swallow some tea and fall into her hammock, Caerdrys shut her eyes upon the ravages of the day and girded herself to meet the phantom battles that would haunt her dreams all night.

The following day brought troubles of its own, which Caerdrys met and conquered as best she could. The healthy youths and children of their band were assigned chores and made themselves useful, seeming to shake off the shock of their losses in the immediacy of the tasks. The adults, both newcomers and residents, found it much harder to set aside their grief. For Min and Caerdrys, it was as though the palace were haunted. They had spent many decades of their youth here in these very halls, but throughout the days that followed, all their queries concerning friends and companions came back with the same response—their lives had been claimed in the battles.

Even after long days of hard, unfamiliar work, Caerdrys found herself wakeful and restless. By moonlight, she paced the familiar, empty halls and courtyards and mourned her lost friends, their childhood, their way of life. Always an active person, Caerdrys was impatient to *do* something, to take some definitive action to relieve their trouble. She admired Aelric, sensing a like spirit in the seething passions restrained by his cool composure. Bitterly, she missed the bright, brave warriors she had grown up with: Rablorn, who had feared nothing; Laslorn, with his ready laughter; solemn Theo, the lodestone they'd all turned to; Aoneth and his skill with the sword; the twins, Glimring and Geltheon; her own cousin, Talrys, who had perished only ten days ago, defending their home. Of their old friends from the City, only Aelric and Domel now remained, though Caerdrys was grateful for an acquaintance with several more. And, of their families, the bare bones that had survived were the children, some of the youth, and those, like Min and herself, who were barely over their first century.

Without the guidance and support of their elders, how were they, barely adult as they were, to keep the others alive and flourishing? Restlessly stalking the dark corridors, exchanging unblinking stares with the moon, Caerdrys wondered what Aelric would do, obscurely comforted by the fact that, whatever action he chose, it must happen soon.

Chapter Two

The Elven Council Chamber, a stately, well-appointed room, was not huge, but its size dwarfed the few Elves gathered there. Six were assembled at the command of the prince, but they were standing around the table awkwardly, not talking to each other. Robse shifted uncomfortably and wondered if the others felt as insignificant as he in this symbolic place.

The chamber was round, hewn from the same warm stone as the castle itself. Its walls were elaborately carved in a pattern of stylized trees and leaves, blending into gracious arches near the high ceiling. A patina of age gilded the carvings, like gentle sunlight in the evening of a long and lovely day. Like most things Robse had grown up with, it was delightful to look upon; beautiful, balanced, subtle, the product of the most skilled artisans of a long-lived people.

He had been in this chamber before, of course. Often, when it was empty, he and his friends had played in the light from the great arched windows. Occasionally, as a page, he had attended his father or some other noble during Council sessions. Robse shivered at the echoes of voices that would never be heard here again. In the absence of the many wise guides, rich in the wisdom of years, who had fallen in the last battle, it seemed almost disrespectful, even arrogant, for him to be here now accepting the position and responsibility he had been given.

Robse looked about him at the others, wondering who they were. He knew that all the Council members who had served King Beregos so well had died in the battles, save Gaelcar, and he knew that Prince Aelric had asked Gaelcar to help him to form a new Council. He recognized a few of the faces but could not readily put names to them. A raven-haired Elf with a direct gaze and an impatient stance stood nearby, her companion slightly shorter and standing quietly in her shadow. The smaller one met Robse's gaze and nodded politely. Her violet eyes were serene and gave Robse an obscure sense of peace. At her notice, her tall companion turned eyes the color of rain to meet Robse's darker gray ones. Taking a step closer to him, she initiated a conversation, extending her palm for him to cover briefly.

"I am Caerdrys Gaelathnalienn. This is my *amia* sister, Minlienda," she said to him as she tipped her raven head toward the Elf on her right. "Though we lived in the foothills northeast of here, we were often at Court. I recall seeing you, but I cannot remember your name."

Robse nodded politely to them.

"I am Robse Lyserea. I believe I have seen you in Court before. You probably knew my older brothers, Laslorn and Theomanus."

The rain-colored eyes lit, then saddened, their quick emotions echoed in the violet eyes of her quiet shadow.

"Yes, we did know them. Then you are Riende's son?" Caerdrys asked.

"Yes, I am," Robse responded, unable to mask his grief at his father's sudden death. He was embarrassed to show his feelings so openly before ones older and wiser than he, but he had not yet mastered the control that allowed Aelric to keep his features still.

Minlienda saw the pain in his eyes and well understood how difficult the past few weeks must have been for him. She spoke then, compassion touching her quiet voice with tenderness that was balm to the young Elf's bereaved soul.

"I am so sorry for your loss. It was a grave loss to all of us. He was very strong."

Robse's gray eyes moved to meet hers. He lingered for a moment, savoring the peace in their violet depths. He struggled to sound natural as he answered.

"Yes, he was."

There was a brief silence. Robse strove without success to fill it.

Caerdrys's clear, almost clipped tones sounded, even as Robse's attention was drawn to a small stir near the door to the chamber.

"So, Robse, why were you appointed to Prince Aelric's Council?" she asked. Before he could answer her, Robse saw Aelric coming toward them, a determined look in his golden eyes. That the prince had heard Caerdrys's question was apparent. With unconscious grace, he bowed over the slender hands of the two ladies, replying easily to Caerdrys's inquiry as he did so.

"After the battle, I appointed Robse as my Champion."

"Your Champion? Really?" Caerdrys's normally strong voice was uncertain.

"Yes," Aelric responded firmly, not wanting to be challenged at that time. He turned the conversation to more personal matters.

"Have you and Minlienda been brought up to date about the battle and its aftermath?"

"We haven't heard much. We just arrived a few nights ago. There was so much to do to organize what was left of our homes and get the survivors here to the City. We too suffered grievous losses in the fight to defend our homes in the northeastern foothills, even as far from the Court as we live. The Goblin forces must have been massive," Caerdrys responded.

"They were much larger than anyone could have expected," Aelric confirmed. "The fighting was brutal, and, as I'm sure you've heard, we lost many of our bravest warriors during the battle. We also lost many of the ships that my father had prepared for us to take to our island. But I will speak more about that in a few moments. Ah, there's Gaelcar."

The young prince turned, his gaze sweeping the small group, his vital personality commanding their instant attention. With a curve of his arm, he indicated the oval council table.

"Come, friends, let us be seated and on to the business of the day. I have much to share with you and am eager for your reports." There was a moment of shuffling, as the eight of them were seated about the table, Gaelcar at Aelric's right, Caerdrys at his left. Robse found himself almost at the end of the oval, with a clear view of the pretty, shy Minlienda. He cast an apprehensive glance about the chamber, his uncertainty about his right to be there underscored by Caerdrys's skeptical tone. Aelric cleared his throat, and Robse realized with some surprise as he focused on his prince that, in spite of his air of confidence, Aelric was uncertain too. They all bowed their heads as Aelric's voice led them.

"We are met in Your name."

They raised their eyes to meet the burning amber ones of their leader and were swept along in his wake once again.

"I thank you all for coming so swiftly to my call. I have several reasons for summoning you here today, but the first is sheer necessity. I must become king soon, and I must have a Council to guide me. Each of you has been chosen for a specific reason, which I will touch upon in good time. I am asking you to leave your homes and join me, to be my eyes and ears, my feet and my voice, to help me and to serve me. I am asking you to be the company of my Companions. Will you do this?"

The hawk eyes were piercing, but underneath their strong intent, Robse could see the shadow of vulnerability. Without considering his action, he found himself on his feet, right hand fisted over his heart in the warrior's salute to his commander. In a belated wave, the others stood and gave their allegiance likewise. There was a suspicious brightness to the prince's eyes as he waved them back to their seats. It could have been the lingering rays of the setting sun slanting through the high windows.

Aelric stood, gesturing to his right, and began to acquaint them with one another, though most had met at some time in the past.

"You all know Gaelcar Talathaem, my *amios* cousin and a member of my father's Council. He is known for his wisdom and for his superb ability to organize." There was a gentle chuckle around the table, for Gaelcar was known to take this trait almost to obsession. Aelric continued.

"You laugh in friendship, but in truth it is largely due to Gaelcar's efforts that you gather here today, with rooms prepared and food ready to nourish you. I have great respect for my cousin's skills, for, as a good Companion should be, he is strong where I am weak, and thus, together, we shall better serve my people. Here and now, I name Gaelcar my

Seneschal!" The ring in his voice could not be mistaken, and all the Companions sat straighter, a desire rising in their hearts to fit into this team and to serve in a manner deserving of praise.

The look of pleased surprise on Gaelcar's face was almost comical as he rose to bow in acknowledgment of the honor given him. It was a task well suited to his skills, for it would put him in charge of all the prince's household, possessions, and provisions.

Aelric, tense in the performance of his formal duties, did not smile, but his gravity sat well upon his young face. Next, he turned to face Robse.

The younger Elf knew the moment he dreaded had come and surreptitiously wiped the moisture from his palms onto the thighs of his leggings. All eyes turned curiously to him, for he was young indeed to be admitted among them, a stripling, still within his first century. Robse raised his chin defiantly. None of them were above two hundred summers, except perhaps Gaelcar. Besides, it wasn't as though he had put himself forward into this position. Aelric had chosen him. And, he reflected, his momentary pride deflating, his father had commissioned him to the task. He must not fail, though he barely knew how to proceed. He wrenched his attention back to his prince's words.

"You all knew Riende Lyserea, my Guardian. Many of you know his second son, Robse, though it may have been some time since you have seen him. Like his brothers before him, Robse has become a strong Elf, a skilled warrior, though he would be the first to tell you he does not love war." Robse looked up, startled, to see Aelric's knowing eyes upon him.

"Yet, I ask of him, young and seemingly untried as he is, to take on the task of Champion to me, though it goes against his nature. I realize he looks too young to bear this burden, and you may well cast up his lack of experience as well, but I tell you he has been tried and tested. In the last great battle, in which so many perished, Robse Lyserea passed his test and acquitted himself impressively. He is my choice! I name him my Champion!"

In the silence after Aelric's words, Robse stood to acknowledge his position, bowing once more with hand over heart, in the age-old gesture of fealty and loyalty. He sat again, hearing the ringing echo of Aelric's voice, wondering if he would be able to serve with honor, or if he would fail at this task for which he felt so unprepared.

Minlienda sat composedly, observing the events of the memorable meeting. She was aware, with heightened senses, of the history they were making. Never before in the long annals of the Faeltheon had there been so crushing a defeat as the one they had suffered bare weeks ago.

She looked about her, sensing the vanished presence of those whose right it had been to sit here. Gone now were the great heart and genial smile of good King Beregos. Gone, too, were the steadying support of Riende, the prince's Guardian; Pellegos, the aged but hale Seneschal; Rearys, the king's Champion; Elrad, Seer and Kythos to the Court. Still, she reminded herself, as the shaken young Champion seated himself again, Elrad had gone missing last fall, along with Riende's other sons; Laslorn of the Merry Heart, and his adopted brother, Theomanus Quaeliom, who had been the heir of her own tribe.

Contemplating young Robse, whose fair hair so reminded her of his good-humored and mischievous brother, Min found herself trying to remember just what had happened to them. It had been something to do with their Faerie Kin, across the Western Woods and down near the Falls. There had been fighting with the Goblins on the Southern Border of the Great Birch Forest nearly three years ago. Queen Aelwyn had sent messengers to ask for aid, and many of the young Elves had gone to fight. Theomanus and Laslorn had gone, followed loyally by their friends, Aoneth, Rablorn, Glimring, and Geltheon.

She thought she remembered hearing that Rablorn had fallen in the same battle that had taken Queen Aelwyn and her consort, Gael. That double blow had been a heavy one for the Faerie people to bear and had left young Elwyn as queen; she who was barely out of childhood, decades younger even than Robse. Of the Elves Min had known who had gone to assist in that war, none had returned to the City of the Elven king. Living in their home in the foothills, away from Court these last few years, Min couldn't remember if they'd heard whatever had happened to their friends.

She felt Caerdrys stir beside her, impatient as usual. Caerdrys was so full of energy and fire. She was always eager to know, to experience, to do! Min had had ample experience of Caerdrys's softer side, but none of it recently. With all that had befallen them, Min's protective *amia* sister was fairly bristling with the desire to strike a blow against the absent enemy. She had little patience for the more mundane tasks of living and little liking for formalities, especially if her curiosity was stirred. Min suppressed a smile. Caerdrys must be fairly eaten up with wanting to know why they had been summoned to the Council and what Prince Aelric planned to do.

The prince was speaking again now, and Minlienda focused herself on his words, his voice, and his manner, seeking to know more than just what passed on the surface of this complex Elf.

"I have asked the rest of you to company with me as my Council because, of all of those left to us, you are the strongest and most able to represent the Five Tribes. Domel Minquallen, like myself and Gaelcar, is of the line of Rysaelf."

The dark-haired Elf, of middling height, stood and bowed, his golden eyes solemn. As his name suggested, he had a reputation for finding the right words to diffuse tense situations. He would be an asset to the Council, thought Min candidly, her eyes traveling from the high-strung prince to her fiery sister. *Between us, we have more than a fair share of youth, inexperience, and hotheadedness!* Minquallen's "gentle speech" would be a welcome balance alongside Gaelcar's quiet steadiness. Now, Aelric turned to his left.

"Lady Caerdrys is now the heir of House Gaelathnalienn." He paused while Caerdrys stood and bowed and was seated again. It had been a blow to lose so many from their tribes in the battle. Their mountain home had been destroyed, leaving only a remnant of grieving members to carry on. It had been a bitter reckoning that had found Caerdrys the oldest remaining member of her family. Min knew that it was not grief alone that caused Caerdrys to chafe under this new responsibility. She wondered if her feisty sister realized that young Robse was in a similar strait. Perhaps she wouldn't have been so disapproving earlier if it had occurred to her. Aelric's voice went on.

"Cerlim Swyren represents House Ammastea." Min saw Robse's form stiffen slightly and remembered that his mother was an Ammastea. The Elf who rose was bold, with the manner of a warrior, his blond hair braided back and caught in a golden clasp, his green eyes roving the group attentively. The longbow for which he was named rested casually against the wall near the door. He sat again, supremely confident, apparently at ease. But for the look of fierce loyalty he had directed to his prince, Min would have thought there was one to challenge Robse's new title.

"Randelos Ommgeon speaks for House Ruachliende," Aelric said, and they all fell silent a moment, missing keenly the wise sage and Seer, Elrad, who had been eldest of that tribe until last fall. The slender, wiry Elf stood briefly, tossing his dark hair out of his amber eyes. His eyes were so dark as to be nearly the color of honey, deep and enigmatic, an unusual color for the Faeltheon. Min didn't know him, though his air of suppressed energy made her wonder how his personality would affect the dynamic of the company.

Then Aelric was gesturing to her. Surprised, Min nearly missed her cue to stand and bow. She had for so many years been merely Caerdrys's shadow that she had neglected to wonder why she too had been summoned. The hard truth was that she, like her *amia* sister, had been the eldest remaining of her Tribe after the fierce fighting in the breached mountain strongholds.

"Minlienda Elashar joins us on behalf of the House of Quaeliom." Blushing furiously at the attention, Min managed to stand, bow, and reseat herself as quickly as possible.

"Together I name you my Council, the Companions of the King. It will be your duty to advise me as wisely as you can and to give me aid as needed in the protection and keeping of what remains of the Faeltheon. This will be no easy task, as the dangers and difficulties now before us have never faced our people in all the long ages we have lived in this land." His golden eyes pinned each of them in turn, measuring, assessing, approving. Min felt a warm glow rise in response to his charisma and knew that he had the makings of a great king, if he could learn to discipline his erratic temper and his wild, sometimes heedless spirit. As if he'd heard her earlier thoughts, Aelric's next words rolled over them all.

"This will also be a challenging call because we are all, save Gaelcar, so young and so inexperienced. We must now, all unready, step into the shoes of those wise elder folk who guided us all so well mere weeks ago. There will be times when our personalities will clash, when the sum of our judgment and experience will not be sufficient to our people's need. I call you to set aside your differences, to set aside the long years of our youth, though unspent, and to grow up with me now into the roles we must assume, to help me to lead this remnant as well as we can, by the grace of the Creator."

There was a brief silence, as those present digested the young prince's words and tested their hearts to see if they were able for the task given. When there was no protest, only a firming of features and a straightening of backs, Aelric continued.

"Now, there are other matters I wish to discuss with you. Before we turn to plans for our future, let us discover all we can about the events of our recent past. Most of us have been out of touch, living in the northern mountains and northeastern hills. I know many of you must be wondering if we have any new information on what happened to our Kin beyond the Western Woods. Unfortunately, we do not. The scouts that my father sent out before our last battle found only a ravaged castle and destroyed homes. There were no Faeltheon left in all the Great Forest area. They did bring back with them a few important items they found there, including those portions of the Ancient Scrolls Master Elrad had taken with him and a ring that belonged to your brother, Robse."

Aelric paused and searched in his belt pouch, bringing out a signet ring with a deep green stone, which he handed to Robse. The younger Elf took it mechanically, fresh grief surging through him at this tangible reminder of the loved ones he'd lost. It was Theo's ring, of course, as Riende's ring now reposed on Robse's right hand. As Robse slipped it into place on his left hand, he wondered if it should now go to Minlienda, as she had been named to the Council on behalf of the Tribe Quaeliom. He wondered briefly who was now that Tribe's head. It hadn't occurred to him before, used as he was to considering Theomanus as his own brother, but Theo had been the son of the head of House Quaeliom. As he had been adopted as a boy upon the deaths of his parents, Theomanus had not been confirmed in his hereditary role. When he had grown old enough to take up his responsibilities to his Tribe, it had been agreed by the Council that he should be released from this duty to seek out the answer to the prophecy over his life that had given him his name. Robse's thoughts were severed as Aelric continued.

"Theomanus and Laslorn must have been at the castle at some point, though what became of them is still a mystery."

Min noticed Robse only had to swallow once before he spoke and his voice was remarkably steady.

"What of the legends of Marliondolen?" he asked. "Elrad believed in them, and it would explain their disappearance."

Aelric's golden eyes were sympathetic as he answered the younger Elf.

"He did believe them, though my father didn't. I suppose we'll never know now."

Min was surprised to hear her own voice speaking then.

"What of the prophecy over Theo's life? Don't you remember? He was named Theomanus, Hand of God, because it was prophesied when he was born that someday he would be used of the Lord to save his people."

Robse's gray eyes turned to her with a grateful light, but Cerlim's strong voice broke in.

"If he was to be used of Aematlon, it seems to me he missed his chance—he should have been here for this last battle, saving the lives of those we lost here!" Min saw the sudden motion of Robse's body half rising from his chair, but a quick movement of Aelric's hand stilled him and he subsided, his hot, young eyes challenging Cerlim's presumption. Aelric spoke, his voice betraying just a hint of exasperation.

"Cerlim, it is obvious you never knew Theo, or you would not speak thusly. He was one of the best, most honorable Faeltheon it has ever been my privilege to know. You can be sure that he fulfilled his prophecy—whatever it was. Perhaps it led him to his doom, or maybe he did save our Kin, somehow leading them all into Marliondolen's mythic glades! We will likely never know, but the worth of the Elf Theomanus Quaeliom shall not be debated by those of us left here!"

Cerlim nodded his head submissively, not noticeably repentant. Domel's quiet voice interceded.

"Perhaps he has become the Master of Marliondolen," he suggested.

"That's just a legend!" protested Randelos, but without heat.

"So is Marliondolen itself," returned Domel, unperturbed. "Yet, Theomanus was not wont to leave his family's ring from off his hand. For it to be found in so obvious a place suggests he left it there apurpose, for us to find. This implies that he knew he was leaving and planned to go without the ring, leaving us a message by it. What say you to my theory, Robse? You knew him best of us all."

Robse nodded his head, grateful for the short Elf's quiet logic and support.

"It would be like him to leave what word he could. My father and I . . ." His voice failed him for a moment, but he recovered almost immediately. "Received a note from Las, claiming they suspected this fate for Theo and planned to stay with him. I do not know why Theo did not leave a written message explaining their plans at the end, but I would guess he knew the Goblins were coming and did not want to call attention to their whereabouts."

Domel spoke again, turning his golden eyes to the prince's, so like his own.

"Whatever the truth of the matter, for them all to have vanished, leaving no survivors and abandoning their treasures, suggests both haste and a plan. If they did indeed find Marliondolen, I pray they are safely there and happy. As for us, we did not believe them. We did not seek to go with them, so, according to the legend, Marliondolen's gates are closed to us now. Our enemy is stronger and more cunning than ever before, and we are weakened beyond the ability to win another battle. What shall we do?"

Aelric nodded and resumed control of the meeting.

"The other reason I have called you all together is to give you my plans for the upcoming days. Nearly all of the wounded have regained the majority of their strength, and we should be ready to leave within a few days." He paused as voices echoed his last statement. Min noticed that of them all, only Caerdrys did not seem startled by the idea of leaving the Land. There was, in fact, a light of satisfaction in her bright eyes. Aelric signed for quiet and got it. "You all know of my father's plan to take such Elves as were willing and sail away in search of the island home where we were created. Of all the ships he commissioned, only a few have survived the destruction of battle. Fortunately, there are enough left to carry the few remaining Elves. I plan to take us on my father's quest; to find for us a new home in the oldest home we have, and, hopefully, a place so far removed from our enemies that we will be safe there. We must leave immediately, in case the Goblins discover that we are still here and decide to send another army and destroy us utterly."

"I agree." Caerdrys spoke up, her clear voice ringing in the dim chamber. "We cannot lose any time in leaving. The Goblins have shown much more cunning and courage than usual in the past few months, and it's true that they may be bold enough now to send more troops after us."

Minlienda nodded in agreement. Then Randelos was on his feet, with Cerlim a second behind him.

"Leave the Land!"

"Leave? Are we to be foresworn, then? The Creator gave us a task here—do we simply abandon it now?"

Aelric stood, eyes blazing. The force of his personality and the sheer command in his bearing silenced the protests, and under his molten gaze they slowly resumed their seats. When Aelric spoke, it was with a passion and force that caused even Gaelcar to sit straighter. Even good King Beregos, who had commanded loyalty through love, could not have matched the driving force of his fiery son's demeanor. They were held spellbound as his words poured from him, ringing with truth, his voice marred by the rasp of pain and loss that echoed in their own hearts.

"We *will* leave these shores! We *must*—think you we could stand against another Goblin attack? Though we left no enemy survivors on that last grim day, which of us shall ensure that breed of vermin are no more? I cannot! Therefore, to preserve the remnant of the Faeltheon, we must leave! Surely the Creator knows what we face. You cannot think He would have us remain, tilling fields and tending trees, to be slaughtered in a month, or a season, or a year? My own desire is to stay and fight until that evil race of Goblins is destroyed, but… I no longer live unto myself. With the death of my father…" Here the passionate voice faltered slightly, then went on, even stronger and more assured. "I became responsible for the lives of the Faeltheon who remain. I cannot protect them here, but on the seas we have a chance. My father believed we could search out that island which was our birthplace. I have to believe that we can find safety there."

There was a moment of silence, as the newly formed Council considered Aelric's words, ears ringing, heads bowed in thoughtful consideration. One by one, their eyes rose to meet his, acquiescing. Before the silence could grow awkward, Gaelcar cleared his throat.

"I understand the need for speed in the present situation, but we must not overlook important details in our haste," Gaelcar interposed. "Prince Aelric, have the remaining ships been inspected to be sure that they are completely seaworthy? While I have reported to you on the condition and quantity of our stores, do we have enough to sustain everyone until we can reach an island where we can get fresh supplies? And have you considered how to apportion the remaining Faeltheon on the ships?" There was a sigh of good-humored relief. Gaelcar's passion for detail dispelled the tension and allowed them to focus on ways to help.

Aelric paused to think before he answered. "No, the ships have not been properly inspected yet. I do know, however, that we have plenty of water and preserved foods in our supplies, since my father had already begun to stock up for the journey, and we will not need as much as he gathered, now that there are fewer of us. His notes were most helpful in this regard. I would like for you to use your skills to settle the question of who will go on which ships, Gaelcar. You may requisition any help you require, of course. There are four ships that seem able. Please let me know what you find as soon as possible, as I wish us to embark within a few days."

"Yes, my prince," replied Gaelcar, eager to tackle this new challenge.

"Should we have your coronation and the formal instatement of your Seneschal and Champion before we leave?" asked Minlienda.

"Yes, that would be wise. It must be simple though, as we don't have much time," Aelric responded. Min could see the veiled impatience in his face. It was obvious that the preparations were going to take longer than he had hoped. He turned to Gaelcar. "Can you also make plans for the ceremonies, old friend?"

"Yes, of course," responded Gaelcar, clearly in his element. With a smile, Aelric dismissed them and strode from the darkling chamber.

Chapter Three

Gaelcar advanced purposefully through the devastated ruins of what had once been the beautiful capital City of the Elves. He was ready to send the messenger birds out to summon the last few Elves who, because they lived in scattered households spread throughout the rural regions of the Elven kingdom, had survived the tremendous slaughter the Goblins had inflicted. These scattered few were the only remaining Fair Folk not already in the Elven City, and they must be gathered in before King Beregos's audacious plan, now taken up by Aelric, was set into motion. Most households had already arrived, trickling in by whatever means they could over the past week, since he had sent out the first summoning messages. But he knew the wounded and weak would be traveling more slowly and would not know of the plans to leave in the ships.

Gaelcar shook his head again at the breathtaking idea that the Faeltheon should depart from their precious Land forever. It was to these shores the Creator had sent them, long ages ago. He had given them a commission to guard and nurture the Land, and they had happily settled into their appointed task. Though their heritage was meticulously recorded in the Ancient Scrolls, telling of their creation upon that mythical isle in the seas to the south, their departure from their island home for the lands to the north, and also their arrival and the creating of the Twelve Peoples, Gaelcar was well aware of the maddening gaps in the records. Things not recorded, perhaps because they were so well known it had not seemed necessary, were the very pieces of information he needed now to help Prince Aelric prepare what was left of their nearly destroyed people to return to that island of their birth.

It was with a heavy heart that Gaelcar once again came to terms with the limping, aching fact that there were no longer any of their Faerie Kin to accompany them. He had reviewed the messages sent from Elrad, Elwyn, and Laslorn, along with the pieces of evidence received from King Beregos's scouting parties. It seemed certain that the Faeries, along with any Elves residing with them, had either departed to the legendary realm of Marliondolen, had faded completely away in the dread power of Men, or had been killed in an ambush as they fled the Men and Goblins pursuing them. Then had come their own dreadful battles and losses. There was no time now for regrets, nor even the necessary healing of grief. Once the remaining Elves were away and safe from the Goblins, they would have time enough to grieve.

Gaelcar arrived at the birdhouse, or what remained of it, and entered, hoping he would find that some of their winged helpers remained within. Much to his relief, there were ten birds left, all strangely quiet, grieving in their own way for the extraordinary number of Elves that had perished at the scaly hands of the Goblins. Gaelcar lost no time skillfully gathering the birds, relaying to them the message he needed them to carry throughout the kingdom, and urging them aloft to carry out the task.

That done, he turned to his next duty. He knew how heavily Prince Aelric depended upon his Seneschal's ability to gather and sort information. Gaelcar was now responsible for updating Aelric on their progress in several areas. His daily reports concerned the current strength and number of the Elves, the progress the shipbuilders were making inspecting and readying the ships, the gathering of all the straggling Faeltheon survivors into the City, which included provisioning them, setting cooking details and other household chores, and all the other related minutiae that kept the refugee City functioning.

He was also coordinating and organizing the monstrous undertaking of transporting the entire Elven population to their new home. Already, he had estimated the number of ships the Elves would need in order to leave their home, and had put all the able-bodied Elves he hadn't assigned to other tasks to assisting the shipwrights in preparing the three vessels. Still, there were matters he had yet to address, such as the distribution of healthy and wounded Elves in the ships. It would not do to have one ship full of those who could not help themselves, much less each other. Unfortunately, there seemed to be fewer healthy Elves than injured at the moment, but Gaelcar had still to take into account those who had not yet arrived in the City.

Preparing supplies for the journey was another task he seemed to have too few hands to accomplish. The Faeltheon lived primarily on a diet derived from plants, supplemented by fish, eggs, and dairy products. Unfortunately, the Goblins had burned much of the cultivated lands. While a great portion of the preserved supplies had been stockpiled during the winter months, according to King Beregos's plan, much of the fresh food, fodder for the animals they would take along, and plants to be nurtured and transported were destroyed or not within easy distance. Gaelcar had already detailed work teams to take wagons several miles up the coast to glean what they could of the needed supplies and bring them back to the City, but he felt he was running out of time. He figured that a good portion of their diet would, of necessity, come from the sea. He also held cautious plans for trading with Human outposts, if they could manage it without the Humans' powerful disbelief draining the Faeltheon of their strength and life.

Gaelcar shuddered, remembering the horrifying messages received from the Faerie queen last fall about the coming of Man into the Forest and the resultant fading of the people that had begun. That ancient curse of the *Finnal Izhodan*, the fading death brought about by the narrow minds of Men who could not accept creatures different from themselves, had devastated the ranks of the Faerie Border Guards by the time the urgent messages had reached the Court of King Beregos. The cold finger of fear did not leave the back of Gaelcar's neck, for the Faeries were all gone, and the Elves knew not the manner of their passing, and now the Elves themselves were left alone in the world of Men.

Gaelcar shook his head briskly. Such thoughts would not get his work done, and he must not fail his young prince. Pondering his many duties, Gaelcar hastened on, striding across the shoreline to his next task.

Aelric sat alone in the large, round office that had belonged to the king, flipping through the pages of his father's journal. The Faeltheon did not normally have to think about time. Their lives were so long that they rarely had to do anything in a hurry. Now Time stretched out his cruel hand to squeeze out the very breath of this remnant of Elves.

Pondering and planning for the future was another foreign task. The Faeltheon had lived in this Land for ages, believing they always would. Nothing had ever happened that could threaten their way of life, but now there had been a paradigm shift in their place in the world. During the past few months, so many strange things had happened. The Faeltheon had been discovered by Men; the Faeries had mysteriously vanished; their lifelong enemies, the Goblins, had grown more cunning and seemed to have a strange driving force behind them; and finally, the spring had brought that endless-seeming army to destroy what was left.

Aelric's own life had been through the same sort of shift. His father had perished in battle, and Aelric had been left no time to grieve but had been thrown abruptly into the role of king in this most uncertain time for the Elves. His restless soul chafed at the great responsibility thrust upon his shoulders. In his secret heart, Aelric was concerned that he, who had always been out of step with his people's peaceful way of life, would be unequal to the task of caring for them all. And yet, the very perilous nature of the circumstances fired his spirit with a determination to accomplish great things, to pull success out of the ashes of defeat. In the rashness and passion of his heart, the young prince did not find the future so dim as some did. It was uncertain, of course, but, by that very uncertainty, not necessarily devoid of hope.

Their most ancient works told of the perfect peace of the time before the Creator had sent them out from that island birthplace. The tales spoke of long periods of walking and talking with the Creator, simply and naturally, like favored children in a lovely home. In the midst of the tragedy and ruin of the past half year, Aelric yearned for such peace as these legends recounted.

He had not believed, as his father had done, that finding that island again would necessarily allow them direct interaction with the Creator, as it had been in the days before the Fall of Man. Yet, now, out of the rebellion of his shocked and harrowed heart, a great striving rose within him to take his people to such a place of peace and refuge. It must be true! He needed it to be true. Somehow, he would make it true.

He was determined to finish what his father had begun, so that the Elves would once again be allowed to walk and talk with the Creator, away from the sin and corruption of Goblins and Men and the fallen world they had made. By the flaring light of this dream, it seemed to Aelric that, for the Faeltheon, it was not the end of time, but the beginning.

Seeking guidance, or at least wisdom, Aelric thumbed through the pages of his father's journal until he came to a place, around the time of the Goblin Wars three years past, where Aelric saw his own name. There, in the strong, bold script, was the hidden secret that Aelric had long suspected.

The king had not understood his son.

Beregos himself was such a peaceful man, he could not comprehend the spirit that drove his son to glory in battle, even the mock battles of a warrior's training. It was necessary in this fallen world, harried by Goblins and wary of the ever-encroaching nearness of Man, to train up the young to be able to defend the Faeltheon people and way of life.

Beregos, like his people, had no love of war. In his own hand, he had declared his sentiments. The king had been an Elf whose serene heart did not welcome the fierceness of a fight. His merry soul found no beauty in the dance of battle, the vivid parry of elegant swords, the swift and deadly arc of the arrow in flight. His blood did not rise to meet the challenge of opposition. The closest the king had come to understanding what moved his quicksilver son in such times was to embrace the necessity of fighting to protect that which he held dear. Yet, in the bold words left behind for that son to contemplate, Aelric could see clearly the passion with which his father loved the people and homes and lifestyle he would fight to save. It was not the same, but it was enough to form a common ground very welcome to the bereft son in those lonely hours.

War seems to me a twisted and hideous insanity, Beregos had written. *A fate to be shunned and avoided if possible. But Aelric…* The penned words wavered as if the hand that wrote them had trembled in the writing. *Aelric, my son and heir, seems to find a mad kind of joy in the very combat itself. He does not stop begging to be allowed to fight. He has been this way all his life; a warrior from birth. I do not know how to succor his embattled spirit, for I cannot find its equivalent in myself.*

The king's words further acknowledged that he knew it hurt his son to be locked up in the City while the other Elves were out fighting to protect their people, but Aelric was next in line for the throne. Beregos did not have any other children, of course. The king, the passage concluded, could only hope and pray that the Creator would use his son's fierce spirit for some good purpose one day.

Aelric closed the book and sat back in his father's old chair. He himself had never understood why the Creator had given him the heart of a warrior. He had always believed that the Lord would use it someday, but that day had never come. Now that the Elves were seeking to return to a place of peace and fellowship with the Creator, it seemed that that day would never come. Silent, grieving, answers still beyond his reach, Aelric bowed his head to pray for himself and for his people.

Chapter Four

Corot stroked his long fingers over the dark mustache that began at the edges of his sculpted lips and curled dangerously down to frame his hard mouth. His short beard, black as midnight and meticulously curled outward, thrust like a defiant chin before him. His eyes, so dark as to be nearly black, regarded him mercilessly from his polished metal mirror.

He contemplated the familiar features before him; the heavy brows, the high, sculpted cheekbones, the slightly hollowed cheeks, the proud nose, thin as a blade and curved like the tearing beak of the desert hawk. There were no moles, or spots, or even wrinkles to mar his austere visage. His scrutiny could find nothing to mar his perfection, save the one scar, high on his forehead, which parted his glossy dark hair with a lock of white. He had received the blow that scarred him when he came to manhood, many years before, and that cursed white lock had been with him since it had healed.

He hated that lock of hair, both for the memory of the one time he had come close to failure and for the impudent way it blazed forth in his otherwise perfectly dark composition. Over the many years since receiving that cut, he had tried dying the hair, shaving it, even plucking out the strands, but the stubborn lock continued to return, as white as the accusing finger of a ghost. He hated white, hated any form of light, with a depth that in a normal man would indicate mental imbalance.

But Corot knew the ultimate secret: darkness was all. Darkness was safety. Darkness was familiar. Night was his favored realm and light an anathema. Even as a child, growing up in hotter, sun-baked lands far to the south and east, Corot had been aware of the power of darkness. He had felt at home in the shifting shadows of the desert nights and, from an early age, had roamed the cool, marble corridors and silent gardens for hours, when others thought him asleep. He became adept at entering rooms where others slumbered, becoming one with the darkness, returning to his own chambers with a prize pilfered from chest or table. Eventually, he had moved closer to the sleepers, taking pride in removing objects from their very bedsides. Some time later, it had been very freeing to realize that he did not need to take anything at all to prove to himself that he could walk the night.

One who walks the night. The phrase was one of Corot's earliest memories. He thought it was his father's voice he heard in that memory, but he wasn't sure. What he did remember clearly was the unmistakable ring of pride and identity in the man's voice as he spoke it. It was a man's conversation, one to which a young boy had not been invited. But, hovering in the shadows of the pillared courtyard, he had listened greedily, yearning with all his being to be one of the powerful men seated around the small fire sipping strong, thick coffee, deciding with almost casual grace who lived or died.

One who walks the night. In the ancient tongue: *Lemyuran.* In time, he had come to understand that this word was an identity, the name his people associated with themselves. By then, he had made himself accomplished at the feat of becoming one with the night, moving through its familiar darkness like a silent fish through deep waters. By the time he was old enough to comprehend some of the nuances of what his people were, he understood himself to be the epitome of his people's culture. He took fierce pride in his own abilities, even as he began to despise the powerful around him for not recognizing him for the tool he could be. He saw, with an instinctive recognition, what sorts of skills would favor darkness and clandestine activities.

He already knew that ultimate power rested in the hands of those who could command death, so he began to train himself in ways of silent killing. The knife and the garrote became his favored tools, though he never could bear to forsake the shuddering, raw pleasure of feeling the life force depart under the pressure of his bare hands. At first, for practice, it was various small creatures of the desert night; fleeting, unimportant lives no one would miss. Then, as he grew bolder, needing to harden his heart, to become invincible, his victims became household pets, strangled, gutted, skinned.

That first death hadn't occasioned much attention. After the second, servants began casting frightened looks over their shoulders and the women stayed in their quarters. Pleased with his power to inspire fear, Corot left his next kill on the pillow of his younger brother. This created a much greater stir, as he had known it would. The household was in a frenzy, the mother of this brother petitioning Corot's father to protect her son, servants going about armed. Corot took careful note that his father didn't seem particularly worried: after all, he had eighteen sons. But he seemed interested to discover who had these talents and such daring courage. Corot swelled with pride, but only inside, where it wouldn't show. He despised his father and all his cohorts for being unable to discover his identity, for not sensing the raw power he felt within himself.

The young Corot began to study the history of his people in depth, with an intensity his tutors wished he would apply to all his studies. He reveled in the discovery that they were an ancient people, whose history stretched back into the mists of time. They had been given the title Lemyuran from their inception. Originally intended as an insult, his ancestors had treasured the name and had delighted in making their enemies see it as a warning, a name to be feared. Corot found entries in the histories that hinted at allies of tremendous power but was frustrated when all his diligent study revealed no more than those tantalizing hints. He learned that the Lemyurans had ranged and spread over all the region, often infiltrating a settled area and existing, unsuspected, as a subculture within the parent culture of the area. Often, their skills were hired for mundane tasks, such as assassinations, but the branches inclined to such work tended to exist on the fringes of the heart of the Lemyuran people.

Over the ages, the Lemyuran name had undergone subtle shifts, as men who suspected their existence picked up hints of their presence, and as the ancient tongue began to dissolve into the various dialects of men. In some places, they were Lemurans, in others Lemurians or Lamurans. In lands far to the south, a branch of his people was teaching gullible men to try to predict the future from the patterns of the stars. Though the stars were placed and maintained by the Creator, the Lemyurans did not hesitate to twist this sign of the Creator's glory into a tool with which to mock Him. In that place, his people's influence was beginning to make itself known.

In all the lands of the region, as men sought power and fought to keep it, more and more it happened that their closest advisors were men of the Lemyuran people. Power, ever marked by the presence of wealth and the right to command the deaths of others, began to be associated with the practices and mores of Lemyuria, though the uninitiated remained unaware of this cultural infiltration. The caravans who traded there and brought word to other lands had mangled and mumbled their half-understood tales until the rest of the civilized world could pick out but a syllable of the name of power: Ur.

Corot smiled to himself as he contemplated the careful piecing together of his own empire over the years. As he had grown to adulthood, Corot had learned the lessons of his people, had drunk deeply of their dreams, had made himself the living icon of their hopes. That he had now lived longer than the average Human life span was a carefully maintained secret, known only to him and to his closest allies, those mysterious powers hinted at in the ancient records. Though he had seen sixty winters, Corot possessed the vigor and healthy body of a man in his prime.

In his rise to power, he had methodically eliminated obstacles to his assumption of power: first, all seventeen of his brothers; then his father and his uncles. By the time he had the beginnings of a downy beard on his chin, he had ruled his father's small world with an iron fist. It had not taken him long to realize that the Lemyuran influence extended as far beyond his father's ruling as the sea ventured beyond the shoreline. With this realization came the natural extension of his plans, and he had set himself to the task of ascending to the apex of power.

Over the years, he had found and formed alliances with all manner of men and other creatures. He had learned more about the Lemyuran purpose than any other man living, he believed. He knew that they were opposed to the Creator, and this knowledge did not dismay him, for he was confident in the powers he would someday command. Of all creation, there remained only one people, the accursed Faeltheon, who still held fast in fidelity to the Creator. For this, Corot, and all Lemyuria, despised and hated them. They were a small group, with almost no power in the world, but they were a living, festering sore in the plans of the Lemyurans. One element in Corot's campaign of power was to eliminate the Faeltheon and their hideous influence. This piece of his carefully constructed scheme was to happen soon.

The chiseled lips curved faintly into a sardonic smile. It was all coming together as he had planned. Soon, even greater power would be his. Already, he wielded more power than any other single Lemyuran, though they were slow to realize this. Corot had made sure that any whose shrewdness jeopardized his plans died a mysterious and painful death. Those remaining either did not understand Corot's intent to rule or were wise enough to be content with a supporting role.

Vividly, Corot remembered the day he had discovered the ultimate goal of the Lemyuran purpose. Filled with certainty that he himself was fated to make it come to pass, Corot had confronted his father. Though his father had to have known by now that Corot was the cause of his brothers' deaths, the older man had been slow to defend himself. It was as though he were so used to being the ultimate power among his people, he could not comprehend his jeopardy. Corot had quickly forced the desert ruler into a defensive position, and from the first move, it was clear to Corot who would be the victor. In the midst of the slashing saber strokes, an interruption had cost Corot an instant's hesitation. His father's blade had swept under his guard and laid open a stinging cut on his forehead before Corot had smashed it aside.

Fury at his first marking had driven Corot to finish the farce, despite the biting blur of blood in his right eye. In a moment, it was ended, his father's severed head rolling across the patterned marble floor of the private courtyard, the look of horror and surprise forever frozen across his face. Dismissing him with contempt, Corot had commanded that the body be flung outside the walls and the head mounted on a pike at the gate as a warning to all that Corot was now in charge. Consumed with fear, the servants had scuttled to do his bidding.

Corot had turned to survey the cause of his momentary distraction, shaking his head to fling the offending drops of blood out of his way. In the arched doorway to the courtyard had stood the frozen forms of the head steward of the household and the peculiar visitor who had caught Corot's attention. The visitor at first appeared to be a bent and wizened old man but, upon closer scrutiny, was revealed to be no man at all.

Instead, it was a hideous creature with a bulbous, mushroom-like head, covered by a stiffened leather helmet. Its eyes were small and red under exaggerated brow ridges, its nose squat and blunt, its mouth a lipless slash above a chin that receded into its scrawny neck in the manner of a frog. Its body was stooped, with a concave chest, a protruding, knobby spine, spindly legs, and large, leathery feet with long toes. Patches of sparse, wiry hair adorned it randomly, as did various moles and spots. Its arms were long, ending in proportionately large hands, with long, strong-looking fingers, tipped with sharpened, horny claws. It was truly repulsive, and the sulfurous odor that emanated from it seemed disgustingly appropriate. Corot had been taken aback at its very existence, as well as its appearance in his father's home. Fastidiously moving upwind, he had gestured for the creature to be brought into the courtyard.

After extensive questioning, which the visitor survived in a surprisingly hardy fashion, Corot had learned that it was a Goblin, one of a race of creatures living in the cold countries to the north. It had come in response to a summons by Corot's father, as its people had always been part of the Lemyuran culture. The Goblins' own legends told of their creation by dark powers opposed to the Creator and His Light. Even more than Humans, they considered themselves to be children of the night, ones who walked in darkness. That they were allies had been obvious. Whether they would prove useful in the long run was less certain, but Corot had allowed this one to live, that he might return to his people and tell them of Corot's rise to power. Corot had maintained contact with the filthy vermin and, over the years, had persuaded them that his was the only Human voice that need be obeyed.

Now that he himself had traveled to the cold lands in the far north and had heard the reports of the Goblin scouts, he was ready to set this phase of his rise into motion. The cursed Faeltheon were badly crippled now, after his brilliant plan to lure Humans into their midst had taken its initial toll. The Faeries were obliterated, according to the latest reports. Thanks to his own tireless efforts, the Goblins were better trained in the arts of war and were set to destroy the remnant of the Faeltheon, the Elves in their fastness to the north and west.

The massive Goblin army had departed, confident in the promise of Human troops to follow and back them up. Corot had no intention of risking his troops, however. In fact, it was his fond hope that the Elves and the Goblins would destroy each other in this last battle. He had no love for the Goblins, filthy creatures that they were, but, as a master strategist, Corot had other plans he could set into motion should any Goblins survive.

Corot smoothed his mustache once more, contemplating the intricacies of his plans for dominance. He knew that his most powerful allies would be delighted at the annihilation of the Faeltheon, though they might be less than pleased at the destruction of the Goblins. Overall, Corot felt it was an acceptable risk that would yield him more power. Never for one day had Corot forgotten the secret he had learned in the day he had confronted his father. *The most ancient and important purpose of the Lemyurans was to gain power over all creation.* Never did the ultimate goal of thc Lemyurans stray from his mind. Power was his god and his goal. One day, they boasted, one of their own would control the entire world. Corot had decided that *he* would be that man.

He would rule the world.

He stepped back from the mirror and contemplated the picture of his face as a whole. Aside from the cursed lock of white hair, he was satisfied. Taken altogether, his was a handsome face, swarthy and severe, the face of a man in his prime, a man to be feared and respected; a man in control. Considering the multitude of secrets his face did not reveal, Corot was pleased with what he saw. Carefully, he replaced the polished metal disc on the shelf behind his imposing carved chair and turned away.

A timid knock upon the closed door drew his attention.

"Come," he commanded in his customary cold voice. A household servant peered cautiously around the doorframe, licking his lips and shifting his eyes quickly to the floor, lest he be accused of boldness. He cleared his throat.

"The Goblin emissaries wish an audience with you, my lord," the nervous attendant divulged.

Corot looked up, no hint of surprise in his expressionless face. To the messenger's relief, his ruthless leader responded placidly. "Tell them I will see them … after they leave their pitiful weapons outside my residence."

The servant nodded and left the room to complete his errand. Corot straightened slowly to his full height, intimidating inches taller than any other living man he had seen. Power and evil intelligence emanated from his every feature. Though coldly handsome, his face was also terrible and frightening. He knew his unreadable dark eyes dominated his expression, giving every appearance of piercing into the very soul. He took pride in this impression and cultivated it to good effect. Corot's intimidating appearance was in no way softened by the strangeness of his left hand, for it had not five fingers, but six, an oddity common in his family line. Corot clenched his hands into fists and waited for his repulsive allies.

The Goblins slunk into the room, some anxiously running their hands over their fragile skulls, now unprotected by their customary helmets. Corot began the meeting, well aware of the depth of their fear of him.

"Why are you in my house?" he demanded. *And why are you alive?* The Goblin who apparently had been elected spokesperson for the delegation stepped forward and angrily answered him.

"The Elves slaughtered us! We were helpless without the reinforcements you promised us. Where were your promised Men?"

Corot responded harshly, his tone reproving them for their arrogant manner.

"They were coming, you fools! You *children* attacked too hastily. Had you waited a mere few hours, our combined powers would have overwhelmed them for our own glorious victory." Corot smoothed his tone, seeing the Goblins flinch in fear. He knew that the gullible creatures would believe anything he said simply because he wielded so much power. Given the forcefulness of Corot's manner and voice, it would never occur to the Goblins to wonder why they hadn't met the following troops on their return journey. Corot lowered his voice to the tone of a wise, understanding father, and continued.

"You realize that only by working together can our two races cause Lemyuria to rise to world domination, now that the Elves have been defeated. That is why our alliance and the good of your warriors mean so much to me. I hope that, regardless of your rashness, the Elves *have* been defeated?"

In response to this, the Goblin general, encouraged by his leader's mobile voice to believe that Corot had no intention of harming him, sneered at the frailty of Elves and nodded an affirmative. Corot eyed him suspiciously.

"Is *every single one* of them dead?" His voice oozed with potential threat. The Goblin suddenly lost his confident attitude.

"I… I think we killed them all," he finally stammered.

Corot nodded, outwardly calm and compassionate toward the vermin, internally seething. *What you think does not amount to anything! The Elves should have eliminated you, even as you annihilated them! You are complicating my plans!*

"I see." He soothed, but his eyes remained hard as obsidian. "But our plan will fail if even a small handful has survived. You must send a party of Goblins to survey the damage and be sure that no Elf escaped."

"Why must we investigate the dead? Why don't the Men work for a change?" another of the Goblins grumbled. His companions elbowed him roughly and he subsided, but Corot's voice took on overtones of the displeased warlord, making them all cringe away from him.

"It is not Human error that created this situation. I expect the report to come to me quickly. Your blunderings have already cost me much."

The Goblins hissed and glared at Corot with their hideous red eyes. Not the least affected, he met their stares with his own cold eyes and signaled that their meeting was over. Even as the Goblins shuffled from the room, Corot turned back to his interrupted plans. He had not anticipated any Goblins surviving the battle, but that problem would be solved quite easily, thanks to the Goblins' gullibility.

He sighed. Soon, he would not need to deceive the Goblins with ridiculous lies. Soon, these simple animals would be his slaves and would do his bidding, no matter how dangerous. He smiled as he pondered the ease with which he was gaining his rightful power.

Chapter Five

Elwyn laid down her armful of gossamer garments on the bed cover and turned to watch her companion. The beautiful Faerie held a swirl of translucent russet up before her and surveyed the effect in the long mirror. Elwyn bit her lip to keep from smiling too broadly. It was a source of fresh delight to her to see her mother acting so young and happy. Aelwyn caught sight of Elwyn's suppressed mirth in the mirror and stuck out her tongue. The gesture surprised a slightly scandalized laugh from Elwyn. Aelwyn joined her, strong alto blending with clear soprano, in a merry sound of pure joy. With a sudden gesture, the mother tossed the floating garment to swirl about her daughter's shoulders. Elwyn stroked the shimmering fabric, fingers lingering on the intricate amber beadwork along the edges.

"It's not my color, but wouldn't this be lovely on Nausika?"

"Indeed it would," her mother agreed, holding up a length of clear amethyst. "Now *this* is you!"

"Oh, Mother, I don't need any new clothes! I have several beautiful garments already, as well as everyday clothing."

"True, but these are stunning work, and I have my reasons for wanting you garbed as befits your status."

"Mother!" protested the young Faerie, blushing slightly. "We are in Marliondolen now; we no longer have queens and kings, nor even High Families."

"Maybe not," her mother agreed placidly, admiring a length of shimmering aqua trimmed in clear crystals. "But we who were once royal will always represent the people we served. Besides, there is someone I wish you to meet, and I wish for you to look your best when you do."

"Well, of course, Mother; I would not disappoint you, but—"

"Darling, don't argue with your mother."

"Yes, Mother."

"I think the lavender, with this pale gold overtunic and the deep purple trim."

"Yes, Mother."

"And stop laughing at me! I think you will look very well in these."

"Yes, Mother." Elwyn tried to hide her twitching lips without success. She obediently took the lovely garments from her mother's hands and tried to pursue the more interesting aspect of the conversation.

"So, for whom am I to be so extravagantly dressed?"

"That's for me to know and you to discover!" replied Aelwyn tantalizingly. Elwyn laughed outright at this oft-employed response from her childhood.

"Watch out, or I'll sic Nausika on you! She could always get you to tell!"

Aelwyn shrugged delicately and met her daughter's eyes in the mirror once more. A small, faintly smug smile warned Elwyn her ploy had failed.

"Oh, I'm way ahead of you," replied her mother. "I've already told Nausika."

Two days later, just at midmorning, Theo came looking for Elwyn where she knelt in the clearing behind their home, tending the garden plot. Sensing his suppressed excitement, Elwyn squinted up at her beloved through the bright sunlight.

"Come," his rich voice beckoned. She reached up and grasped the hand he held out to help her to her feet.

"Where are we going?" she asked, bemusedly, trying to figure out what it was that had her usually self-possessed husband aquiver. There had been so many delightful discoveries since they had entered Marliondolen; one never knew what new wonder might be waiting for one.

To Elwyn's surprise, Theo led her inside their small home and back into the tiny chamber that held their garments, hanging neatly upon their hooks. Once there, he gestured to the new outfit her mother had chosen for her.

"It's time," he said, as though that explained everything.

"Time for what?" Elwyn demanded, not wanting to be too surprised by whatever her mother had cooked up. Theo didn't answer, as he was buried in the tunic he was pulling off over his head. Elwyn laughed when he got stuck and patiently untangled him, knowing he was being deliberately clumsy to try to distract her.

Unable to get more information from him, she changed into her beautiful new garments and helped straighten Theo's new clothes. She hadn't seen this outfit yet and admired both the rich colors and fabrics used, as well as the way they set off his straight, broad-shouldered, slim-hipped figure. Not for the first time, Elwyn allowed herself to dwell on the handsome picture her husband made.

A faint color stained Theo's cheekbones as he stood under his wife's regard. She tugged the deep golden tunic straight and fastened his purple cloak at his shoulder with a beautiful cloak pin, made in the likeness of a spreading oak tree, each leaf picked out in tiny amber stones.

Satisfied, she stepped back and would have gone on admiring the fine sight he made, but he forestalled her by reaching for her hairbrush, turning her to face away from him and stroking it through the waves of her pale hair.

Finally, he fastened about her slender throat a delicate necklace of amethyst and tourmaline, carved to represent birch leaves. Watching the leaves flutter with the beat of the pulse in her throat, Elwyn turned to Theo and laid her slender hand on his chest.

"What are we doing? What's all this about? I would really rather know than be surprised, Theo!"

He chuckled goodnaturedly as he escorted her to the door.

"We are finally getting around to meeting some of our ancestors! They are all here, you know, and many's the time we've said we must look them up. Well, your mother and Ethaniel decided to arrange an informal gathering so we could all meet one another."

Elwyn glanced down at the finery swirling about her, and a smile tugged at her lips.

"But nothing's ever that simple with those two, is it? An "informal gathering" has probably grown to enormous proportions by now!" At the mischief twinkling in her beloved's golden eyes, Elwyn felt a laugh gurgle up from her throat.

"Hmm. Something like that, I believe. But *it's all under control!*"

Elwyn laughed outright at his deft mimicry of Ethaniel, and so they arrived at the meeting place on a wave of silvery mirth.

In a large, fairly level field near their home, open tents had been erected to provide shade from the midday sun. These enclosures were little more than bright billows of woven or dyed cloth, intricately patterned, stretched over carved poles sunk into the turf. Garlands and bunches of bright meadow flowers adorned the poles and the swags of cloth, shedding their delicate perfume upon the gentle breezes.

Within the pavilions were pleasant groupings of tooled wooden benches crowded with plump, colorful cushions. Beside these were small, curiously engraved and shaped tables, decorated with meticulous patterns inlaid with polished bits of stone, gems, shells, and woods. These were invitingly set with tea and fruit and small cakes.

The canopies were set in two long parallel rows, with a broad green swath between. Already, many people sat under the awnings and stood in clustered groups, chatting animatedly. Musicians played enthusiastically at the far end of the stretch of tenting, though Elwyn couldn't see them from her vantage point.

Almost immediately, Elwyn and Nausika spotted each other, and Nausika hurried toward them, the skirts and demi-cape of her new outfit swirling about her energetically. Elwyn was pleased to see the cape and underskirt were indeed the lovely russet fabric she had recommended to her mother. The gold-embroidered leaf green tunic worn over the skirt was belted about her slim hips with links of copper set with carnelian and fire opals. Her hair was adorned with a *bhrudam,* a brow-band that encircled the back of her head and nearly, but not quite, met across her white brow. The delicate jewelry was a flowing, sinuous swirl of copper and gold wires, beaten and etched and intertwined to form a lovely setting for the girl's fiery hair. Elwyn hadn't seen her *amia* sister look so radiant since their wedding ceremony. Exuberantly, she hugged her dear friend, whose excitement was contagious. Laslorn joined them then, splendid in his own finery.

"This is so exciting!" Nausika exclaimed, still holding Elwyn's hand. "I can't wait to meet all these who went before us!" Elwyn laughed at Nausika's energy, even as Laslorn goodnaturedly fished a lock of her floating curls out of his mouth and tried again to kiss his wife. Suddenly, there was a stir among those seated under the tents, and many people began to line up along both edges of the long greensward, jockeying for position. Laslorn led Nausika toward where Ethaniel and Elamani stood on a slight rise to the left, watching. Elwyn moved to follow, but Theo held her by him.

"Wait," he murmured, and she focused on the panoply unfolding before her. When it seemed that everyone who was going to join the double line had done so, the musicians must have received a signal, for they began to play a lively, happy tune that had smiles flashing all along the queues and in the great crowds massed on either side of the lines under the canopies. As Elwyn watched the people in the double line that stretched before her, she realized that they were paired, male and female, and clearly all dressed in their finest. The faces of those closest to her seemed different to her eyes, but she couldn't place just how. Fleetingly, she was reminded of Elrad, and, as though her thoughts had summoned him, he appeared on her right, smiling slightly.

When the music stopped, Elrad turned to her and bowed deeply. Flushed and a little confused at being so singled out in this company, Elwyn curtsied in return and accepted his proffered arm. The fingers of her right hand rested on the teal velvet of the Seer's sleeve, even as those of her left hand laced with Theo's, suddenly seeking security. He squeezed them gently and reassurance flooded her, restoring her smile.

Snapping her delicate wings up and out, she walked between the two Elves to the head of the double line.

Drawing her attention to the first couple on her left, Elrad began to introduce Elwyn and Theo.

"Elwyn, Theo, this is Elenfea, the first Queen of Faerie, and her Consort, Lasnov. Elen, Nov, may I present the Master and Lady of Marliondolen."

Elwyn drew her breath in sharply and for a moment felt a sudden disorientation. *This was the legendary Elenfea!* She was the first in the Elenthea line, and the one who had set up the seven First Families to guard the Great Birch Forest. This Faerie had come to the Land on the great ships that had been built on that lost island home where the Faeltheon had been created! It was a wonder beyond delight to be standing before this legend, and Elwyn suddenly felt very small. In a flash she remembered her feelings of deep connection as she'd put on the wedding dress this Faerie had made for her own daughter countless centuries ago.

Even as she sank into a deep curtsey of respect, Elwyn's cheeks flamed with the shaming knowledge that she had been unable to save the nation this brave queen had created. As her two gallants raised Elwyn from her curtsey, Elenfea reached out and enfolded the confused young Faerie in a warm embrace.

"Thank you for being faithful," she whispered in Elwyn's ear. "Thank you for bringing my people home." Sudden tears sprang to Elwyn's lashes. Then Elrad and Theo were turning her to her right and the couple waiting there. So overwhelmed was she that she nearly missed the names Elrad was speaking.

"This is King Amadthalos and his queen, Hadara. Thal, Dara, the Master and Lady of Marliondolen." Elwyn was slightly better prepared to meet the first king and queen of the Elven peoples, but it was many introductions later before she felt anything like her usual composure. Elenfea, Silvana, Amadthalos, Bregos, Dremwyn, Amiel: all the familiar litany of famous kings and queens of the past, plus many others whose names she knew not, were there before her in person! Uniformly, they were all pleased to meet her and Theo, though she couldn't comprehend why. She also couldn't understand why they were the only couple being singled out for the honor of being presented to this august receiving line.

Finally, after a long daze of names and faces, the end of the double line came into sight. Though she was faint from the two hours of presentation and trembling with nerves and excitement, she made a small sound between a gasp and a sob when she saw the final pairs awaiting them. Good King Beregos and his gentle wife, Ashwyn, smiled upon her benignly, even as Elwyn wondered why Elrad was formally introducing them. At last she turned to the final pair. Aelwyn and Gael barely waited for Elrad's words before enfolding her in their loving arms. Elwyn was more than surprised to see tears on Aelwyn's cheeks. She barely heard her father's gruff, "We're so proud of you, dearling," before she was led, still between Elrad and Theo, to stand facing the other direction down the long double line.

Gazing down that impossible length of monarchs, Elwyn saw the passage of centuries represented by their lives. In their faces and forms dwelt the elegant, brilliant, dynamic culture of her people. She realized then that she had not met, in this incredible ceremony, any folk from before the period her people had spent in the Land. Looking down this long gauntlet of leaders, Elwyn realized that she and Theo, standing at their end, represented the closure of this phase of the lives of the Faeltheon. As Elenfea, at the far end, was the first queen of Faerie, she, Elwyn, was the last. In this stretch of faces, all turned toward her in a blur of friendly intent, was the length of the *Tallalduri*, the Age of Stewardship. That age was over now. What would come to her people next, Elwyn wondered.

She snatched her attention back to her surroundings when Elrad began to speak once more. He was using his "official voice," so she knew whatever was behind all this ceremony was about to be revealed. Nervously, she squeezed Theo's fingers and felt the reassuring pressure in return. He didn't seem at all nervous, so Elwyn relaxed and listened.

"Rulers of old, faithful friends, companions and blood-Kin, whatever plans the Creator has for those of our Kin left behind, the Age of Stewardship has ended."

Elwyn started to hear her thoughts so clearly stated in the Seer's deep, resonant voice. Theo, feeling her movement, glanced down at her. She smiled back into his eyes, secure in his love. Elrad's voice continued.

"We have now been led into this haven of Marliondolen, where we have found peace and plenty, love and laughter. We do not yet know what the Creator plans for us here, but our knowledge of Him assures us that His plans will be for our good. He Who has made a way for us will surely guide us in that way, that His plans for us will bear good fruit in His timing.

"So, as we lay aside the Age of Stewardship, we lay aside the need for kings and queens, though not for leadership. Revered ancestors, lords and ladies, good friends—I give you the Master and Lady of Marliondolen!"

Elrad, clearly enjoying playing up the moment, waved his arm in their general direction, and the crowd exploded into thunderous cheers and applause. Crimson with embarrassment, though pleased at the show of good will, Theo and Elwyn were quickly lost in the swirling crowd of well-wishers.

The gathering resolved itself into a vast entertainment with music, dancing, food, and drink. The former kings and queens were besieged with folk eager to meet them, and the convivial atmosphere lasted well into the evening.

Theo, returning to Elwyn with a laden plate of savories and two forks, sat beside her just in time to hear Nausika exclaim, "We should do this often!"

"Do what?" asked Laslorn, arriving with a tray containing a steaming pitcher and a handful of earthenware mugs with beautiful glazing. The drinks were poured and deftly handed round as Nausika explained her thought.

"We should set times when we will gather like this to meet people we don't know! Earlier today, I spoke with a tesseler who had laid much of the floor in the Great Hall of Elwyn's castle! He was fascinating to talk to and promised to introduce me to the artisan who designed the patterns of the columns."

"That is a good idea, Nausika! There are so many people I want to meet; many of them the artisans who designed and built the palace over the ages," agreed Elwyn enthusiastically. Theo nodded, swallowing his bite.

"Yes, and I'd like to meet the people who designed and created the beautiful coronation pieces in the Elven Great Hall. They've long been favorites of mine."

"Well, let's do it, then. We could arrange gatherings like this every so often, I should think," Laslorn approved, popping an entire berry tart in his mouth at once. Nausika laughed at his efforts to chew his mouthful, and Elwyn went to find Aelwyn and Ethaniel to thank them for their delightful arrangements and to convey their suggestion.

Chapter Six

Aelric stood before the throne of his fathers, gazing out at the humble gathering of the remains of his race. The Hall was so grand; the remnant of Elves so meek. Gaelcar's lofty words echoed throughout the Great Hall, deepening the empty feeling of the room.

Aelric was greatly saddened to think that this would be the last formal gathering in the beloved Hall. Many generations of Faeltheon had labored to build it, and they had not ceased decorating it over the long ages it had served them. Its carved and gilded benches had seen guests from the realm of Faerie come to visit their Kin, as well as the mundane daily affairs of audience, supplication, and reports from scouts. Its echoing ceiling vaulted beyond the reach of the light from the windows, its arches and groins shrouded in dim and brooding mystery above. The elaborately carved walls gave the impression of a clearing in a copse of trees, the leaf and flower patterns echoed in the tiered seating along the long walls and in the beautiful stone mosaics upon the floor.

Aelric's golden eyes scanned the walls, dwelling in turn on each of the tapestries and mosaics that lined them. They depicted the coronations of his ancestors, each filled with bright colors and peaceful faces. It was an age-old tradition that, after the coronation of a new king or queen, weavers and tesselers would spend the first century of the new reign creating an elaborate image from the coronation. Some portrayed the crowning, others the appointment of the ruler's Council, still others the celebrations that followed. In his youth, Aelric had spent many long hours examining every one, letting his imagination take flight as he pictured his own ceremony, never envisioning that it would be so different from the rest.

Today there were no bright colors, no great crowd, no cheerful faces. His own face lacked the lines of experience he had expected to bear on this day, nor was his father by his side. They had chosen to forego the normal celebrations, not only because the mood was inappropriate, but also due to the pressing of time. Aelric felt himself growing more uneasy with each day their departure was delayed. Gaelcar assured him all was progressing at the best speed they could manage, but they had many things to attend to before they could set sail.

His eyes fell upon the small crowd of Elves who huddled in the center of the room, as if they felt the need to draw closer together in this trying time. Every Elf who had not died in the battle was present, many still in bandages or on crutches, yet it was hard to believe that they were all that was left of the blessed race of the Faeltheon. Their expressions, whether fearful or hopeful, all showed uncertainty. Now, more than ever before, they needed a strong king, but Aelric was just as uncertain of himself as they were. He was young, inexperienced, and vulnerable, but he was determined. His followers were looking to him for guidance, and he would do his absolute best to lead them.

He took a deep breath and reminded himself that the Creator had placed him in this position for a purpose. Suddenly, he felt himself suffused with passion to lead his people well. He would search for their beloved island home, as his noble forefathers would have done, and he would not fail.

Gaelcar reverently held aloft the jeweled crown, and Aelric turned to face him. He saw behind the throne the brilliant tapestry of his father's coronation. How he wished Beregos could be here to give his blessing and crown his son! That tradition of the retiring ruler crowning the rising sovereign had always held more than the simple transfer of power from parent to child: it had also been a mark of confidence, a sign that the leader felt his offspring was ready to care for his people. Aelric had hoped that he would make his parents proud when his time came to shoulder the mantle of responsibility to lead his people well. Although Beregos had been confused by his son's fierce and passionate nature, Aelric was sure his father had never doubted that his child would rise to the occasion. Aelric had treasured the anticipation of that moment and the look he'd hoped would shine from his parents' eyes. Now, that hope burned like bitter ashes in his heart.

"Aelric Rysaelf, son of King Beregos and Ashwyn, his queen, will you accept the responsibilities of leadership over these Elves here assembled and over all your people?" Gaelcar's voice intoned ceremoniously, awaking modest echoes in the vaults above them.

Aelric, crossing his fists over his chest, bowed his dark head. Gaelcar nodded and Aelric sank down on one knee.

Lord, please be with me. Guide me, lead me, that I may lead them aright.

Aelric felt the cool weight as Gaelcar placed the silver crown on his head.

Creator, watch over us in our desperate need. We need You now more than ever. Without You, my people have only me to lead them. May it never be so! They are loyal, Aematlon, but You know how inadequate I am to lead them safely. Be my Guide and Guard, Holy One. Be closer than my next breath, that I will not endanger them in my ignorance!

"Aelric Rysaelf, with this crown upon your brow, symbolizing your elevated state among us, I proclaim you King of the Elves! Remember to lift your head high as you represent us before the throne of Aematlon. Remember to bow your head humbly as you bring us before the might and greater rule of Aematlon, the King above all kings. Be all that is best in the Faeltheon, and ever lead us in the paths of truth."

Creator, help me! I must not disappoint them! I wish Father and the others could have been here. Comfort us in their absence, my Lord, for we are naked and shivering in the wind of their loss. Be our sustenance in this hour of need, for I am not the strength my father was!

Fighting back tears, Aelric rose to his feet and turned to face his people. In silence, the Elves slowly and reverently bowed to their new king. Aelric tried his hardest to look as kingly as possible, suppressing his doubts and fears and forcing himself to exude an air of confidence. He *would* lead his people to their destiny.

Somehow, he would.

The Great Hall was strangely silent in the first long moment after Aelric was crowned. The usual deafening roar of cheers, clapping, whistling, and happy laughter that had greeted every other newly made monarch was conspicuously absent. Robse darted a nervous glance around the occupants of the Hall, trying to gauge their mood, wondering if they shared his feelings of being dwarfed by both the Hall and the circumstances. The faces he could see were solemn; some reverent, some hopeful, some still blank with the shock of the past month's losses.

Robse let his gaze rest once more on his king and saw the same solemnity in those golden eyes. It looked oddly out of place in a face that habitually wore a look of barely restrained passion. Yet, as he searched Aelric's visage, Robse saw a face refined by grief, in a manner aged by care. A new maturity sat upon the drawn countenance of the young ruler. The fierceness of his nature still glimmered from his amber eyes, but the past month had conferred upon him the weight of responsibilities he had not thought to take up for centuries. Now, at this moment, when all eyes of his dependants were upon him, as he officially took upon his soul the vows to protect and care for them to the best of his ability, he stood tall before them, strong and well able to sustain this weight he must bear. Yet, as closely as Robse stood to his sovereign, he could discern, beneath the proud stance and lifted chin, the youth and inexperience that made this king so much more vulnerable than any in the long line of his ancestors.

Robse's gaze was drawn beyond Aelric, standing in the pool of many-colored light that cascaded through the tall window at the head of the Chamber, to the dimness of the vast Hall. The Great Hall, with its dais and thrones at the head and its waterfall and pool at the foot, had for untold centuries been the site of coronations, birth announcements, and state receptions. On the occasions of other coronations, the Hall had been packed to capacity, with two thousand eager Elves participating in the rites of fealty and noble Faeries witnessing. Many more thousands would be massed outside the Hall, patiently awaiting their turns to bow before the throne and give their loyalty to the new ruler. Traditionally, the Ceremony of the Swearing would take days, all good-naturedly swathed in feasting and song.

Now, by contrast, as if to underscore the dreadful circumstances in which they found themselves, all the Faeltheon left alive were clustered dejectedly in the center of the Great Hall, trying to take what hope they could from the survival of their king's son, now their new monarch.

Robse swallowed again to see them there, so few, so silent. Gaelcar's final count of survivors had been given to the Council last night. Two hundred twelve remained of all the many families and tribes of the Faeltheon upon the Earth. Two hundred twelve souls, including the king and his Companions. They would need only three ships tomorrow to take them into their uncertain future.

Aelric was speaking now, the formal phrases rolling through the nearly empty Hall, investing Gaelcar Talathaem with the role and duties of the Seneschal. Gaelcar knelt before his new lord, his hands clasped palm to palm, resting between Aelric's own palms.

"*Í, Gaelcar Talathaem, ven ergashat ír rysaros an Faeltheon anaon íraem aon ceilihten domar aím, a'aia í neademar yehon ergashai.*" The new Seneschal's voice was steady and clear as he accepted his duties, vowing to serve the king and the Faeltheon with all that was in him, for all of the days given him, until he was released from service.

Aelric accepted his vows and released his hands, pulling him to his feet. Gaelcar bowed and Aelric took him by the shoulders and bestowed the kiss of the king upon Gaelcar's brow. The older Elf quietly resumed his place in the row of the king's Companions, and Robse knew it was his turn.

Trying to cover the fine tremor in his hands, Robse stepped forth in response to the summons in his sovereign's voice. In a moment, as he bowed before Aelric, Robse had a sudden deep desire that pierced him like a sword thrust that his family could be here with him to see and to share in the honor being given him. Yet, hard on the heels of that thought came the painful knowledge that if they had been present, he would not be up here receiving this honor, for it would have gone to his father. Riende, the faithful Guardian would have become Riende, the trusted Champion. In that bitter moment, Robse would have given all he had left to make it so.

Aelric's hands closed warm and strong about his own, and Robse looked up to meet the knowing sympathy in the golden eyes. A rush of affection for the young ruler lit Robse's eyes, and the sudden light in them gave Aelric confidence, both in his choice and in his future. Robse relinquished his hands to Aelric's grasp, symbolizing placing his hands, his whole being, into the king's hands to be used as he saw fit. The ceremony continued, including the proffering of Riende's sword to Aelric and its return to Robse, consecrated to his king's service.

Robse remembered the words of King Beregos, which Aelric had shared with him last night after the Council had dispersed. *I love not War. I do not admire its various aspects: the arrow with its swift accuracy, the sword in its flashing elegance. I do not seek the glory of a warrior in battle. The fierce blood of battle does not rise in my heart at the thought of a fight. I cannot so easily dismiss the desperate fear of those forced to War, the cries of the wounded, the tears of the bereaved. I love instead the things I fight to defend: my people, their homes, their fields and flocks, our ancient culture, and our peaceful way of life. Yes, for love of these things, I will War, if I am forced to it to protect them. For love, I will take up arms.*

The old king's words echoed in Robse's mind as he bowed his head in prayer. He was a young man who loved poetry and music, carving and working with his hands, but he was being asked to make his life's work one of war. He had spent all last night on his knees before the Throne of the King of kings, seeking to still the voices of protest in his own heart, so that he might, with clear and serious mien, take upon himself true vows today to serve his lord in the capacity of warrior and Champion, despite his personal disinclinations.

Fresh from his vigil of the night, with Beregos's words for a guide,

Robse gave himself in service to his young sovereign with a whole heart. *I love not war…*

Lucina and Davin had chosen to spend the day together, enjoying each other's company in the beautiful meadows of Marliondolen. They planned to spend the entire day alone, as Davin insisted they had not had sufficient time with one another since their marriage. They had packed a picnic lunch to share and had already begun on sweet conversation as they walked hand in hand toward a lovely valley some distance away from the forest where the Faeltheon had settled.

Lucina, in the midst of a rare laugh, had turned to send a playful comeback to a mischievous comment her husband had made when an odd sparkling gleam caught her eye. Years of training sent her mind and body into alert. Play dropped from her like a cloak, and her husband saw the Border Guard he had married reappear. Though Davin's mind knew there was no danger of Goblins or any other enemies lurking in Marliondolen, the expression on Lucina's face gave him pause. In an instant he was by her side, but more relaxed than she, for he could not believe harm would come to them here.

Together, they watched the spectacle that materialized before them. A window-like image shimmered in the air, though around it the meadow went on unbroken, unperturbed. Within the opening, the two perceived a vision of their old Land, though it seemed to be an area beyond the Great Birch Forest, nearer the sea. It appeared to be the Elven kingdom, though much of it stood in ruins. Horrified and amazed, Lucina and Davin approached the portal to observe more closely this message from the Creator.

Davin exchanged a speaking glance with Lucina, and she knew he was thinking of the tale Theomanus and the others had told of a massive Goblin army they had seen in a window like this one. In that earlier vision, the hideous army had been approaching the Land. The recent massive influx into Marliondolen of dazed and weary Elves slain in mighty battles had confirmed to its inhabitants that that monstrous force had arrived and had attacked the Elven holdings.

Peering closely, the former Border Guards could now see shapes that quickly resolved into Elves boarding great ships drawn up to what was left of the fishing docks. Around them were the burned and shattered hulks of many other ships. The Elves marching slowly onto the three ships standing ready did not appear to be as glad to be embarking upon their quest as the Faeries had been to enter Marliondolen. Their heads drooped, as if they were too weary or burdened with grief to stand tall. Some were helping others, who seemed to be wounded, and several appeared to be weeping as they climbed the long planks into the vessels. Silently, Davin pointed out the unusually great proportion of children.

As the window widened, Lucina broke the silence in a voice that hurt Davin to hear.

"They are few, *far* fewer than they were."

Davin nodded, his eyes blinking at the enormous devastation the window showed them. The charred remains of ruined ships littered the shore; bits of burnt and broken homes were strewn about the beach. There were many large patches of freshly turned dirt, evidence of massive Elven burials. It was horribly obvious that these few were all that were left on Earth of the once mighty Faeltheon people. The Faerie couple fell silent, in mourning with their Elven Kin, as they watched the last Elf limp slowly up to his ship.

Their concentration was broken abruptly by the sound of soft footfalls in the meadow grass behind them. Lucina whirled, her taut emotions making her overreact. Davin was merely wary, expecting no enemy, yet still on edge from what they'd just witnessed. Before them stood the Elven Seer, Elrad, whom they had sometimes glimpsed during their stay in the royal palace during their final days in their old Land.

"It is impossible to surprise a Border Guard." The aged Elf greeted them with a small smile. "I often come this way to enjoy fellowship with the

Creator. I did not expect company today, but I have felt a deep stirring that pressed me to come here. You have seen what the Lord is showing you?"

They nodded, but Lucina's direct gaze was as troubled as Davin's.

"Do you know what He has shown us?" questioned Lucina softly. The old Elf nodded solemnly, acknowledging their trouble.

"Yes. I, too, have seen it, in a vision given long ago."

"Has it happened? Is this a true vision?" asked Davin, his throat tight as his eyes turned back to the shimmering window.

"If you mean, is this happening right now, I believe it is," replied the Seer. His face was beautiful, timeless and still, as if he felt himself in the presence of the Creator, but his eyes were old with a deep pain in their turquoise depths.

"What will become of them?" Lucina ventured.

Elrad's eyes met Lucina's, full of wisdom that could come only from long years spent learning from the Creator. "Even I cannot tell the future, child. It is not for us to know what will befall anyone, except as the Lord reveals it for His plan's sake. I do not know what will become of them. They cannot stay behind in the Land, for they will be discovered and destroyed by their enemies. No matter what happens, they cannot turn back to the lives they led before."

Lucina nodded slowly, inwardly grieving for the plight of her Elven Kindred. Elrad was right: it was obvious the remnant of the Elves could not return to the happy, peaceful lives they had enjoyed before the terrible alliance of Men and Goblins had been formed against the Faeltheon. They would certainly perish if they remained.

"He is taking them from this Land, leading them elsewhere. What He wants them to become, only He knows," the Elf concluded.

"What if they cannot find what He is leading them to?" Davin asked, eyes on the departing ships. Elrad smiled wearily.

"The Creator has already proven to us that what He wills will happen. Their future depends upon their readiness to respond to His desires for them. He will make a way to enact His plans, which may include preserving them. I sense that the path He has chosen for them will not be easy, but I cannot perceive what it holds. One thing is sure, though." He paused and looked them each in the eye, weighing his point. "As our Kindred proceed along the way He has made for them, they can grow in only one of two ways: stronger or weaker."

Lucina nodded, understanding the wise Elf's message. She felt a chill, though the sun lay warm upon the meadow. Davin's hand enfolded hers as he moved to stand between her wings in an unconscious gesture of protection. She nestled her cold fingers into his warm clasp. She might not know what lay before these cousins, left behind when the Faeries departed for Marliondolen, but she could pray that they would grow stronger. Her eyes turned with Davin's, and they watched the three ships move slowly out of the harbor into the sea, taking what remained of the Faeltheon away from the Land.

Elrad left the young couple in the sun-drenched meadow and headed for the cool shadows of the forest. Within their friendly shade, he knew he would find those he considered his close companions. Now that his vision had been shown to others, he felt an urgency to gather with his friends and pray for their Kin. He tried to remember how long it had been since he'd seen that frightening and puzzling vision, but the years ran together like dew poured from a goblet. He had not spoken of those haunting dreams to anyone, save his friend Beregos, and then only as a possible warning. He'd been unable to imagine events that could reduce his people to this ragged remnant, fleeing the shores of the land they had been given, forsaking the trust laid upon them in order to save what was left of their Kindred. He was glad he had not awakened from this dream with a pressing need to tell of it. In the absence of the need to speak, his heart could take refuge in the belief that the events he saw were just a dream or perhaps a thing that might not happen, at least not for many years.

There was one thing he had not told Beregos when he had shared the dream with him. Many of the Elves boarding the vessels had looked up to the small group of figures standing at the quarterdeck rail of the lead vessel. They had looked with eyes full of wary, desperate hope upon the tall, still figure in the purple cloak. Their king had returned their gazes, steadfast and strong, the stars on his brow winking in the sullen light. One thing had stood out in Elrad's mind as he'd awakened, shivering, from the dream. Though the face of the king had been familiar, it had not belonged to Beregos. It had been the visage of his son, Aelric.

Stirred once more by the grief of the terrible losses sustained by their people, Elrad knocked upon the door of the pleasant cottage that housed Beregos and his wife, Ashwyn. Receiving no answer, he walked around the cottage to the garden in the back. Several of the snug structures had been built in a curve around a natural hollow. As all the homes backed onto this same grassy spot, sheltering and protecting it, the inhabitants had chosen to plant it together and share the garden.

As he'd suspected, Elrad found his friends gathered here, under the shade of the large trees they had incorporated into their homes. Elamani was seated on a moss-covered rock, with her husband, Riende, at her feet. The crown of flowers she had been weaving lay discarded beside her. Beregos sat on a stone bench near them, his wife's hand in his. Seated on a low, curved branch, hand in hand, were Aelwyn and Gael. Perched on the little bridge that arched across the stream sat Nausika and Elwyn, their feet trailing in the cool, chuckling water. Laslorn was crossing the garden toward them, from Riende and Elamani's home, carrying a pitcher and a stack of earthenware cups. Theomanus was standing on the bridge. Elrad noted that his stance between Elwyn's wings was protective. Sensing their tension, Elrad's steps faltered.

Elamani saw him first and jumped up to draw him over to her rock. She seated him there and sat in the cool green grass at her husband's side. Laslorn handed the Seer a cup of melon juice, laced with honey. The light drink was just what he needed to refresh himself, and the drinking of it gave him a chance to regain his composure. When the others had all been served, and Theo had stashed the pitcher in a shallow pool of the cool stream, Elrad found all eyes upon him. Theomanus spoke for them all.

"We've had another window," he began, amber eyes darkening with the memory of what they'd seen. Elrad was struck with the resemblance between Theo's eyes and those of his cousin, Aelric, as he'd stood upon the high deck of his ship. He nodded.

"You saw them board the ships then," he confirmed quietly. Their startled looks restored his sense of humor and balance. Smothering a chuckle, he waved a hand at them. "No, I've no special powers to read your minds! I've just come from Lucina and Davin. They were given the same vision." Theo and Laslorn exchanged glances, weighing the importance of a vision shown to many. Beregos turned to Elrad.

"Speaking of visions, my friend, did you not See this years ago? I seem to remember you telling me of something very similar. It has haunted me this past hour, for I could have acted on your warning and much of this grief might have been prevented."

Elrad laid his hand on his troubled friend's shoulder.

"I did See this, Beregos, and I did tell you of it. Certainly, things would have gone much differently, if we had known then what we know now, but there was no way to guess what would befall our people to bring them to this pass. You cannot know what would have happened had you taken action at my words, so stop berating yourself, my friend."

Beregos shook his head, but Riende spoke into the small silence.

"We all made choices that seemed right to us. You," he gestured toward Elrad and the two younger couples, "chose to believe in Marliondolen and the grace of the Creator to provide for us in our need. You were right. Our dream of finding our island birthplace and returning to the fellowship with our Maker, which we knew before the Fall of Man, was a vain and empty one. It is as you told us, Elrad: we cannot go back. As a people, we must go forward; we must grow in wisdom and understanding. Only then, I believe, will we find that sweet communion with the Lord that we crave."

Elrad was nodding with his friend's words, and Theomanus looked as though he wanted to say something but felt the time was not right. Elrad made a mental note to pull him aside later and ask what was on his mind.

"Yet now, with the threat of the alliance driving what is left of our people away from the Land, what is left to them but to seek for the island?" asked Elamani, as ever unafraid to ask the hard questions.

"They will likely do just that," replied Elrad, unperturbed. He felt a familiar warmth flare within him as he continued. "But even if they do find their roots, life will not be as it was when we dwelt there before. They will be forced to make changes and to learn new ways. They will become different, though I do not know in what way." Elrad felt their gazes upon him, as the slight flush of power faded. Sometimes a vision would come upon him suddenly, but this had just been a strong but vague impression rather than a full vision. He shook his head as he handed Laslorn his cup for a refill. "I'm sorry; that is all I've Seen."

Elwyn's hand came up to lay over her husband's, where it rested on her shoulder. Her head raised, her chin jutting with a shadow of defiance. Her violet eyes sparkled as they met Elrad's waiting gaze.

"Then we will just have to trust Aematlon to make His perfect plans come about! We have seen His faithfulness to us. He will not abandon our Kin any more than He did us. He will bring them safely home."

Riende's eyes smiled gently at her for her passion.

"Indeed, He has been more than gracious to those of us who did not believe in His provision. He allowed us to come here to this haven, in spite of our foolishness and stubbornness. His steadfast love has strengthened our faith. Truly, we have reason to give thanks."

The three Goblin spies drew close to the anticipated site of the battle, their nervousness increasing as they neared their destination. Each Goblin had tied to his waist a pouch containing various body parts of small animals, which they were consuming with rapid haste, as though they feared the gruesome meal might be the last they would experience. The shortest, scrawniest of the three was babbling pitifully to his cohorts in the brief pauses between his convulsive gulps.

"We will die! If the Elves are not all dead, we will have to report it to Thragsmor, and he will take it out on us, of course!"

The Goblin's whining voice ceased for a moment as he stuffed what appeared to be a rat's hindquarters into his wide, nearly lipless mouth.

The next of his companions hissed, "Even if all the Elves have been killed by our great forces, we are still humiliated at being forced to come here at the command of that *Human*!"

The tallest Goblin joined the conversation, smirking, as though briefly forgetting his possible death at the hands of his leader.

"Soon, Men will not be so cocky. They think that they are in command of us. They think that they are able to use us, to insult us, and to threaten us forever, but they are wrong. Our minds are far greater than they dare to imagine, and we are developing superior warriors under their training faster than we are allowing them to know. Soon, *they* will be yielding to *our* demands."

Sneers spread across the faces of the other two Goblins as they pondered the ingenious method that they had just now learned they were using to take advantage of the Human race. The sneers quickly disappeared, however, as they topped the rise overlooking the battlefield. Six blood-red eyes anxiously scanned the strip of seaside land which was barren and scarred and stained with dark patches that still reeked faintly of blood.

Finally, the smallest of the three exclaimed with relief, "No Elves!"

The scout nearest to him immediately administered a bone-cracking whack to his helmet, and he yelped and cowered away. The larger spy pointed off to their right. The taint of old smoke lay heavy on the sea breeze, and now the other scouts could see the remains of a large pit. From the smell, it had been used to burn the dead. Goblin dead, undoubtedly, as the Elves buried their own dead, instead of eating them, as decent, civilized folk did, thus keeping the strength of the fallen warriors within the people. The largest spy turned on the smallest with contempt.

"No Elves at all, you fool! No living Elves and no dead Elves. Who dug the pit and burned the warriors? Did the dead Elven bodies walk away?"

The subdued Goblin once again searched the field desperately. He began to tremble slightly as he realized the full significance of the lack of Elven bodies. Instantly, his bony fingers dipped into his pouch, seeking comfort, and he began stuffing his mouth with the dried frog's intestines he had hoarded against such a time. He hated being the smallest! Resolutely, he munched, hunching away from the repeated blows as his larger comrades continued to whack him.

Part II

The Sea

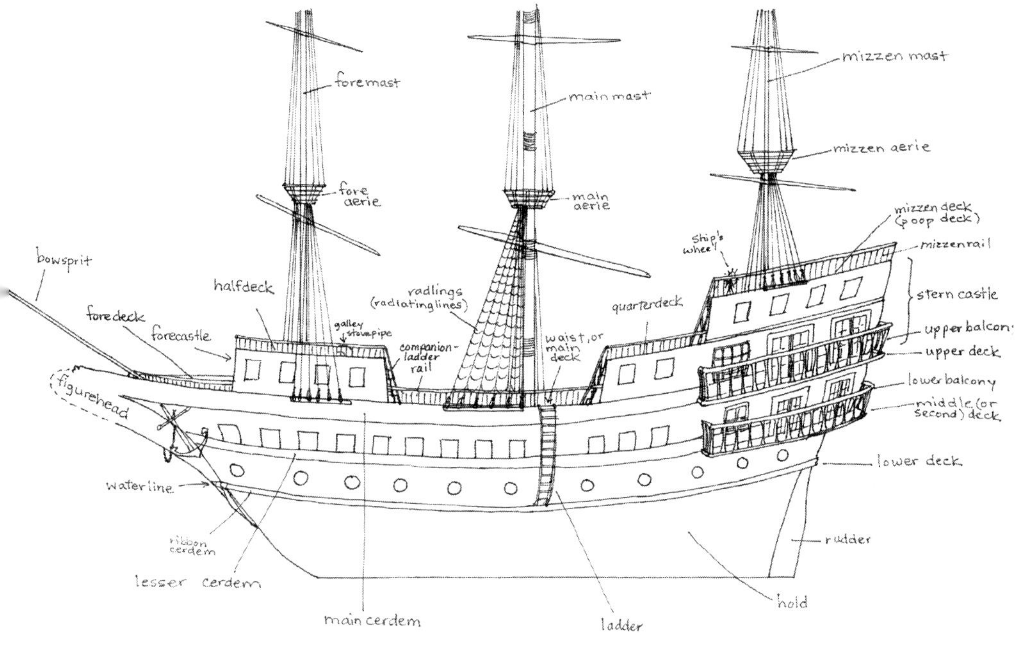
foremast
main mast
mizzen mast
mizzen aerie
fore aerie
main aerie
mizzen deck (poop deck)
mizzenrail
Ship's wheel
bowsprit
halfdeck
radlings (radiatinglines)
stern castle
foredeck
forecastle
galley stovepipe
companion-ladder rail
waist, or main deck
quarterdeck
upper balcon·
upper deck
lowerbalcony
figurehead
middle (or second) deck
lower deck
waterline
ribbon cerdem
rudder
lesser cerdem
hold
main cerdem
ladder

Chapter Seven

Gaelcar unconsciously touched his fingers to his throbbing temples and groaned. Some days it seemed that he would never quite be through with his official duties. It had been a daunting job to portion out the able-bodied with the recovering wounded and the orphans, especially as he had tried to keep families together as much as possible. Somehow, he had succeeded in dividing the remnant more or less equally. The *Cethastea*, the lead ship carrying the king and his Companions, held seventy-one Elves. The *Dridelphanen* carried the same, and the *Gaelrandel* shipped seventy.

Now that the entire Elven race was spread evenly throughout the three ships, Gaelcar needed to assign tasks and duties to the individual Elves. Though the rotation of duties and the changing of tasks would fall to leaders aboard the other ships eventually, in the beginning of this perilous journey, with the shock of their losses still hard upon them, there was no one else old enough or capable enough to see to the initial organization.

The Seneschal would have preferred to have accomplished this portion of his duties before they had set sail, but the urgency riding King Aelric had forbidden them to linger beyond the time it had taken the ill and injured to be well enough to be moved aboard. Even now, when they had been at sea for some days, many were unfit to take up any duties as yet. Therefore, as he assigned tasks, Gaelcar must also consider those who must care for the ill, and those who, being strong enough, must take on the duties of the bedridden, as well as their own chores.

This task of settling initial duties was especially complex because not only must he be able to assign each Elf a job based upon his abilities, but he had to make certain that no one would be overwhelmed with work, at the same time assuring that there were enough assigned to see each task covered. Though the willing messenger birds fluttered and murmured in their wicker shelters on the deck, Gaelcar had decided to send Elven messengers by ship's boats to the various families living aboard the other two ships to find out the jobs for which each individual was best suited.

Those with the aptitude to learn to handle the large ships were in demand, as the Faeltheon had never been a major seafaring species prior to their exile. Small fishing boats had met their seagoing needs for generations, so there was really no one skilled enough to guide them on this journey. They must simply learn as each occasion presented itself. Gaelcar himself, with several others, was learning how to run the *Cethastea,* so that they might serve as relief commanders when Captain Lysion and his first mate were off duty. He knew others were taking similar training aboard the other two vessels.

Healers, too, were needed, since many of the Elves on the ships were still recovering from wounds received in the battles against the Goblins. Worse than the wounds themselves were the deadly diseases that took advantage of the victims' weakened states. Even before they'd set sail, a new fever-like illness had claimed the lives of several injured Elves, and Gaelcar feared that the disease would sweep from the beds of the sick to the healthy Elves aboard the vessels, especially the fragile children who made up a large portion of the survivors. He needed to organize a group of healers quickly to ensure that there would be no epidemics aboard the floating sanctuaries.

Gaelcar also noted that patient and gentle Elven "parents" would be needed to tend to the crowds of children, the majority of whom were now orphans. Many of them now ran unsupervised about the decks. One of the youngsters could easily slip and fall from the ship, the Seneschal realized, and the busy young adults would not even notice that he was missing until long after the child had drowned. These foster parents would also have the task and duty of teaching the children; passing down the history, customs, and arts of their ancient race to this newest generation of Elves. The Elven people may have been exiled from their homes, but they certainly would not forget their heritage!

In addition to these important tasks, Gaelcar also needed to organize teams of Elves who would produce various necessities and perform other mandatory chores on the ships. Since they could no longer rely on the bountiful forests to supply their food, fishing lines needed to be set and artificial gardens planted to produce the nutrition the Elves needed. Gaelcar decided that he would put the teams of unskilled laborers on a rotating schedule that changed every two weeks, so that no one team would be forced to do the less savory duties for very long. These were ones who would do tasks such as keeping the ships clean, tending fires, drawing water, distilling seawater into fresh, tending the plants and livestock, and cooking. Those who were skilled in their jobs, like the healers, teachers, and sailors, would work on a more permanent schedule.

Gaelcar rose from his seat and stretched his weary back. He had to bend his arms at the elbows to keep from bumping the low ceiling of his office, but the stretching of his cramped muscles helped. As he gazed from his large window out to the brilliantly blue sea, he was grateful for the space to work. Aboard ship, space was at a premium, and having his own office in the upper level of the sterncastle made his duties easier to perform.

He turned as the first of his messengers returned. The young aide bowed slightly in respect for Gaelcar's high position, then handed him a rolled scroll on which he had scribbled the names and special talents of those whom he had visited. Thanking the youth for his hard work, Gaelcar opened the scroll and began to read the long lists of Elven recruits. As soon as the messenger left, the Seneschal sat down to begin organizing the task forces. It was very likely that he would be awake long into the night with this assignment, but he was determined to see that it was finished as soon as possible and his people able to settle into their new way of life.

Minlienda paused to rest her arms. The burning sensation gradually faded, and she took up her task once more. The monotonous pull and grasp, pull and grasp was punctuated by the squeaking of the chain at each turn of the crank. The muffled thumping of the wooden bucket as it bumped the hull cautioned her, and she slowed her pace slightly. It seemed a long time but was really only a few minutes before the brimming bucket of seawater was level with the open porthole.

At its appearance, little Doma reached her hands for its rim and carefully tipped its sloshing contents into the trough below the porthole. This was the third bucket full, and their careful handling had spilled little, so that the water made daring dashes at the rim of the trough but did not spill over onto the damp floor. Min gave the child a smile of thanks and sent her on to one of the other chores suitable for small hands.

Ciella came up behind Min, with a bucket over one strong arm. With a quiet word of thanks for the water, she scooped out a bucketful and headed off to finish scrubbing the deck of the second level. Min laid her hands upon the spokes of the winch once more, but they were joined by larger hands. Glancing back, she saw Lashar, *amios* cousin to Domel, grinning down at her.

"My turn, little song," he remarked cheerfully, taking the wheel from her. Glad to pass on to another task for a while, Min returned his smile and slipped out of the trough alcove.

As she turned to enter the large, open all-purpose room that dominated the second level, a gust of salt-scented air blew in through the open port, lifting her hair. It was strange to her to smell the salt air all around, though she knew it seemed almost normal to those who had lived along the coast of the Land. In her snug home in the foothills of the mountains, the air had been cool, scented with wildflowers in spring and the crisp snap of turning leaves in the fall. For a moment she stood, unaware of the rolling deck beneath her feet, transfixed by the memory of a brisk fall day, gathering late apples, the cry of a hawk on the wind a wild, sweet portent of winter. In a moment, the memory was swept away on the salt breeze and the myriad creaks and groans of a living ship.

Minlienda moved briskly past the main companionway, pausing a moment in the center of the broad, all-purpose dining-recreationworkroom, to see if anyone working there had a need she could tend on her way. The spacious room was graceful, if low ceilinged. The walls curved up to meet the beams of dark wood that had been secured there in a grid formation to form the hanging gardens that sheltered their plants and cuttings. The herbs and seedling were in a similar hanging structure in the workroom on the port side, ahead and on Min's right, as she was facing astern.

Across the passageway from the smaller workroom, she could hear the chanting of a group of children's voices as they learned by rote one of the traditional lays. She listened for a moment and identified one of her favorites: the "Saga of the Three Sisters." She had always loved that tale of the triplet sisters who had chosen to die at their enemy's hands rather than to betray the Faeltheon people. Legend told that when they'd died, burned to death by Goblins, there were no remains, not even bones, but that a beautiful cluster of three bright stars had appeared in the night sky where they had not been before.

The song, poignant and haunting, roughened her skin with goose bumps. She glanced around the big common room and met the knowing twinkle in the eyes of one of the Elf women, who rubbed her own arms with a small smile. Others, busy braiding rope, had stopped their chatter to listen. No one indicated a need, so Min drew back to the forward companionway and climbed to the upper deck, emerging through the forward hatch onto the broad planking.

There the sea breeze was no idle companion. The wind was full and invigorating, belling the sails and making the canvas snap. The rope eyes spliced into the corners of the canvas sails and secured by thicker ropes to the sides of the ship groaned and muttered, sounding like giant sleeping dogs. The tackle securing the sails to the spars far above creaked and sang, and the wind boomed in the canvas, making Min aware that they were tacking into the wind.

She turned her eyes astern, past the mainmast, over the quarterdeck, up to the sterncastle deck. She smoothed her whipping hair out of her eyes, squinting to see Lysion, the captain of the *Cethastea*, at the great wheel. The ship listed slightly to port, and the great booms near the bottoms of the mainmast and the foremast swung in a smooth, synchronized arc to take up their new positions, belling once again with the fierce wind. Min could see the familiar shape of Gaelcar standing beside Lysion, Cerlim behind them.

In a pleasant ceremony a few nights before, Gaelcar had been given the honorary rank of captain, though it was understood that Lysion was in command of the vessel and her operations. This new rank conferred upon Gaelcar the rights and responsibilities of a captain in the absence of Lysion or his first mate, Rannel. It also enabled Gaelcar to represent the *Cethastea* when they went ashore to deal among Humans, as it seemed they would have to do soon. Still, the positions to the right and left of the ship's wheel were becoming the typical places to find Gaelcar and Cerlim, who had quickly become enamored with the mechanics of sailing the ship. Min knew that Lysion was training them and any others who showed interest. Soon, they would be pulling duty watches unsupervised.

Minlienda turned to face forward, moving to her left, skirting the goat pen and the distilling apparatus, and leaned out over the port rail, looking ahead. The endless sea rolled on before them, beautiful in the midday sun. Behind her, she heard a door open and turned to see Aelric emerging from the sterncastle, Robse in his wake. She chuckled to herself at this nautical metaphor, but her eyes lingered on the second form. She couldn't be sure, but it looked to her as if Robse had grown over the past month at sea. He was nearly of a height with the king now, if less broad. Peering critically, she decided that his shoulders matched Aelric's in width, but the younger Elf still had something of the stripling about his gangly length. Aelric was intent on his errand and climbed up the ladder steps to the quarterdeck, then on to the mizzendeck, but Robse's eyes swept the ship first, seeing her and nodding politely before he followed the king.

Min let her eyes play across the main deck once more. Behind her was the sterncastle, including the lower level roofed by the quarterdeck. This lower level contained Aelric's office, quarters for the Companions, and a common room, used as a conference room and private dining room. In order to be housed together, to be available at all times to Aelric, the Companions had chosen to share the cabins, though they were slightly cramped with two. Aelric and Gaelcar had the sternmost cabin, with Robse and Domel across the aisle from them. Min and Caerdrys were between the king's cabin and the common room, and Randelos and Cerlim were across from them. The upper level of the sterncastle housed the captain's cabin and his office, Gaelcar's office, and the first mate's quarters. Above these quarters, reached by the ladder steps Aelric had just ascended, was the sterncastle deck, from which sprang the mizzenmast and, nearby, the ship's wheel.

Facing forward, Min watched the Elves-turned-sailors as they swarmed in the rigging, neatly reefing the upper topsails on the fore and main masts. They seemed at home climbing the ladder-like radlings, a shortened term for the radiating lines that swooped from the tall yards to the aeries and then to the sides of the ship. Min supposed it was much like climbing trees back home, only requiring one to keep balance with the swaying of the ship.

She could see the lookouts, posted in their aeries in the middle of the three masts, and waved back to young Cethlas in the mizzen aerie, when he caught sight of her and enthusiastically gestured. It warmed her to see how these new tasks and responsibilities were giving the people, especially the very young, a sense of accomplishment and interest to balance their collective grief and the futility and emptiness of death.

Ahead of her, beyond the goat pen, the deck rose by means of another ladder stair to the half deck that roofed the "crew's quarters." These were the rooms reserved for those few whose interest in the functioning of the ship was full time and required them to be near the sails as much as possible. On the surface of the half deck, the chickens and guinea fowl roosted quietly in their hutches on the port side, and the blunt, rounded chimney of the cookstove from the galley below poked up near the starboard side. Sharing the space below the half deck with the crew quarters were the galley and the pantry stores, which opened out ahead onto the small, triangular foredeck.

Noting the time by the position of the sun's shadows on the deck, Min hurried forward. It was her turn to help with preparations for the evening meal, and feeding seventy Elves, even in shifts, was no light matter!

"Aelric!" Gaelcar caught the king's attention as he passed.

"I assume that you have noticed the port?" Aelric responded, turning to face him, while gesturing toward the distant isle visible on the horizon. Even from this far out, the presence of many ships could be discerned, clustered and swarming around one end of the island like bees around a green hive. Gaelcar nodded and turned to walk with Aelric toward the helm.

"I know we have discussed the fact that we need to stop soon for provisions and anything we can find in the way of maps, but do you think it wise to stop here? We will need time to prepare ourselves before we reach the port."

"We will need time to prepare," Aelric agreed, nodding his dark head sharply. "We need to inform everyone of our plan of action. We need to assemble our party and brief them on the protocol we are to use in the presence of the Humans." He paused as they approached the helm. "And we need to pray." He turned his attention to the ship's captain.

"Lysion, how long before we reach that island?"

"I estimate we could be there by nightfall," Lysion responded.

Aelric looked out over the ocean and ran his long fingers through his hair. "Is there any way that you can give us more time? We would like to get there early tomorrow morning." He eyed the older Elf hopefully.

"We could tack a wider arc of approach," the captain mused, stroking his chin with one hand. "And if we furl the mainsails, we'll make slower time. However, we would have to do it quickly."

"Then do it now, Captain. That should give us the time we need to prepare." Gaelcar and Lysion nodded to Aelric. The king turned to Gaelcar. "I'll gather our party together and bring them to the common room, if you could make sure that other ships know our plan. Come as soon as you can."

Aelric's party consisted of Gaelcar, Robse, Caerdrys, Minlienda, Randelos, Domel, and Lysion. They all filed into the small, low-ceilinged room and took their respective places. There was an air of nervousness and excitement as Aelric began to explain his plan.

"When we go ashore, we will be wearing hats lest our ears arouse suspicion. We must be observant, looking for and adopting the mannerisms and customs of the Men around us. The last thing we need is to stand out in the crowd," Aelric began.

"For what will we be trading?" Caerdrys asked.

"Fresh water is presently of the highest importance to us, but we should also trade for grain, and maps or information," Gaelcar responded.

"What are we taking to trade?" Minlienda inquired.

Aelric numbered their goods on slender fingers. "We have carved buttons, woven fabrics, and a few silver items. We'll just have to hope that it will be enough."

Robse shifted restlessly in his chair, hesitant to ask that most important question no one was addressing. Receiving a look from his king, Robse put into words their greatest concern.

"What about the Men's disbelief? If we are in contact with them for too long, we may not even be able to make it back to the ship."

Gaelcar took in a deep breath before responding. "We Elves have never been in direct contact with Men before. We cannot know how severe the effect will be or how long it will take for us to weaken. This venture is extremely dangerous because we know so little."

Aelric spoke up. "Given what we *don't* know, I suggest you pray and get a good night's rest."

Chapter Eight

The next morning, just past sunrise, the *Cethastea* warped into the primitive harbor of the island. According to the plan devised last evening, the other two ships remained out at sea, but close enough to come to their compatriots' aid, should the *Cethastea* signal for help. For the previous half hour the Elves had been able to see, hear, and smell the masses of Humans in the dock front city. The place had begun to bustle at first light, though many of the Men shuffling about were ending their night's activities rather than beginning the day's work. By the time the Elven ship drew close enough to jockey for position in the harbor, the noisome place was bustling, reeking, and resounding with shouted profanities.

The trading party stepped down onto the stained and filthy dock, only to be surrounded immediately by a mayhem of tanned, leathery-skinned Men shouting orders at one another with harsh voices. There were cursing captains threatening their men with drawn swords, slaves struggling under immense loads, sweating laborers, and hawking vendors. The chaos was incredible, the noise and stench enough to overwhelm the Elves at the outset. They tried their hardest to walk nonchalantly down the dock and to conceal their horrified expressions. Fortunately, the Humans were unlikely to notice the strangers' looks, for they seemed to care for nothing beyond their own affairs. The Faeltheon party walked in a compact group, with Aelric at the front and Robse bringing up the rear.

As soon as they entered the marketplace, Robse's senses sharpened even more. He knew that, as Champion, the safety of the king, if not the whole group, was on his shoulders and that any relaxation of alertness on his part could cost them everything. He forced himself to maintain constant awareness of the state of every member of the group and to scrutinize carefully anyone who approached them. As his eyes scanned across the party, he noticed that Caerdrys looked more high-strung than usual, as if she might snap at any moment.

In truth, Caerdrys felt smothered. The marketplace was so crowded that dirty, noisome Men were constantly bumping into her, and every time her shoulder so much as brushed one of theirs, chills ran down her spine. The cacophony pounded inside her head. Never before had she heard so much shouting and bellowing in one place. As she followed Aelric, she was amazed at how he managed to keep his appearance so calm.

Aelric was focused on the task at hand. He watched and absorbed his surroundings, attempting to learn as much of Men's culture as possible in the short time he had. He stopped near a vendor who sold fresh water and watched as a customer tried to make a fair trade.

"I'll give you three of my large spools of rope fer five barrels of water," the customer offered.

The vendor leaned over the counter to judge the rope. He stroked his beard and pondered the offer. "I'll take seven spools of rope an' no less, mark my words."

Gaelcar raised his eyebrows in disbelief. The offer had been far too low, and the counteroffer far too high.

"Are you mad?" the customer shouted back. "This is good, strong rope. You'll not get seven spools out of me, that's for sure!"

"Well, then you're not going to get five barrels! You can die of thirst, for all I care."

The customer grunted and clenched his fist. "Fine! I'll give you four spools for six barrels."

"You'll give me six for six or nothing, you filthy scum!"

Gaelcar balked again. The logic didn't make sense. This was the most unethical trading he had ever witnessed.

"Well, maybe I'll just go somewhere else then!" retorted the customer. "Your water's probably not fit to drink anyway."

"There ain't nothin' wrong with my water! It's the best water you can get! It's six for six, or you can get water from somebody else an' end up drinking mud!"

The enraged customer turned to leave, then paused. He growled and turned back around. "I'll give you five for six, but it's a lot more than you deserve, you scurvy rat!"

The vendor looked at the rope again, his expression sour and his voice disgusted. "Fine, then. I'll take it, but I'm being generous."

Aelric was astonished. They had both begun with ridiculous offers, then screamed at each other for a while, ending up with a deal that seemed to satisfy neither party. Yet when the transaction was over, and the Men turned their faces away from one another, each seemed proud of himself. The whole process was foreign to Aelric. Puzzled and a bit apprehensive, he led his group over to a dirty outdoor eatery, where grubby customers sat. Most of the Men appeared to be swilling ale at a much greater rate than they were consuming the unappetizing food. The Elves settled uneasily in a relatively secluded corner where they could discuss their plan of action.

As they sat down on either side of a table made of rough-hewn planks set athwart a pair of rickety braces, Randelos took note of their nearest neighbor. He was a large, burly, thickly bearded sailor gnawing on a greasy turkey leg. The fetid grease ran down his beard, and he stopped to pick some skin out of his teeth. Randelos's stomach began to tie itself in knots at the ghastly display. He placed a hand over his mouth.

Robse, who'd noted the Man and Randelos's observation, saw that Randelos was turning a sickly pale color. The young Champion was concerned about his companions drawing attention to themselves by their more overt reactions. Shooting a warning glance at Randelos, Robse turned his attention to Gaelcar. The Seneschal was fastidious by nature and, though he was the more mature and experienced member of their party, even Gaelcar hadn't had any more contact with Men than the rest of them had.

Gaelcar was having a very hard time concealing his thoughts and emotions. His face mirrored his disgust at everything he saw around him. Customers and vendors shouted on all sides, cursing foully and spitting copiously. Common sailors settled almost everything with insults and fists; and everywhere Men drowned themselves in sour ale. Fortunately, Aelric interrupted his thoughts.

"I do not want to linger here long, but we need to discuss how we are going to get the water we need. I don't understand the process those Men were going through at all."

"Nor do I," Gaelcar responded. "It made no rational sense. Also, we appear to be overdressed. These people seem not to care about their appearance whatsoever."

Minlienda spoke up. "Caerdrys, have you noticed the odd looks they have been giving us? They stare at me like I don't belong here."

"Although I can hardly notice anything with all this noise pounding in my head, I've seen the looks, too," Caerdrys responded.

Lysion interjected on the ship's behalf. "We have to get water and information on the currents. We'd best do it quickly, as we can't leave everyone on board hiding below decks forever." He added, "And I can't stand this horrid stench much longer."

"I agree, Lysion. We cannot delay here any longer. Gaelcar, how much do you think I should offer them?" Aelric asked.

Gaelcar pondered the question for a moment. "I think that ten of the carved buttons and a roll of the dyed woven cloth should be a fair exchange for six barrels, but let him make the first offer just so we know what we are dealing with. My offer may be too low, as we don't know how much our goods are worth to these people."

Robse had been quiet through the conversation, but he took this opportunity to speak up. "I have been noticing the strange looks they have been giving all of us, and they seem very suspicious of us. With their volatile tempers, I'm concerned that the situation could become violent very quickly."

Aelric rose from the table. "Well then, I guess we had better hurry and get what we need."

The party followed Aelric to the same vendor they had watched just a few moments earlier. He took a deep breath of the foul-smelling air and resolutely approached the counter.

"Good morning," he offered.

The vendor sneered at him. "What do you want? I haven't got all day."

Aelric cleared his throat. "I need six barrels of water, please." He counted the carved buttons out of a small leather bag at his waist. Gaelcar proffered the bolt of cloth. "I have these to trade."

The vendor took a step back, eyeing the goods as if he had never seen anything like them before. His wonder turned quickly into suspicion.

"Who are you, and whence came you, that you bring such fine goods and clothe yourselves so richly?" he inquired.

"Where we are from can be of no concern to you. We simply wish to trade for some water," Aelric responded, hoping this merchant would not ask too many questions.

The Man looked bewildered by their party and quickly took the defensive.

"For starters, I won't have you tellin' me what my concerns are, and if you want to trade, you'd best begin by making an offer," he challenged belligerently.

Aelric did not want to upset him further, but he honestly didn't know what their goods were worth to this trader.

"I was hoping that you might make the first offer," he responded.

The vendor squinted his eyes at Aelric. "You trying to twist things about? Seeking advantage, are ya? The customer always makes the offer: that's how it goes, and I won't have you threatening my honor!" He slammed his fist on the counter.

Honor? I can find no honor in their trading methods! I cannot even find courtesy, let alone honesty! The thoughts ran through Aelric's head, and he couldn't think of anything to say to the Man.

Gaelcar stepped forward. "We are certainly not trying to threaten anyone, sir. We just don't know what our goods would be worth at this port."

"Same as they'd be at any other port! And I wasn't talking to you anyway, squid!" the uncouth merchant replied.

Gaelcar gasped at his rudeness. "I beg your pardon? That was not very—"

Aelric quickly pulled Gaelcar back from the counter and stepped in front of him.

"We'll give you ten of the buttons and a roll of the cloth if you will provide us with six barrels of water and maps of the currents in this region," he offered quickly. However, the merchant was now discussing their party with the vendor from an adjacent booth. They whispered with each other, frequently glancing up toward the Elves with looks of disdain. The newcomer turned to address Aelric.

"I bet you're from one of them big, fancy ships out there," he accused. "We think you're up to somethin.' We don't much like people who keep secrets from us. Who's yer backer and why are you so anxious to look over our goods and docks? You'd best not be plannin' no raid, for we won't stand for piracy an' such! Just tell who ye are and where ye came from, and you can have yer water and be on yer way."

Minlienda stood at the back of the group, watching Aelric and Gaelcar exchange confused glances. Clearly, they had no idea what the merchant was talking about. The tone of the trader's voice was becoming more hostile, and their little party was becoming the focus of a tense scene. Robse stood next to her, shifting his weight from side to side, as if he were ready to pounce at the slightest sign of violence. She noticed that the Elves were beginning to look paler and weaker as the tension rose.

Her attention was diverted from the scene when a Man carrying a large basket tripped and lurched into her. Instinctively, she caught his arm to help him.

"Are you all right?" she asked. The Man was startled to hear a woman's voice and looked up. He locked eyes with Minlienda and gasped. Her violet eyes with their vertical pupils were a definite shock.

A surge went up Min's arm and through her entire body, causing her to let go and fall backwards. Robse caught her and brought her quickly to her feet, lest they draw too much attention.

"Min? Are you all right?" he asked urgently, in a low voice.

She felt her energy somewhat renewed, though she still braced herself on Robse's arm.

"Yes—I'll be fine," she answered quietly. The Man grabbed his basket and scurried away as quickly as possible, shaking his head as if to wake himself from a dream.

Robse looked toward Aelric and heard shouts coming from behind the counter. He had been nervous before, but Minlienda's encounter made him trust his instincts. "We need to get back to the ship. We are too much at risk here." He caught Caerdrys's eyes and nodded to the pale Minlienda. Instantly, the taller Elf joined her sister, putting her arm supportively around Min's waist, although she felt weak herself.

Robse strode to the front of the group and caught Aelric's arm, turning his king to face away from the grimy booth. "We need to leave. Now," he said with such authority in his voice that it grabbed Aelric's attention. The golden eyes widened with understanding.

"We aren't getting anywhere with this. I'll take the lead; you bring up the rear," the king responded. "We'll take the quickest route to the docks."

Abruptly, they departed the scene, leaving the baffled and suspicious vendors to denigrate their manners in loud voices. Domel joined Minlienda, bringing his strong arm to support her on the other side from Caerdrys, and Min still tried her hardest to stand on her own two feet. She could tell that her sister was becoming weak. In fact, it seemed as though all of them were. Aelric and Robse appeared strong, but Min suspected the illusion was maintained by sheer willpower.

Aelric led them to the ship, weaving in and out of the crowd, but still trying to keep to the most direct route. He tried his hardest not to make eye contact or brush shoulders with anyone, because every time he did he could feel himself becoming weaker.

Word of the odd party's presence spread through the crowd like ripples on a suddenly agitated pond. Robse looked back to see many people pointing at them, with looks of suspicion and hostility. He wrenched his attention back to their little group. As they stepped onto the dock, he saw Lysion stumble, shaking his head as if to rid himself of a persistent dizziness, but Randelos quickly lent his support to the captain. Robse watched them weaving like drunken Men and knew that if their party had lingered any longer, they likely would not have made it back to the ship.

Cerlim, on duty on the *Cethastea's* deck, saw their desperate expressions as they approached and ordered two of the crewmembers to untie the ship. The other hands practically carried the party aboard, and they departed immediately to the dwindling shouts of the growing crowd on the dock front.

As soon as he knew they were safe, Aelric allowed his discipline to give way. He bent over with his hands on his knees, breathing hard. His limbs were trembling as though he had just performed some massive task of strength. Glancing up under his brows, he assessed the other members of the party. They were sprawled on the deck, slumped against the side of the ship like so many broken dolls. Robse was the only one still standing, bracing himself against the rail. Minlienda looked as though she would not be able to hold her head up much longer. All were pale and gleamed with moisture, and most had an alarming grayish cast to their skin.

Those clustered around them wore worried faces, hovering uncertainly, wanting to help, but not knowing what was wrong. Aelric knew he had to find a way to restore his closest friends without panicking the rest of his people. With an effort that seemed immense and out of proportion to his actions, he straightened and forced his voice to be as normal as possible.

"Everyone go rest. Meet me in my office at dusk to discuss what just happened," he managed to get out between breaths.

Minlienda had suffered the deepest drain, and she could barely conjure the strength to stand. Caerdrys tried to help her but no longer had the strength. Robse signaled for help, and Cerlim came forward and picked Min up in his arms to bear her away. Robse gave Caerdrys his arm as a support, and she leaned hard upon it, though he could tell it galled her to be so needy. He struggled briefly with a flare of jealousy that Cerlim had the honor of carrying Minlienda, but dismissed the feeling, too weary to fight that battle. Certainly, *he* didn't have the strength to carry anyone right now.

Soon enough, the women were in their cabin. After that, Robse forced his trembling body to make the rounds of the other Companions' rooms, to be sure they were all safely where they belonged. It was only after he had seen the king asleep in his hammock that Robse finally allowed his body to give in to the weakness it had been resisting.

Robse stumbled into the cabin he shared with Domel, trying to be quiet, though Dom was already deeply asleep and likely wouldn't hear him. He fell into his hammock and tried to analyze the day's events. He guessed the reason Minlienda had been affected more than the others was because of her gift of seeing into people. She had not only come into contact with these Men physically, but also spiritually. When he had caught her, he'd felt some of his strength pass to her and only wished he could have given her more.

His frustration finally came into focus as he forced himself to face the thing he'd been hiding from his own heart. The day's fiasco had been his fault, at least in part. He had been uneasy long before the others had seemed to notice. He had been tempted to say something to Aelric earlier, but had remained silent, reluctant to put himself forward. Now, he wished he had spoken up. If they had departed the docks sooner, their energy wouldn't have been so taxed, nor would they have drawn so much attention to themselves. His failure to trust his instincts had placed them all in greater jeopardy than they need have been; in truth, his self-consciousness had almost cost them their lives. They had so very nearly failed to make it back to the *Cethastea*.

As Champion, it had been his responsibility to watch out for the safety of the king and his Companions. By not speaking out when he should have, he had placed them at risk in a way his father never would have done. He had failed in the performance of his duty.

He was not old enough or experienced enough yet to realize that his self-evaluation was harsh. None of them had had contact with Humans before today, so there was no precedent, no experience to guide him and to help him know how and when to act upon his new duties.

Feeling a welling of bitter despair, Robse struggled to stay awake long enough to pray. His heavy eyes closed and his last conscious awareness was of Domel's gentle snores in the other hammock.

Chapter Nine

Aelric and his Companions, gesturing Cerlim down from his post at the ship's wheel along the way, filed into the king's office chamber and crowded round the table. The twelve-by-fourteen foot space was cramped holding all of them, but it was the same size as their common room and had the advantage of privacy. In spite of their long rest, the weakening of their powers had alarmed the young ruler more than he wished to admit. Aelric sighed dejectedly and leaned back into his chair as Cerlim closed the door and joined them.

"Well, that went terribly," Aelric remarked grimly. Cerlim looked surprised but waited for the news.

"It was our first encounter with Men, sire. It could have been worse," Gaelcar responded, trying to think positively. Robse looked up at him with one eyebrow raised.

"Really?"

"We just need to learn from our mistakes," persisted Gaelcar. "We were behaving in the correct manner for a trade, but they seemed to think we were being … too polite." Randelos snorted with grim humor. Aelric nodded, looking perplexed.

"Perhaps they don't trade the same way we do," Robse offered. "I mean, their customs may be different. There must have been some tradition we neglected, or … something," he finished lamely, flushing slightly with embarrassment at how weak his suggestion sounded. Domel nodded in agreement, ignoring the flustered look. Caerdrys turned to include Cerlim in her observations, disgust tingeing her voice.

"So it would seem. That Man in front of us was practically screaming at the water merchant because he wouldn't lower his price. I thought that was terrible, but it seemed as though everyone else was doing it too. The buyer kept trying to get the seller to lower the price, and the seller kept trying to boost the price higher. They went on and on, until they finally came to an agreement that it seemed *neither* of them was happy with. And yet, as soon as they turned from each other, each smiled unkindly, as if satisfied he had gotten some advantage over the other!" Others nodded, having observed the same thing. "The whole process was incomprehensible to me! What was the point?" She flung up her hands in a typical exasperated gesture and then had to make a grab for the lantern she'd set swinging with her unguarded blow. Minlienda ignored the outburst, pondering the strange customs they had seen.

"Yes, they were unkind in their treatment of one another, and it did seem as if each was trying to gain from the other's loss. And yet their hostility rang false, and there was a sense of mutual understanding between them even as they shouted and quarreled. I think they were playing a game," she ventured in her soft voice. They all paused to listen to her, Domel nodding as if his thoughts had kept pace with hers. "I think it was all an elaborate game of greed—one with rules and measures that should not be overstepped, and the skill of the player is marked by how closely he can walk the edges of acceptable margins."

Several members of the party nodded in agreement as they considered her idea.

Aelric sat forward suddenly, snaring their attention.

"We were fortunate this time," he interjected. "As ignorant as we were of their ways, we deserved to rouse their suspicions and their dislike. It is their typical response to anything that is not like them, remember? It is fortunate for us that we sustained as little damage as we did. It is my fault for not thinking this through more carefully before sending a whole party ashore! I should have scouted ahead, learned their ways, and returned to make a more careful plan. Instead, I didn't think, and I failed to plan for your safety and for the safety of us all." His golden eyes pierced each Companion with his solemn intent. "Will you forgive me for my thoughtless leadership?"

There was a quiet shuffling among them as they pondered his words. The desire to excuse Aelric rose to Robse's tongue, but he kept his lips firmly closed. Much as he desired to support his king, he couldn't deny that what Aelric said was true. After a moment of awkward silence, Domel spoke for them all.

"My liege, I will forgive you freely, if you will forgive me in turn, for failing in my duty to advise you on this matter." They all drew relieved breaths as Aelric nodded. Once again, Min reflected upon the perils of their youth and inexperience.

Gaelcar added, thoughtfully, "I, for one, still feel a great weakness upon me. It was all I could do to return to the ship. Have we been permanently weakened by their disbelief? If so, how badly? How will it affect us? Will we recover our strength or will we fade? We must consider the concept that if we are going to be around Humans, we are going to encounter their disbelief, unless we can convince them that we are no different than they."

"Actually," said Robse, "I was thinking about that. We know that the Faeries had a Human living inside the palace, but she did not affect them adversely. Perhaps we can be safe, as long as the Humans are not actively disbelieving in us."

"I think we may be on to something. As long as we look and act enough like Humans that we do not arouse suspicion, it seems to me we should be safe. If we're going to pass unremarked, we will have to disguise ourselves as Men, dressing like them, mimicking their habits and customs," Gaelcar concurred.

"Perhaps we should work on conducting ourselves more like they do. If we try not to be so polite, and try to—what did they call it?—*bargain* more, and to blend in with other Men, they may not be so suspicious next time," Caerdrys offered.

Gaelcar had also noticed the absence of women on the docks, but he refrained from commenting on it, as he wasn't ready to fight that battle with Caerdrys yet.

"But will that counter the effects of their disbelief already leveled against us?" asked Randelos. They exchanged glances, and more than one of the Companions wished for the vast experience and kindly guidance of Elrad in this uncertain time. Finally, Aelric spoke.

"I do not know what lasting effect this encounter will have upon us, Randelos. Clearly, we were all somewhat affected by the force of their power. It is to be hoped that another good sleep will restore us to full strength, but I think we are not finished here yet. When we are," he added, turning to Cerlim, "I will ask you to remain in command of the vessel until we have rested, as you were the only one of us not subjected to their presence." Cerlim nodded briefly.

"There's one more thing I want to understand," Caerdrys put in sharply. "I want to know why they were so surprised that Min and I were with you. What is so unusual about that?"

Gaelcar suppressed a groan. Trust Caerdrys to pick a time when they were all weary beyond tact to bring up what would likely prove an uncomfortable point. Gaelcar could see where this would lead, although it seemed Aelric had not yet.

"Apparently most sailors don't bring women with them," Aelric said. "I don't recall seeing any women on the docks at all. Do you?" he asked of the Company at large. There were various headshakes around the table, and Caerdrys's dark brows lowered over her eyes dangerously.

"Does that mean that all sailors are males?" Caerdrys asked with mock sweetness.

"It would seem so," Aelric temporized, obviously just realizing where this conversation was headed.

"How can that be?" Caerdrys asked, scorn vibrant in her voice. "What woman would stand for being forbidden the lifework she chooses? And what kind of culture would so restrict a woman?" Her logic rang true in their ears, but these were Humans, and their customs and beliefs were alien. Gaelcar knew he would have to try to calm the rising storm. He cleared his throat to gain attention and spoke in his most soothing voice.

"In the reports I have studied of the Human culture—at least, those Humans observed near the Land of Faerie—the women are reported to stay home and raise the children and keep the home, while the men work at various skills and trades to support them."

"I know their lives are short," Caerdrys was obviously trying to be patient. "But what about when the women are finished raising the children?"

Gaelcar looked uncomfortable. "Well, then they stay home, cook, clean, and help raise the grandchildren."

Caerdrys was not the only Companion to look nonplussed.

"So they never do anything else with their lives? They are not permitted to pursue their dreams, their talents, to learn about the Creator through the act of creating?"

"Many of them engage in domestic skills such as weaving, cooking, preserving, and such. Rarely, I have heard, one or two females will become healers or practice some other form of skilled employment, but it is not encouraged, beyond midwifery and simple herb-lore. Indeed, it is apparently looked upon as not quite decent. I do not know, of course, if the average woman feels fulfilled. If their actions are anything to go by, they don't seem to mind the restrictions of their lifestyle very much." Gaelcar wound down, looking from one blank face to the next around the small table. Clearly, they could not conceive of such a life. Seeing no way out of the inevitable conclusion, Gaelcar spoke firmly, but not unsympathetically.

"Caerdrys, you and Minlienda cannot accompany us to the docks any more. In fact, if we are to appear to be an unremarkable trading vessel, all the women and children are going to have to stay below the decks when we come in sight of a port."

"What? No, Gaelcar, you have to let me come with you to bargain with the Humans!" Caerdrys protested. "I'm part of the King's Council, one of the Companions! I should be down there with Aelric, ready to help and aid him. It's my duty as much as it is yours! I cannot do any good waiting beneath the decks!"

"I'm sorry, Caerdrys, but it is imperative for everyone's safety that we do nothing to rouse their suspicions," Aelric responded, though he didn't look any better pleased at the decision than she did.

"Wait! I can disguise myself as a male!" The Companions were polite enough not to snort in disbelief, though there was a suspicious muffled sound from Cerlim's direction.

"Caerdrys," Aelric intervened, his voice kind, but brooking no argument. "You know as well as I do that you could never manage to look like a Man! I'm sorry, and I know it's not fair, but I agree with Gaelcar and that's my ruling."

Caerdrys took in a breath, about to defend herself further, but stopped, realizing that she would be challenging the king's orders. She released her breath in a resigned sigh instead. "All right. I'll stay below decks with the rest of the women and children," she surrendered with as good grace as she could muster. Gaelcar felt they had gotten off very lightly.

Robse resisted the urge to scratch the back of his neck, where the rough woolen shirt was chafing against skin irritated by wood bark dye and a judicious application of dirt. He hoped the disguises would be sufficient to make this contact go more smoothly than the last. He looked critically at his companions. Aelric, as their leader, wore cheaply made finery, with soiled lace at his wrists and throat. Gaelcar was similarly attired but did not have the gold braid stitched along his hems. The other male Companions were dressed as common seamen; their nearly threadbare garments barely hid their dirty, scruffy bodies.

Over the past few weeks, an oily dye had been perfected, after several less-than-successful tries, and it imparted a darker, greasy sheen to their too-fair skin. Lacking the wherewithal to provide the stench of unwashed Men, they had liberally daubed themselves and their garments with rank fish oils, mixed with sheep's dung, hoping that would suffice. Between the itching, the stink, and the annoying flies that had begun to swarm as they got close to port, Robse had to call upon all his strength of will not to betray how appalled he was by it all. *It must seem natural*, he reminded himself yet again. *I must act as if this has always been my natural state.* Momentarily, his eye was caught by Gaelcar's expression of horrified and outraged fastidiousness. *And I must not laugh…*

Loud and boisterous dockhands caught the ropes flung down from the *Cethastea* and made her fast to the dock. Briskly, a plank was run out, as they had observed other ships doing, and no sooner had it settled on the uneven wooden surface than Aelric was striding down it. Robse's eyes narrowed as he watched his king.

The day before, in an unofficial Council meeting after supper, Gaelcar had raised the subject that had worried at the edges of Robse's mind, even creeping into uneasy dreams, since their last attempt at contact. If their disguises were not enough to protect them from the power of Man's crippling disbelief, the quiet Seneschal had pointed out, it would not do to risk losing the last heir of the royal bloodline. The measured voice had bravely put into words the very sentiments that had plagued Robse. Aelric, declared Gaelcar, should not go ashore with them.

There had been a moment of silence around the table, each of the Companions arrested in the midst of his or her actions. All eyes had gone to Aelric's face. Surprisingly, he had not burst forth with vehement denials or vigorous arguments, as expected. With apparent calm, he had finished chewing his bite of honey cake and taken a small sip of pear juice. Only then had he raised his eyes to Gaelcar. It was obvious from the molten gold of his gaze that he was holding back his reactions with a self-control they could but admire. The heat of that gaze had not been permitted to leak into the king's voice as he responded to Gaelcar's comment.

"I am the king. I will go. Not only will I go, but I will go *first* into danger. It is my privilege and my responsibility." His gaze swept them all, scorching in its intensity. The unusually calm voice continued. "If you are concerned about the succession, let me relieve your minds. If I fall, Gaelcar will rule after me, being closest kin. After him, should there be a need, would come young Dahlrys, with Domel as Regent, until he is old enough. Does this answer your need?"

Reassured by the quiet manner and the exhibition of control, as much as by the words, they had nodded. As the king's Champion,

Robse knew it was his duty to see that the monarch came to no harm as he led them into danger, yet his concern for Aelric's safety was balanced by relief at his sovereign's words. It was true that they could ill afford to lose him so soon after losing his royal father, and yet it was equally true that it was Aelric's place to lead them.

Now, as they stood in their uncomfortable disguises, preparing to embark on a risky quest that could spark disaster, Robse's eyes were scanning all the dockside area, noting and cataloguing potential threats to their ruler. Though they had all seen the control shown by Aelric last night, the royal temper was notoriously uncertain, and much of their fortune rode upon the success of today's enterprise. With all the annoying aspects of their disguises added to the already high stress levels, Robse was unsure of Aelric's mood. There was vigorous energy in the swing of his long legs down the plank. Robse hastily stepped up behind Gaelcar. It wouldn't do for the king's Champion to be too far behind his sovereign to protect him.

As his feet contacted the bobbing plank, he nearly lost his footing. He had become so accustomed to the rhythm of the ship's movements that he had forgotten to compensate for the jarringly solid land on the other end of the makeshift bridge. The plank dipped wildly under him, mocking his footsteps, but he was on his guard now and easily compensated with his natural grace. He gained the dock in time to see a rakish gleam in Aelric's eye as he turned to follow the pointing arm of a dockhand.

Aelric was enjoying himself.

Robse stayed close to Aelric as they made their zigzagging way between standing piles of goods that were waiting to be loaded onto ships bobbing at anchor or transported into the nearby warehouses. They dodged the sweating, swearing dockhands who wrestled great loads of barrels strapped together with broad leather bands. They wove in and out of the swelling, milling crowds of seamen on leave, businessmen come to see their goods loaded, gawkers watching the ships come in, and hawkers stridently proclaiming their wares. The noise, bustle, and confusion of it all was surpassed only by the unbelievable stench of unwashed Humanity, heavily cloaked in some by liberal applications of perfumes and pomades.

Robse caught sight of the unguarded expression on Randelos's face and jabbed an elbow into his side. The dark amber eyes beneath the shabby cap were quick to take his meaning, and the unfamiliar dark face schooled itself to bored patience. Robse saw Gaelcar struggling to hide his reaction, somewhat less successfully than Randelos, and wondered if it might be wiser to leave Gaelcar behind aboard the *Cethastea* next time. Still, his skill at knowing what they needed and what they had to trade could not be denied. They needed Gaelcar along on these missions. He would just have to learn to hide his reactions better.

Robse's eyes went forward to Aelric once again, and he bit back a smile at the fierce light in his king's eyes. The broad grin on his darkened face made his teeth flash in the sunlight. He looked like a pirate about to enjoy a merchant for lunch.

Robse's eyes were busy, darting all about them, taking in everything of the confusion and bedlam, noting the faces that bothered to notice them, keeping track of their route away from the *Cethastea*. He was on full alert, but so far he had seen none of the arrested, open-mouthed looks they had received at their last docking. *So far, so good*, he thought. *We don't seem to have attracted any undue attention yet. Maybe this will work. I feel no weakening of my power either. I think they believe us to be what we seem.*

They drew up at last before the rough wooden table of the dockmaster, set in the open double doorway of a large warehouse. A dirty scribe, in a shirt that had once been red, barely looked up as they stopped before him.

"Name, ship, intent," he mumbled, dipping a scarred quill pen into an inkwell made of stained horn and preparing to record them onto the much scraped parchment before him. According to their agreed-upon script, Gaelcar stepped forward.

"I am Captain Talathaem of the *Cethastea*. We're here to take on water and provisions." Robse held his breath as he waited for the Man's reaction. Would he notice the note of restraint in Gaelcar's voice, the quality of politeness that the tall Elf just couldn't seem to abandon, even to act his part? Would he look up and see that the dye on Aelric's face had begun to trickle at the left temple? Would he think it unusual for all these seamen to accompany their captain to the dockmaster's registration? Robse had just noted that the other seafarers seemed to be coming and going in twos and threes, making their party of six painfully obvious, at least in Robse's mind.

The little Man didn't even look up again. His split nib scratched and spluttered its way across another line of parchment, detailing their information phonetically in weak brown ink.

"Water casks refilled at south end of harbor. Buy and sell trade goods in central marketplace. No drunkenness permitted outside dockside taverns. Enjoy your stay." The words came out in a monotone with no noticeable punctuation. The scribe waved them on, without even looking up again. As they turned away, they heard him address the next Man in line.

"Name, ship, intent."

They exchanged quietly exultant glances as they headed off to the south side of the great harbor. Robse kept close behind Aelric, whose walk had quickly become a swagger. Behind him, Domel, Randelos, and Cerlim tried not to stagger on their "land-legs," as they shuffled the packs of trade goods they carried and hurried to keep up.

Robse stifled the impulse to laugh once more as the success of their stratagem buoyed his spirits. He wondered if Aelric's throat would be sore from the deep growl he affected in his rude, raucous trading banter.

By the third time they had to make port, the mass of women and children confined below the decks of the *Cethastea* during these ventures accepted their role as routine. They worked busily, talking quietly among themselves. Most of them were in the large, open workroom in the center of the second deck, though many of the children and a few teachers were in the roomy chamber where the children took their daily lessons.

Caerdrys fidgeted on her stool, her hands holding the large, loose loop of yarn for Min, who was briskly winding it into a ball. Around her, women were engaged in carding, spinning, weaving, sewing, mending clothes, splicing ropes, mending sails and fishing nets. Across the broad, low room, more women were engaged in making trade goods of carved buttons, tooled leather belts, beaded belts and necklaces, carved wooden utensils, and sturdy, colorful woven cloth.

Moving through the narrow passages between busy workers, other women were tending the many plants in the hanging arrays above them. On the level below, where the open space was smaller and mostly taken up by stored goods, the overhead lattices supported the cocooned and hibernating colony of pod dragons. The portable apiaries were on that level as well, the bees snug in their hives and dormant until warmer weather.

Caerdrys shifted again, chafing at the rampant domesticity all around her. She longed for the freedom of the upper decks and the sea breeze. Her cramped muscles ached to reach and pull, to climb the radlings to one of the aeries. She had never been comfortable for long with confined spaces and had never been suited to the quieter domestic tasks. She could do them, though her sewing was very basic and lacked skill. She just found them tedious, preferring more demanding physical tasks.

She turned aside her resentment at her confinement: they all had to suffer it and none were complaining. The tasks had to be done anyway, and while they were confined, they chose to make it a social occasion, moving all their chores to the central location, so they could talk and visit while they worked. At least they could go back to the surface in a few days. It never took more than three days to resupply and to take on fresh water. Most ports could accommodate them in two days. And, fortunately, they didn't need to make port more than once every three or four weeks. Still, it was irksome being trapped below!

Chapter Ten

Only the brightest stars remained visible in the velvet firmament above, as false dawn pearled the edges of vision. The silent watcher bid farewell to the many fiery points as the lightening sky masked their brightness, one by one. Soon, the light of their own star would flood the sky, and day would be upon him again, with all its joys and perplexities.

With a sigh that was part peace, part undefined longing, the observer lowered his golden gaze to the dark shape of his home, not far away. His senses, so attuned to the quiet pre-dawn darkness, felt the moment when his beloved stirred and, waking, sought him. A few moments later, he saw the door open and her slight figure come out. Though the light was still faint, there was quite enough for him to drink in her beauty, her grace.

Unerringly, her violet eyes found him in the darkness, and a sleepy smile lit her face. She crossed to him, where he stood near a clump of chestnut trees, facing out into a broad field. He brought her to his side, and she tucked her pale head into the hollow of his right shoulder and turned her face up to the vanishing stars.

Though the skies of Marliondolen held a vast array of spangled glory, and the eyes of that realm's inhabitants were keen enough now to discern so much more than they could on Earth, many of the Faeltheon had been disappointed not to find their familiar friends above them. The night skies were splendid indeed, with a wealth of bright and colored points of light, and some had already begun to fashion new constellations of their arrangements. The moon was present in her phases, but she, too, was altered from the familiar face they remembered.

Some debated that the skies were the same, but their own enhanced senses made so much more available to their sight that they could not recognize the old patterns. Others thought they had been moved to a different location, so that the star patterns were ones they had not known before. Still others believed, though they kept their thoughts quietly among their closest friends, that the realm of Marliondolen existed outside the realm containing Earth, and that the skies they saw above them now were not even in the same world with Earth.

Despite the many views, the truth could not be known at this point, and, familiar or unfamiliar, the sight of the stars above did not inspire fear or concern in any inhabitant of Marliondolen. For one thing, as had been observed in the recent past, they could not seem to feel fear of the unknown here, even if they tried. The sense of security and safety was too prevalent to permit that sort of worry.

After a few moments of companionable silence, Elwyn murmured, "Do you know what I miss most from these skies?"

"Hmm?" Theo encouraged.

"The Three Sisters constellation. That story has always meant so much to me. The sacrifice of those three Faeries gave me the courage to face so many trials, both the minor ones of my childhood and the very real ones toward the end of our time there."

Theo nodded, wrapping his strong arms around his wife to show he understood. She settled lightly against him, infinitely precious, trusting him to guard her, even when there was no threat. After a time of watching the slowly brightening sky, she turned to see his face above her.

"Why were you out here, beloved?"

Theo shifted slightly, putting his back to the early morning breeze, for it was cool and Elwyn was dressed lightly. Trying to put his thoughts into words, he sought for a reply that would answer her real question.

"There is nothing wrong, my heart. I heard no calling, nor felt any deep compulsion to "brood" as Las calls it." Elwyn snickered faintly, and Theo smiled. "I just wanted to come and see the sky and the stars and to feel the peace of the quiet night. I was praying for our Kin still upon the Earth, that they might find a safe haven, learn whatever the Creator has for them to learn, and then join us here."

Elwyn nodded in her turn, for she too lifted these prayers. While she did not know most of those still wandering the Earth, she knew how deeply Theo and Laslorn and others missed their Kin and desired to have them brought safely home to Marliondolen.

The Master and Lady of Marliondolen stood close together as the morning dawned with opal fire. When the bright sun had shot, laughing, over the horizon, they turned to meet Laslorn's cheerful greeting. Nausika joined them a moment later, and the four friends agreed to break their fast together in the common garden behind their homes. Nausika, sensing the Elves' need to be with friends this morning, sent a passing finch to invite Aoneth, Rablorn, Glimring, and Geltheon.

When they had all assembled a short time later, their guests began to arrive, bringing fruit and nuts and flowers to add to the repast. With Aoneth came shy Michal, accompanied by Cador, Kier, Davin, and Lucina. They all made a merry group, settling by the banks of the stream that flowed through the garden. Dew, mixed with the juice pressed from ripe plums, refreshed them, and the fruit, cheese, and fresh scones, spread with cinnamon honey or ginger preserves, were shared with great pleasure.

There was much laughter and teasing in the bright, sunlit morning, but Nausika could still see the faint darkness that haunted the forest depths of her husband's eyes and was echoed in the amber shadows of Theo's gaze. She knew they were missing their younger brother, Robse.

When the feasting was ended, they lingered in each other's company, talking and even singing a few songs together. As they were finishing a beautiful and complicated madrigal, Nausika looked up to see Elrad coming around the side of Elwyn and Theo's home, leading three Faeries she did not recognize. Theo saw him then and rose with a glad shout to welcome the Seer to their midst. They all rose and clustered about Elrad and his guests, herding them toward the picnic cloth and pressing food and drink upon them.

When the generous hospitality had been extended and the exuberant welcome somewhat stilled, Elrad laughingly protested that he was not being allowed to introduce his guests, whom he had brought specially to meet them. With goodnatured speed, the others settled about him, composing themselves to listen, as Elrad rarely came among them without a story to relate. Nausika was not the only one to notice the twinkle in the turquoise eyes and the sense of suppressed elation that accompanied the older Elf's speech. Whatever he had to share with them, Elrad was enjoying it immensely.

"Thank you, my friends, for your hospitable welcome! This is a fine feast, indeed! Let me begin by introducing my three friends, for I think that you will want to hear their story as much as they have desired to share it with you!" With this intriguing start, Elrad then paused to savor a mouthful of juice, pretending not to hear Laslorn's smothered exclamation of impatience. Nausika and Theo laughed, and Elwyn saw their guests supplied with fresh pistachios, as though she were not as eager as they.

Gesturing to the tallest of the three Faeries, Elrad executed a seated bow to show his respect of her. The crowd of friends sat up and took sharper notice at this.

"This is Drythiela, also known as Lienda."

The grave-eyed Faerie nodded her head to them.

"Here is her sister, Dashiela, called Hleafa."

The second Faerie echoed the greeting nods, giving a smile, which was returned by many. They still did not know who these Faeries were, but the family resemblance was strong, so if all three were sisters, they must be from far in the past, from the days when the Faeltheon had been blessed with several children in a family.

"And this is Domiela, later named Lisea," finished Elrad, with another bow to the three. Before Elwyn could extend a proper greeting, the Seer continued, speaking to the three newcomers.

"Allow me to present to you the Master and Lady of Marliondolen," he began. They knew by his formality, if they hadn't guessed it by his very manner, that these guests were significant. As hosts, Elwyn and Theo presented their hands, palms up, to receive the hands of their guests. When the gesture had been completed, Elrad introduced the others present. When the Seer had finished, looking very pleased with himself, Theo spoke his part, knowing what was expected of him.

"Will you share your story with us?"

The first of the three nodded, and there was the usual bustle of refreshing everyone's drinks and plates before they all bowed their heads together, then settled back to listen with absorbed interest.

"As you heard, my name is Drythiela, though I am usually called by my second name, Lienda." She paused here, and the sober gray eyes lightened as she momentarily allowed herself to be diverted by an aside. "I have noticed that most of those born in later years were not given second names. Did this practice die out?"

Lucina, who found herself strongly attracted to the atmosphere around the three Faeries, answered thoughtfully, "I do not know of anyone with a formal second name, such as you three have. Sometimes we are given a nickname to describe a particular characteristic, such as King Beregos the Good."

"Or Clever Nausika," put in that woman's husband mischievously. Nausika awarded him a sharp elbow in the ribs, and he laughed at her crimson face. Elwyn interceded.

"Are your second names given later in life, for a trait you have displayed?"

The eldest of the three Faeries nodded, looking pleased. "Yes, that was common in our day. As a child grew, if she showed a gift or tendency toward something, she was given a descriptive name, which became her commonly used name after that."

They all nodded, pleased with having learned something of the past customs of their people.

"But I must continue with our story," Lienda went on. "I am the eldest of the three of us, but only by a matter of minutes. We are triplets, you see, and even in our time, this was an extremely rare occurrence."

As Lienda began to tell of their childhood, Elwyn felt a rising shiver of gooseflesh stalk the fine hairs on her arms and neck. Wide-eyed, she met the knowing, almost smug gaze of Elrad.

***

"... and the Goblins became very restless in those days. We had heard, of course, of battles fought with them in the past, but no one we knew had met them in battle. After several seasons of raids and general unrest, the Goblins finally attacked in the early spring of our eightieth year."

"We were not yet adults, yet no longer children, so we were hidden away with the other young folk in the northern part of the Great Birch Forest, while our elders went to war," continued Lisea, picking up the narrative from Hleafa. Their wide-eyed audience was listening intently, for this was indeed their most beloved legend come to life. "Our mother remained with the group of refugees, for she was best suited to nurturing, not fighting, and someone had to help organize us all. Our father, uncle, and *amion* uncles and aunts had gone to the fighting and, by the end of that summer, we had had no word from them. Our mother became ill with a fever that swept through our camp. We lost three younglings to it, and many others were ill. One of the young women, Amiela, set out for the castle to bring the queen, if she could be spared, for she was a great healer. My sisters and I agreed that we would travel south for a ways and try to determine what had become of our kin."

"So we set out one evening, traveling mostly by night to avoid being seen by any enemies, though we had no reason to suppose them so far north," resumed Lienda. "We traveled hard, and by the end of four nights, we could see the hills that separated us from the southernmost parts of the Great Birch Forest. That night we could smell a stench that warned us we were near to danger. The choking scent of heavy smoke and the awful reek of burning hair and flesh grew stronger as we pushed cautiously southward. By morning, though the sun was well up, we could see little for the heavy, greasy haze that clung to everything."

She swallowed against the dreadful memory that followed and could not continue. Lisea put an arm about her, and the sisters bowed their heads together for a moment. Hleafa's clear voice picked up the threads and resumed weaving their story.

"We came to a clearing that opened onto a small field, and they were there. The bodies. The corpses were scattered and piled all about as they had fallen, and the blood that stained the ground turned all the earth red. There were flies and carrion birds and the skulking shapes of Goblin scavengers moving about in the throng. At first, we were too faint and sick to heed anything else, but soon, in spite of our quailing hearts, we began to recognize people we knew. The faces of our beloved kin looked so different; empty and robbed of life. We hardly recognized our own father when we found him there, fallen beside our uncle, his brother."

Lienda resumed the tale, her voice as hoarse and strained as her sister's was clear. "We laid ourselves down upon their bodies and wept. Never again would they return home to mother or family. In our grief, we forgot to guard against danger, and so we were found there by a commander of the Goblins. We were young and strong, so we fought with all the grief and wrath in our hearts. We slew many of them that grim day. The commander, one Grimswrath, retreated then, but returned later as if he could not stay away. Not many would come with him, for we had fought fiercely, and they did not care to continue a battle they felt they had won before we arrived.

"Finally, on the third morning after we arrived to find our kin, Grimswrath came to us under flag of truce. We did not trust him, but he came alone within our bow range, so we let him speak. He told us that he wanted to keep us for himself. He claimed he would be willing to convince his cohorts to end the war if we would agree to be his.

"We did not trust him, but the chance of ending the terrible war was too great to ignore. We finally agreed that if his allies would come with him to swear this peace to us, we would agree to come with him. That evening he returned with several other warriors, who swore they would end the war if we would come with them and not fight them. We took counsel together and bowed our heads in prayer, but in the end we could see no other path, so we agreed."

"He took us back to their camp, a noisome, filthy place of low tents and screams of torture from their victims," Lisea went on, bravely taking up the horrific tale in a voice that shook slightly, but persevered. "Here he kept us for several days for, though he was powerful among the Goblin warlords, he did not have sufficient strength to dictate his own terms without argument from the others. Some of the others objected to him having such a sign of power when they did not and clamored to share his prize. Others of the warlords insisted we should be killed, but they fell to quarreling among themselves as to how we should be killed and whether we should be eaten afterwards." She gave a shudder, echoed by several of her hearers. Hleafa took over the tale here.

"Finally, there was a terrible quarrel which escalated into a bloody fight. When it was over, Grimswrath and a few of his followers were slain. The most powerful among the remaining warlords decided we should be burnt to death, in retaliation for the way we burn their dead instead of eating them as they do. By that time, we didn't much care if we were to die at their hands. It was, indeed, preferable to sundry other fates we might have suffered among them. Our greatest concern was that the Goblins would not keep their word to end the war, and our deaths would be for naught. Still, there was nothing we could do but meet our fate as bravely as possible.

"So, they took us back to that grim field where our kin had fallen, and they put up a thick stake and tied us to it. They piled great faggots of wood and bunches of brush about its foot, then soaked them with rancid grease. As we awaited our fate, we realized that others of the Faeltheon had come to that place, for we could hear their voices high in the surrounding trees. They were grieved and cried out against our capture and fate. Some even tried to parley with the Goblins to get them to release us, but they would not.

Finally, after much argument and discussion, our people threatened to carry the battle over into the Goblin lands if we were not released.

Then the Goblin warriors looked worried and consulted among themselves, for they did not desire this, being tired of the war they had begun. They came back to the Faeries and Elves who waited near us and declared that we had offered ourselves as a sacrifice to end the war. If we agreed to die in their fire, they would swear to go away into their lands and trouble our people no more.

"The noble Faerie speaking on the queen's behalf refused their treaty, but we had been speaking among ourselves all the while and had come to a decision. Lienda cried out for the three of us that we would allow this treaty, but that if the Goblins who swore this oath broke it, we would curse them with a hideous death from the world beyond. The Goblins turned quite gray at that threat and proceeded to bring lighted torches to bear upon the grease-soaked wood."

Lienda's voice took up the story, and she was steadier now. "Our people cried out against this deed, but it was done. The smoke rose sullenly while the flames were still small at our feet. We were scared but also filled with a wild kind of glory. With one voice we began to sing the ancient 'Praise Hymn' and then 'We Await Your Will.' The flames were cruel, but the heavy smoke was our great foe. We could scarcely get the words out for the choking smoke. Soon, we could not get air to breathe, and then we knew no more."

Hleafa finished triumphantly. "A little later, when we awoke, it was to this beautiful place and to the joyful faces of our kin whom we had last seen dead upon that field! We searched among them and found all who were lost and also those who had been back home. At first we were confused, but great was our joy when we found our parents reunited once more, and all were content. Some time later, we were told about the stars that appeared in the heavens the night we perished and about the song that was sung of our deeds. It is a bit embarrassing, actually, but we are glad that our choice gave peace to our generation and that the things that befell us provided inspiration for others."

Elwyn shook her golden head.

"No, my friends, it was not what befell you that inspired us; it was how you responded to what befell you! While your story has always been one that made me desire to be courageous and faithful, hearing you tell it, knowing you even this little bit, has made it all the more compelling!"

Others agreed with her, assuring the sisters that their tale had been a treasured gift that would not soon be forgotten.

Lienda stretched out her hands and enfolded one of Elwyn's and one of Theo's. "We have heard your tale as well. We are agreed that while the manner of our death was ugly and hard, we were grateful to be spared the fate of having to *live* with those evil creatures. We have great respect for you, Elwyn Elenthea, for you showed courage and faithfulness in a time of dreadful trouble, bearing up and continuing to live a worthy life in the midst of the destruction of your people. We admire you both, and we salute you for having the faith to seek for Marliondolen and the courage to lead the way here, that we may all have a place in this welcome sanctuary! Yes, we know that the Creator planned and provided this place for us," she said with a smile as they began to protest. "But it took your sacrifice, your faith, your steadfastness to open the way for us to enter in."

Elwyn and Theo were so abashed by this praise, they didn't know where to look, and Elrad laughed at them. The others, still shaking their heads in amazement at the triplets' story, gathered about to ask questions and share their feelings. After a time of talking together, the group finally separated with lingering thanks and promises to gather again soon.

As Elwyn and Theo retired hand in hand to their home, she was reminded again about Theo's starlit watch that morning. She leaned against him, feeling his arms surround her with their heartening strength, and thought of their Kin still adrift on the seas of Earth.

"We have listened to a tale of sacrifice today," she murmured, knowing he listened. "And, much as I admire them for it, they attributed the same to us. I hope Robse and the others left behind on Earth don't have to make such sacrifices."

"So do I, my love. Yet, if they must, I pray they will be strengthened by the Presence of the Creator and able to do with faith and fortitude whatever they are called upon to do."

Chapter Eleven

The cool breeze lifted the hair that had come loose from the braided thong at the back of Robse's neck, blowing the fine strands into his eyes and mouth. Resignedly, he pulled out the tie and raked his long fingers through his hair. It had grown in the past few months, and he reminded himself to ask one of the women to trim it for him.

It had been the habit of the young Elves to wear their hair long, pulled back into intricate braided ties, or left to hang straight down their backs. Their hair, whether sun-fair like Robse's or midnight dark like Aelric's, had been a feature much admired by the opposite gender, but the need to impersonate Humans had required uncompromising gestures. All the male Elves, whether Companions who went ashore or "deck hands" who remained aboard their ships, needed to appear to be Men, so the long locks had been ruthlessly shorn, not without some sighing on both sides.

It had taken Robse a while to get used to hair that curled at his shoulders and wouldn't stay tied back when the sea breeze blew, no matter what his efforts. His dark-haired compatriots had it a bit easier, as their hair was naturally heavier and inclined to lay flat and smooth. Unfortunately for him, fair hair among the Elven folk meant a lighter texture and a tendency to curl when short.

Still, Robse reflected, yanking his recalcitrant hair back once more, at least he didn't have Faerie hair. The fair-haired among his Faerie Kin had hair that moved without a breeze, often drifting as if in water. He bit his lip in vexation, both at his annoyance with his hair and at how it jarred him still to remember that the Faeries were no more. In the midst of an ordinary conversation or routine thought, the loss of his Kindred would stab through him like a well-aimed knife, bringing with it the hot torture of the loss of brothers and father.

Despite the months the day count said had passed, Robse's grief would not ease. The pain of losing his family continued to eat at him like a canker in his soul. His frustration mounted when a handful of locks was tugged free by the wind and whipped into his eyes again. He blamed the sting of hair for the tears that rose, and lowered his arms to rest on the starboard half-deck rail.

He was wrenched back from his black aloneness by a firm voice behind him, followed an instant later by two small, capable hands.

"Here," said Minlienda, smoothing his hair back for him and braiding it deftly, tight to his nape, and tying it off with a bit of string. It was so quickly done, he had not time to protest, nor even to dwell on how the feel of her hands on his hair, startlingly intimate and yet so commonplace, had made the hot color flood to his face. The wind tugged and played, cooling his telltale cheeks, but his hair stayed firmly in place. Surprised, he turned to face her.

"How did you do that?" he demanded, trying in vain to see what she'd tied his hair with. She laughed at his efforts to see the end of his short braid, and he was arrested again at the beauty of her laugh, her generosity, her simple friendliness. He checked his thoughts quickly, refusing to allow his attraction for her to be acknowledged, even in his mind. She was older than he, they were adrift on a wild quest to try to save their people, he was subject to ravaging bouts of grief, and ... well, he was sure he could think of many more reasons to keep his thoughts away from Minlienda Elashar.

Besides, he thought, triumphantly coming up with the perfect reason, *she has given no indication of interest, and it is the woman's role to initiate any relationship deeper than friendship*. Belatedly, he realized he was still caught by the depth of her violet eyes. Flushing again, he wrenched his gaze back out to sea.

"It's treated," she said, as though she fully expected cognizance from him.

"What?" He had lost the thread of the conversation.

"The string," she explained, tugging on his braid. "We treated it with *linte* sap, so it would grip the hair. It will be sticky, but the sap will wash out of your hair." Robse's left eyebrow arched at the clever idea, prompting another smile from Minlienda. Turning, she made her way briskly down the companionway ladder to the galley door.

"Dinner in an hour!" she called back.

Slightly bemused, as he often was after talking with her, Robse turned back to the vivid sunset he'd been watching. It had been difficult to learn to become sailors, Robse reflected, watching the sea roll in a jumble of silver and gold and shimmering shards of flame. The sky deepened to amethyst, and the first stars stood out from behind the horizon's cloudbank. Learning the tasks that kept the ship afloat hadn't been particularly taxing, just a matter of practice and concentration. The salt air and the rolling decks had become ordinary in time, too. The sudden storms still caused some damage and seasickness, but they were getting better at protecting themselves from the sometimes violent tossing of the ships.

The days were filled with chores and tasks designed to keep the ship running efficiently. He candidly acknowledged that many of the tasks were also designed to keep their little community running as smoothly as possible. Their biggest challenges were boredom, confinement, and a steady diet of fish. Robse wasn't particularly fond of fish to begin with, but it had become a staple in their diets aboard ship. He had never realized how many different ways there were to prepare fish!

Still, it was the tedium that chafed at him most. While each had specific duties, their free time hung heavy on their hands at times. Many of the tasks were unique to their shipboard life, such as hauling seawater, purifying it, learning the ropes, hauling, trimming, and furling the sails, scrubbing the decks, and cooking for seventy. Yet, many of the chores were commonplace, too. They tended the plants they had brought, harvested their food, and tended the livestock, including the bees in the portable apiaries and the delicate pod dragons. They taught the children, mended clothing, wove, sang, carved, sewed, and braided rope.

Even the masquerade as Humans, while annoying and uncomfortable, had at least provided a change of pace, a sting of danger. Although, he thought wryly, he wasn't sure which danger was greater: being discovered by Humans or having to live confined aboard a ship with Caerdrys for the days it took to restock when they made harbor. To give her credit, she never complained aloud, but it was obvious that she chafed at the restriction more than most, and her temper was as volatile as Aelric's for days afterward. He snorted with humor, but his smile never reached his silver eyes.

In truth, the hardest adjustment for all of them was the confinement. There was some privacy to be had in one's quarters, of course, though many of them shared quarters with a friend, but there was no room to stretch, to walk for hours under the cool trees, to see new faces and to visit friends. And some faces would never be seen again. Always, it came back to this ever-present pain: so many were gone, abruptly snuffed out, and life forever gapped over their absence like the hollow flapping of a luffing sail as it tacked into the wind.

The sharp sound of the ship's bell calling the first shift to dinner pulled Robse from the rails. They had been sailing for months with no sight of their goal, though the record Scrolls indicated that the original journey north had taken but a handful of weeks. How long would they continue at sea, in these floating communities that never quite felt like home? And if, or when, they found their island home and were freed from the confines of the ships, what would await them next? Could they make a home for themselves in a strange place?

That question was too much for him to grapple with on an empty stomach. Robse turned away from the rail and descended the companionway to join the others gathering for the meal. As he crossed the deck to the common room in the sterncastle where the Companions ate their meals, another question haunted Robse.

What if they never found their island?

In all of the time Gaelcar had spent on the sea with his fellow Elves, he had never experienced a storm quite this violent. The *Cethastea*, sturdy as she was, seemed fragile as she creaked and groaned in the grip of the merciless torture of raging wind and waves. Several times, Gaelcar had been sure that she would overturn completely, drowning every Elf crammed into her damp, dark belly. He didn't want to think of those serving valiantly up on the deck, who might be swept off into the turbulent sea in an instant and lost to them forever. When he had been forced below decks a few hours before by a direct order from his king, reinforced by a bellow from Lysion, they hadn't lost anyone yet, but the storm had been raging for several days, and they were all becoming too exhausted to continue.

In the spacious workroom on the second deck, where Gaelcar and most of his shipmates were anxiously awaiting the passing of the storm, poorly secured objects flew down the empty central passageway as the ship was tossed first one way and then another, like a helpless rag doll in a giant's temper tantrum. An unpleasant stench reached Gaelcar's nostrils, alerting him to the fact that one or, more likely, several of the miserable Elves in their cabins had lost their share of what little food they'd managed to eat the previous day. Their faint, heartfelt groans echoed down the passageway. He tried to rise to see if he could help, but his weary muscles refused to respond. He saw the slender forms of Minlienda and Ciella moving in and out of the cabin doorways in short, calm rushes of movement between the fierce rocking motions of the ship. Another smaller form, one of the children he thought, emerged from a cabin, carrying a basin of water and a cloth, but a sudden lurch of the *Cethastea* flung the child to the passageway floor. She slid almost to the foot of the companionway, her water splashed all about her.

At that moment, a soaking wet figure reached the bottom of the companionway from the upper deck and lifted the child to her feet. She seemed unharmed by her rough treatment, only leaning against the taller Elf until she could retrieve her basin and totter off for more water. The dripping, exhausted Elf turned to join the huddled group in the workroom, and Gaelcar saw that it was Robse. The younger Elf met his eyes and shook his head slightly as they exchanged a weary, nearly hopeless look. Robse shivered convulsively, and Gaelcar wished he had hot soup or tea to offer the young Champion, but there was nothing hot. They had not been able to risk a fire for the past three days.

Well built and sound as the *Cethastea* was, she had not sprung a leak, though with the amount of water the storm was flinging down the companionways, they were all at least damp. Gaelcar, Robse, all those who had been doing all they could up on deck to try to keep the great ship afloat, had been soaked to the bone for longer than Gaelcar could reckon up in his present state of mind. He watched Robse stop and look dazedly about the room. A trio of young boys in the corner lifted the edge of their blanket in invitation, and Gaelcar watched the weary Champion stumble across to them and drop thankfully into their warm cocoon.

They would all help one another to survive this storm, each doing what he could. With what little strength remained to him, Gaelcar lifted up yet another prayer that the Creator would preserve them out of the storm, that their losses would be few and small. He sighed and, rolling into a miserable ball, tried to wait patiently for the end of the storm.

Two exaggeratedly long days later, the violent winds began to veer off and the towering waves to subside. By that time, few of the Elves were still on their feet, and none were in good shape. Gaelcar, once more above deck and directing those few who could still function, perceived a faint lightening of the heavy skies above them.

A few hours later, the winds whipping them were no fiercer than those of an ordinary storm. The rain fell in blinding sheets onto Elves already so inured to being wet they didn't even notice the added indignity. Lashing rain was better than the towering cliffs of waves that had smashed down upon them for days. Doggedly, they continued wrestling with sails torn to ribbons by the winds and ropes that had snarled into massive knots, hindering their tasks.

Gaelcar didn't notice the lessening of the rain, until Cerlim, up on the half deck, shouted to a companion, and Gaelcar realized he could actually hear Cerlim over the rain and wind. He looked up and was surprised to find he could distinguish patches of sky amidst the heavy clouds.

Noting that the wind was not unusually strong now, he gestured the waiting Randelos up to the main aerie to look about them. Gaelcar looked critically about the *Cethastea's* main deck, assessing the damages. The mizzenmast was snapped off an elf-height above the deck. They had lost it the second day of the storm. Its burden of canvas, yardarms, and rigging lay sprawled in an unnatural tangle across the mizzendeck and draped over the stern rail. The other masts were intact, though they would need to be inspected for soundness. The main sails were still neatly furled against their yards, but the two fore-topsails were rent full of great tears, the upper one streaming in long tatters in the wind. Fortunately, they had managed to move the livestock down to the lower deck before the worst of the storm had hit. Looking at the storm-swept deck, Gaelcar knew they had come close to losing all their sheep and fowl.

Gaelcar turned as Caerdrys joined him at the wheel, picking her way across the debris from the mizzenmast. Her dark hair was tightly pulled back, but still the wind plucked loose strands to sting her cheeks. Gaelcar noticed the dark circles under her rain-colored eyes and knew he must look as weary. She swept the destruction on the deck with one assessing glance, but her eyes held hope and an indomitable spirit as she turned back to him.

"We have broken bones, bruises, cuts, chills, and weakness from sea-sickness, but we have lost none of our complement."

Gaelcar released a breath he hadn't realized he'd been holding, and relief made his eyes tear. Domel arrived at their sides with a bandaged splint on his left arm and a quiet smile on his pain-etched face.

"The king is sleeping," he reported. "Finally."

Caerdrys chuckled, and Gaelcar spared a grim smile. Throughout the entire six days of the storm, though he had rested when his body forced him to, Aelric had not closed his eyes in sleep. It was as though he would not allow his attention to waver as long as his people were in such danger.

"The *Gaelrandel*! Where is the *Gaelrandel*?" The sudden hoarse cry erupted from Randelos up in the aerie.

Gaelcar groaned before turning in the direction of the new challenge. The pale, tired Elves who had been climbing out into the fresh air of the decks began to question one another in alarm, moving to the rails to search the calming sea. As the ship erupted into confused chatter, a very pale Gaelcar rushed to the port mizzen rail and gazed out across the water intently. Several other Elves, their faces ghost white, were doing likewise, scrambling to many different sections of the ship in hopes of glimpsing their missing comrades. A few agile youngsters swarmed up the radlings, in spite of their mothers' pleas, trying to locate the ship from afar.

Though their longest eyes sought diligently all the afternoon, as did those aboard the *Dridelphanen* limping alongside, their search availed them naught; the missing ship simply could not be found. At last, with the shades of twilight beginning to shroud them, Gaelcar called off the search and dispatched several lookouts to the aeries with orders to shout at the first sign of their sister ship—or its wreckage.

The remaining healthy Elves were already hard at work, repairing the ravages of the storm. The galley fires were burning again, sending Elves with cups of steaming tea and restorative soups to the many injured and ill still below decks. Others were cleansing the ship's hold of the many messes left by frightened livestock and nauseated Elves. Still others bent to tasks assigned by Lysion after he had examined the ship and determined what measures they would need to take in order to repair it. It had soon become evident that they could not effect all the repairs needed while afloat—they would need land.

Gaelcar rubbed his throbbing temples and sighed dismally. Despite the good news that they had lost none of their own crew, the reckoning of damages and the loss of the *Gaelrandel* had taken an awful toll.

Though some of the Elves around him were buoyed with hope, many were dejected, pulled down and made vulnerable by their exhaustion, and overwhelmed by the enormity of their new challenge and the grief of losing one-third of their remaining Kin.

The newly calm sea was burnished with sunset's brassy gleam, its very peace mocking the dreadful week of storm. Gaelcar sighed as he descended the companion-ladder to the quarterdeck and then to the main deck. He turned to enter the sterncastle, reluctant to do what must be done. Though it had only been a few precious hours, in light of the loss of the *Gaelrandel*, Gaelcar knew he had to wake the king. He wasn't looking forward to it.

The next morning dawned clear and breezy, as though to deny the violence of the previous week. Robse stood his watch in the forward aerie, scanning the horizon as the stars paled in the growing light of the approaching sunrise. He had been unable to sleep the night out. As weary as his battered body was, he had been awakened by restlessness. Leaving his cabin, he had climbed to the mizzendeck to confer with Cerlim, who had the wheel. Knowing how shorthanded they would be, with so many ill or injured, Robse had volunteered to stand the dawn watch, and Cerlim had gratefully agreed.

In the creeping light, all around him was painted in shades of gray and slate. Robse could make out the dark bulk of the *Dridelphanen* off the port bow. He thought he could make out small, flashing forms ahead of her but couldn't be sure. Intently, he looked down at the purling sea before their own figurehead and thought he could make out flashes of movement there as well, but they were elusive and he could not be sure of them. Before the light grew strong enough to be certain of what he saw, they were gone, if they had ever been there at all. This was not the first time Robse had sensed the shimmer of movement ahead of the ship, but as it always seemed to occur on the dawn watches, he didn't mention it, unsure if it were mere illusion in the uncertain light.

The light was stronger now, allowing pale cream and faint yellow into the palette of sky and sea. The sky was clear of clouds, and Robse relaxed in the knowledge that the storm was truly past. The colors of the *Dridelphanen* were becoming identifiable, and the sea stretched before them like a carpet of pod dragon silk.

Robse turned his gaze to the starboard side, watching the *Cethastea's* shadow take shape in the growing light. In the distance there was a shimmer of movement along the horizon. Robse sharpened his gaze, then reached for the longeye he had slipped through his belt. Balancing its slender, cool weight in his fingers, Robse searched the horizon for the object. When he found it, it took a moment for him to interpret the shape of the spiky hulk. Then he gave a loud cry, alerting Cerlim to his find.

"Ship on the starboard horizon!"

A moment later, even as Elves tumbled onto the deck and Cerlim began to shout orders to unfurl what sail they had and tack to starboard, the *Dridelphanen's* lookout echoed Robse's cry. Those not engaged in turning the ships were crowded, silent and tense, along the starboard rails, wondering if they would find their lost companions or a watery graveyard. Their apprehension turned to gladness when they drew close enough to see that the wandering ship, battered horribly, yet stubbornly afloat, was still populated by their rejoicing Kin.

When the three ships formed up close to one another, the lost Elves shared the bare bones of their tale by shouting to their comrades across the water. It became apparent that the ship had come very near to sinking. She had taken considerable damage, including losing two of her masts and being holed. They had done their best to patch her leaks, but if the storm had raged another day, it was probable the ship would have broken apart, leaving her company to the mercy of the angry sea. The storm had ceased in a timely fashion, however, and they were grateful to be saved. Battered by the winds and weary from the long, hard fight to stay afloat, the Elves had surveyed their surroundings and, in a panic, realized that they were completely alone. Fearing that the other two ships had not been as fortunate as they had been, they had done their best to repair what damages they could and had searched for their companions.

The need to discuss the state of the ships necessitated the arrival of the other captains to consult with Lysion and the king. The *Gaelrandel*, which appeared as though it would not last many more days in the water, was in most urgent need of land, but they would all need to replace masts and repair damages. All the ships reported loss of fresh water and forage for the livestock, and their own food supplies were growing short. Lookouts were posted yet again to shout at the first sign of an island on which they could land and make repairs, and all able hands busied themselves with tending the injured and preserving their ships until they found land. Even so, it was nearly a weary week later when a cry was raised from the aerie of the *Dridelphanen*, and an excited Elf pointed out a tiny pinnacle of land on the horizon. Late the next day, the crippled ships anchored in a shallow cove, and their relieved inhabitants rowed quickly ashore, staggering about humorously on the solid ground.

Gaelcar, ever the Seneschal, set about organizing the work and assigning duties immediately, since it was obvious to him that they would be delayed there for several weeks. In the back of his mind loomed the thought that if they did not find their island home soon, they would not survive the winter cold upon the open sea.

Chapter Twelve

Domel stood on the high bluff on the westward side of the tiny island. The wind, rising as evening approached, chilled him and snatched his hair from the tie at his nape. He ignored the discomfort, keeping his eyes upon the shifting sea. In a moment, his patience was rewarded as he glimpsed the shining silver backs of the fish leaping at the edge of his sight. The creatures were large, their dorsal fins reminiscent of sharks, but their swimming and diving patterns were different. Sailors at the various ports they'd visited had spoken of the creatures, calling them ship-fish for their habit of swimming ahead of smaller craft, especially fishing boats. Some of the sailors had insisted the creatures were smart, but others had scoffed at the idea of a fish doing anything on purpose.

Domel had been fascinated by the arguments of the Men, drawn toward the chance to observe the elusive creatures himself. He had had fleeting glimpses of them along their journey, especially at dawn and dusk, but had never seen them up close. He felt an odd pull toward them, a deep sense of curiosity, a reaction he thought was a bit strong in response to a fish, even a big one.

He didn't sense from them the same cold predator's pragmatism he had sometimes gleaned from sharks, but he was beginning to wonder if his heightened curiosity was all on his part. Perhaps he was sensing *their* reaction to the Faeltheon? All his life, Domel had enjoyed and employed his gift of sensing the thoughts and feelings of the creatures they had served and nurtured in the Land. He wondered if his gift would serve them again, here on the sea.

His sharp ears picked up the sounds of a party of children returning from their afternoon's foraging along the inland brush. The deepening of evening's shadows and the voices in the camp around the northern curve of the island warned him it was time to return. He bent and retrieved his sack of olives, feeling it to be sure the small pouch of precious seeds was still nestled down the side. Until his broken arm healed, he'd be useful only for forage and tending the sheep. He sighed, knowing the injured, like himself, were sorely needed to accomplish the tasks they had yet to complete to be seaworthy again. He chafed at the limitations of his healing arm, but he stifled his impatience, knowing it would do no one any good.

As he picked his way down the rocky slope, feeling for his footing in the shadowed scree, Domel realized anew that this tiny island, haven though it was to the desperate Faeltheon who had hailed it with joy three weeks ago, would not be able to support them much longer. The island was kidney shaped and barely half a mile across at its widest point. Its eastern slopes were gentle and covered in varied foliage, a boon to the poor sheep, which had been turned out of their pens to graze there almost immediately. At the summit of the first rise, a long fold ran the length of the island, a few date palms growing like a straggling cowlick on its crown. Down the western side of the fold, the hill's slope was steeper, clothed sporadically with a variety of trees and scrub grass.

Now that the pounding storms had ceased, the Faeltheon had had some success with forage, finding herbs and roots they needed to supplement their dwindling supplies, as well as a few hardy plants they had uprooted and transferred to their hanging nurseries aboard the ships. There had been no flowers, though it was warm for the end of October. They had found dates, figs, and olives on the harvest-heavy trees, as well as a few late apricots. They had welcomed the strange foods to their diet and rejoiced in the Creator's provision for them.

Domel was as grateful as any, but he could see, as could the other Companions, that winter approached, and the fruits on the tiny island would feed them for a short time only. In the gentle valley between that slope and the rising bluff at the western edge of the island, they had rejoiced to find a tiny stream of fresh water. It was small, in places hardly more than wet ground, but they had used it to refill their casks and for drinking and cooking. It was awkward, driving the sheep over the rise and into the valley twice a day for water, but the grass near the stream was sparse.

He rounded the curve at the foot of the high bluff to see the large communal fire of their camp leaping against the purple dusk. Figures of graceful women and laughing children were silhouetted against its glow as they welcomed tired men and women from their tasks of felling, trimming, and shaping the new masts and repairing the hull breaches. Domel hastened to join them, misgivings set aside for the time.

Aelric scooped up a handful of sand and let it sift slowly through his fingers. Although the ocean breeze whipped his hair around into his face, he had surrendered to the inevitable and ignored it. The sun matched his golden eyes as it settled onto the horizon, marking the end of another day on the little island. Yesterday, he had spoken at length with the three ship's captains and had received the long-awaited report that they were stocked and seaworthy again.

Although he had yearned for the repairs to be over so that they could continue their quest, he knew that many of his people had become attached to this island. In truth, he, too, had been grateful for the shelter and provision it had given them for nearly six weeks. The first three of those weeks had been miserable, as their makeshift shelters and some of their repairs and harvests had suffered damage from the frequent heavy storms. They had all been grateful to be on solid ground for those tempests. Now that they were entering into the heart of winter, Aelric suspected they had seen the worst of the storms predicted by the sailors in the last few ports. They had been warned that the worst seasonal storms attacked through the fall and early winter in these parts.

The Faeltheon had been intrigued to note that, as they had followed the great sea gyres southward, the Humans at each port seemed to grow darker of skin and eye. Such variations of skin color were not unknown among the Faeltheon, but the green, lavender, and bronze tints common to their people tended to occur in their Faerie Kin, while the skin of the Elves was mostly pale golden. According to the reports of Elrad and young Queen Elwyn, the Humans of the Land had been paler creatures, with skin like unbaked bread dough for the most part

Now, as their travels through the summer and fall had taken the Elves so far from the Land, they had met Humans whose skin was the color of the polished dark wood they traded. These folk, who lived along the northernmost edge of the great vast land to the south and east, had spoken a strange, clicking tongue, which had taken the Elves some time to interpret. These dark sailors had been the ones to warn them of the approaching fall and winter storms and of the sluggish seas to the west that captured unwary ships. Still, they had also confirmed that the great sea gyres did indeed turn westward there, and thus, if the Faeltheon were to continue following them, they, too, must turn into the setting sun.

They had done so, running before fair strong winds for a little over a week before that dreadful storm had overtaken them. Now, though Aelric was not precisely sure where they were, those among them who could interpret positions from the night skies had told him that the constellations at night showed that they were far to the southwest of their old Land.

Today, he had drawn apart from his people to wrestle with the problem of whether to go on searching for their island or to remain here. Aelric knew his own heart greatly desired to continue their journey. He felt that finding their ancestral home was a quest laid upon them by the Creator, and he was eager to resume it, though it was an arduous and dangerous journey with an uncertain ending. Yet, in spite of that, he knew himself to be strong willed, and he didn't want to make decisions that affected his people based solely upon his own desires. He knew his shortcomings and earnestly wished to be a good and wise king to what remained of his Kin. So, he had spent the day going over the advantages and disadvantages in both plans, striving to make a fair and wise judgment. Now, in the evening of a frustrating day, he felt he was no closer to a clear answer.

Behind him, down the headland to the beach, he could hear the Elves laughing and telling stories as they gathered about the fires for the evening meal. This small island had provided a much-needed refuge for them and had allowed them to rest and even to heal a bit from the grievous hurts their spirits had taken a season ago. The little community had grown somewhat stronger, and his people were happy to be together again. Aelric hated to take that away from them, yet he was haunted by his father's dream of finding the island on which they had been created. This dream had given them heart and hope in the aftermath of the destruction of their people and their way of life. This was the task Aelric and the people had set out to accomplish. Was it right for them to abandon it simply because they found something that made them happy?

"I thought I'd find you out here." Caerdrys's familiar voice startled him, so deep was he in his thoughts. She sat down next to him. "Has your time apart given you clear direction for us?"

Aelric smiled wryly. "No. Unfortunately, the Creator doesn't always answer me in a booming voice." Aelric shook his head. "I'm completely torn. I don't know what decision is best for the people." Caerdrys nodded her dark head, as if she'd expected that answer. Aelric wondered if she'd come up against the same quandaries as he had.

"Let us approach the problem logically," she said, mimicking Gaelcar and making him chuckle fondly. Her rain-colored eyes glinted with humor as she went on, but her voice was serious as she listed the items Aelric had considered repeatedly. "We know that, for now at least, we have this island all to ourselves. We've seen no signs that Men have landed here in the past, and it is far enough to the south and west to be fairly far from the main shipping routes. The island we're searching for may be located near the trading routes of Men."

"True," Aelric conceded. "And we actually know where this one is. None of us know much about currents, and the Scrolls are lamentably vague about how we are to follow them. So far, we have faithfully followed the gyres, both south and east, and they are now leading us westward! We have been at sea for the whole summer, and it is now into the cold season, though the Scrolls claim our ancestors traveled upon the sea for only a handful of weeks. With only these stories to guide us, who knows how long it may take for us to find our island."

"We have good supplies here," Caerdrys added, watching his face.

"Yes, but they are limited, and fresh water could become a problem, as the only source is so small," he returned. She nodded, not mentioning the obvious fact that they didn't know what resources the island of their origin would provide, assuming they could find it.

"People seem to be getting back to a normal way of life," Aelric mused. Caerdrys nodded once more, thinking of the buoyed spirits of the tired Faeltheon as they interacted with one another to make their temporary refuge a home.

"Yes, but this island is inadequate to support us all, let alone for us to grow and to spread out as we did in our 'normal' life. How normal will our lives ever become if over two hundred Elves try to remain here on an island barely half a mile across?"

"You feel it too, eh?" Aelric grinned at her, for he had been chafing already at the confined spaces available to them. "Though these lands so far south seem to stay warmer than our northern home, I do not know how severe a winter to expect here," the young king added.

"So…"

"So, I am torn between an unknown and unpredictable journey to an uncertain end and the dubious safety and contentment to be found here. There are many among us who urge remaining where we are, and in some ways, that seems a sensible and safe alternative, but…"

Caerdrys nodded. "Well, now that we're done being safe and rational, what does your heart tell you?"

"That we cannot give up hope, that we have a *need* to continue to search for our island," Aelric responded with a sigh.

"Then, for what it's worth, I think you have found your answer. Unlike the race of Men, we are unfallen. Though we may not always see clearly the path the Creator would have us take, the desires of our hearts are still aligned with His will. Even the folk who urge staying here do so with reservation, for they see that what is adequate for a temporary refuge is not sufficient for a new home. Also, the Creator is still in charge: He will provide for us a place to meet our needs. Why should we choose to settle in a place obviously lacking in the abundance He has always shown His people and dwell here with restless hearts that clamor to complete the task we were given?" Caerdrys asked practically.

Aelric grinned and shook his head. "You know, I really wish you had come down here earlier."

Caerdrys laughed, tossing back her heavy mane and scrambling to her feet. She reached down a strong arm to haul him up. "Come on. Maybe we can get back in time to hear Gaelcar surrendering to the pleas of the children and telling a story of King Amadthalos and his Champion Ethalion for the eighteenth time!"

"What! *Again*?" Gaelcar's long face expressed surprise, his fair, winged brows rising even farther, his tall forehead wrinkling in mock dismay.

"Yes!" shrieked the crowd of young children with glee. It had taken both parties some time to recognize the delight they could take in one another's company. The normally stiff and correct Seneschal had unintentionally intimidated the youngsters, who were already abashed by the traumatic loss of their families and Kinfolk. Yet the young of any species are resilient, and under the watchful and loving care of those who remained, these children were beginning to regain a measure of the ebullience of youth.

When they had discovered what a good storyteller the tall, apparently grim Elf was, one of the boldest of them had begged him for a story. Caught off guard, Gaelcar had submitted. Somehow, in the telling of that first tale to the children, some hard and frightened thing, hidden in the Seneschal's heart, had melted, and his audience had sensed his difference toward them. No more were they afraid of him, even when he was grim, for they knew they held a place in his heart.

Three or four children now took possession of Gaelcar's hands, and the crowd of them surrounded him, escorting him to the rock near the central fire, which he used as a seat. As he settled himself, pretending to be exasperated at this interruption to his work, many of them pressed against him, leaning confidently on his arms and back and knees.

They laughed and giggled, full of joy that they had caught him and made him come join them. Several cried out for a story, and Gaelcar allowed his face to relax into the smile he kept just for them. With a whoop of relieved laughter, those who had been standing around him stopped patting and coaxing him and rushed to settle in the crowd at his feet. One mite of four or five summers calmly picked her way over to him, climbed up on his rock, and settled herself into his lap. The older children, and a few nearby adults, stifled snorts of amusement at the look on the usually dignified Seneschal's face.

Ignoring his now disheveled appearance, Gaelcar put his arms somewhat gingerly around the child, hoping she wouldn't slide off. She nestled into his lap, content. Turning to the expectant crowd of grinning faces, he started their evening ritual.

"All right, *which* story of Amadthalos and Ethalion do you want?"

One of the little girls stood up, pulling a small boy with her. His left hand was bound with strips of cloth that had once been white but were now no cleaner than the rest of the child.

"Freos was hurt today while helping to gather shellfish. Let's let him choose the story!" The other children nodded, and Freos smiled with bashful joy. He was a small, skinny child, so it was no surprise when he made his choice known.

"Please, Lord Gaelcar, tell the story of how Ethalion was chosen to be Amadthalos's Champion!" There were wriggles of happy excitement at this, for the tale was a universal favorite. Gaelcar nodded his fair head, and the children sighed on a note of bliss. Gaelcar's flexible voice took on the nuances of the storyteller as he took them with him back into the mists of time.

"Back in the Elder Days, when the Faeltheon had just come to the Land, Amadthalos was still just a child, like you. Among his close friends he counted three: Stealiht, Pellos, and Ethalion. Stealiht was as delicate and beautiful as her name, and the boys adored her. She was a Faerie, for this was in the days before the Kindred split apart to found their kingdoms. It was as well for her that her wings could carry her wherever the boys ventured, for she was lame, due to an accident aboard the great ships that had brought them to the Land. Pellos, as broad and tall as Amadthalos himself, was a fleet runner and loved games and swimming. Ethalion, much the smallest and slightest of the four, was several years younger than they, but was a good and true friend.

"One day, when the children were out playing on the mountainside, Amadthalos and Pellos decided to have a race. They set Stealiht at the starting line, for she could fly to the finish and not miss the race, and placed Ethalion at the finish line to determine the winner. When all was ready, Stealiht shouted, 'Go!' and off they went! Faster and harder they raced. Closer and nearer they came to Ethalion, who was hopping up and down with excitement. The two friends were level with each other for the better part of the race, then Pellos began to draw ahead.

"Suddenly, just as Amadthalos put on a burst of speed, the ground disappeared before his feet! Pellos, a single pace ahead, lost his footing and tumbled to the ground, but Amadthalos was gone from sight!

"Before Pellos had regained his feet, Stealiht and Ethalion had rushed to the spot. Carefully they approached, not wanting to disappear themselves! As they drew close, the children found that a pit had opened up in the ground. It was a fairly large hole, perhaps four feet deep and as many wide. It had been covered by years of leaves and forest detritus, so that they had not noticed it at all.

"They crept close to the rim of the pit and called down to their friend, but he made no answer. Pellos, very much afraid for his fallen friend, raced away to find adult help. Stealiht wanted to go, too, thinking her wings might be swifter, but Ethalion screamed at her not to leave him, but to fly up and look into the pit and tell him if it was safe to try to help Amadthalos. Stealiht fluttered above the hole and peered down inside it.

She called down to Ethalion that she could see Amadthalos, but he was lying at the bottom and there was much blood around his head.

"The children were frightened, of course, but Ethalion feared the loss of blood more than any other injury. He crept up to the very rim of the pit, trying not to rain dirt and debris down on Amadthalos. With Stealiht guiding him, he crawled over the edge and slid down into the hole, keeping well to the side away from Amadthalos's head.

"When he crouched carefully beside his friend, he saw that they were right to be worried. Amadthalos lay crumpled and pale, a great wound in his head. Blood was still coming from the gash, and Amadthalos's lips were taking on a bluish hue. Glancing up, Ethalion could see the rocky outcropping in the side of the pit where Amadthalos had struck his head when he fell.

"Carefully, he felt over Amadthalos's limbs, but none seemed to be broken. Realizing that there could well be injuries he could not see, Ethalion feared moving his friend, but he wondered how long it would be before Pellos would return with adult aid. He shouted up to Stealiht.

"'Fly above the trees and tell me if you see help coming!' Instantly, the Faerie vanished from his sight. While he waited, Ethalion searched for some way to staunch the dreadful bleeding. There really was nothing to use, so the boy wriggled out of his tunic and tried to wrap it about his friend's head. The first few tries did not work, as the tunic was cumbersome and the blood slippery. Ethalion was surprised by how heavy his friend's head felt as he tried to raise it with one hand while wrapping the tunic around it with the other. Finally, he succeeded in swathing Amadthalos's head in the tunic and secured it with his supple leather belt. Amadthalos groaned pitifully, though Ethalion was as careful as he could be.

"'I'm sorry! I'm sorry,' he whispered, trying to wipe the blood away. He looked up to see if Stealiht had returned but could not see her. Ethalion straightened Amadthalos's limbs as best he could in the cramped space. Already his tunic bandage was showing ominous dark stains.

"'Ethalion!' came Stealiht's cry at last. 'Pellos is running as fast as he can, but he is not yet near the village!'

"Ethalion bit back his tears of fear and called out to her. 'Come and help me get him out of here. They will come soon, but the closer we are to them, the faster Amadthalos will get help!'

"The Faerie flew down until she hovered just above the pit. She could not come farther down or her wings would hit the edges. Ethalion summoned all his strength and pulled Amadthalos over his shoulder. He tried to stand up, but the weight of the older boy was too much for his poor legs and he could not do it. Panting, trying not to cry, Ethalion crawled over to the side where the rocky outcrop was imbedded.

"'Come stand on this rock and I will try to get him up that far!' he called to Stealiht. Obediently, she let her feet down until her sound right foot touched the rock. Awkwardly, she crouched there, extending her strong young arms to help pull Amadthalos up. With Stealiht taking some of the weight from his shoulders, Ethalion was able to stand nearly upright, and together they wrestled their friend up and over the lip of the hole. As they rolled him over the edge, much of the dirt and ground around crumbled and rained down on Ethalion. The two friends kept their grip firmly on Amadthalos, so he didn't slide back down into the pit with the loosened earth.

"When they had him safely up on level ground again, Ethalion scrambled up, using the rock as a bench. He lay panting on the cool earth for a moment, then remembered Amadthalos's wound. Rolling over, the boy checked the tunic. It had stayed on during their struggle, but it was wet with blood now. Feeling an uprising of panic at the grey tone of Amadthalos's skin, Ethalion rose and caught Amadthalos under the arms. As carefully as he could, the younger boy dragged his friend over to a nearby boulder. With Stealiht's help, they pulled the older boy up onto the rock. Ethalion stopped for a moment to catch his breath.

"'What are we going to do?' asked Stealiht, watching the dark stain grow on the tunic bandage. 'We can't just wait here. He'll bleed to death!'

"Ethalion nodded. He scrambled to his feet again and bent over the body of his friend. Grasping him by the arms, Ethalion heaved until he had Amadthalos over his back and shoulder once again. Stealiht helped to steady the burden. Bent almost double, the younger boy began to stagger down the mountainside.

"'Go up,' he grunted to the Faerie. 'Guide me so I don't drop him!'

"It was a long and arduous struggle down that rough mountainside. Ethalion thought his back would surely crack, and his lungs burned to draw in air. His vision was red and hazy, but his steps were dogged. He would not stop. He would not give up.

"After a time, he could not even hear the directions called down by Stealiht, and once his foot came down in a small dell, nearly dumping both boys to the ground. With a great wrench, Ethalion recovered his balance, but his legs were burning and shaking with fatigue by now.

"A little while later, he found he could not move forward, no matter how hard he tried. He seemed to have come up against something unyielding, but he could not force his eyes to open and see the problem. He felt Amadthalos starting to slip and took a firmer grip, but it was no use. Something was pulling his friend from him. With a sob of despair, Ethalion fell to his knees, trying to cushion Amadthalos as much as possible.

"Somehow, Amadthalos didn't seem to be falling, though. When Ethalion had drawn in enough air to dispel the dizziness and open his eyes, he found Amadthalos lying on the ground next to him, his father kneeling beside him and one of the women removing the bloodstained tunic. Another adult came to him and held a flask of water to his lips. Suddenly aware of his burning thirst, Ethalion drank.

"The younger boy was unaware that he himself was pale and shaking, beaded with sweat and streaked front and back with his friend's blood. Now that help had met them and his desperate errand was finished, Ethalion's overtaxed body reacted, and, for the first and last time in his life, the child fainted.

"Later, when he awoke in his own bed, the pain of his wrenched back was severe, and the vicious cramps in his legs made him bite his lips, determined not to cry out. His injuries were not severe, but the healing took some time. He was kept to his bed nearly as long as Amadthalos.

"Amadthalos was badly hurt, but the healers were able to make him well again. Ethalion, because of his great love for his friend, had carried the larger boy on his back for nearly a mile, getting him to help just in time. Thanks to the courage and fortitude of his friends, especially the smallest and weakest one, the life of the future king was saved. It was only a few weeks before he was able to be up and about with his friends.

"As soon as he was well enough, Amadthalos asked to see Ethalion. When Ethalion came to him, Amadthalos told him that when they were grown up, and he was king, he would appoint Ethalion to be his Champion.

"And so it was."

"Poor scrawny little boy!" Shouting with laughter, Stealiht shoved at Ethalion's muscled arm with no noticeable effect. Red-faced with embarrassment, he pushed her back, and she tumbled head over heels, only to right herself and flutter back down to land on her two good feet.

"Did the story really happen like that?" asked Nausika, turning from the vanishing window to the four friends. Amadthalos, laughing to the point of tears, had fallen backwards into the tender grass, and could not answer. Pellos, chuckling at the Champion's discomfort, nodded. Stealiht, laughing too, settled back down next to Ethalion, who was muttering under his breath and looking everywhere except at his companions.

"That was one of my favorite stories as a child," remarked Laslorn meditatively. "Probably because I was so scrawny and short as a boy."

"Of all things to be remembered for!" gasped Amadthalos, between wheezes of laughter at Ethalion's red face. "They couldn't remember him for his incredible deeds in battle against the Goblins or for his feats of heroism during fires or floods! No, they have to remember him as a skinny little boy—"

"—Risking his own life trying to save his friend against all odds. Going beyond his natural strength because of the love he bore! In short, displaying the best and truest that lies in the hearts of the Faeltheon people … *of course* he is remembered for this deed. It is epic. It is what we all wish to be, in our secret hearts. It is the hope of every child, weak or strong, to be able to do such deeds for friendship's sake," put in Theo passionately, stopping Amadthalos's mirth and Ethalion's blushes. Elwyn's gentle voice picked up the words as she completed her husband's thought.

"You are both remembered for your later deeds as fell warriors and good leaders. Your names are synonymous with loyalty and friendship. Many stories are told of your rule and of your friendship, but none is more cherished or more often requested than this tale, for if a *child* can so enact the essence of friendship, there is hope for each of us to be so courageous. We needn't be strong or skilled; we need only be steadfast and true and willing to give all we have for the sake of love."

The last shimmer of the window faded away amidst a profound silence, as they each considered the words of the Master and Lady of Marliondolen.

The next morning Aelric gathered all the Elves together. They all sat before him on the sand, anxiously awaiting his decision.

"After much prayer and deliberation, I have decided that we will continue on with our search for our island home. We will not abandon the task we set out to accomplish. However, this island was certainly a blessing from Aematlon. We have waited out the storm season here and have made all repairs we needed to the ships. According to the Scrolls, we should not have to travel much farther, if everything goes well and we follow the currents. We will depart as soon as the ships are watered and we have stocked all we can carry."

The people's reactions were varied, but all stood and immediately began to gather their possessions and to organize the repacking of the ships. They might not all agree with Aelric's choice, but he was their king. They had sworn to obey him, and they trusted that he was not making any decisions without seeking the Creator's will first.

Corot sat alone in his dark office, anticipating a message from his mightiest allies. He had been warned to make himself available for their messenger, and, as powerful as he knew himself to be, he did not dare to defy them. His black eyes, usually so piercing and alert, were gazing blankly into space, and he had not made any movements for hours.

Finally, he sensed a familiar dark presence nearby. Only then did Corot rouse himself and look expectantly about the room. His eyes finally found the dim figure lurking in a corner. It approached him, and he rose to greet it, carefully lowering his eyes so that they would not meet what passed for eyes in the creature's face. Corot seldom feared anything, but even the mere emissary of these allies intimidated him. The envoy's smooth, cuttingly contemptuous voice broke the silence, filling the chamber, while remaining menacingly quiet.

"Your rebellious 'partners' are pitiful! Pitifully trained, pitifully equipped, and pitifully outnumbered. You were foolish to align yourself and your cause with them. They are vermin, pleasingly offensive to our Enemy, yet not much good to us. What potential you see in them escapes me! Still, they gather to overthrow you. Their miserable attempt will begin in exactly one hour. Prepare your soldiers, and you will crush them utterly." With that, the envoy quit the room, departing as suddenly as it had come.

Corot suppressed the shudder that rippled over his skin, controlling his expressionless face, lest the minion still be lurking nearby, spying on him. It would take a longer time than he had yet spent in their company to control his traitorous body's response to the presence of these masters of evil, but he knew better than to show his fear.

Inwardly, he seethed at the creature's assessment of his intelligence and acumen in the matter of the Goblin alliance. He felt his confidence return, with an edge of contempt reflected back at the emissary for not being able to see what was plain to Corot. The 'alliance' was merely an intermediate step to pacify the Goblin leaders into a habit of compliance with Corot's will. When he judged there had been sufficient time to teach them to fear and obey him, he would dispense with this ridiculous notion of equality, of partnership, and force them to submit to his plans. They would make very useful slaves and would furnish a key element in Corot's designs.

Smoothing down the spotless front of his unrelieved black robe, Corot turned and strode sharply out of his private office into the anteroom where his highest-ranking officers stood, waiting to receive his orders.

Little over an hour later, Corot stood on the bloodied battlefield, hearing the report of his commanders. The rebellion, if this petty revolt warranted the term, had lasted less than fifteen minutes, and every Goblin commander had either been slaughtered in the initial battle or summarily executed shortly thereafter. Corot could count on the fingers of his left hand the number of his own men who had died in the conflict. The few Goblins leaders who remained cowered within the tight circle his men formed around them.

Corot approached them, being careful to stop on a slight rise, which, coupled with his own unusual height, caused him to tower over them. He waited in grim silence, his cold eyes boring into them until they shifted uneasily, whimpering in fear. Corot knew his aspect to be terrifying, and he played on their guilty knowledge that they had betrayed their alliance in seeking to overthrow him. When he judged them sufficiently cowed, he addressed them, his quiet voice lashing them like a whip of ice.

"Your uprising has been justly squashed by the pure might of my soldiers, which you forced me to unleash upon you. You are surely aware now that there is no way to defeat us. Alone, we are too powerful for you, and we have other powerful allies as well. How could you think to betray the rest of the Lemyurans? Do you understand nothing of what we stand for? However, even though there was no possibility you could have endangered me, you have managed to lose my trust. Our alliance is betrayed; our partnership destroyed by your rash actions.

"Although it would have been of great advantage to you to remain allied with the Lemyuran might, only a fool would trust you now. Remaining partners with you would be dangerous, for you are slow to learn and would most likely undertake another amusing, though irritating, attempt to seize power. Since I cannot trust you as partners, yet find your small services somewhat useful, I have no choice but make you my slaves. From this day on, I have absolute control over your lives and the lives of your people. All orders come from me, and you have no choice but to obey them. Do any of you object?"

There was no sound from the cowed Goblins. The pointed spears of his soldiers ensured their compliance. Corot compressed his lips into a tight, humorless smile and finished his duplicitous speech. Even as he had castigated them for their betrayal and cited the common drive of Lemyurans everywhere, he'd gloried in the secret knowledge that they had played right into his hands, just as he had anticipated. It would not be necessary to betray and enslave them to do his will; they had accomplished the task for him.

"Wise choice. Your decision will benefit you, even as it will serve me." Coldly, he left the prisoners to his men.

Several days later, two of his personal guards and a single small Goblin interrupted Corot in his work.

"What do you mean by this intrusion?" Corot snapped testily, for he hated being disturbed nearly as much as he disliked their presumption in daring to disturb him.

"Them newly appointed Goblins leaders felt it would be wise to send you a gift, sir," one of the men replied, with a snicker. "Since they don't own nothin' anymore, they sent this worthless bag o' bones!" With that, he shoved the hapless Goblin with his foot, sending the scrawny creature tumbling to the floor in a tangle of bony arms and legs.

"I suppose that means that they are awed by the swiftness of their defeat and hope that they can cajole me into giving them their power back," Corot muttered. "What a repulsive creature it is. Do you have a name?" he inquired of the little Goblin, who was rapidly regaining his footing. It was small, with scrawny limbs and a pudgy body, topped by a round face. Corot was trying to decide what was different about this one, from other Goblins, when it looked up brightly and began to respond to his question, as though being addressed flipped a switch that started his mouth.

"Greetings, Your Worship! My name is Gren, and I'm to be your new personal attendant! I really like your house. Well, that's not entirely true. I don't really like your office, you see, because—"

A sharp thwack to the skull ended Gren's opinion of Corot's office, and the second soldier, who had administered the punishment, promptly explained. "They said that hitting him usually makes him stop, sir. They also would like to assure you that, other than a slight speech problem, this Goblin is the most loyal, dutiful, and efficient slave you could desire."

"Really?" remarked Corot dryly, raising his left eyebrow at the young Goblin. Usually, that gesture was enough to make his strongest soldiers blanch with fear, but the round-faced creature seemed to take it as permission to speak again.

"Indeed, Your Worship, that's what they said. I heard 'em. But I think they were lying, because before they brought me here, my last master said that I was the worst, most dimwitted, annoying slave he ever acquired. Of course, he really wasn't a very nice person at all. I'm not sure you could trust his assessment. I think maybe he had a difficult childhood. You know, that would explain a lot, like when—" *Crack!* The soldier's arm shot out and once again silenced the alarmingly social Goblin.

"How kind of them to bestow such a ... valuable ... gift upon me. I think perhaps I should just return it. Still, it could be amusing, I suppose," Corot grumbled. He suspected the creature might be a spy of sorts, but it did not seem clever enough to manage such a task. Still, Goblins were cunning. Perhaps he would be wise to keep it around long enough to ascertain its true mission. He glanced at his desktop and was recalled to the pressing matters of his work, and his annoyance at the interruption was renewed. He addressed his soldiers sharply.

"You are dismissed."

With alacrity, they turned and departed the room, seeming to Corot to be searching for a safe place where they might snicker at his plight. The slave began to chatter once more.

"Oh, good! They're gone. That one fellow seemed to enjoy hitting me a little too much!" Gren suddenly ducked, nimbly dodging Corot's fist, which sailed harmlessly over his large cranium. "I think I'm going to like you; you hesitate a little before you strike."

"I'll try to work on that," Corot promised sarcastically, with the sinking feeling that he would likely be getting a lot of practice. Already, his head was beginning to ache in anticipation of Gren's constant chatter. "Aren't you supposed to bow submissively and to speak ingratiatingly, and only when necessary?" he inquired of his voluble property.

The round face bobbed in agreement and the bright voice chirped. "Yessir! I sure am. I never could master that protocol stuff, though! No matter what they tried, it never would stick—you know: how to hold your hands and how far to bow and when to whisper and when to whine! If I didn't have my helmet, I bet my brains would have been dashed out years ago! Why, I—"

The little Goblin with the annoyingly persistent voice stopped suddenly, as Corot held out his six-fingered hand for the helmet.

Chapter Thirteen

The long, tiring day, filled with so many tasks, finally wound down to making cider and pies with her mother. Chassidy had had hardly any time to think. She wiped the sweat off her forehead with her rolled-up sleeve as she stepped abruptly out of the steamy kitchen into the swept dirt yard, seeking a moment of solitude.

Her mother had noted how reserved Chassidy had been lately and it troubled her, for a mere year ago Chassidy had had the boldness to venture into the unknown to rescue young Chloe, but now the girl seemed too quiet. There was even an air of sadness about her, which her mother, a practical woman, put down to Chassidy's leaving childhood and entering womanhood. The melancholy, so unusual in her bright, energetic older daughter, made the mother impatient and brusque. The older woman's forehead bore a line of anxiety and a frown of disapproval for the precipitous exit.

However, Chassidy noticed neither her mother's concern nor her disapproval. The young woman, lost in deep thought, walked on blindly until she realized her feet had taken her to the place which, a year before, she had found to be a most dangerous location for picnics. Baby Chloe had been snatched from this very spot, stolen away, to the dismay and heartbreak of her loving family. But Chassidy, driven by her deep need to find the baby, had taken all her courage and indomitable spirit and had ventured into the forbidden and frightening Great Forest to seek for the lost one. None had known then that little Chloe's kidnapping had been a vital part of an evil plot conceived by an alliance of Goblins and Humans bent on the destruction of the Faeries who made their home in the nearby Forest.

Of course, when Chassidy had discovered all this during her attempt to rescue Chloe, she had known it would be folly to try to speak of it, for none would believe her. Or, at least, none would believe her sane. So, throughout that exciting, amazing, frightening, sorrowful time the girl had stored up all she had seen and experienced, until her heart was full to overflowing with a greater reality than the one presented by her everyday life. Yet, since her return to that ordinary existence, she had been unable to speak of any of it, restrained from sharing the wonder, the joy, the grief of meeting and then losing those incredible Faeltheon, except as make-believe stories spun for her little sister.

She sat down mechanically, as if sitting were an involuntary action, for her mind was engrossed in her musings. There, surrounded by fall's wealth of golden and russet leaves, Chassidy longed for the Faeltheon, who had written an eternal mark on her memory. She tugged gently on the fine silver chain about her neck, revealing her gift of golden stars from their hiding place under her dress. As her melancholy thoughts swept through her, she finally resolved to enter the Forest again. In her heart she cherished a faint hope that if she could just speak a final farewell to her dear friends, she might find solace for her sense of loss. She also hoped she might discover what had become of their Elven Kin who had not accompanied the Faerie folk into Marliondolen but had remained in their homes in the mountains near the northwestern coast.

Chassidy was aware that she had but two seasons before she would be wed to an affable young man of her parents' choice. While the match was entirely appropriate and Chassidy had no intention of arguing, she could not help but think that they were not well enough suited to each other to fill the longing in her heart for a love deep and true, such as she had witnessed in the white castle of Elwyn, the last Queen of Faerie. Further troubling her lately was the realization that with her rapidly approaching marriage and the new status her married state would impart, she would be forced to put aside or, at least, cease to acknowledge, her childhood adventure.

She could not speak of it now, for none would listen, uncomfortable as they were with the Forest itself, let alone the unmaidenly and inappropriate actions she had taken last fall. Most of the women were unwilling to speak of it; either not wanting to distress her over what must have been a dreadful and frightening adventure, or not wanting to encourage such outrageous behavior in a young maiden. Many of the men, though Chassidy could not know it, were secretly filled with admiration, and not a little jealousy, at her bravery in breaching the fearsome Great Forest to search for the babe. The fact that, when she'd finally been located far to the north, she had had the missing baby with her, safe and sound, was miracle enough to excuse her very vague and unsatisfactory explanations of the weeks she'd been missing.

Chassidy's wandering thoughts kept circling back to the same place, like a messenger bird seeking its home roost. The passage of time pressed her to find what answers she could as soon as possible. Decisively, she concluded that tonight, once all others in the home had surrendered to slumber, she must set out into the Forest one last time.

Late that night, Chassidy lay awake in secret, waiting impatiently for stillness. She could hear her mother's restless movements and knew she was awake and, likely, worried. Chassidy had felt her mother's gaze upon her all the evening and knew she was wary of her daughter's odd mood. However, Chassidy's will was firm tonight, and she waited until, at last, the stillness of the household assured her that her time had come. So, much better prepared than she'd been on her former journey, having left a note on her bed disclosing her location and begging that no one be made to follow her, Chassidy made her escape.

The journey to the palace was both shorter and less challenging than it had been before, for the magic wards no longer opposed Chassidy's speed and determination, and the way seemed plain before her feet. Although she questioned herself about the possibility of a Goblin presence in the Forest, she pressed onward, for she no longer feared the Forest itself.

At sunset, four days into her journey, as Chassidy lifted her eyes, the slanting copper rays gilded the watchtowers of the castle with fire. Ignoring her exhaustion, she quickened her pace toward the familiar shapes. Soon she was through the great gate and into the inner bailey, so strangely silent and lifeless. Panting and choked with tears, she embraced one of the gracefully carved columns and sank to her knees in the rosy light.

It is still here! I knew it would be, she assured herself. She had almost begun to wonder if the Faeltheon *were* just a dream or a story as her small sister, Chloe, believed. At barely four summers, Chloe had no clear memory of the Faerie child she had befriended last fall. Although Chassidy had told her of the Faeltheon in a far different tone than that which she was accustomed to use for storytelling, Chloe, in her simplicity, assumed that story was just an elaborate kind of fairy tale. The loneliness of being the only one she knew to believe in the departed Faeries was far weightier than the young woman had anticipated, and her heart often echoed hollowly.

Chassidy was not surprised to find the palace's treasures shattered and spoiled, for she had known of the advancing Goblin army. Even though the Goblins, in their hatred of all things beautiful, had torn down the intricate hanging tapestries and had defaced the carved stone pillars, the beauty of the palace still mesmerized Chassidy. It was as if the very air of that place was filled with a different spirit from anywhere else she had ever been, and the breeze through the trees, which lulled her to sleep, seemed to echo still with the sound of Theomanus's joyous voice as he had entered into Marliondolen.

When Chassidy awoke the next day, in the cold light of pre-dawn, her face was stained with tears of mingled sorrow and joy. After splashing her face in the cold water of the nearby River Fleet, she began to explore the remnants of the palace. Debris was scattered across the ground, but the frame of the castle itself was not greatly damaged. The palace no longer teemed with light and laughter and bright, sparkling colors, as it had before in the days when Elwyn Elenthea, the last Queen of Faerie, had lived there with her beautiful Court. The earth itself seemed to cry out to Chassidy, throbbing under her feet, as if in protest of a great wrong done. She paused to savor the realization of how richly God had blessed her, allowing her to know such a wonderful people, even for so short a time, yet the emptiness in her heart seemed a terrible price to pay for that fleeting joy.

Chassidy's footsteps echoed inside the great palace, emphasizing her aloneness, until the rising of the sun prompted the chirping of birds, which gradually filled the building, swelling to a magnificent symphony. The palace already seemed warmer, and with each new room she entered, Chassidy could not suppress the expectation that she would find one of her friends, even though she knew they had gone long ago.

Daringly, she entered Elwyn's own suite of rooms at the top of the Queen's Tower. There on the carved dressing table, coated with the dust of a year's neglect, she found a dainty silver brush, a beautifully inlaid hair comb, rich with carvings and gems, and a silver-bound book, left carelessly open, facedown on the dresser. With reverent hands, Chassidy picked up the little book and smoothed the leaves closed, setting it down again. Her fingers trailed over the stylized birch trees and graceful runes incised into the front cover, wishing she could read its message. Leaving the precious book, her eyes swept the room.

On the floor, near the draped and carved bed, Chassidy's eyes caught the glimmer of one of Elwyn's necklaces glittering against the rich green rug. She picked up the delicate treasure, holding it clasped to the breast of her homespun dress, letting the echo of the queen's kind voice come to her through the long months of solitude. Chassidy moved to slip the piece into her pocket to remember Elwyn by, but paused to consider.

If I were to keep this, it would surely be found someday. It would cause a mad treasure hunt, and what is left of this beauty would perish in the hands of greedy men, with no thought to the holiness of the lives lived here! She lifted the necklace once more, examined it closely, that she might always remember the tiny leaves, fashioned in autumn colors from copper and gold and bronze, then set it under the broken mirror on the dresser, safely hidden forever.

As she exited the lonely Tower an hour later, she took with her two treasures only: her memories and a tiny braided ring she had twisted from the strands of moonlight hair caught in the brush.

She's crazy! Aye, I'm marryin' a crazy 'un, 'n' I only got six months to get myself out o' it! Nicholan thought, more to distract his mind from his fear than to actually denigrate the sanity of his betrothed, though he *was* beginning to question it. After all, what sane, well-bred young woman would venture out unescorted, let alone into the Forest! She was developing quite a reputation for wandering in the Forest, and it disturbed him that this otherwise perfectly respectable young woman should show a penchant for the forbidden. It seemed almost defiant, in a way, though he wasn't sure if he meant defying custom and protocol or defying his suit by making herself less than respectable, now they were promised.

Chassidy's recent disquiet, added to her having no comprehensible reason to be in the Forest, made her behavior, and his task, all the more uncomfortable. Nicholan knew no more of last year's queer adventure than anyone else in the village, but he was beginning to wonder if he oughtn't to probe her father more determinedly for the details. It was downright odd her going off like this again.

According to the story that had been the gossip of last winter, the girl had had a valid, if headstrong, reason for her actions then. Her bizarre action of venturing alone into the Forest to seek her lost sister had been somewhat justified by the fact that Chassidy had indeed recovered the missing child. Still, what possible reason could there be for this latest jaunt?

Nicholan felt a niggling suspicion there might be more to the story than he had yet been told. He didn't want to be tied for life to a daft woman. Headstrong was bad enough, but daft was out of the question. *Perhaps I should've pursued the hand of the baker's daughter… She wouldn't have dragged me from my work on some wild errand into this dangerous Forest!*

Still, it's a boon to partner with the Cooper, for he's the best in four counties, and my livin' will be secured w' a good reputation like that! I must think o' my family and future. I've trained as a cooper, not a baker! Further, I've several years paid work to my credit. I'm not an apprentice to spend more years toilin' under the man while waitin' for his youngest girl to grow old enow to wed. No, it's this lass for me, and a bonny one she is, too. If only she weren't so fey!

Across the River Fleet, near the Western Woods, Nicholan retraced the path of last year's search party. He recalled the journey taking much longer last fall. The Forest was not as intimidating as he remembered either. So far, he had not found her, and he had lost her trail yesterday, but he doggedly strode on, hoping to find her where they had found her last year. If he did not, he would retrace his way back to where he had last been sure of her sign and try to pick up her trail again.

His fear was shifting from nervousness of the forbidding Forest, through fear for her safety out here alone, to exasperation at her costing him this journey. The tale of it was sure to get around, and he had no mind to be the butt of jokes in the pub all winter. The girl had best have a good explanation for this crazy stunt… one that he could use to turn aside the mirth of his companions.

They have *to be around here somewhere, unless they did not survive the Goblin attacks.* Chassidy refused to entertain the notion that all the Elves had perished. Yet, it could not be denied that there were no signs or markings anywhere suggestive of a path or trail used to get from the Realm of Faerie to the Court of the Elven King. She had never been farther than this wide meadow where, on a bright autumn day nearly a year ago, she had watched in amazement as Theomanus had made of himself a shimmering doorway, opening into the fabled realm of Marliondolen. The Faeries and their Elven Kindred who had chosen to accompany them, along with the People of the Horn, unicorns of surpassing beauty and wisdom, had vanished one by one, passing through the very form of Theomanus into their sanctuary. When all save Chassidy and Chloe had passed through, Theo himself had turned, a twisting shimmer of rainbow joy, and had disappeared as well. She and Chloe had been left alone in a meadow as empty as it was today.

Recalling the desolation of the few days they had waited until their father's party had found them, Chassidy felt a chill that had nothing to do with the weather chase itself down her spine. She looked around her now, seeing again the familiar landmarks she had memorized in that lonely time. Feeling hollow inside, she decided to go in search of the little stream she had used the last time she was here. It was getting toward late afternoon; it would be well to gather supplies and make a camp for the night before the sun went down.

Chassidy knew it was not hunger that caused the hollow feeling in her middle, but, being a practical sort, she realized that keeping busy at necessary tasks would be better than succumbing to the dreadful sorrow that haunted the edges of her soul, especially in this place. She crossed the wide meadow and went just into the first trees of the Western Wood. There, as she remembered from last winter, was the little stream, cold and clear, burbling and brisk. Chassidy knelt at a low place in the bank and scooped the cold water into her hands to drink. It was refreshing, though cold enough to make her back teeth ache. She reached for her pack and the leather water pouch tied to the side of it. Untying it, she held the lip under the water and waited patiently while the bag filled. Full pouch restored to its place, Chassidy turned her attention to gathering twigs and small fallen branches for firewood. Arms full with enough to warm her the whole night through, pack and water bottle over her shoulder, Chassidy returned to the open field. It didn't occur to her to be afraid to camp out in the open. The prospect of harm from wolves or other predators never occurred to her. This was, as best she could remember, the site of the Faeltheon's passage into fabled Marliondolen: where else would she stop?

After standing with her squinting eyes to the lowering sun that sat upon the rim of the Western Wood, Chassidy did a bit of scouting and quickly found the small circle of rocks she had set up for a hearth last winter. Dropping her armload of kindling, she set about laying out her cloak and blanket, her food and water. Returning to the edge of the Woods, she found springy bracken growing in dense clumps under the lower trees. Collecting an armload of this, she carried it back to her campsite. Several more trips accrued a wealth of the springy, fragrant fronds, which she piled up under her blanket. She would sleep comfortably this night with fresh bracken for bedding. Another search, somewhat longer, finally yielded two sturdy, forked sticks and a longer, nearly straight shaft to use as a makeshift spit over her hearth fire.

By the time the sun had set, Chassidy had a cheery small fire going in her rock pit. Suspended above it on the spit was a skin bag such as hunters used in the wild. In this bag, made from the hide of some small kill, probably an otter, she thought, was water from the stream and a handful of leaves to make an herbal tea. With two sticks held as pinchers, Chassidy fished a small rock from the heart of the fire and dropped it into the skin bag. The water hissed a bit. She repeated her task three more times before she saw wisps of steam curling from the top of the skin.

Careful not to spill, Chassidy dipped her horn cup into the bag of steeping tea and drew out enough to begin to warm her. Setting her flat-bottomed cup down beside her, she picked up her water pouch and added more water to the skin pot. Now that she had added the fresh water, the contents of the bag were little more than warm, so she reached her hand in and fished out the small stones, tossing them back into the fire to reheat. By the time she had consumed her frugal meal of apples, cheese, and tea, the water in the skin bag was hot enough for another cup.

When she had finished her meal and cleared away the spit and supplies, Chassidy added more wood to the fire, building it carefully so that the larger sticks and small logs would gradually catch and burn through the night. Rolling herself in her woolen cloak for warmth, she lay down upon her bed of bracken and blanket, face to the fire. For all the night was cool, she was warm enough . . . at least on the outside.

Now that her activities had ceased, Chassidy had to face the memories that crowded hot and hard against her heart. The bright, beautiful faces, the luminous, tilted eyes, the graceful forms and lovely garments of her lost friends pressed round the girl in the firelit night. The music of their voices, the lilting of their speech hovered just beyond her hearing, though her mind perceived them clearly. For many hours, as the fire burned down to glowing coals, Chassidy lay surrounded by precious, painful memories, heedless of the tears that streaked her cheeks and trickled down to soak the edge of her cloak.

Finally, near dawn, she drifted from waking dream to exhausted slumber. Aching with fresh grief at her loss, she was unaware that she continued to weep in her sleep.

Chapter Fourteen

Elwyn gently wiped the tears from her own cheeks as the small window before her shimmered and faded away. She shook back her gilt hair and felt the late afternoon sun of Marliondolen warm upon her shoulders. Her breaths were still a bit uneven, for she was more shaken than she had realized by this small glimpse she had been shown.

Wishing that Theo were near to discuss the vision with her and to comfort her, Elwyn began carefully to gather her materials. She had come out to this spot to collect some of the herbs and flowers that grew in the sheltered copse near the little waterfall. The little grotto was not far from their home, perhaps half an hour's stroll, and was a treasure trove of medicinal plants.

She finished placing the last of her harvest into the small gauze bags she had labeled for them and tied their tops with the knots peculiar to each. This ensured that she could find the correct plants, even in the dark, just by feeling the knots of the cords that bound the bags. Putting the bags into her gathering basket, Elwyn stood and left the pleasant clearing, heading for home and family.

Before she had flown half the distance, she recognized the distinctive upright carriage and sleek dark head of her husband walking below her, and her heart gave a happy leap. A few more moments and they had converged, Theo claiming a kiss.

He tucked her against his side, gathering her left hand into his.

"You've been crying, my heart. What is wrong?"

The memory of her vision flooded back, and Elwyn's throat tightened. She leaned hard against his strength, and he slowed to give her time to collect herself. She swallowed hard and found she could speak of it.

"I was given a window," she began. Theo drew in his breath sharply. Clearly this was not what he had expected. "In it I saw Fyrenfyld, the meadow from which we entered Marliondolen. At first there was no one in it. But then, as I watched, a small figure came walking, all alone. Theo, it was Chassidy! I watched as she made camp and lay awake all night on that meadow. I could see her face, her tears. But, even if I could not have seen them, I knew that she grieved. In her heart, that Human child still grieved for us as though we had just departed!"

Theo was silent, taking in what she had said and hearing what she did not say, in the manner of perceptive lovers. Elwyn rested against him as they walked, thankful anew for this quiet Elf, with his steadfast love and support. Finally, as they drew near where some of their friends were waiting, he spoke softly into the floating hair above her ear.

"Beloved, the Creator's mercy and kindness allowed the meeting between this small Human and the Faeltheon. We learned much that was good from knowing her, and she has retained a strong impression of us as well. For all the sorrow she feels at being left behind, the memories she holds of us will comfort her and will bring her wisdom in her later years, I hope."

Elwyn nodded within the shelter of his arm. His voice continued in a different tone, making her smile once more with love for him.

"Still, this is the first window that has shown us a Human! I wonder why the Creator wanted you to see this vision."

Still smiling, her equilibrium restored, Elwyn replied.

"Probably so we could pray for her. Life for Humans is short and hard enough without this added burden of grief. How lonely she must feel, poor child."

Before Theo could reply, Laslorn's voice reached them.

"Hurry up, you two! Everyone's waiting and we can't start without you!"

"Everyone? Waiting for what?" Elwyn exclaimed, tilting her head to see Theo's face. Theo chuckled, quickening his pace.

"Laslorn's exaggerating again. There are just a few friends, mostly those who lived before us, who desire to hear the story of our entry into Marliondolen."

"Oh, how nice! It's always so … *renewing* … to dwell on that adventure!"

Theo hugged her tightly, bestowing a last kiss on the top of her head as they reached the group. "It is indeed, my heart," he agreed.

The "few friends" turned into a crowd, for few who heard the tale could resist hearing it again. As they found places beside the great cracking fire that had been built against the sheer rock face of the hillside at the far end of the meadow, there were closer to sixty than forty in the party. A festive air circulated with spiced hot cider, and foodstuffs were shared about liberally.

As though they had rehearsed it, Elrad began the tale, then Elwyn chimed in, with Nausika, Lucina, and Kier adding bits along the way. When Nausika reached the part where they had first discovered that the legend of Marliondolen, their hoped-for haven and refuge, had come to them in a dream long ages ago and might not be real at all, a light, clear voice called out.

"*I* had that dream! It haunted my sleep for weeks before I could get anyone to listen to me!"

All eyes were now turned upon a slender, fair-haired Faerie woman, seated on a moss-green cloak spread upon a convenient boulder. She smiled, her dark eyes flashing in the firelight, as she raised her goblet to Nausika and Elwyn. "I dreamed of this place, this land! It was *just* like this: safe and happy and loving. The dream was as much about the spirit of the place as it was of its purpose." Her face softened as she looked upon the gathering of friends, old and new. "I never dreamed I'd get to be here though."

"The Creator always exceeds our expectations, doesn't He?" murmured Elrad, and many heads nodded in agreement.

The tale continued, told in the somewhat nasal tones of Silverlight the unicorn, until it wound down to the arrival of the company at the meadow called Fyrenfyld, and the transformation of Theomanus into the living portal that had opened Marliondolen to the refugees.

Many then took turns describing their first impressions of the wonders of the land the Creator had made to shelter them. In growing excitement and energy, they told of their joy and delight in all the good things that awaited them. Even those who had died many years before were encouraged to tell of their initial impressions.

Replete with satisfaction and renewed faith, they fell silent after a time, each one dwelling in his thankful heart. The contemplative silence was broken at last by the lazily inquiring tones of Laslorn.

"Why do you suppose the meadow Fyrenfyld is called "Fiery Field"? The reason for its naming is so far in the past that even Elrad didn't know when I asked him." There was a goodnatured chuckle from Theo, but before Rablorn could lob a handful of acorns at Laslorn for breaking the mood, a voice answered Las's idle question.

"Why, I can tell you that! A good story it was too, and I and my friends were there!" Eager for another story, many voices called out encouragement. Fresh drinks were poured all around, and everyone sat up to listen to the latest in the string of "new" old tales.

"It was during the reign of King Qualdruth the Second," the Elf began, warming to his tale. Many couldn't place the era but left the question for later, not wanting to interrupt the story. "There had been a score of hard winters in a row, and the flocks were being kept in the lowlands, the highlands of the mountains being harsh with snow. Much of the mountain game also moved south, and their predators with them, to the depredation of our flocks. We had begun keeping watches over the flocks and were able to drive off the wolves and big cats and such. But one hungry creature found our gathered herds to be most tempting and attacked again and again, until we despaired of keeping enough alive to continue them.

"The creatures we couldn't stop were dragons. Wild mountain dragons, they were, driven down from their peaks and caves by hunger. Now, in those days, there were many such creatures, though they did not band together, nor live in groups. Solitary creatures they were for the most part, keeping company only to mate and raise their young.

"Canny creatures they were, too. Able to speak the Old Tongue when they had a mind to. We tried on many occasions to treat with them, to beg them to leave our herds and flocks alone and to hunt their accustomed prey, which could still be found on the slopes of the lowland hillsides. But the great beasts found our herds much easier prey than to hunt deer and such through the trees of the forested slopes. They heard us, but they would not parley." The speaker paused to take a refreshing draught from his mug of cider, and eager voices pressed him to continue.

"Finally, the king instructed his Champion, Caerbryht, to seek out one of them and to talk with him and come to an understanding. Now, Caerbryht, being a canny and clever Elf, sought to prepare himself in such a way as to have a chance to say his piece before the dragon could reduce him to a pile of ash." The storyteller paused, waving a hand in the general direction of a group of Elves.

Caerbryht was easy to spot, for his cheeks were much ruddier than could be accounted for by the heat of the fire. The broad Elf at his side, who laughed heartily and slapped him on the back, was King Qualdruth himself. Reluctantly, poking fun at himself, Caerbryht took up the tale.

"Aye, I thought myself very clever, I'm sure!" he began, his light tenor laced with humor. "First, I set a dragon trap. Now, I had no idea how to trap a dragon, so all the credit for the success of the trap goes to Ergos, the smith who helped design and build it." Caerbryht smiled over at a wide, dark-haired Elf who sat with his lady by his side. "The trap was fashioned in a clearing. A huge net was made, which was hidden in the foliage of the surrounding trees. Now, as you all know, dragons breathe fire when they've a mind to get their own way, so no ordinary net would hold one. This net was cunningly woven of hundreds of slender metal wires, twisted together to make ropes. Those ropes were then spliced together in a cross pattern, like a giant fishing net." There were murmurs of approval at this clever move and nods to Ergos for creating it.

"Well, the dragon came for the bait," Caerbryht continued, "assuming himself safe. When he landed and found the succulent sheep in the clearing was a sheepskin on a wooden frame, he was a bit... annoyed, shall we say? Immediately, he set fire to the surrounding trees. This was a hasty move and not well thought out, for the only fire that can harm a dragon is dragonfire, so of course he had to wait awhile for the trees to be consumed before he could fly away. So, he waited there while the trees burned, but before he could depart, the metal net, deprived of the supporting trees, fell on him." There was some appreciative laughter, and the Champion went on.

"Well, he was not best pleased by this, as you may imagine, so I knew I'd have to speak my piece quickly. Not wanting to be reduced to the aforementioned pile of ash, I had cleverly encased myself in several layers of leather armor, which I had soaked for three days previously in cold water. While it was unlikely that my protection would catch fire, I had forgotten to calculate the effect that three layers of soaking wet leather would have on my mobility..." There was outright laughter now, and the Champion smiled and shook his head at his remembered folly.

"*Ah well*, I thought as I staggered forth to face the angry dragon, *at least I'll keep my cool*. Unfortunately, I didn't pay as much attention to my feet as to my burdens. Halfway across the clearing, I stumbled on a tussock of grass and fell flat on my face. This was scarcely dignified, and I struggled to right myself, but to no avail. The soaked armor was too heavy. I couldn't lever myself upright, no matter what I tried." By now, many were in tears of laughter, their mirth goodnatured and sympathetic.

"All in all, it was a fortunate thing, that fall," Caerbryht resumed. "The dragon was so taken aback at my appearance that he paused in his roaring long enough to notice me. When I fell, and didn't get up, he assumed I was prostrating myself as a gesture of reverence and respect, and this did much to lessen his temper. Mollified, he was willing to hear me speak. At least he would have been if he could have understood me through the turf in my face! He kept roaring at me to speak up, and I kept trying to get my head lifted clear of the ground so I could yell my message at him.

"Finally, I managed to roll onto my side, where I reclined, pretending relaxation, and delivered my message. The idea that he and his kind were to stop killing our flocks or we would be forced to meet them in battle provoked such a noise from him that it was some time before I realized he was laughing. When he finally quieted and I was able to convince him that I was serious, and this was not a joke but a war challenge, he became most agitated.

"Still, in the end, he bought his freedom with the promise that he would take our challenge to every dragon in the mountains. As dragons are entirely truthful, once you get them to commit to anything, he was freed from the net and allowed to go.

"A week later, a message stone was dropped into the courtyard of the castle in the Elven City. The runes scratched upon it indicated that the dragons were more inclined to fight us than to submit. With a minimum of fuss and messengers, we set the time for three days hence, and the place the meadow east of the Western Wood.

"When the morning of the engagement dawned, our lines of battle were drawn up at opposing sides of the field. The Faeltheon had chosen the southern end, as it was closest to the Silverin Stream, and we thought we would need the water. Mindful of my misadventure, our regular leather armor was covered in only one layer of soaked padding. It was not likely to protect us for long but might give us some small advantage.

"The battle was joined and was fiercely fought. We did not wish to kill the great beasts, though they had made themselves our foes. We sought instead to disable them by making such wounds as we could later mend, aiming for wing membranes or the powerful rear legs they used to launch themselves skyward.

"They fought out of pride, intending to show us their power and our insignificance. Many Faeltheon took grievous wounds that day, but our best healers were present and saved nearly all. In the end, after a long day of fighting, the dragons were wearying. They were not accustomed to having to exert themselves for any length of time. They could not sustain their flames much longer, and their great bodies needed food to replenish the vast energies they had squandered in the battle.

"They gathered themselves for one last effort, intending to finish us entirely. Acting in concert, the whole mass of them let loose their fire toward us at once. The rage and the heat of it were greater than I can tell. In that instant, the entire meadow was consumed in flames. Had we not retreated to the Silverin and thrown ourselves bodily into it, we would surely have perished in that great conflagration.

"When the roar of flame had ceased, we came out from the water to survey the damage. The meadow was a blackened mass: not one blade of grass remained green upon it. The dragons were all at the other end of the field, their wounded behind their line. Having spent their fire, they had no more. Having used all their remaining energy in that last flagrant gesture, they could not summon the strength to fly away. They had sealed their own doom by their actions.

"They expected death at our hands, but they knew us not, for that is not our way. In exchange for their lives, they swore to the king that they would no longer prey upon our beasts, and that, as further evidence of their desire to live in peace with us, henceforth they would pay a portion each year from their troves to the royal treasury. When this had been sworn by each one there and to be binding upon all their kin for all time, our healers set about doing what they could to mend the damages and ease their discomfort." There were sighs of satisfaction as Caerbryht paused to wet his dry throat.

"After that time, there were no more troubles with the mountain dragons. In fact, one or two of them became quite fond of Elven music and would visit the City for weeks at a time when delivering their annual tribute. Much of the gold and jewels that adorn the Great Hall and other buildings of the City came from the dragon troves, though in later years the numbers of dragons in the mountains dwindled and we saw them seldom. From the date of the battle and truce with the dragons, that meadow has been known as Fyrenfyld, the Fiery Field, in memory of that last blast that bought lasting peace."

Chassidy shielded her eyes with her sun-browned hand and peered toward the dark green shadow that was the Western Woods, knowing that the Elven lands lay somewhere beyond its cool, secret depths, but unaware of how to find her way there. She wasn't even sure if she wanted to go that far. It could be a journey of some days or weeks farther, even if she didn't get hopelessly lost. Already, she began to feel that she was running out of time. It was unlikely that her family, good, solid, conventional people, would leave her in peace to make this questionable pilgrimage.

As she stood, irresolute, she paused to glance to the south. Movement beyond the tall grass caught her eye, and she waited until she was sure it was traveling in her direction. Whatever it was, it walked upright and was too short and stocky to be an Elf, and it didn't move like a Goblin. That didn't leave many possibilities. With a sigh, she folded her arms across her chest and watched his approach through narrowed blue eyes.

When he was close enough for her to discern the fiery hair and the sun-kissed face, there was no mistaking who it was. *Nicholan, did I not ask my father not to send you after me?* She shook her head in disappointment. *Somehow, I knew he wouldn't listen. And I know you wouldn't understand. I suppose now I will never know the fate of the Elves. My time for chasing fantasies is over. This chapter must close.*

When he finally sighted his elusive fiancée, Nicholan was relieved to know that he was no longer alone in the Forest. *I don't much see the point o' my havin' to come rescue her when she's less afraid of the Forest than any man alive! Look at her, standin' there waitin' for me like she was mistress of a grand house and me come to tea!*

He paused to mop the sweat from his face and to study her again before he was close enough for conversation. She stood straight and proud, her slender figure in the simple homespun dress outlined by the brisk fall wind, her dark curls escaping from the confining braids to dance about her face.

Suddenly, his heart squeezed with affection for this funny, proud, beautiful, misfit girl, who barely reached his shoulder. Nicholan's face reddened from more than exertion, but, man-like, he wouldn't speak his affections aloud. In a moment, he thought he would burst from the conflicting feelings rising in him; impatience at the inconvenience she had caused him, annoyance that he had been forced to fear for her, exasperation that she didn't seem to acknowledge his efforts on her behalf, even seemed to regard them as unnecessary and unwelcome, to judge by her expression. And, reluctantly, affection for the stubborn lass crept into the mix as well, causing Nicholan's first words to her to come out much more roughly than he really intended.

"What do you mean, goin' off like this? Don't you know the trouble you've caused!"

Chassidy's calm eyes regarded him with an expression he would almost call resigned.

"Good afternoon to you, too, Smith Nicholan," she said coolly, beginning to walk past him, back toward the Forest and home. A moment he stared at her, his jaw dropped at her cool impudence, but then realized she hadn't meant it for impertinence. Still, the sting of rebuke had been in her tone for his lack of greeting.

Yes, she had annoyed him, and cost him a week's work by the time they were back home, but she was such a brave little thing, to have dared so much and come this far alone, whatever her reasons. The breeze blew up suddenly cold, and he saw her shiver; his heart bade him forgive and protect.

"Forgive my harshness?" he asked gently, covering her with his cloak. Chassidy's eyes met his, and the strong, purposeful look in them assured him that she was sane, perhaps more so than most. As they journeyed home, for the most part in silence, he saw the profound sadness in her, and the firm resolution, and he wondered anew what had happened to her in that silence-shrouded adventure last fall and what had brought her out here now. The reserve in the deep sky-colored eyes caused him to hold his questions until the morning they came within sight of the village. Then, in the early light, he stopped her, turning her to face him.

"Someday, will you tell me about it?" he asked, with a note of respect that heartened the weary girl. She gave him the best smile she could muster, as her heart bade farewell to the Faeltheon.

"Someday, perhaps."

Chapter Fifteen

The last woven rope was finally secured, and, at Laslorn's shout, Theo pulled with all his might on his end. Slowly, ponderously, helped along the way by many willing hands, the massive structure of intertwined tree limbs and support branches was raised aloft into the upper third of the large, spreading chestnut tree.

After what seemed a very long time of strenuous pulling, Laslorn's second shout alerted Theo and his companions that the last load had arrived at its destination. In a few moments the line they held steady went lax in their hands and the friends released it, to wipe the stinging sweat from their faces and gratefully accept the cups of chilled tea proffered by Nausika.

Once the first draught was down, Theo sipped more slowly at his second cup, sharing grins of satisfaction with Aoneth and Tal. Theo thanked Nausika, returning the cup, and then began to climb the slight steps and handy limbs that provided access to the upper reaches of the great tree. He knew Aoneth was at his back, and he could hear the deep rumble of Finrandel's tones conversing with Elrad and Tal below. After a time of climbing that loosened limbs stiffened by the strenuous pulling of the past two hours, Theo reached the broad branch that led into the home of Lucina and Davin.

Within the encircling and skillfully woven screen of branches was a cozy home. It consisted of two rooms: one for living and eating, and the other for sleeping. As was common in Faeltheon tree homes, the sleeping room was situated on a slightly higher level than the common living area. There was also a smaller space for storage tucked away within easy reach of the living level.

Theo and Aoneth continued through the living room and up into the sleeping chamber, from which could be heard sounds of laughter, voices, and the busy *tap-tap* of Laslorn's hammer. Crossing the airy, open room, the two friends came to the scene of the activity. Resting on the large support limbs that extended beyond the walls of the sleeping room was the structure they had helped haul up to the height. Now that various materials had been removed from the main piece, it was revealed to be a small, gracefully shaped platform, or flet, of planed planks, skillfully joined. Around the edges of this flet, living branches of the chestnut were being coaxed, woven, and tied in place to fashion support posts every three feet or so.

From below the flet came the sounds of Glimring and Geltheon knotting the sturdy ropes and vines through the cross-supports of the flet and around the larger branches on which it rested. The creaking of the ties as they were pulled tight could be heard even above the chatter all around. Las was kneeling at the intersection of the flet and the sleeping room wall, tapping whittled pegs into holes drilled for them in the planks.

Theo's view of the workers on the flet was momentarily blocked by Elwyn and Linnallia, who stepped into the new doorway to measure it for the drapery they were fashioning to fit there. As they moved away to mark their measurements on the beautiful cloth, Theo allowed the backs of his fingers to caress Elwyn's cheek. She smiled and slanted him a loving look but continued across the room with Linnallia.

Theo and Aoneth stepped out onto the flet, placing their feet carefully to avoid the many tools scattered about. A hand reached over the edge of the flet, groping for the end of a vine that had been fed through between two intertwined support branches. Theo stepped forward and placed the trailing end into the seeking hand. Gently, he held the slender, curving limbs in place as the vine was coaxed to weave in and out of the two branches. The many graceful support posts were living branches that had been trained into these positions over a period of several seasons. The patience and artistry of the work justified the high esteem in which Laslorn was held as a home fashioner.

In another hour, the flet had been secured to both the lower support branches and to the smaller, intertwined uprights, which had then been woven into their places for added stability. With a great shout and many willing hands, the long, braided branches that had been carefully shaped into a top rail that echoed the shape of the flet was lowered onto the uprights and securely lashed into place with vines, ropes, and supple, living switches of the chestnut.

By the time the sun was at midday, Lucina and Davin rejoiced in a new balcony off their sleeping room, one which echoed the style of the beloved outpost flets of their former Border Guard stations. The many workers who had helped to set it into place departed in twos and threes for other tasks, chatting and laughing happily among themselves.

Laslorn remained, carefully going over all the curving, interwoven branches that made the structure, checking for stress points and places that might rub away the bark of the living tree. Before he left, he would also place soil into the hollows and joints of many parts of the balcony, and plant seeds there, so that, in due time, many flowering vines would grow to cloak the structure and add to its beauty. Elwyn and Nausika also stayed with Lucina and Davin, putting the finishing touches on the matching tiebacks that would hold the door drape open when the couple desired the breeze to enter their sleeping room.

As Theo descended the chestnut, he found a group of Elven men at its foot, helpfully stacking the limbs, planks, and tools that were left over from Laslorn's work. Theo prepared to greet them and to thank them for their help, but before he spoke, he realized that the faces of two of the Elves were unfamiliar, and two more were only vaguely so. Of course, there were so many of the Faelthcon in Marliondolen, Theo couldn't know them all, even by sight, but most of those who lent a hand in this sort of project were friends of the homeowners, and Theo thought he knew all Davin and Lucina's friends better than that.

One of the Elves looked up and saw him, raising a hand in greeting. Puzzled still, Theo returned the gesture. A robust Elf, one of the two Theo almost recognized, nodded to him with a cheerful grin.

"Master Theomanus! Just the one I was looking for!" At Theo's politely raised brow, the older Elf continued. "When we saw that you were engaged here, we thought we'd join the effort. Will you join *us* now, for a time? I, for one, would welcome a dip in the stream to cool off. Afterward, perhaps we could talk?"

"Thanks for your help! Yes, I'll be glad to join you for a swim. That sounds refreshing! I am sorry that I cannot remember your name, for I'm sure we've been introduced," Theo responded.

The Elf and his companions laughed comfortably at that. The second one, who seemed familiar to Theo, clapped his companion on the shoulder, smiling at Theo.

"You had many introductions that day, lad," he chuckled, his eyes creasing at the corners. "This is Amadthalos, and I am Ethalion, once his Champion. These are our friends, Maegos and Vyggos."

Theo exchanged handclasps with each, inwardly embarrassed at having forgotten the face of Amadthalos the First. They set off together for the nearby stream. When they arrived in the shade of a clump of leafy willows on the bank, they stripped off their tunics and trews and splashed into the fast-running water, shouting like children at the chill of the water, though it was welcome relief from the heat of their labors. Amadthalos swiped his broad arm through the choppy surface ripples, sending a sizable wave into the face of his erstwhile Champion. In the ensuing water fight, all awkwardness was forgotten. By the time they were all soaked and exhausted and had laughingly dragged themselves up the bank to rest in the warm sun, they had been joined by Laslorn, Elrad, Riende, Beregos, and Thalleam.

Lying on the grassy bank, eyes closed against the bright sunlight, Theo listened to the desultory deep-voiced conversations of his companions and marveled to himself that he was there in such august company. Never in his most vivid dreams had he imagined himself and Las in the company of the first Elven king of the Land, that king's renowned Champion, one of the wisest Seers his people had ever known, Theo's own father, whom he had lost to the sea when he was but a child, King

Beregos the Good, and Riende, Theo's beloved *amios* father. He was recalled to himself when Laslorn's elbow nudged his ribs and he realized that Amadthalos had just addressed a question to him.

"How are you finding the tasks of leadership, Master Theomanus?" the former king asked. "I understand that you were raised at the Elven Court for much of your life, but you were not destined to rule, so this sudden assumption of leadership could be quite a burden."

"Indeed," Theo agreed slowly, his golden eyes seeking the turquoise depths of his mentor's gaze. "There are some challenges, to be sure. I suppose I am what they call a 'natural leader,' for I have never lacked for loyal friends, but this … this task is different, I think, from any we have encountered before, and I confess, it often baffles me to know how to go about it." He cast a rueful smile at his father and foster father. Shifting his gaze to the first king of the Elves, Theo sought for any insight the renowned ruler might have to offer. "The part that still plagues me is the same question we had before we even entered this place: What is the Master of Marliondolen to *do*?"

A sympathetic chuckle went around the little group, but no one had any advice to proffer. Before any of them could speak, Davin's voice was heard, hailing them.

"Theo! Bring our friends up to the clearing by the chestnut! We're fixing supper, and Nausika is making her famous bean soup!"

They all sat up eagerly at this summons, being hungry, and Theo wasn't the only one to laugh at the speed at which Laslorn headed for the clearing and his wife's soup.

Later, replete with good food, excellent company, and a gorgeous sunset, Theo was recalled to their earlier conversation by a remark from Amadthalos.

"I don't think you need worry overmuch about your role as leader here, Theomanus," the former king stated as he mopped the last of the soup from his bowl with a piece of fresh bread. "You know the Creator will show you what He wants of you, and you have the temperament to wait for it. Now, my friends and I had a harder time of it, I think, for we are fiercer by nature than most of the Faeltheon, and it is hard to understand the role of a warrior's heart in a race of peaceful people."

There was a slight stir, as a few of those around them showed interest in the conversation. Lucina poured fresh hot tea into Amadthalos's mug and returned it to him with a keen glance from her amber eyes. Beregos sat forward and brought his attention to bear on the older king.

"Tell us what you learned of this, Amadthalos, for I, too, have struggled with this same issue for many years."

"*You*?" The question was surprised from Ethalion's lips, for what they had heard of Good King Beregos had not led them to suspect aught but a gentle nature. Beregos shook his head, his arm going around the slender shoulders of his sweet wife, Ashwyn, who sat at his side.

"Not for myself. My son, Aelric, is restless, competitive, even combative on occasion, which trait has worried me considerably as he grew up. With such a ... seething ... nature, how is he to fit in among our people, let alone be fit to rule them, for a ruler must be self-controlled and peaceful to guide the people."

Amadthalos exchanged a glance with his companions and nodded knowingly.

"It is true we are a peaceful people, Beregos, and the traits you describe are important in a ruler. Yet, there can be more. As I mentioned before, sometimes one of us is born with a warrior's heart, a passion to protect and to defend, a willingness to go to battle, if necessary, to preserve that peace for which our people are known. It is never easy to have such a spirit, for it seldom allows you to rest and enjoy the fruits of that peace." He paused a moment, seeing that he had the attention of all the company. Then he gestured to his three companions, seated loosely near him.

"Still, as I have found for myself, and as my friends here also discovered, this fierce nature is given us by the Creator as surely as others are given gentler temperaments. As each of us can attest, those with warriors' hearts are born for the times in which the Creator places us. Into each of our lives came a time of testing, of war, of the need for battle and strong leaders to bring our people through it. We were shaped for those times, to meet the needs of the Faeltheon during those struggles." His gaze moved about the group, lingering at the vindication in Lucina's bright eyes, then going on to meet the concerned visage of the father.

"The Lord knows what purpose He has for your son, Beregos. He makes no mistakes, no errors in judgment. He has given each leader exactly the tools he needs to lead our people through the times and circumstances in which they live. Theomanus was chosen to be Master of Marliondolen because he is the one the Creator has fashioned to meet our needs here. Aelric has a warrior's heart because Aematlon knows his people will have need of a warrior to lead them."

Into the contemplative quiet after these words came the rich voice of the Seer, the cadence of his tones telling the experienced that Elrad was Seeing more than the faces about him.

"The remnant of our people left on Earth will have need of Aelric's warrior's heart before they complete the journey before them. Be thankful, therefore, that the Creator has made Aelric to be different, to be able to lead them through the dangers they must encounter before they can return to us and find peace and safety."

Chapter Sixteen

Captain Jed Haggert tipped back his head and drained the last of his rum. Rubbing his red, worn knuckles, he allowed his thoughts to wallow in the dourness of his current circumstances. The prospects of his ships, the *Cutlass* and her two smaller sisters, were looking grim, indeed. It had been months since their last plunder, and even then the paucity of their spoils had made it a gloriless conquest. Pirates with their sort of history and reputation should be doing better. For the past decade his fleet had been the major threat on the waters; the sort of ships that assured that every decent sailor said his prayers each time he left port. *Look at us now. Barely more than drifters.* He punctuated his thoughts with a disgusted snort.

If Jed wasn't careful, the empty holds might become the least of his worries. He lifted the clay bottle back to his lips and, finding it empty, hurled it into the corner. They had been out at sea so long they were running dangerously low on provisions, but he hesitated to go into port for fear that if he stepped off his ship he would never get back on it again. His ears had not been deaf to the whispers running through the crew; they were restless, and a mutiny was stirring in their thick blood.

Just beyond his cabin doorway, he saw the large shadow of his first mate moving steadily toward him down the passageway. In no mood for a confrontation, he rested his feet on the corner of his desk and tilted the wide brim of his hat down over his eyes, as if he were sleeping. Everyone knew better than to wake the captain from one of his increasingly frequent naps.

As he feigned sleep, Jed's thoughts turned from the grimness of his situation to its unfairness. The crew had no right to blame him for this streak of bad luck. He had captained these ships for the past eleven years, and no one could have done a finer job. They had made a fortune raiding port towns and pillaging the coasts. That alone would have been enough, but Jed had also led them on over a hundred attacks on heavily laden merchant ships, which had produced the majority of their wealth. Under his command, the *Cutlass* had never seen a dry spell such as this one. His suspicion was that one of the crew had done something to offend Fate, for what else could explain their change in luck?

Luck must be to blame, for their empty holds were certainly not due to a lack of effort. They simply had not spotted another ship on the sea that looked like it held anything worth stealing. He felt a tingle in his spine as a new thought crept into his rum-soaked brain. Perhaps that was the problem; maybe he had been too picky. They hadn't even *attacked* anything in months, regardless of spoil. The men in his crew drew their energy from the smell of burning wood, the sound of clashing blades, the look of fear in their victims' eyes. The men were restless, and they needed a good fight to stem the monotony of life on a stinking, crowded pirate ship.

Propelled to action, Jed was at his door in three long strides. He grabbed a passing cabin boy by the shirt and whipped him around to face him. Jed saw the boy stifle a startled shout and brace himself for whatever was about to come his way.

"Aye, Cap'n?" the lad managed.

"Run and tell the watchman to inform me immediately if he sees anything with sails on the horizon!" Jed barked his orders, giving the youth a shove toward the mainmast. The boy thanked his lucky stars for a painless escape and made all haste toward the watchman. Killern, Jed's first mate, saw the exchange and slowly walked back toward the captain's office, awaiting an explanation. Jed lowered his voice and let a grin creep over his face.

"The next ship we see on these God-forsaken waters, we *take*."

The sea wind ruffled Aelric's ebony hair as he paced along the deck of the *Cethastea*, staring out at the waters that, he prayed, would carry them to their island home. He seemed at peace, but anyone who looked closely enough would have noticed the fine crease between his dark brows, a clear sign that the Elven King was deep in thought.

His sleep had been restless last night, and he had risen before the sun, nagged by a sense of coming trouble. It was nearly noon now, and he had spent all morning watching the empty ocean, trying to find some sign as to whether his feelings were correct. He had seen nothing that would warrant concern, nor had he noticed that anyone else shared his trouble. Aelric shook his head and looked down at his rope-callused hands, which had for so long practiced and trained for battle. Privately, he wondered if this present feeling was merely the imagination of his warrior's heart; that perhaps, though he hated to think it, he actually *wanted* a fight.

Laughter to his right banished the wayward thought and drew his gaze. Standing nearby, elbows perched on the railing, Caerdrys, Minlienda, and Ciella were enjoying pleasant conversation. He watched them for a moment, appreciating their beauty, savoring their diversity. Though they were similar in coloring, they were very different in personality and skills, and each had worked hard to make herself a valuable member of his party. Aelric knew he would never be able to express his appreciation for them and for all the Elven women on this journey.

It amazed him that Human sailors refused to take their women aboard ship, willingly going months without the joy of a full community of men, women, and children. From what he understood, Men held to a superstition that it was bad luck to have women onboard. In Aelric's experience, there was no such thing as luck. The idea of trying to establish a community at sea without the women and children seemed both ludicrous and foolish to him. The Elven women on their ships had been of such a great help to them that Aelric could not imagine sailing without them.

Noting the cool breeze and goose bumps on the girls' arms, he approached with a warm greeting and offered them his cloak. Min and Ciella accepted it readily and huddled together under its warmth, as it was more than broad enough to fit around their slender shoulders. Caerdrys politely refused, rather enjoying the chill air. Minlienda's sharp eyes studied Aelric for a moment.

"The skies are clear today, and yet there are storm clouds in your eyes, King Aelric. Is something troubling you?"

Aelric smiled and inclined his head, deciding there was no harm in revealing his thoughts to one who already seemed to know them.

"Yes, I am troubled, but I'm still waiting to discover what is causing my unrest. However, my current company brings much happier thoughts. You all are enjoying the morning, I see." He was answered by three nodding heads, and took up a spot on the rail next to Caerdrys, returning his gaze to the sea.

"We were just recalling the time on the island when Gaelcar had to tell the story of how Ethalion was appointed Champion—five times!" Minlienda offered, and Aelric remembered the events with a fond chuckle.

Not yet engaged enough in the conversation to lose his alertness, out of the corner of his eye Aelric saw a young Elf approaching. Radlas's long sight had recently led him to be employed as a watchman in the ship's aerie. He was young for the responsibility but had proven steady and dependable in his task.

"I apologize for the interruption, my lord," Radlas said with a quick bow. "I have a message for you from the midday watchman. We've spotted another a fleet of three ships, sir."

"How far away are they?" Aelric asked.

"Still quite a ways, sir. They certainly can't see us yet," the youth answered.

"Very well. Please inform me when they are closer, and I'll send out the order for the women and children to go below deck," Aelric responded with a nod of dismissal. He heard a soft sigh from Caerdrys as she propped her chin in her hand, grudgingly accepting her fate in the belly of the ship.

Instead of returning to his post, however, the messenger remained and shifted his weight nervously.

"There's more, Radlas?" Aelric prompted.

"Yes, my lord. The watchman requests that you come take a look, sir. He would like... your opinion."

"Of course." Aelric nodded an apology to the girls and followed Radlas up to the main aerie, wondering if this news was somehow related to his restlessness.

"Greetings, Aelric," welcomed the watchman on duty. "Have a look at this, my lord." He handed him the longeye and pointed toward a small dot on the horizon.

"They carry a lot of sail and look incredibly fast," Aelric observed.

"Aye, that was my first thought, too." The watchman nodded his head toward the other ships again. "But do you see all their scars, sir?" Aelric furrowed his brow in suspicion and looked a second time.

"No. They are still too far off for me to distinguish anything." The watchman nodded his head in agreement.

"I can't see them either, but Radlas's sight is longer than most, and he tells me that the ships, though sound, are littered with battle scars—especially the flagship. It has clearly seen more than its fair share of fighting."

"That doesn't bode well for us, does it?" Aelric said, clenching his jaw as he considered what to do next. "Our ships were not built for speed, so I see no way that we could outrun them, should they choose to pursue us."

The watchman nodded sharply again, gesturing at the distant mote. "Radlas also tells me the ships are foul with barnacles, which should mean that they're running low and slow in the water. But, from what I can see, this is not the case. The only reason I can figure for the anomaly is if their holds are light."

Aelric's brows drew together as the watchman's implication struck him. "So, if they mean us harm, an empty hold will make them determined at the least. Let me know the minute that fleet comes within the Humans' sighting distance, and we will reassess the situation."

"Aye, my lord," the watchman responded, and Aelric climbed back down to the deck to look for Gaelcar and Robse. He spotted the golden heads near the helm. Crossing to the sterncastle and climbing to the mizzendeck, he greeted them with a firm hand on Robse's shoulder.

"My friends, my Champion and Seneschal, I have need of your counsel."

Robse's winged eyebrows soared at the use of his formal title, and he wondered what would require his service as Champion, but he kept the question to himself as he and Gaelcar followed Aelric down to the king's small office in the sterncastle.

The three Elves settled around the table in the center of the room, and Robse poured them each a goblet of fresh juice from the pitcher on the sideboard. They listened carefully as Aelric informed them of the possible threat.

"This morning I awoke before the sun with a restless heart, my friends. The air was heavy with a sense of danger, and I felt a strong instinct to defend my people. At first I wondered if this was merely an overflow of my warrior's heart, or if there was something more sinister at hand that required my action."

Understanding, Gaelcar nodded for him to continue. He had seen his king's earnest struggles with this subject before, but he also knew the power of the Creator's stirring in one's spirit.

"But then I heard news from the watchman." Aelric continued, telling them of the number and speed of the approaching ships, as well as their unnerving battle scars. Hearing the seriousness in Aelric's voice, Robse's senses sharpened immediately and his mind sprang to action, analyzing the threat and the implications of an attack. Gaelcar's pale brows creased and his mouth became tight.

"Aelric, do you remember the warning we received from that vendor with whom we traded at the last port? He spoke of three ships of that very description, although he did not mention the scars. He said they were known to operate in this area—the cruelest pirates on these seas. He had not heard reports of any attacks in recent months, but his fear of them had not lessened. It reminded me of the response we received on our first foray into the ports of Men. I had thought their reaction to us was simply one of disbelief, but, remember, they were suspicious of us before they had treated with us. I wonder if they thought we might be those three pirate vessels. Do you think it possible these are the same pirates?"

Robse's grey eyes widened at this thought, and he nodded in his turn, for he had been about to mention the recent incident but had not made the connection to the earlier event.

"I had not remembered that last warning, and I am grateful once again for your sharp memory," Aelric commented. Considering for a moment, he dismissed Gaelcar's possible connection, for it did not affect them now. Deftly, he returned them to the main point of the discussion. "This certainly could be that fleet. This afternoon I'll gather a council of captains, first mates, and others who can help us organize an effective defense. We need to prepare plans and ready our fighters for tomorrow morning, as arrows will be our strongest weapon, and we won't want to let them get close enough to board us, if indeed they are hostile."

"How long until they reach us, if they turn to pursue?" Robse asked, wondering how much time he would have to prepare a defense.

"At present speeds, less than a day," Aelric answered, seeing Robse's mind at work. "What do you think are the chances they will attack us?"

Robse shook his head. "It's difficult to say. Our ships are not modest, and if these are truly pirates, they will wrongly assume that we carry vast wealth. That will certainly tempt them, but our ships are also much larger than theirs. I cannot imagine being the captain of a normal ship and daring to attack three of this size."

Gaelcar nodded but added wryly, "It would seem to me a foolish move, but I have seen the extent of Men's greed and fear it may outweigh their better judgment."

"I agree." Aelric nodded. "I've been wrestling with the same thought. I'd like you both to prepare plans for our defense while we wait to see what these Humans are going to do. I'll let you know as soon as we know more. But do it quietly," he added. "I don't want to raise alarm amongst the people unless and until there is a real danger."

"Of course. I'll send word to the captains and first mates of our other ships and have them gather their weapons and prepare for the women and children to go below," Robse responded, rising from the table and exiting the room swiftly.

Gaelcar arose as well, setting his goblet and Robse's back behind the rail on the sideboard with the pitcher. At the door, he turned back to see the king standing behind his big desk, staring out the bulging, multipaned window at the distant sea.

"I will arrange for the afternoon council," Gaelcar offered. Aelric turned back to him with a grateful smile. "And Aelric ... it is wise to remember that our best defense is not arrows, but the strength of the Creator." Aelric's smile deepened and the stiffness of his broad shoulders eased perceptibly. With a brisk nod, the Seneschal left the chamber, and both turned immediately to their respective tasks: the Seneschal to plan and the king to pray.

Just at sunrise, Jed Haggert heard the news for which he had been waiting. His luck had changed! To think that in the very same day they had spotted not one, but three ships traveling together! It gave him the leverage he needed with the crew. His blood racing, he didn't even wait to take a look at the ships himself—the report that they appeared very rich was all he needed. The captain lost no time in summoning his men onto the deck to announce the good news.

"Gather round, gents!"

The whole disheveled lot of them looked up at him with the same disdain their eyes had held for months. They crossed their leathery arms and squared their broad shoulders, boldly daring him to say anything against their liking. Jed took his time, carefully planning his words to work to his greatest advantage. He had set up men to relay his speech to the two other ships, but he knew the fiery passion with which he spoke would be lost.

"For months now, the tyrannous hand of Fate has worked against us. First, she stole the wind from our very sails, leaving us to drift in the blistering sun. Then the cruel Lady blew our canvases again, but not in kindness. Nay, rather to draw us away from any ships worth the taking. Fate destroyed our very livelihood! For so long our loyal mistress, she left us rotting with empty holds and empty bellies." He had their attention now, and he raised the volume of his voice so none would miss his argument.

"Can you remember why you chose to follow the infamous Captain Jed Haggert?" he shouted, a grin and a spark in his eye. "You came to me to pursue the promise of wealth and adventure! You came to me because you crave success and would settle for nothing less than the best! And I will keep my promise. A man of my word, I will prove to you that you were not fools when you signed aboard these ships!" He watched their expressions start to change and their weight begin to shift. He sucked in a deep breath and raised his volume another notch. Time to whip them up.

"For who other than Captain Jed Haggert could conquer Fate, could crush her brazen efforts, and bring you a glorious feast of *three* ships at once, undoubtedly laden with the finest riches? It has been far too long since you gents had a good fight! There is a fire pent up in your veins! As your captain, who wants to see these holds filled as much as you do, I offer you this perfect opportunity! When we come upon those ships tomorrow, they will feel the full force of our wrath! We will show them why they sail armed and clutching amulets for luck and protection about their scrawny necks! *Who's with me*?"

As if by some unknown force, his last words came with a gust of wind that filled their sails to bursting with a snapping boom, whipping through the crowd of sailors like a seal on his promise. Full throated, their ugly shout rose from the decks, answering their captain's call.

Just before sundown, Aelric met once more with Gaelcar to be sure all the details they'd discussed in the afternoon council meeting were being carried out without trouble. His heart had not settled since that morning, and though he wondered if he was overreacting to the presence of the other fleet, he could not shake the gut instinct that caused him to raise his guard.

Throughout the day, they all had been making ready for whatever would pass tomorrow. There were the usual provisions set up below decks, and the women and children had been asked to sleep there tonight and not to emerge until the all clear was sounded the next day. Everyone was handling the potential danger calmly.

Robse had briefed the captains and first mates during the meeting, and the arms masters of the three great ships had made sure of their stock of bows and arrows, which would be their main hope for avoiding casualties if they were indeed attacked. Aelric had been in close contact with the watchmen, who faithfully kept him abreast of every move the forbidding fleet made.

The king had felt a sense of urgency calling him to make the safety of his people his first priority. Though he was unable to know the intentions of the Human leader, Aelric's highest duty was still to protect his people, and he had been restless until he knew that all they could muster for defense was in place. Now, as the sea breeze chilled in time with the setting sun, he felt the need to take some time with his most trusted friend.

Gaelcar returned his greeting composedly and fell in beside the long strides of the king as the two friends paced the deck of the *Cethastea*. Though he had meant to ask many questions, Aelric found himself walking in shared silence. If there had been problems or concerns, Gaelcar would have voiced them. His silence held a measure of serenity, so Aelric found his own tension easing. The busy day had been broken by several times of heartfelt prayer, and the atmosphere of that communing lingered about the Seneschal now, laying Aelric's final fears to rest. Whatever would happen tomorrow, his people would not be out of the shelter of the Creator's Hand, so whatever He willed for their fate, Aelric would accept with calm grace. Fleetingly, he wondered if the young Queen Elwyn had had to reach a similar hard-won peace as the safety of her people was compromised last year.

Gradually, the king's pace slackened to his normal vigorous stride. A small smile played at the corners of Gaelcar's generous mouth. At the door to the sterncastle, he bade his lord goodnight.

"Try to rest tonight, cousin. We will all need our strength tomorrow."

Aelric nodded.

Jed's thoughts were a whirlpool as he peered through the spyglass at his kingly target. After his speech to the crew, he had boiled with pride at having secured his position as captain of the *Cutlass* and had immediately gone to see their new booty with his own yellowed eyes. His mood had turned gray once again as he saw that these ships were monsters compared with his! If he had known how large they were, he would have been wary to suggest an attack. Boiling no longer with pride, but with anger, he felt a strong urge to seize the watchman by his shirt and heave him overboard. However, as he did not want to show his fear, he suppressed the urge. He kept his language and demeanor arrogantly confident. What was done was done; if he went back on his word now, he would surely walk the plank.

But now, as they grew closer, his eyes took in the quality of the wood, the intricate carvings, and the painted bows and cerdems of his prey. Never in his life had he seen anything so fine. This was without doubt the fleet of a wealthy man, laden with unimaginable riches. Beyond their beauty, he also saw that the ships were not weak. If the pirates followed their usual tactics and planned to ram the big ships, their targets would eventually smash to pieces, but it wouldn't happen in a moment.

But, no, he thought, devouring them with his lustful gaze, he could not ruin something so fine, waste something so grand. He closed the spyglass with a determined snap and thrust it back at the watchman. They would be a boarding party, and he would seize the ships for his own.

His decision made, his boot heels pounded menacingly on the wooden planks as his long strides brought him to the side of his first mate. Jed's previous fears were completely overridden by the promise of wealth as he gave the order not to ram the ships.

"But Cap'n, we always ram the ships," Killern protested, not understanding the order. He, too, had noticed the size of the fleet and could not comprehend this new madness. "It's our best means of attack."

"Are ye too stupid to change battle plans? I don't want any harm to the ships, so we'll be a boarding party, I tell ye!" The captain growled back his response.

"Cap'n, there's a reason our bows are plated in iron! It would be foolish not to use our best weapon," Killern retorted brazenly, fearing for his life if the attack failed.

"Don't question me, scoundrel, or I'll have ye keel hauled! There'll be no damage to those ships, and that's an order!"

The pirates were rapidly approaching, and there was no longer any doubt of their intentions. Aboard the *Cethastea*, Aelric organized and instructed fighters on the main deck in preparation to repel boarders. Robse placed bowmen in their positions up in the radlings, instructing them to fire upon the enemy as they approached and to focus on any pirates attempting to board the ship. Gaelcar had made the suggestion of using flaming arrows to set fire to the enemy's large sails, and he was helping several bowmen wrap the tips of their arrows with oil-soaked cloth. Domel and Randelos oversaw the placement of half barrels of water and sand about the decks. If the pirates fired the *Cethastea*, sand would be needed to smother the burning pitch, and water to douse the sails and wooden planking. On the *Gaelrandel* and *Dridelphanen*, the captains and first mates performed the same tasks.

Aelric went in search of Caerdrys below decks, for he had a special duty for her. He found her in the main workroom on the second deck, helping Minlienda to organize the women and children, making sure everyone had what she needed and reassuring the wives of the Elves who would be defending them. He caught her elbow and drew her to follow him. He led her to the main companionway and stopped at the foot.

"Caerdrys, you have an important role today." She raised one sable brow, urging him to continue. "Several of our fighters will be stationed around the hatch at the top of these stairs to ensure that no enemy comes down, but I want you to remain here. Get your sword, and if any enemy makes it below deck and tries to come down these stairs, take him down. Many of our women are unarmed, and the children cannot defend themselves. Anyone who wishes them harm stops at you. Understood?"

"Of course, my lord," responded Caerdrys, accepting her duty with a fierce gleam in her eyes. "And Aelric … thank you." She nodded to him, grateful for an active role to play.

A shout came from above: "They are almost within range!"

Aelric bounded up the companionway and proceeded to the front of the formation of Elves on the deck. Below, Caerdrys ran for her sharp sword.

The king nodded up to Robse. "They have been warned through signals and have not stood down?" His Champion gave an affirmative response. "Then give the order to fire."

"*Aerweon*!" At Robse's shout, the bowmen loosed their first round of arrows, sending them like rain upon their attackers. Their eyes were sharp and their aim was sure, and just as soon as their arrows were released, new ones were on their strings. They managed three volleys, causing much damage and consternation among the enemy before the pirates were close enough to board.

The rusty iron prow of the lead pirate ship, a slovenly looking vessel with *Cutlass* painted crudely on her bows, swung toward the *Cethastea*. Most of those waiting in the forefront to board the *Cethastea* were struck by the arrows of the bowmen before they reached the Elven ship. There were so many Men packed aboard the smaller vessel, however, that a goodly number were still prepared to give battle. The first boarder to make it over the *Cethastea's* railing was struck down by the king before his feet hit the deck.

The first attackers were so greatly outnumbered that they were easily taken down, though the fighting Elves could not help but notice the shock on many of the Human faces as they looked into the eyes of their prey and found them non-human. Some of the Elves worried that the Men's disbelief would cause the defenders' strength to begin to fade, risking the safety of those precious ones hidden below decks.

Though the archers' bows still sang from the radlings above, more boarders came in greater numbers, and the real fighting began on the main deck. This wave of attackers brought the captain and first mate of the *Cutlass*, Jed and Killern, aboard the *Cethastea*.

Inevitably, the captain met the king and a fierce fight began. Their blades clashed together, and Jed saw the jewels inlaid on the hilt of Aelric's sword and allowed himself to gloat over the wealth he thought to find in the holds. He was confident that he would bring down this rich man, for Jed was nearly as tall as his adversary and much bulkier. This insolent rich pup was but a stripling and should be easy prey! Using his weight, he pushed against his opponent, seeking to unbalance him. Jed tipped his head back slightly and looked up into the stern young face to search for fear in his adversary's eyes, but he found none there.

Instead, he found two flaming golden disks with almond-shaped pupils, burning with anger and determination. The pirate captain turned his face away and shook his head, as if to wake himself from a dream. Wrenching his attention back to their fight, he suddenly felt the life draining out of him. Looking down, his shocked eyes beheld the coveted jeweled hilt protruding from his ribcage. Belatedly, there came a wash of agony, then his coldness swiftly settled into eternal night.

As Aelric freed his sword, he reached out to steady himself on the railing, feeling his strength ebb sharply, then return again. Unable to spare the time for worry, he summoned what strength he could to face the next opponent on the crowded deck.

As soon as Killern's boots hit the deck, he had but one purpose. The promise of becoming captain had been ripped away from him yesterday, but today he was determined to get to the treasure first, certain there would be something there he could take and use as leverage to power. He headed straight for the battened hatch that led below decks. The guards, already fighting fiercely, saw him coming, but between the weakening of the Humans' disbelief and the enemy already engaged with them, they could do nothing to prevent his actions. Killern's booted foot kicked away the securing hasp and his burly arms wrenched open the latticed hatch cover. The companionway loomed dark and inviting below him. Treasure awaited.

From the foot of the companionway, Caerdrys heard his approach and readied herself. As Killern hastened down the stairs, his eyes could not adjust from the bright daylight above to the darkness below, but he heard the swift slip of forged metal ringing free and flung himself backwards just in time. Willing his eyes to adjust, he raised his sword above his head to dispatch whoever was in his way, but his shock at seeing a fiercely beautiful woman before him caused a fatal hesitation. Caerdrys ran him through, but as his body fell toward her, she found she did not have the strength to fling him off, and they tumbled together down the stairs.

Killern was gasping for breath as his back hit the floor. He felt himself choking on blood and turned his head to the side. Not a foot away were the wide eyes of a young girl and her small brother, staring at him in horror. He realized the screams he heard were those of children and was filled with confusion and disbelief as he sighed out his dying breath.

The bowmen on the *Gaelrandel* and *Dridelphanen* had sent their flaming arrows into the sails and onto the decks of the pirate ships attacking them, and the *Cethastea* followed suit. Not wanting to kill those who did not directly threaten them, Aelric had ordered the archers to spare one of the pirate vessels to carry the living enemy away, so the flaming arrows from the *Cethastea* had not targeted the broad sails of the *Cutlass*.

Seeing their sister ships engulfed in flames and choking on billows of greasy black smoke, the sailors still aboard the *Cutlass* rushed to put out the fires on their own deck. They succeeded, and all those pirates still living seemed to realize that they were beaten, and badly at that. Sensing it was time to retreat, they flung themselves into the sea and swam furiously to the *Cutlass*, swarming to be taken aboard, even as the remaining ship from the once-feared pirate fleet limped away while it still could, without glory, without riches, and without a captain.

That night the atmosphere was still tense on the Elven ships, though they praised the Creator for their victory. Weary, but finally at rest in the common room, Aelric listened to the reports from Robse, Gaelcar, and Caerdrys, while he ate his long-overdue supper. None of the Faeltheon had been killed in the battle, which was a blessing to be sure, but several Elves had suffered injuries and some were severely weakened.

The worst *finnal* was found in the two children who had locked eyes with Killern as he died. Their frightened mother had pulled them back as quickly as she could, but the damage had already been done. Fortunately, they were strong and healthy children and would come around soon. Everyone predicted a full recovery, but any harm done to their children pierced the Elves like a knife.

Caerdrys in particular took this injury hard, blaming herself for the children's exposure. Aelric tried to set her self-recriminations aside, but she did not seem to hear his words. Finally, it was Gaelcar's voice that seemed to calm the excitable Elf, and it was not much later before Min came to take her sister away to bed.

When all the reports had been made, Aelric dismissed Robse and Gaelcar to bathe and rest. Though all was now calm aboard the Faeltheon ships, Aelric recognized that his warrior's heart, while at peace, was still racing with the events of the day. As the stars came out, casting their faint silvery shine about the decks and sails, the king paced the *Cethastea* from prow to stern. Not until he had looked in on every one of the seventy charges aboard his vessel did Aelric seek his own bunk.

Chapter Seventeen

"With no wind, we cannot go on."

The captain's uncompromising words brought every eye to rest on him. He stood before the round table in the common room, his fists resting on his wide sash belt. Lysion was not a particularly tall Elf, nor was his appearance striking, but his air of quiet confidence and the command in his steady voice brought instant obedience and respect from all aboard the *Cethastea*. They looked to him now to help solve the problem of the still sea they had encountered. For three days they had been becalmed in a sea near as smooth as a lake. The warnings of the old sailors at their last port echoed in Robse's ears, but he did not speak.

In private council with his Companions and the three captains before they had left the repair island, Aelric had sought advice to prepare them for the months ahead. Gaelcar had reminded him of the sailors' warnings of the still seas to the west, but Raros, captain of the *Gaelrandel*, had pointed to the passage in the Ancient Scrolls that had described the journey of their ancestors to the Land. The Scrolls clearly stated that the Faeltheon vessels had followed the major currents of the sea. They had debated the point for a time, but with an increasingly familiar undercurrent of futility, for once again, those Scrolls left out so much they needed to know! In the end, Aelric had decreed that they would provision the ships as fully as possible and then continue west, following the major current.

Now, two weeks later, they were mired in a crystal sea by lack of wind. The sea was a deep, clear blue, patched with golden brown, because of the sea plants that grew so close to the surface. Their efforts to pull up seawater and to take soundings had shown them that they floated on a shallow bubble of warm water, with dark, cold depths below. The warmth of the sun meeting the air at the surface of the calmed water promoted vigorous growth, and vast mats of intertwined plants surrounded them, in a nearly unbroken mass, as far as their long eyes could see.

The odd brownish plants looked like miniature bent trees with strange round fruits. A sampling of them showed that the 'fruits' were hollow air sacs that kept the plants afloat in the warm water. Experimentation had proven that the plants, though edible, were not particularly tasty, but that they provided a nutritious thickening agent, useful in fish chowders, vegetable stews, and all manner of pies. The stringy fibers left over after the boiling were sturdy and tough. When stripped from the stalks and dried, they were a handy addition to the fibers used to twist ropes and ties of various types.

All this was very interesting, of course, but in spite of the variety of fascinating flora and fauna in the becalmed waters, the fact that they could not make headway was of paramount concern at the moment. Lysion's flat statement merely confirmed their unease. Not only was their progress to their goal delayed by this becalmed water, but many were still uneasy at the thought of pirates catching them at a disadvantage. Aelric was quick to respond, not wanting his or anyone else's concerns to gain the upper hand.

"What *can* we do?"

"Aside from praying," came the clear, calm voice of Minlienda, "we can wait."

"Wait? Wait for what?" asked Cerlim, his voice a little rougher than he intended. He shot her a look of apology, even as Gaelcar cleared his throat to answer.

"Wait for the seasonal winds, of course. We have successfully weathered the storm season and are now experiencing a calm. According to the sailors who advised us about this area, the seasonal winds will pick up again within a month."

"A month? What are we to do becalmed for a month?" cried Randelos, restless as ever.

"There is much to be learned here and many new things to explore," began Minlienda soothingly.

"It's not as if we'll be staying here forever!" exclaimed Caerdrys with typical fire. Aelric and Min exchanged amused glances over Caerdrys's dark head. "While we are here, we can rest and visit with one another and learn what there is to learn about this part of the Creator's world. It's not as if we have great stores of knowledge about the sea!" She waved a slender hand at the Scrolls resting in their netting on the shelf above the desk in the corner. Cerlim's snort expressed their feelings on the shortcomings of the Scrolls' knowledge. Robse cleared his throat diffidently.

"This seems like a good time to visit with the other ships and to rest after the storm season; a time to rebuild our community somewhat. Aside from our brief sojourn on the repair island, we've not had much time together since the War, to become one people again and to heal the hurts we all received. Perhaps this calm is the Creator's way of giving us the gift of time: time to grow together and to become a people, instead of a remnant." He stopped when he realized all eyes were fixed on him. The quality of their silence made him wonder if he had said something offensive, and he flushed slightly, unsure. Domel's quiet voice rescued him from his confusion.

"I believe Robse has given us the answer. This time is a gift. Let us not waste it."

The late-morning sun poured down on the quarterdeck like liquid heat. It bounced and splashed over the surface of the water, throwing the brightly painted sides of the two accompanying ships into sharp relief against the golden blue of the sea. The Companions were scattered across the quarterdeck, scanning the distances, port and starboard, to the other ships. The vivid peacock blue and gold that marked the *Dridelphanen* stood a bowshot off the port rail. The *Gaelrandel's* slightly battered scarlet and sky blue was just aft of the *Cethastea's* starboard rail, level with her emerald and purple stern.

The three ships were moving sluggishly in the almost non-existent current, remaining level with one another with no effort. The great sails were furled on the yardarms, and quite a number of the Faeltheon had taken advantage of the slack time to climb up into the rigging, as though it were the beloved trees of their lost home. They perched, relaxed, chattering, like so many brightly colored birds, Robse thought idly.

His attention was caught by the conversation behind him. Aelric, Gaelcar, and Lysion were trying to decide how to facilitate communication between the three ships. The signal flags were adequate for short messages, as were the efforts of the ten messenger birds shared across the three vessels, but the thought of rowing the ship's boats back and forth every time someone wanted to visit was inefficient and wasteful. There were not enough boats to convey the number of people who would want to visit, and the amount of rowing would be exhausting, not to mention time consuming.

Robse could tell from their voices that the three were becoming frustrated. Caerdrys had wisely removed herself from the conversation, knowing her quick temper would not be of service. She had gravitated to where Minlienda leaned against the port rail, studying the *Dridelphanen*. Though Robse could feel them close by, he did not turn his gaze to them. He didn't relish what sharp-tongued Caerdrys might say if his eyes betrayed what his heart was beginning to feel for gentle Minlienda. Instead, he focused on the problem they were all wrestling with: how to convey to the other ships what this gift of time might bring to them as a people—and then how to make it happen.

He smiled as he saw members of the *Dridelphanen's* compliment aloft in their rigging as well, some even waving to members of the *Cethastea's* crew. *Too bad these ships' masts aren't the trees of the forests and woods back home,* he thought. *Then we'd have rope bridges linking us and all this fuss would be unnecessary.*

Caught by the sudden inspiration, Robse turned abruptly and called over to Lysion, interrupting the conversation.

"Captain! Are our three ships all caught in the same current, mild as it is? Will we remain at these distances, relative to one another?"

Lysion wasn't the only one to blink and sort out Robse's meaning, but he replied quickly enough, a tinge of impatience shading his voice.

"Aye, as much as we know anything about these odd waters, it seems we will. Why?"

Robse, excited by the possibilities of his thought, didn't answer him directly. Instead, he turned to Caerdrys.

"Caerdrys, you're the best shot with the bow. Can you send an arrow, with a stout rope attached, to the *Dridelphanen's* main mast, just above the aerie?"

The tall, dark-haired Elf considered him for a moment, her rain-colored eyes narrowed.

"I can. Why should I?" Her tone was not nearly as sharp as her words. She was curious, interested. Robse hastened to explain, his words tumbling over each other in a manner uncharacteristic of the normally self-effacing young Elf.

"If we can send ropes across, then we could build bridges, like we had among the trees back home! We could link the ships in a way that any of us could travel. We could be together. We could—"

"We could become a village," Min finished for him, as he became tongue-tied at the attention. He shot her a grateful glance. Aelric's expression was becoming hopeful, even while the more sober and thoughtful Gaelcar still showed skepticism. Domel's relieved laughter showed he believed it could be done, and Cerlim was mentally measuring the distance between the vessels.

Caerdrys reappeared at the foot of the companion-ladder to the quarterdeck, her bow and quiver slung over her back. They hadn't even noticed she'd gone to get them from her quarters beneath them. After some discussion, they decided to begin by shooting a linking cable between two of the vessels and seeing how it held with the movements of the ships.

Armed with a coil of stout but lightweight rope, Caerdrys mounted the radlings to the main aerie, startling the lookout on duty there. Once perched securely on the basket-like flet, Caerdrys took aim and let fly. Her arrow flew true, trailing its cargo of rope behind, to land with an audible *thunk* in the *Dridelphanen's* main mast, two feet above the lookout's head.

Fortunately, Gaelcar had thought to advise them via signal flags while Caerdrys was climbing to the aerie, so no one was caught off guard. An impromptu cheer went up from the *Cethastea's* deck, echoed a moment later from the other ships as the people began to perceive the reasons behind the unusual action. They all watched the slender cable intently for the next few minutes. It moved with the motions of the ships, its curve changing gently from a shallow arc as the ships rocked apart to a deep hammock-like curve when they listed toward each other. The movements were slight, however, as there was no wind beyond a gentle, fitful breeze.

Before anyone could think to caution him, Robse crowded into the main aerie with Caerdrys and the lookout. In another moment, he was up on the rope and running lightly across to the waiting *Dridelphanen*, trailing something behind him. Several Faeltheon held their breaths as he skimmed across the not quite taut rope, but, as Gaelcar caustically remarked to Aelric, the worst that could happen would be a fall into the warm water, from which they would have to fish him out. This slightly acerbic observation caused the watchers on the quarterdeck to laugh. They could tell Gaelcar was trying to cover his initial alarm at Robse's seemingly reckless act, for he was quite fond of Riende's remaining son.

Safely arrived at the other aerie, Robse untied the end of his burden from around his waist, shook out its folds, and made it fast to the *Dridelphanen's* main mast with the help of their lookout. As the small breeze teased the watchers again, it revealed a sturdy rope bridge swaying gently between the two aeries. Caerdrys's rope, which Robse had run across, stretched above the slender bridge at chest height, to be used as a guardrail. Another cheer went up, and people began to scramble for rope and rolled-up ladders, stored away against a time of need.

By midafternoon, six or seven rope bridges ran from the *Cethastea's* main deck, on both port and starboard, linking the three ships, and the traffic upon them was steady and joyful.

Minlienda swept the wayward strands of her dark hair out of her eyes and laughed with more than simple pleasure at the sight of the pack of Elven children scuttling up and down the radlings of the mizzenmast. Their wild game of tag was an exuberant echo of the joyous hearts of their elders. She called to them that the evening meal would soon be ready. Her suggestion of a communal time of singing and storytelling on the main deck after supper had been greeted with joy, and the other ships had quickly taken up the idea. Savory smells were wafting on the breeze from the galley, hinting that some were preparing special foods to celebrate the joining of the ships. It was wonderful how a few rope bridges created a community. For the first time since they had departed the Land, Min felt the *Cethastea* was home. It was amazing how the simple idea of linking the becalmed ships had sparked new life into the tired, grief-weighted spirits of the Faeltheon. It recalled the linked homes they had shared in their woods and forests. Even those who had built homes on the ground had known the deep and casual welcome of walking the arching spans from tree to tree to visit with friends and neighbors. The freedom to move about from one ship to another, to see friends and relatives whenever they chose, was a delight to the confined Elves.

In a way, their losses, so sudden and devastating, had created an isolation of the soul, even while they were crowded into ships with no way to escape each other. Min wondered if the confined spaces and forced inactivity had even strengthened that sense of isolation. Some bore it better than others, of course. The naturally outgoing, and those who had lost few close relatives, provided a calming, cheerful balance. But some, those hard hit by losses, and those naturally reticent or desiring more solitude, had become too quiet. Some had withdrawn enough to be called reclusive, though few among them had noticed, Min thought. They had all been overwhelmed with the tasks of dealing with their own griefs, adjusting to a new way of life, and leaving forever the Land that held all their memories. Min found herself wondering if any of those gifted with healing talents had survived. She felt increasingly sure that some of those more heavily crushed by grief might need more help.

Her eyes searched the ships until they fastened unerringly on the graceful form that was Robse, dropping effortlessly to the *Cethastea's* deck from the radlings above. She had seen the tightness of his jaw and the weariness in his gray eyes that increased day by day. The loss of father and brothers had hurt him deeply and had left him somehow defenseless, vulnerable to dark thoughts and a lack of confidence, both in the Creator and in himself. She knew that he was not naturally a warrior, though she didn't know him well enough to say what his talents were or what his dreams had been. That necessity had called him into the position of Champion, that his anger and despair had made him a fell warrior, that there had been no relenting of the grief that rode him, were all combining to work a change in him, Min was sure.

She could not see how to help him. She did not have the skills of a trained healer, to be able to guide him back to the person he had been, but she watched, helpless and grieving, as the fine boy he'd been was swallowed up into a being who seemed to have no identity of his own. It was as though he were trying to be too many other people: wise like his father, Riende; loyal as his brother Laslorn; as honorable as Theomanus; and courageous as a Champion. There was nothing wrong with his aspirations, Min reflected. It just disturbed her that in the many facets of the person Robse seemed determined to become, she could find no trace of Robse himself.

She shook off her somber thoughts and made a note to herself to seek Gaelcar in the next few days. He would know if they had any healers still among them and where they could be found. There might be others, like Robse, who were dealing with their sorrows in a way that could be potentially unhealthy. Min felt herself so inadequate to deal with problems like these. She longed again for the reassuring presence of older, wiser, more skilled Faeltheon. They had been the secure backdrop in the weaving of her life, seldom noticed, often unknown, but sorely missed now that they were gone. The fabric of their lives was destroyed, ravaged, tattered, and it was up to those who remained to repair it with what skill they could devise.

Their former life, with its expansive freedoms, was gone forever, vanished with the lingering smoke of the charnel fires that had burned the dead Goblin bodies. Never more would the voices of the multitude that had perished be heard in the Land. Never again would they see those beloved faces.

Bitterly, Min regretted the choice that had turned them away from pursuing fabled Marliondolen. Now that the Faeries and those Elven Kin who had shared their Forest home were gone beyond recall, it seemed obvious to her that Marliondolen *must* exist. Surely the Creator had provided a place of refuge for them all. Her soul cried out in despair that she and the rest of the Faeltheon had not heeded the voices of Elrad and others, warning them that the time to trust and to flee was at hand. If they had listened, they would all be together now, wherever the Faeries had gone.

She wondered again if the legends of Marliondolen were indeed true; if it was a place of surpassing beauty and safety, created just for them by their loving Creator, a place of refuge from the rising tide of Man. She wondered longingly if those who had disappeared had found their way there. Perhaps it had happened as Robse seemed to believe: that, somehow, the answer to the prophecy over Theomanus's life had been for him to become the Master of Marliondolen. She wondered afresh what that might mean, what duties that role would require of Theo.

Chapter Eighteen

Theomanus ran his long fingers through his dark hair, adding new furrows to the disorder he'd already created. *Master of Marliondolen*. What did that title entail? As often as he and Elrad, sometimes joined by others, had wrestled with this question, he could get no firmer grip upon it than that he was meant to lead them somehow. Elrad remained steadfast in his insistence that Theo would be shown by the Creator how to lead the Faeltheon in Marliondolen into the next stage of their becoming.

Theo thought that was entirely possible, though the idea left him dry-mouthed with apprehension, but what did it *mean*? What was he to *do*? Though the concept of time moved differently here in Marliondolen, the fact that they had been here awhile and he was no closer to understanding his role left Theo feeling he was missing something, some clue as to what he was to be doing. Exasperated and frustrated with his own inability, Theo had left his home early this morning, determined to thrash it out.

Wakened in the night by the feeling that he'd been called, he had risen in the darkness and gone outside his home. He had found no one there but the silent stars, so he had slipped back to his wife's side, determined to recapture his dream. But sleep had refused to return. An hour before dawn, he had risen resigned, packed some food in a bag, written a short note, kissed his sleeping wife, and left the house for a distant patch of woods and the solitude to wrestle with himself.

Now, as he sat at the edge of the woods, watching the dawn light the horizon with the colors of the sea, he was gripped with a wave of nostalgia so sudden and powerful it was like a blow. He remembered standing at the edge of his world, where sea met Land, the salt breeze whipping his hair, the spray dashing into his face, so that he could not tell his own tears from those of the ocean.

Suddenly, it was as though he were there again, a lonely, hurting child, battered and confused and lost. Powerful emotions swirled in him, threatening to destroy him if he flinched, if he showed by any sign the deep betrayal of his heart.

How could this have happened?

How could it be true? He could not make it real. The Elves had come and extracted him from where he lay sleeping in a friendly tangle of arms and legs with Laslorn and Rablorn and Glimring and Geltheon at Riende and Elamani's home. The boys had played and sung and wrestled late into the previous night, and the indulgent parents had decided for once to let them remain where they had fallen asleep, like a litter of puppies.

But the warm hands and voices that had summoned him from his sleep with the awful news had felt cold to the young Elf. It had seemed to Theomanus that no warmth could reach him, that he was encased in ice and couldn't break out to be enfolded in the living warmth of Elamani's arms or to be touched by his friends' wretched silence.

An accident, they had said, their words bouncing off him like small, sharp pebbles. The boat had been caught in a sudden storm and capsized. Only one among the four had been saved alive from the restless sea. Their words had poured on, a relentless flow that held no meaning beyond the truth that had shattered Theo's world: his parents were dead.

The following dawn, the silent child had left Riende's home in the corridors and passages of the palace, had left the still-sleeping City itself, had crossed the sand, pale gray in the muted light of predawn, and had come to confront the sea. He'd stood, his feet lapped by the encroaching waves of the incoming tide, and waited for the sea to explain why it had taken his parents. He had waited, while the sky behind him took on the aspect of a pearl. He had waited for a very long time, until the slow tears had finally melted through the ice and coursed down his stiff face, and the sea had wept with him.

With that melting had come the pain—deep, engulfing, bewildering, shattering. He had felt so lost. He had never felt so young. He had never before known fear, even with the prophecy that had haunted his steps since birth. Always, he had been secure in his parents' love, in the love of their friends and *amia* family, in the love of the Creator. The thundering hurt of betrayal had wrenched through him, twisting his face, tearing at his heart. His parents weren't *supposed* to leave him! They were supposed to stay and love him forever, like the Lord did. Then the deeper hurt mutated into anger, and Theo had flung his head back and screamed at the pale sky.

"*How could You take my parents from me? I thought You loved me!*" Shocked at the force of his anger and the terrible implication in his wild cry, Theo had sobbed until his strength gave out and dropped him limply to the sand. He was deeply shaken at the thought that the Creator might not love him as he'd been taught, and he felt guilty for even thinking it. He wanted to apologize to the Creator, to ask Him to bring his parents back, but he knew that wouldn't happen.

Gradually, Theo had stopped begging to have his beloved parents returned and had instead turned to the Lord for comfort. He had found, no matter how it hurt to lose his parents, he could not just abandon the faith they had lived and had spent his lifetime instilling in him. In a deeply hidden part of his soul that Theomanus had never needed to find before, he knew beyond doubt that his Maker loved him.

Clinging to that lifeline of comfort, Theo had gone through the days following the loss of the three Elves with a calm that worried his elders and awed his friends. Riende and Elamani had taken him in and adopted him as their own, even though he was the heir of the Quaeliom house. No one had objected, for the prophecy over his life had cast some question over his availability to head the Tribe as an adult.

Now, shaken by the intensity of the memories, Theomanus shook his head sharply as he watched the sun rise joyfully over the rolling green hills in Marliondolen. He wondered why he had recalled those days at this time. He became so swamped in reliving them that he almost missed the answer: that time in his life, though it had been dreadful and had seared his soul with sorrow, had been a defining moment in his faith. He had been tempted to turn away and hide his heart from the Creator, to blame Him for the sadness of loss, instead of trusting Him to know what He was doing, even when it hurt a small boy. And yet, through the faith of his parents and the example of the Lord's love in his life already, Theo had been able to turn *toward* his Maker instead, to take refuge in His infinitely greater strength, to be warmed by the love that would never fail. Having come through that crisis with his faith intact, Theo realized he'd never doubted the Creator again, even in the face of some unnerving situations.

Before he could pursue that thought, Theomanus found himself plunged into another memory. Recognizing this time that the Lord was speaking to him, Theo set himself to remember clearly and to glean from the memory whatever his Creator would have him understand.

In his memory, Theo saw the familiar stripes of light and dark that barred the corridor of the palace, caused by the shadows of the carven pillars alternating with the moonlight that poured between them. The inlaid flagstones were cold against his hurrying feet, their bright patterns muted in the flat light of night. It seemed to him that it was really the clenching fear that gripped his insides that caused all color and light to be dimmed, and that fear was echoed in the harsh breaths of his brother beside him. The two boys fled silently down the endless-seeming corridor that led from their friend Aoneth's home in the south wing.

They had been so happy earlier that night, with permission given to spend the night and partake in Aoneth's birth-feast. Permission had been given readily by Riende, as Elamani was so near her birthing time. The miracle of a second child was so rare, Riende and the boys had been unwilling to let Elamani out of their sight for the past eight months! Laslorn, several years Theo's junior, was beside himself at the thought of being an older brother.

That night had been so happy. They had celebrated Aoneth's feast with all their might, eating far too many sweets, staying up late to listen to tales and songs, finally succumbing to sleep in spite of themselves.

The six boys had crowded into Aoneth's room to sleep, festooning themselves in the extra hammocks like so much tree moss.

Then Theo had awakened to Laslorn's muffled cries as he tossed fitfully in what appeared to be a bad dream. Theo had gone to him and shaken his shoulder, expecting to hear that Las had a stomachache from the sweets, but both boys had shouted, startled, when Laslorn had sat bolt upright and fallen out of the hammock onto Theo. Two of the other boys had wakened at the commotion, but had rolled over again when they saw that Theo was awake.

Theo had struggled out from under Laslorn, hoping his brother wouldn't be sick on him, but when he'd turned to see Laslorn's face in the moonlight from the window, a deep cold had settled in his middle. Laslorn's eyes were open, but his gaze was distant and his normally merry face was a mask of pain and fear. Almost afraid of his reaction, Theo had reached out to touch Laslorn's shoulder. When this elicited no response, he shook the younger boy slightly. Laslorn blinked and turned slowly to meet Theo's eyes, and Theo wished he hadn't. Something was very wrong.

"Las!" he'd whispered, trying not to wake the other boys. "Las! What is it?"

"I don't know, Theo," the boy had replied, sounding very young and frightened.

"Where does it hurt?" Theo prodded, needing to know whether to wake Aoneth's mother. The wide green eyes fastened on his in the pale light, and Theo felt Laslorn begin to tremble. The fine tremors radiated out from the child's torso, until his hands and feet were shaking and his teeth chattered.

"It's not me. I think it's Mother."

Theo hadn't stopped to question Laslorn. He'd just stuffed him into his discarded clothing, yanked on his own, and led him toward home at a fast pace. Laslorn's breath had grown harsher, and the occasional whimper escaped him as they ran. Theomanus knew something was wrong by Laslorn's behavior, but he felt it confirmed in his own gut as they neared Riende's home.

Lamps were lit and there was a sound of bustle and muted voices as they drew near. The pale moonlight faded beside the warmth of lamp, candle, and hearth flame. There were adults there, moving briskly, talking and working as if nothing were wrong. The very normalcy of their demeanor soothed Theo's nerves some as he sought among those present for his adoptive father. Spying him by the hearth, Theo half led, half-dragged Laslorn to him.

"Father," he began, knowing he was interrupting, but too worried about Laslorn to heed protocol. Surprised, Riende turned at the sound of his voice.

"What are you two doing here?" he exclaimed, but before Theo could answer, the father's eyes noted his sons' distress. He gathered them to him, Laslorn's face pressed against Riende's middle, Theo glad to lay his head on the man's shoulder. "What is it, my boys? What is wrong?" the beloved voice prompted. Laslorn raised his deep green eyes to his father's and the tears spilled over.

"Father, something is wrong with Mother! I woke up with such a pain in my tummy! I couldn't get a breath, and I felt such fear! What's wrong with her? Where is she?" The boy's eyes were frantically searching the room now. Riende's large hand stroked his son's fair head.

"Shh, shh, son. It's all right. Mother is in her bedchamber. I don't know how you became so attuned to her, my child, but she is having the baby tonight. Do you still feel the pain?" The father's eyes searched Laslorn's carefully, but the child shook his head.

"No, Papa, not anymore. Is Mama all right? Why did I feel so scared? Is the baby here yet? When do we sing?" Riende laughed at the fusillade of questions. It was apparent his normally ebullient son was none the worse for his unsettling experience. He disengaged from their arms and sat in his chair, pulling Laslorn onto his lap, while Theo perched on the arm, swinging one bare foot. Now that Riende was in charge and Laslorn seemed better, Theo tried to relax. Laying Laslorn's blond head against his chest, Riende began answering the questions in the quiet, patient voice Theo knew he often used at bedtime to put them to sleep.

"Mama is fine, my dear. I do not know why you felt fear, but we will talk about it tomorrow, for I think perhaps you forgot to ask the Creator to help you, hmm?" The sleepy head nodded, and a huge yawn showed Theo a glimpse of his brother's healthy tonsils.

"The baby is not here yet but is coming," the deep voice went on as the fair lashes fanned onto flushed cheeks. "And when he arrives and your mother and I have held him and given thanks, then we shall sing the Welcome Song for him. Sleep now, my son. It will be a while yet." Almost before he had finished speaking, the late night and unusual excitement had combined to send Laslorn into deep slumber.

Riende looked up to meet Theo's eyes, but what he saw there caused him to rise and put Laslorn into the chair. He took Theo's shoulder and urged him away from the hearth, so their voices would not wake the tired boy. Understanding what Riende wanted, Theomanus told him of the odd awakening and Laslorn's reactions. Riende didn't seem troubled by the incident, so Theo assumed it was not something he need worry about. As he finished his tale, he hesitated and Riende prompted him to share all his thoughts.

"You said all is well with Elamani," Theo began, troubled by the chill inside that would not be comforted. "But I am still uneasy. If I had been alone in the woods, I would have said danger approached. I am cold inside. So cold," he whispered. Riende's dark green eyes grew wide at Theo's words. Grim lines appeared around the mouth that so often smiled. He gripped Theomanus's shoulder hard, in a man's grip, and Theo straightened to meet it, knowing what strength he had was needed now by those who had become his family. At that moment, the healer's attendant came quickly to them, stopping by Riende so abruptly that her skirts swirled around Theo's legs.

"Riende," she said quietly, "there's trouble."

The green eyes turned once more to the golden ones.

"Pray, Theo," he said and followed the attendant into the bedchamber, shutting the door behind him.

Theo had prayed. He had prayed harder than he had since the morning of his parents' death. He was still praying when Laslorn woke and came to join him, looking scared again. They prayed together, their arms around one another, seeking the Anchor that could hold them both in this storm.

With the first rays of the sun, Riende came to them, blood on his tunic, tears on his face. The boys cast themselves into his arms, and the three rocked together in their pain, tears mingling. Finally, Riende pushed them back, a hand on each boy's shoulder, and looked them in the eyes. His eyes held a pain familiar to Theo, but Laslorn was too young to comprehend the truth so quickly.

"She is gone," Riende managed before tears closed his throat. He struggled for a moment and managed to go on. "She has left us, my boys. The Creator has called her and she has returned to Him."

"Will she come back?" Laslorn asked, afraid of his father's eyes. "We prayed, Papa. We prayed *hard*!" Tears rolled down Riende's face, and he made no move to wipe them away. It was as if he were unaware he was crying.

"What did you pray, my sons?" Riende looked at Laslorn and Laslorn at Theomanus. Theo had to clear his throat in order to answer the grieving man he loved so much.

"We prayed for their safety, and that the Lord would guard them. We prayed that His will would be done."

"And so it is," responded the Elf, with a sigh that broke at the end. Fiercely, he drew the two boys to him again, as if he needed to feel their life.

"What about the baby?" Theo found the courage to ask. Riende relaxed his arms and turned toward the bedchamber door, drawing them after him.

"Come, my sons. We shall look upon them both and say farewell. They shall not return to us, Laslorn, but perhaps someday our Lord will reunite us again. We cannot know what He has planned for us, and we do not know what happens to those who die. Perhaps they are with Him when they are not with us."

The three entered the darkened room and came to look upon the bed. The covers had been pulled up to lay straight and smooth, and all signs of the birthing had been removed. Elamani lay as though sleeping, but she suddenly seemed a stranger to Theomanus. The woman who had taken him in and had become like a mother to him was gone. It seemed odd to him that her body was still there, like a forgotten garment, unneeded, left behind.

In the crook of her arm lay a tiny, pale baby boy. He had been washed but was not yet wrapped in the wee clothes that had been so lovingly prepared for him. His skin was pale, with a purplish cast to his eyelids and lips and fingers. Laslorn pushed forward to the bedside.

"No!" he shouted out, startling them all. Riende reached for him, thinking he was denying his mother's absence, but the youngster eluded him, reaching for the baby. With shaking hands, he awkwardly lifted the infant, hugging him close to his heart. A strange fire burned in his forest green eyes, and Riende checked his own motions to watch him. Not knowing why, Theo began to pray.

"You can't be dead!" Laslorn cried to the still form he held. "You're my little brother! I get to be the big brother! Come back to me! I never got to know you or to show you all the things you need to know! Come on—all you have to do is breathe, like this! Do it like this!" Laslorn put his lips over the baby's tiny mouth and blew a small breath into him. For a few moments he continued to teach his little brother how to breathe, holding him in a tight hug after each breath. Riende watched through his tears, but Theo prayed, asking the Creator *please* to let Laslorn have his little brother. They were both so lost in their own thoughts that at first they missed the joy in Laslorn's voice.

"That's it! That's right! Do it again! You can do it! See, Papa, Theo, I'm a good big brother!" Excitedly, he was showing them the baby, now flushed with pink and emitting the beginnings of an outraged squall. "See, I showed him how!" he proclaimed proudly while the nurse bustled forward and exclamations were heard in both rooms. Theo grinned until he thought his cheeks would split, and Riende's tears flowed steadily through his whispered thanks.

They named the child Robse, *present power*, to remind them of the power of the Lord that filled them and the tiny babe. They sang the Welcome Song, though their joy was tempered with deep sorrow at the loss of Elamani. They heard the refrain picked up by those of their household, and then by their friends, and soon by all the Palace's inhabitants. Within a few minutes, the strains of the joyous song were heard throughout the City, as the Faeltheon welcomed the miracle child into their midst.

The vivid memories began to fade, and Theo became aware of his surroundings and of the tears that wet his face. Once again, the Creator had required him to relive a difficult time in his life, a time when his Lord had met him and sustained him. He was beginning to understand the message behind the memories when another one overwhelmed his senses.

The shouts and cries of the warriors rang in his ears as Theo's memories crashed around him with the force of a gale. Instantly, he was transported back to the chaotic melee of the recent outbreak of Goblin Wars. He and his friends had come to the aid of their Faerie Kindred when Gael, consort to Aelwyn, had sent the call for help to vanquish this latest uprising of their ancient foes. Laslorn was now at his right hand, Aoneth at his left. It took Theo a moment to remember that young Robse was safely at home with Riende. He felt the reassuring presence of Rablorn and the twins at his back as his arms thrust and hacked at the Goblins surrounding them. Even as his thoughts sorted themselves out, a deep foreboding welled within him. He did not want to relive this memory.

The clashing of metal on metal rang a counterpoint to the hiss of arrows from the trees. The burning in his arms slowed Theo, even as he struggled to stave off his opponents. He felt an impact on his left and heard a grunt as Aoneth threw a Goblin off his shield and back into its fellows. Knowing he did not want to turn around, still Theo craned his eyes to the left. Aoneth stumbled and went down on one knee, an axe head buried in his shield rim. Even as Theo raised his sword and dispatched the Goblin on the other end of the axe, he saw the gnarled, mushroom-colored enemy in the middle distance, arm poised to throw a deadly black blade.

"No," Theo whispered to his memory, but it was no use. The past could not be changed. The five-pointed blade flew through the intervening distance and buried itself in Rablorn's throat. In slow motion, Theomanus saw his friend fall, a look of surprise spreading over his fair face. Theomanus caught him as he fell, trusting to his friends to protect them, even as he felt them close their circle, himself inside. He held Rablorn's body as the light died in his friend's eyes.

Cruel grief struck at Theo, tearing at his heart. This was one of his oldest friends, an Elf who was only here because, loyal, as all his friends were, Rablorn had followed Theo, believing in the prophecy spoken over him that he would someday be used of the Creator to save his people. Laslorn, Rablorn, Aoneth, Glimring, and Geltheon, his five closest friends, sworn in a brotherhood to support and help him in his quest, had followed him here, and now Rablorn was dead.

Even as guilt clawed at him, Theomanus began to pray for his friend, that the Lord would keep his spirit and, someday, as Riende had taught him to believe, reunite them again. As his grief and sense of loss welled up, Theomanus felt the steadying presence of the Creator there with him. He struggled with the feeling that it was because of his prophecy that Rablorn had lost his life, but the presence of his Maker would not be denied. In thundering silence, the Creator made it very clear to Theomanus that no thing could happen without His knowledge and that His plan *would* be accomplished. He was reminded that no one but the Lord knew the tally of Rablorn's days, and that no circumstance could thwart the will of the Creator. Reluctantly, but grateful for the underlying peace, Theo yielded up his friend and his troubled heart.

Without pause for contemplation or recovery, Theo's memories shifted to another scene, abandoning the cacophony of the battlefield for the blanketing silence of a garden at night. Struggling to orient himself, it was the scent of rosemary and the muted roar of the distant Falls that told Theomanus he was in the Queen's Garden of Elwyn's palace.

Instantly, sweet memories flooded his mind and heart. This night he had declared his love to Elwyn and won her for his bride. Well, technically, she had trapped him into it, but he was grateful, nonetheless.

In the quiet garden, before Elwyn had joined him, he had struggled to set aside his love for her, because he was sure his destiny would end his life and there would be no time for them together. How right and how wrong he had been, he thought ruefully. The battle in his heart seared him anew as he remembered his shame at the pride revealed within him, as well as the belief that he must not acknowledge his love for Elwyn.

He was tormented with the conflicting desires of his heart. He knew all too well that his path, his duty, would likely make an end of him. Until he had met her, his heart had been at peace with the thought. To save his people, to fulfill the duty for which the Creator had made him, was sufficient to warrant the sacrifice of his single life. He had been confident that nothing would shake him from the cool distance he had always cultivated in his relationships, so that he would remain heart-free to follow his destiny when the time arrived.

Then, in one agonizing moment, all the careful self-control on which he had prided himself had been exposed for what it was: mere dreams of prideful confidence. Throughout his life, he had kept his distance even from those he most loved, to avoid the entanglement and pain of parting, only to become completely entranced by the brave, giving young Queen of Faerie.

In his mind, Theomanus heard the echo of their voices as they struggled with duty, honor, love, and, ultimately, trust in the Creator. The young queen's voice stirred his heart afresh, even now that he'd been married to her for months.

"The adventure that comes to us is not ours to control, and I am afraid many will be hurt, and the courageous may buy our freedom with their lives."

"For those we love to have the freedom to live in peace is a goal worthy of the sacrifice of our lives, Elwyn. Never doubt that. Remember, too, that if these events are not ours to control, they are still in the palm of the Creator. It is He Who ordains and orchestrates the destinies of those of us who serve the people."

Theomanus remembered Elwyn praying there in the little cave where they had trysted. He remembered the peace that had flooded the small space and the serene look in her eyes when she'd looked up at him. He'd recognized that look of restored peace and confidence, for his own face had worn it many times over the years after communing with the Creator. It was the look that came after he had submitted his own will to the calling the Lord had placed on his life.

Finally, the relentless memories released Theomanus. He lay back in the tender grass, exhausted, but at peace. *I understand, Lord. Forgive me for needing the reminder. Again. I will trust You to make Your will known and to use me as You see fit. I will leave the timing to You and trust You not to let me fail You.*

Chapter Nineteen

Gaelcar was so completely engrossed in his task that when he glanced up slightly and caught sight of the still figure standing before his desk, he started. He was used to receiving unexpected visitors, but typically they did not lurk quietly, waiting to be noticed, as this silent girl had.

"Yes?" he asked, a trifle sharply, then smoothed his tunic, quickly recovering his composure. "Is there something I can do for you?"

The girl's solemn mouth quirked slightly in the shadow of a smile, and she replied in a voice so soft Gaelcar almost didn't hear her over the sound of the waves lapping against the ship.

"Yes, thank you. I have been sent from the *Dridelphanen* to report that we may need more food, since our nets have not been extremely productive in the past several weeks, and this morning we found that a fungus has destroyed a portion of our nursery plants."

Gaelcar nodded, and after assuring the girl that he would arrange to have a load of supplies transferred to her ship within a short time, he returned to the neat stacks of papers covering his desk, assuming the meeting was over.

Looking over the piles of scrolls and sheets of vellum stacked crosswise on his desktop, awaiting his attention and decisions, Gaelcar groaned softly, brushing his fingers over his aching temples. Already today he had spent long hours working to make sure that the affairs of the *Cethastea* and the other ships were running smoothly and efficiently. But the mound of work seemed never to grow less. He could not keep up with it all, as well as attend to his other duties. He needed help—but whom?

"Do you need help?"

The quiet voice of the girl broke his frustrated silence as though she had read his mind. Startled once more, he looked up and realized she had not gone beyond his office doorway. As the offer implicit in her words penetrated his busy mind, the shy, slightly awkward young Elf suddenly took on a very welcome appearance. Dismissing his minor irritation at being startled twice in one morning, Gaelcar smiled and gestured to the adjacent table, whose surface was also covered in stacks of work.

"Yes, please, if you can be spared and are an organized person."

The girl nodded and replied in her slightly stilted manner, "I will deliver my message to Gaelneth, then return and assist you."

Gaelcar, slightly bemused by this swift answer to his need, managed an acknowledging nod as she left the doorway. He watched through his propped-open window as her lithe figure hastened across the rope bridge that bound the ships together. When active, she lost her awkward appearance and was as graceful as any of his Kin.

Gaelcar wondered briefly if the way she had held herself in his office, and her stiff manner of speech, were merely shyness. Her accent, though faint, told him she came from the deeper hills and valleys of the mountains. Many of those settlements were fairly isolated, so she might also be unaccustomed to much social interaction. He wondered how the enforced crowding aboard the ships had affected her these past months.

Minutes later, she returned, and this time Gaelcar was waiting to welcome her properly. She introduced herself as Myrandella Durilyse, an Elf whose former home had indeed been in the higher slopes of the mountain ridge farthest from the City. Gaelcar was pleased to have been correct in his initial assessment, and his restored equilibrium was evident in his typical gentle formality. His organized mind was able to place her family name as one of the Tribe Ruachliende. He knew many of these families had lived in greater isolation than was the norm among the Elven people, preferring solitude and wide spaces, so he was unsurprised at her quiet demeanor. It seemed logical to assume she was far more used to conversing with the Creator than with other creatures.

Still, as their time together progressed, he noticed that she was singularly quiet, hardly ever uttering a word unless it was absolutely necessary. During a stretch of quiet work, when the scratching of their pens was the only sound within the office, Gaelcar felt a distant quality to the silence, as though she were deliberately walling herself off from him. He wondered if she did this with everyone. He cast a quick glance over to the small table bolted to the cabin wall, where she worked industriously, her dark head bowed over the scrolls and inkwell. The distancing was more than simple reticence, but her attitude led him to believe that her habits were ingrained over a long time, not the product of the shattering forces of the War. He wondered what secrets haunted her past that she would work so hard to keep others away.

Her silent nature did not bother Gaelcar though. At the end of the day, as Myrandella prepared to leave, he checked her work. It was well done—very well done. The sheer attention to detail with which she had finished every single one of the tasks he had requested of her astounded him. She would be an incredible asset, if she were willing to work with him. Given her help, Gaelcar was confident that he could do his work much more effectively.

He stopped her briefly before she disappeared from the *Cethastea*. His eyes squinted against the bright sunlight after the dimness of his little office, but some of the creases in the corners of his eyes came from his smile.

"Thank you, Myrandella. You are an excellent helper and have been of invaluable service to me today. If it is agreeable to you, would you be willing to transfer to this ship and help me on a daily basis?"

Myrandella flushed slightly in response to his compliment, but replied, "It would be no bother. I can transfer over here tomorrow, if you'd like."

Inwardly, Gaelcar was shouting with joy at the new and unforeseen aid, although his habitual dignity was firmly in place as he thanked her again and saw her on her way to the *Dridelphanen*. In very high spirits, Gaelcar set out to finish one last task of the day—to arrange to have his new assistant transferred to the *Cethastea*.

Caerdrys stood, legs braced, in her customary position at the farthest forward point of the prow, balanced between the slender red-painted rails, above the figurehead of the Elven king with his crown of stars that gave the *Cethastea* her name. Though the breeze was blowing, it was weak and fitful, as always in these becalmed, weed-grown waters. Caerdrys sighed and stepped down from her perch. It wasn't the same when they were hardly moving. She missed the days of balancing there as the ship raced before the wind, rising and plunging into the great troughs of the waves, the fierce wind whipping her long hair about her head. Resigned to their temporary fate, until the currents should pick them up again, Caerdrys turned and made her way to the waist of the vessel, leaning on the port rail to watch the children below.

Lately, it had become the favorite pastime of the many youngsters of the three ships to swim and play in the warm, calm waters. The vessels were moving so slowly that an hour's play would not leave them behind. As always, watchers kept guard, in case any of the children felt distress, and there were more than a few, like herself, watching indulgently in an idle moment. Their splashing and shouting looked like fun, actually. Caerdrys toyed with the idea of joining them, but then thought about the chore of trying to get all the salt out of her hair before the itching drove her mad. It took so long to distill sufficient fresh water for a full bath that most of the Faeltheon restricted themselves to one indulgence a week, taking quick washes from their basins the other days.

Idly scanning the waters below, Caerdrys noticed the slick arch of a gray dorsal fin some distance away. The ship fish often came leaping around the three ships at dawn and dusk, splashing and clicking and squealing in a manner that made Caerdrys feel that she should be able to understand what they were saying. She couldn't put her finger on why they intrigued her so much more than any other fish, but they did. She had noticed others felt drawn to them too.

Suddenly, her gaze sharpened alertly. One of the dorsal fins approaching the playing children was darker and moved in a side-to-side motion rather than up and down. Just as Caerdrys filled her lungs to shout a warning, the lookout cried the alarm.

"Shark! Shark off the port side! Shark!"

The children looked up and around, trying to spot the menace. Some began to make for the ship ladders and others to cry for help. The eldest children were trying to get the youngest ones to safety, but the little ones were panicking and crying. Caerdrys could see that the shark would reach them before they could get to safety. Heart racing, she flung off her outer tunic and grabbed up one of the barbed grapples secured to the side of the *Cethastea*. The long poles, with the wicked hooks on their ends, were used to help drag heavy fish over the side of the ship. She had to struggle for a frustrating moment with the ropes that secured it before she got it free. The precious seconds were ticking away, and the children were in danger.

Climbing to the rail, Caerdrys jumped feet first over the side. Dropping from that height, the warm water hit her like a fist, closing over her head in a cloudy swirl. Desperately, she kicked for the surface, hearing other bodies impacting the water, as more adults leapt overboard to try to save the youngsters.

Surfacing, Caerdrys took stock of the situation. To her right, one of the older girls was towing two tinies toward the ship's ladder, another gamely following in her wake. Directly ahead of her, a boy and another girl were trying to get several little ones to stop screaming and splashing. Beyond them, heading toward them from the *Dridelphanen*, came two Elven men, swimming strongly.

Looking to her left, Caerdrys sucked in a breath and felt her blood run cold. Several yards away were three small ones, huddled around young Netharos, who was treading water, trying to keep all of their heads above the surface. The sinister dorsal fin was rapidly approaching them, and Caerdrys knew she would not be able to reach them first. She wanted to throw the grapple at the predator but knew the gesture would be futile and might harm the children. Aware it was useless, she struck out for them, kicking desperately, hearing the frantic shouts of others behind her.

She swam with all her might, pausing only to fling heavy wet hair out of her eyes. As she drew near, unable to spare the breath to call a reassurance to Netharos, she heard an ominous thrashing in the water and shrieks from the little girls. Her heartbeat choking her, as though her heart had lodged in her throat, Caerdrys sobbed her frustration in harsh breaths. Suddenly, she was there, the water churning and foaming around her. One of the little ones, seeing an adult, flung herself from Netharos onto Caerdrys, and they both went under for a moment.

As she struggled to reach the surface once more, trying to keep the deadly grapple away from the clinging child, the water before Caerdrys's eyes cleared and she saw a remarkable sight. Rising swiftly from the depths beneath her, the sleek body of one of the ship fish sped past. Just ahead was the shark, and Caerdrys watched in amazement as the ship fish sped to the predator and dealt him a mighty blow.

Caerdrys and the child surfaced then, and the churning water resolved itself into four ship fish circling the children, while two more beat the shark soundly, driving it away. Other adults reached them then, taking the children into their arms and praising Netharos, who was quite pale under his tan. The two pursuing ship fish returned and joined the four surrounding the Elves. With clacks and nods and none-too-gentle prods, they herded the Faeltheon over to the *Cethastea's* ladder. The children were handed up and the adults followed, but Caerdrys turned, unwilling to leave such an incredible event.

She hooked an arm in the nearest rung and looked closely at their rescuers. Sleek gray bodies crowded round as soon as they perceived she was lingering with them. Great heads, with long, narrow beaks and bulging foreheads, turned sideways so the gleaming eyes could fasten on her. Caerdrys was sure they were trying to tell her something, but they were all clacking and squeeing at once. She held out her hand to touch one of them. The skin was surprisingly soft and resilient, like a palmful of warm, solid water. They all crowded her then, wanting to be touched.

The largest ship fish suddenly pushed through the rest, bestowing slaps right and left with her flippers. The others moved smartly out of her way. She came up to Caerdrys and lifted the upper part of her body out of the water to look the Elf in the eye. The others were quiet, so when the large female spoke, Caerdrys could hear distinct sounds that seemed like words. She listened with all her might and could almost make out what the female was saying. Wanting to understand, certain that these creatures were trying to communicate, Caerdrys reached out her hand, laying it on the slick head just in front of the blowhole.

"*Eon ashar ímon*," she enunciated carefully. *You blessed us all.* The creature studied her intently for a moment, then vigorously nodded her head, flinging water at Caerdrys and opening her long mouth in a toothy grin.

"*Í-ah ye'he'ehr*," the large creature squealed back. Caerdrys listened hard then was shocked to realize what she was hearing. *Íon yehearm*, the creature had said as clearly as she could, given the shape of her mouth. *We rescue.*

Dazed, Caerdrys looked up at the interested watchers crowding the *Cethastea's* rail.

"They speak the Common Tongue," she reported. Lifting her hand from the warm head and watching another of them surface and blow to clear its airhole, she added, "And they're mammals."

Hours later, a happy, waterlogged Caerdrys was hauled aboard the *Cethastea* by Cerlim's strong arm, and a warm blanket was wrapped around her by Min. She and others had plunged back into the warm waters to join their new friends and to learn about them. Caerdrys had been delighted to find that one of the beautiful creatures, a young male, had remarkably clear speech. They named him Qualneth, Gifted Speaker, which pleased him so much he adopted it immediately in favor of his previous name, Sleek.

They learned that it was the custom among the pods to name a calf for a physical characteristic. This would be his childhood name. But when the calf was a young adult, ready to leave the pod or to become a mother, a new name was given, describing a character trait or attribute the youngster had grown into or accomplished.

Caerdrys learned that the large female who had spoken with her was the leader of this pod. Her name was Ghaerwe, Silver Arrow, and it

suited her as she sped through the water. Caerdrys was so enchanted with these creatures, with their beauty, their friendliness, their sense of fun, that she coined a name for them that stuck: *delphys*, beauty. They loved their new name, squeeing it to each other as best they could, until everyone was laughing. Aelric remarked that it was truly a fitting name, for not only were the creatures beautiful, but they bore and nursed and cherished their young as the Faeltheon did, which concept was at the heart of the word.

For the remainder of their time in the becalmed waters, Caerdrys spent a portion of every day playing and conversing with her new friends, as did many others.

The sunset painted the western horizon in shades of flame so brilliant it almost hurt to watch. It had become a cherished time for many of them, gathering to witness day's end together on the *Cethastea's* main deck. Some were busy with evening chores, of course, but as the task list varied, all who wished to gather were able to do so at least once every few days.

This evening's vivid display was so breathtaking that even many who were still on duty paused to savor its beauty. As the optical fanfare faded slowly into mellow shades of royal twilight, the reverent peace was enhanced by a single piper, high in the fore-aerie. With masterful skill, he wove a melody at once joyful and melancholy, a tune that touched all the listening Faeltheon with hints of the day's hopeful promise and haunting wisps of the losses they'd suffered. As the last of the gold faded into shadowed flame, he overlaid it all with a paean of unshakeable faith in the loving care of the Creator, his young voice soaring pure and high against the embers of the sun.

Fylarai
Íon nedistale
Íron randel

Nean eam
Aematlon
Brygar ím sia
Yo regan ím
Namad

Min was not surprised to find her face wet with tears as the last note faded into stillness and the unending song of the sea. As she looked about her at the faces of her companions, she saw that most glimmered with tear tracks.

Flame was overlaid with streaks of heavy violet as dusk's clouds overwhelmed the departing sun. The violet deepened to muted purple, drawing the eye up into indigo, spangled with the night's first stars. A last ragged tear in the darkling horizon was pierced with molten gold, which vanished into blood-red embers and sank beneath the sea's rim.

With a shared sigh for the throbbing beauty of the sunset, the Elves turned from the rails and radlings and gathered in the center of the main deck, sitting in a ragged, companionable circle. A handful of Faerie wicks had been scooped into the center of their group, and their comfortable bluish glow enhanced the waxing starlight. Though Humans would have struggled to see in such dim lighting, the illumination was strong enough for Faeltheon sight to pick out clearly the faces of their companions. As Min moved to join the gathering, she was astonished to note that the lone piper, whom she could now see climbing nimbly down the radlings, was twelve-year-old Netharos, aptly named 'gifted.'

Minlienda leaned easily against Caerdrys's shoulder. One advantage she had always enjoyed about being the shorter of the two was the ability to make use of her sister as a prop. Of course, in their younger days, Caerdrys had been known to remove herself suddenly and laugh with great glee when Min went sprawling …

Min felt a deep contentment well up in her, born of the song, the beauty of the night, and the closeness of her friends, doubly cherished now that so many loved ones were gone. She lifted up a silent prayer of thankfulness for those who had been spared, and for the blessing of the need that had drawn them together. Feeling contemplative, Min scanned the crowd in tonight's circle, the faces grown so familiar over these past months.

Almost directly across from her sat Aelric, clad in a mismatched tunic and vest. She smiled when she recalled that he had rushed to his cabin to fling on dry clothes after the soaking he had received helping to haul in the day's catch of fish. The sunset had promised to be so lovely, he hadn't wanted to miss any of it, but Caerdrys had insisted that he change from his wet garments before the sun's setting cooled the wind. The young king's hair was in wild disarray from that same wind, and he had further spiked it with his characteristic gesture of plowing his long fingers through it. Min chuckled quietly at the relaxed, disheveled picture he presented. Tonight, he looked like what he was: part of a team of hard-working Elves, trying to stay alive upon the unfamiliar sea. That he was also their king could not have been inferred from his current appearance, however.

On his right sat his faithful Seneschal. Min's chuckle widened to a grin as she took in Gaelcar's contrasting semblance. The older Elf was his usual neat self, his pale hair caught back from his face in two slender braids and falling smoothly to his shoulders. His tunic and leggings were neat and clean and in good repair, the colors muted and coordinating pleasantly. He looked as if he had just stepped out of his office in a stationary, calm castle. Even his expression betrayed no agitation or care, though she knew the myriad details of his tasks would harry any other individual.

By contrast, on Aelric's left sat his Champion. As Min's gaze came to rest on young Robse, she was struck by the sudden impression that she was looking at a stranger. His form was broader and stronger than it had been when they set out, and he sat with a warrior's alert ease of body. His face was set in an expression of guarded calm, much like his father used to wear. It was obvious that he believed his part was to be alert to every nuance of what surrounded the king. It seemed to Min that he had fashioned himself into the ultimate Champion; ever alert, always on guard, even among friends, as though he didn't dare to relax from his duties, lest he betray the trust laid upon him. In the strength of his body and the way he held himself, he unconsciously communicated to her watchful eyes that he had, through endless repetition, become at ease with his own body and the movements required of one who wields arms for a living. Gone was the awkward boy who strove without hope to fill his father's shoes. Gone was the unformed youth whose aptitude with wood and stone had set him apart for further skilled training. In that revealing moment, Min could not quite credit that in less than a year Robse had become comfortable in his role as warrior. It went against his very nature, yet that dichotomy did not show in his manner or bearing. She searched him until her persistent gaze brought his eyes around to hers.

In the gray depths of those eyes, she found what she sought. The tortured passion was aflame there, in the depths he kept so carefully hidden. There lurked the open wounds of grief and self-doubt, quickly veiled by the sweep of his fair lashes. Min wondered how none of them had seen it. As she had suspected, this was one of them who was not healing from the pain of loss. With sudden insight, she saw that he was striving to heal his pain by driving himself to become those he had lost. He was trying to be Riende the protector; Laslorn the older brother; Theomanus, ever faithful to his duty and calling.

He was doing his best to replace their loss with himself, shaping his life and soul to become them, as much as he was able. Min knew it was an impossible task, for he had never been designed to be any of them, let alone all of them! It seemed from the torment in his eyes that Robse sensed his failure too. But, it appeared, he blamed himself for his inadequacy instead of recognizing that it was a task he was never meant to fulfill. Min began to worry, then changed her mind and began to pray, with a sharp intensity, that the Creator would somehow reveal to them a way to stop this transformation before Robse himself disappeared into the shadow person he was creating.

Minlienda moved her violet gaze to another group of her companions, even as she continued to lift Robse up to the Lord. Her eyes rested next upon young Netharos, nestled comfortably between his mother and one of his friends. Though the boy's father had perished in the battle, and his mother had been lost among the wounded, Min remembered the joy of the day they had been able to reunite mother and son. Netharos's two best friends, his *amia* brothers, had been orphaned in that last terrible week. That crushing blow had fallen upon so many of their precious children, and it was one of the deepest griefs her people had to bear. Min was pleased to note that the healing of the three boys was aided by the unstinting love of Netharos's mother, Domiella, who had adopted them all. It had been a rare blessing tonight to hear Netharos's music again, for the boy hadn't been able to play since he had lost his father. Min had great hopes that the undeniable gift of his music would further help him to heal.

Her eyes moved next to her right. Two or three Elves beyond, Min noticed Myrandella settling into the circle. She was glad for this, for she had come to enjoy the shy, almost fierce nature of Gaelcar's young assistant. Certainly, there was more to her than met the eye, even the discerning eye of an Elf, mused Min. There was something more than mere shyness that hovered behind those piercing green eyes. Well, she would not probe, though she would like to get to know the girl better. Perhaps tonight's relaxed atmosphere would be a good time to hear a little about this new member of their company.

Chapter Twenty

Although Myrandella was typically more comfortable when she was alone, she realized with some surprise that she had come to enjoy the evening company of the other Elves aboard the *Cethastea.* Though she seldom spoke during their gatherings, she enjoyed the music and singing and hearing the stories others told of their lives before they were forced to leave the Land. Tonight, she had silently joined the edge of the circle of friends on the main deck, prepared to enjoy another such evening, but for once, her predictions proved false.

The warm, gentle voice of Minlienda began the evening's exchange, as the dark-haired Elf turned to Myrandella with a friendly question, interest shining in her violet eyes.

"So, Randa, what was it like growing up in the higher elevations? My home was on the lower slopes of those same mountains, but I never ventured so high."

All feelings of comfort vanished, and Randa suddenly felt trapped under the friendly gaze of her companions as they smiled at her and encouraged her to share her past with them. She forced her lips to part, hoping to iterate a quick story that would satisfy her friends and divert their attention.

"Well... my home was separated from the nearest neighbor by nearly five miles, through the wilderness," she began hesitantly. Encouraging interest forced her to continue. "I was the only child in the household, so it wasn't often that I saw anyone my age. Sometimes, if we traveled to attend a festival or a celebration, I would meet another young person, but there was never enough time to become friends." Still, Randa smiled to herself, recalling the happy memories she had accumulated at those special occasions.

Recalling her audience, which had grown as latecomers had joined them, she hastened to conclude her tale. "My mother kept a garden, but we ranged all through the forests for the plants she needed. She taught me all she could about healing: which plants could be used to treat diseases and how to cure various illnesses. She knew so much about it; I can't remember more than four days of my life when I was sick. Most of the time, there was no one to play with or to talk to, except the Creator, of course. I liked it though. The solitude never disturbed me."

Randa finished speaking, glad to retire from the spotlight. On the other side of Min, her *amia* sister, the fiery Caerdrys, stirred. She leaned forward to look past Min at Randa. The knowing look in her eyes warned Randa that the Elven woman had heard the tales surrounding her birth and wasn't going to let her go without sharing them. She could not know how painful that attention would be to the shy Myrandella, for there wasn't a retiring bone in Caerdrys's body. Randa's eyes closed, seeking to avoid the subject, but Caerdrys's voice was clear and commanding, carrying across the ring of faces easily.

"Randa! You must tell them of Elrad and the prophecy over your life! Tell of your dreams—you have become his replacement now, after all."

That aroused the interest of the remaining Elves! They turned to her once again, eyebrows raised. Randa had really hoped that she would not be called upon to tell this story—the one tale guaranteed to set her apart from all others and forever distance her from potential friends. At the various gatherings and celebrations her family had attended in her childhood, this story had made others gawk at her and set her apart and murmur among themselves. They were awed and joyful, quick to tell her that she had been given a gift that was significant beyond imagination. But Randa, shy and wanting only to belong, had shifted nervously and attempted to draw attention away from herself. As she'd grown older and resigned to the odd gift and the lack of friends, Randa had ceased accompanying her parents down the mountainside. She had roamed the wild hillsides and had grown ever shyer and more reclusive, until most folks had forgotten her existence.

Now, in the midst of circumstances that forced her to be among people, she had begun to allow the walls of her heart to come down. She had begun to forge friendships with Minlienda and Ciella. Now, with a few casual words of friendly intent, Caerdrys had closed those doors. Just as the others had done at the gatherings in her childhood, her new companions were leaning toward her, encouraging her to tell them the most prominent chapter of her past. Swallowing the lump that was forming in her throat, Randa began to tell the tale, trying in vain to make the story sound as ordinary as she possibly could.

"Before my birth, the prophet Elrad came to my home, following the prompting of a vision. Of course, he was well received, and my entire family waited with anticipation to see what would become of his dream. The day my mother gave birth to me, Elrad joined the rest of my family in watching over me and praying for my healthy childhood. When he saw me for the first time, the Creator spoke to him, and he prophesied that I was the one He had provided to replace the Kythos when he could no longer be with us. Kythos Elrad said that my life would be a bitter journey, a constant striving through toil and anguish toward whatever Aematlon planned for me, hence my name."

The entire gathering upon the deck was silent, every Elf staring wide-eyed at Randa, who deliberately kept her eyes down to avoid meeting theirs. She felt the familiar turmoil rise in her heart as the pregnant silence stretched. She felt again the bitter bile in her throat at the thought that any would hear her story and think she felt worthy of this burden, the "gift" she had been given. She, more than most, mourned the mysterious passing of the wise old Elf, the Seer and prophet of his long generation. She trembled at the thought of filling his place, bearing the vague, haunting dreams and rendering the service of interpreting them when she could. No Seer wanted to bring messages of bad tidings, and she dreaded the visions she would be required to See.

Afraid that the silence surrounding her held condemnation for the recent losses, she flushed uncomfortably and fought with a throat suddenly tight. How could she make these trusting people understand that they could not expect from her the abundant wisdom and insightful knowledge of her predecessor, Elrad? What if they ignored her warnings and still entrusted her with too much responsibility? She would fail them, as she had already failed to save her own family! Finally, she could bear what she perceived as a strained silence no more.

"Please believe me that I had no warning of the Goblin massacre! I knew no more than anyone else! I saw nothing! I don't know why. Surely the Creator would have warned us of such a horrible event, but I swear I dreamed nothing of it!" Her voice was low, but it throbbed with the tortured anguish of one who had blamed herself for a great calamity. At first, no one responded. Randa raised her eyes, fearful of what she might see, but found only surprise in the eyes that gazed steadily back at her. Gaelcar cleared his throat, drawing their attention.

"We know that the Creator does not warn of every event, nor do we know why He chooses the things He does to show to our Kython. Still, if we needed warning of the hostilities to the south, we received them. Elrad himself, and Queen Elwyn, sent warnings to King Beregos. I heard them myself. No one here expects you to have warned us a third time, Kytha."

Randa drew an unsteady breath but saw the truth of Gaelcar's words reflected in the eyes turned once again to her. Relief filled her in a dizzying wave, but she felt it necessary to try to make them see that while she would do what she must, and to the best of her ability, she could never replace the wise, kindly old Seer.

"Since we discovered Elrad was no longer with us, I have had dreams. Sometimes, the Creator will tell me directly what He wants me, or others, to do, but usually not. Mostly, I just wait to understand them, for they are unclear." Many who had heard Elrad speak of his dreams now nodded their heads, for the words were familiar. Randa went on. "Recently, I have been having dreams of an island that appears out of the mist and the sea, less than a mile from the ship. I do not know if this is symbolic or real, but it is what I have Seen."

Randa stopped speaking and, gathering all her courage, looked about the area. The others still were looking at her, their eyes wide with awe. Randa desperately wished that someone would break the silence and bring the conversation back to the light, fun bantering she had learned to love. After what seemed like an eternity, Caerdrys extended her hand to touch Randa's, her eyes filled with respect.

"It is a great honor to share company with a Kytha."

Randa smiled nervously, wishing for the ability to disappear. Sensing her discomfort, Aelric addressed his companions.

"Several years ago, when many had left to join the Goblin Wars in the South, Elrad told me that the Creator had purposefully made me a warrior. At the time, I could not understand the meaning of his words, since I was frustrated and anxious about not being allowed to join the battles. Only now do I realize what he meant. Now, in this time we could not foresee, but which the Lord knew when He created each of us, you have a need for a warrior king, a thing our people have not needed in many generations.

"Sometimes, with the limitations placed on us here in this fallen world, we cannot see how the difficult things we are given can be borne. Yet, He calls them gifts and shows us in His own time how He will use us in His purposes. When we are beset with doubts, let us remind ourselves of what Elrad so often repeated: Aematlon's will shall not be thwarted; His plans shall come to pass. Let us trust in Him to see to our protection and growth. We are not now what we once were, and yet He has given us exactly what we need to continue to serve Him.

"I, your king, am needed as a warrior among my people. You, Myrandella, are needed as our Seer. Our Lord prepared you, not Elrad, to accompany us, and I trust in Him to know what we will need."

Randa looked up quickly, and for a brief second, her vivid emerald eyes locked with Aelric's golden ones. So he had seen her misgivings! Those words were meant for her comfort she knew, even as the other Elves began to ponder their meaning in quiet conversations. But his words were like one of her visions; she had to interpret their meaning carefully, something that required a bit more solitude than the warm circle granted.

Quietly, she rose and moved away to lean on the forward guardrail.

As the remaining Elves pondered Aelric's words, Randa smiled to herself, giving the king her unspoken thanks. She understood now what her rebellious heart had been unable to grasp before. She could not doubt that the Creator had made her a Kytha on purpose, and assuredly He knew her limitations. Though the dreams she would be given would guide the Faeltheon in His ways, He would never expect her to lead His people; that was not the function for which she had been chosen.

A small feeling of comfort unfurled within her, and the heavy burden of the task she must bear lifted slightly from her chest. She still didn't understand why she hadn't been able to save her family, but now she could trust that if the Lord wanted a shy, solitary girl to speak His will to His people, she would submit. The Creator had given everyone talents, and with them responsibilities, as *He* had seen fit. Aelric was needed as a warrior, and she was needed as a prophetess. All that her Maker expected of her was her best effort in fulfilling His work. As her fellow Elves bowed their heads in prayer before departing to their beds for the night, Randa prayed silently that she would always be willing to do just that.

She tilted her head back to see the vast heavens, seeking out her favorite stars. Seeing them brought feelings of comfort, memories of her home, long gone. Randa lowered her gaze from the sky for a moment to eye the black waves, and her heart began to beat faster. She couldn't understand why she felt this increase in tension, but it was unmistakable. She strained her eyes again, seeking the source of her unease. Surely there was something looming out there in the dark. She wanted to call out to the others, to alert them to the strangeness she felt, but she daren't take her eyes from the sea.

There *was* something out there; she could just barely make out a form. She blinked her eyes to make sure that they weren't mistaken, but they weren't. An island loomed in the distance, directly in the ship's path. Randa heard her own voice cry out, and all the Elves crowded around her, eyes wide with hope, each searching the emerald island for the signs that it was to be their new home.

Not knowing why, Randa was certain that it was indeed the home for which they had been searching. Laughing with delight, she leaned forward slightly to see the sunny isle better. What was that on the shore? Silence dropped over the excited crowds on the ships, and her companions gasped as they considered the unthinkable. Shadowy forms were walking toward them, on *their* island! They were smiling and waving a welcome to the Faeltheon, but that didn't change the fact that they were *there*. Randa felt a lump forming in her throat. What could this mean? Were these strange inhabitants as friendly as they first appeared? Were they Faeltheon? But how could that be? And, if they weren't Kin, who were they? How would they react upon learning that the Elves wanted to live on the island?

Stunned with shock, she wrenched her gaze from the sunlit seas back toward her companions on the ship to see what they were thinking, only to find that she was alone in the dark night. A strange feeling settled in the pit of Randa's stomach, and she turned back to the water, anticipating that the island, too, was no longer there. As she had expected, only the endless miles of starlit sea filled her view in every direction.

It had been a vision.

Chapter Twenty-One

The day began early, before the eastern sky had pearled light into the sea. Min pushed up the sleeves of her blouse for the third time in as many minutes as her busy hands deftly twisted the ropes of dough to make the traditional braided sweet bread used in the blessing ceremony. Ciella's long fingers reached over and rolled the errant sleeves up, tucking them securely above Min's elbows. Min flashed her a grateful smile and turned to brush the plump loaves with beaten egg and honey before sliding them into the hot ovens. The galley hummed with activity and happy murmurs as the women worked to prepare the feast they would all share this afternoon. In a few hours, the regular cooking crew would arrive to prepare the first shift of breakfast, so the bakers needed to be finished by then.

An hour later, Min stood upon the half deck above the galley, glorying in the fresh breeze and adding her voice to the morning song that welcomed the sun as it rose. All over the ship, Elves were pausing to note the sunrise and sing praise to the Creator for the beauty of the day. Min heard the clear voices raised on either side as well, as those aboard the *Dridelphanen* and the *Gaelrandel* joined in the song. The seductive scent of sweetness and cinnamon and freshly baked bread coaxed both young and old onto the deck, and Min rushed down the steps to add her voice to the teasing and laughter that protected the feast treats until their proper time.

Later, in their cabin under the quarterdeck, Min sat very still, holding the colored ribbons until Caerdrys asked for them, as her *amia* sister skillfully wove them into Min's dark hair. She was wearing a new dress, one made from fine lavender fabric Ciella had woven during the many hours confined below decks. Min herself had embroidered the deep bands of sylvan designs on neck, sleeves, and hem. She had sat for many evenings on deck, as the stories and songs swept back and forth about the circle and wove them into a community, and her needle had flashed silently in and out, trailing silver and gold, amethyst and amber, crimson and emerald threads, telling their own tale of the beloved Land left behind. Now she finally had an occasion to wear the lovely dress, for Fyllys and Hederos would wed this day.

Min smiled afresh, catching a glimpse of Caerdrys in her new finery, a dress the color of the water in the lagoon to the south of the tiny island where they had taken refuge from the storm. The clear turquoise blended subtly with a shining jade green, colors that complemented Caerdrys's midnight hair and rain-colored eyes. Many hours of delicate embroidery had fashioned the heart-shaped leaves of the *cathelath* vine, which set off Caerdrys's bold beauty perfectly and were worth every loving stitch Min had put into them.

That Caerdrys was not suited to such peaceful, repetitive pastimes as embroidery had long been acknowledged between the sisters. In their long years together, they had companionably fallen into patterns of serving one another in their strengths and compensating for each other's weaknesses. Min remembered fondly the snug little home they had shared, tucked into the foothills of the mountains two days' journey northeast of the Elven City on the coast. The sisters had made a cozy little home, with a kitchen, a sitting room with a fireplace and several comfortable chairs, a few small tables to hold whatever projects they were working on, and cheerful braided rugs. They had had bedrooms in the loft, and had shared a bathing chamber just behind the kitchen, convenient to the hot water.

Min could remember typical evenings before the fire, working on her embroidery or mending the frequent rips in Caerdrys's clothing, listening to her sister's voice as she read to them from a book of poetry, or, more often, some stirring tale of the past. Caerdrys's favorite tales had been of the brave and heroic deeds done by various Faeltheon ancestors, and had often involved scenes of battles fought and lives sacrificed. Inevitably, her voice would burst forth, rich with passion, and she would follow the story to its end, gesturing broadly and pacing before the crackling fire in the hearth. Min nearly chuckled aloud at the thought of Caerdrys's flushed face and shining eyes after such a recitation. How her sister had loved tales of glory and bravery! How she had longed to do such deeds, to be such a one as valiant tales were woven about.

And now? Min wondered. *What now? In the midst of such perils, sorrows, passions, and sacrifices as we are currently experiencing, surely Caerdrys's wishes will come true. I wonder if it feels as glorious to live it as it sounds to read it aloud before a cheery fire in a safe home. Certainly, our hardships seemed to have affected her nature and stamina not at all… except perhaps during our confinement, but that is understandable. In the old tales, Caerdrys loved the scenes of battle and valiant action the best, yet it seemed to me that the heroes in those stirring tales were not particularly brave; they just did what needed to be done when it came up and persevered until it was over. Still, if keeping your head and your spirits, persevering even against terrible odds, and helping others with every ounce of your ability is what it means to be a hero, she certainly is one. I wonder if this is what she thought being a hero would be like.*

Shaking her head briskly, both to dispel her thoughts and to hear the tinkling of the tiny bells woven into her hair ribbons, Min turned her attention to readying Caerdrys for the coming celebration.

As Fyllys lived aboard the *Cethastea* and Hederos hailed from the *Dridelphanen*, Hederos would, of course, defer to her comfort, and so the new couple would live on the *Cethastea.* One of the *Cethastea's* single males was happy to transfer to Hederos's old lodgings, and the young woman who had been sharing quarters with Fyllys moved into another's room to make a home for the new couple.

In the absence of the traditional settings and people, the remnant of the Faeltheon found themselves creating new customs. Neither Fyllys nor Hederos had living parents to speak the words to seal their covenant, the binding of the two into one. And, as their new home had not been built by the willing hands of their *amia* family, it was uncertain who should present the Blessing of the New Home. Finally, it was decided that Myrandella, as their Kythos, would speak the marriage vows for them; Aelric, as their leader, would speak the Blessing; and Caerdrys, as his nearest female kin, would proffer the Gifts of Welcome.

The ceremony took place on the broad deck of the *Cethastea*, with fully two-thirds of the watchers observing from lofty perches in the radlings. If Myrandella was nervous at her first public duties, she didn't show it. Her voice rose, pure and steady, as she spoke the traditional words and lifted in turn the items representing the three elements from which the Faeltheon had been created. The light of a Faerie wick glimmered faintly in the strong afternoon sunlight, as Randa cupped it in her palms to represent starlight. When she released it to hold aloft the silver cup of dew, the tiny Faerie wick settled itself in the crook of her neck, like a misplaced earring, and gently illuminated the young Kytha's intent expression. Lastly, she held up a prism into the light, and, with a mature sensitivity surprising in one so young, angled it so the resulting rainbow fell across the happy lovers. A great sigh of contentment rippled through the crowd as the ceremony closed, for a wedding represented hope and promise of future happiness, and they all took the omen to themselves with jealous joy.

It seemed neither the food nor the fiddlers could keep up with the pace of people determined to wring every morsel of happiness from the occasion. The dancing and singing, the feasting and toasting, the laughter and lightheartedness seemed to go on for days, though it was really only until sunset. As the sun retired behind ragged streamers of clouds whose windy edges were too many miles away to affect them, the revelers dropped by twos and threes into happy clusters across the decks and aeries of the *Cethastea*.

Replete with merriment and good food, they fell silent to watch the miracle of colors that was poured forth to end their happy day. One of those standing at the forward rail lifted up his arms and began to sing an ancient song of praise to the Creator. Many voices joined in, until the song swelled out from the vessel and the other two ships caught on and joined in. A shiver of pure joy rippled up her spine, as Min lifted her voice in the second chorus.

Hlalashel yeon yom ashon russ
Hlalashyom mianatlan domel dyseliseh
Hlalashyom eon amadali eliseh
Hlalash elsaenos, elaem.

A sudden image brought a sting of tears to her eyes. She saw them, as if from a distance, like a gull on the wing; what was left of the once mighty race of the Faeltheon, encapsulated in three tiny ships upon the vast bosom of the sea, joined as one in praise of the Creator and His works.

More Faerie wicks were coaxed to light in the gathering dimness of evening, and the solemn, yet joyful company made its way below the decks, to escort the married couple to their new quarters. Many would not fit down there, of course, so most stayed above, cleaning up the few scraps of leftovers.

Due to the crush of the goodnatured crowd, Min got only as far as the third step from the bottom on the companionway. As it happened, this was fortunate, as it enabled her to see over the heads of her companions to the little ceremony being played out before the couple's door. The two newlyweds stood in the open doorway of their cabin, while Aelric and Caerdrys faced them from the corridor, with the crowd swelling up and down its length. Though the patterned basket her sister held was covered by a brightly woven cloth, Min knew what it contained, for she had packed it with her own hands. Two of the shining braided loaves, a beautifully glazed crock of sweet butter, and a tightly covered mortar containing sugar, ground with cinnamon, comprised the traditional gift for a new home. Caerdrys's hands were trembling slightly, Min noticed, and there was a heightened color in Aelric's face as he began the traditional chant used in so many Faeltheon ceremonies. Wavering at first, his voice quickly settled into its customary rich baritone.

Cybel ash emon
Cybel thal emon
Cyb eron randel
Reg emon doma

Aelric sang all four verses of the ancient song, one of the oldest known among them. When the last note had faded away, Caerdrys held out her basket and Fyllys took it. Caerdrys spoke the traditional blessing.

"Receive from us bread; that you and yours may know no want or need. Receive from us butter; that you may know the rich and abundant provision of our Creator. Receive from us sugar; that your life together may be sweet. Receive from us spices; that your days may be enlivened by joy and pleasant surprises."

Caerdrys looked so relieved when she had successfully completed the ritual that those nearby laughed in camaraderie. Joyful wishes and blessings were shouted out from the crowd, and then the door was closed behind the couple and people began to surge back up the companionways to the upper decks.

A tired Minlienda was heading down the passageway in the sterncastle, hoping to reach the peace of her chamber before another need arose. She knew from experience that Caerdrys would be up most of the night, listening to the tales being told around the main deck, for the stories had turned to the days of old and the glorious deeds done by those now passed away into the uncertain mists of death. Min well knew this sort of evening was nourishment to Caerdrys's very soul, but she herself was weary enough to sleep through the tale of the Three Sisters!

Just as her hand closed around the smooth coldness of her door handle, she heard the passageway door open behind her. Expecting one of the Companions, who were the only ones chambered in this level of the sterncastle, Min was surprised to see Myrandella hurrying toward her. At the look on the girl's face, Min straightened and turned to face her. Before the Kytha spoke, Min knew something was wrong, and her spirit shook off its weariness and rose to meet the new challenge.

"Min, you must help me!" Randa exclaimed, her usual composure dropped away to reveal a nervous fear.

"What has happened?"

"It's good news really—another blessing in a day already full of them—but I need your help!" the young Kytha replied quickly. "Leawyn is birthing and is asking for *me*! I've never been to a birthing before—I wouldn't know what to do! But I'm told you are one of the few of us left with experience in this area. Please come with me!"

Min chuckled at the girl's nearly panicked expression. She felt a fresh joy rising within her at the thought of a new life beginning among them tonight! This would mark the first birth since their exile. And, so far as she knew, the first Faeltheon born at sea!

"Of course I'll come! And don't worry; Leawyn is very healthy and strong. Just let me step into my quarters for some supplies and then we'll cross over to the *Gaelrandel*."

The birthing had gone well, and the tiny newborn looked strong and healthy. Min finished wrapping the stained cloths into the bundle for burning, as Myrandella handed the tiny boy to his father. The look on Randa's face when the newly washed form had been laid in her arms to be blessed by the Kytha had tightened Min's throat and brought tears to her eyes. She recalled that Randa had said she was raised in a remote, high mountain area, so this was the first baby she'd ever held. The miracle of the new little soul in their midst had touched the Kytha deeply. Min knew Randa would forever have a soft spot in her heart for this child.

Tall Ethanos passed his son to his wife and knelt beside her bed to hold them both. They exchanged tender looks and smiles while examining their tiny, perfect son. Then they looked up at Min and Myrandella, who served as both witnesses and family in this event. Leawyn smiled broadly.

"His name is Gaelal, for he was born upon the shining sea," she announced. Then Ethanos laid his hand upon his son and Leawyn placed hers over his and they began to sing the lullaby that welcomed every newborn Faeltheon.

Hlalriel aímon eorsa mynovos
Nov aímon don caertheon
Eorsa ash ímon
Gelig lihti astea
Lulla, nov ayapanos, lindeos
Thallari íron behereti aemm
Gwenna, íroncaer, íronaemm,
Íronagen, íronatlan.

As tradition dictated, when the parents finished the first round, Min and Myrandella picked up the song. As their notes faded, they could hear the voices of those in the cabins on either side and in the corridor picking up the song. In a few more rounds, the melody was carried in to them through the open porthole from the surrounding ships. The singing voices fairly vibrated with sweetness and rejoicing over the addition of Gaelal to their number. It had been a day full of such blessings Min thought she might shiver apart with it.

Laslorn sighed in pure bliss as, replete with good food and congenial company, he flopped back against a slope of lacy green ferns. A moment later, his joy was complete, as his wife nestled her fiery head into the curve of his shoulder. He drew her close and contentedly spit out one of her floating locks. Nausika giggled, knowing he loved holding her so and would gladly put up with her hair in his face. An answering chuckle from the left announced that Elwyn, Nausika's beloved *amia* sister, had witnessed the byplay.

"We are so blessed…" came the soft murmur of Theo's voice. Through his barely opened eyes, Las could see the confirming nod of Lucina's bright head. The goodnatured smile on his face broadened into its characteristic grin as he noticed Lucina lobbing ripe grapes at her reclining husband. Davin was doing a decent job catching most of them in his mouth, but there were a few purple globes scattered down the gentle slope of the bank where the friends rested. A whir of wings caused Laslorn to look up, just as their friend Kier came into view through the willows above them.

"Down here!" called Davin, and Kier gestured to friends on foot behind him. Shortly, they were joined by Kier, Cador, Michal, Aoneth, Rablorn, and the twins, Glimring and Geltheon. The friends made room and all settled comfortably among the ferns and moss of the riverbank. Laslorn was happy to note the soft color blooming in the cheeks of Kier's *amia* sister, Michal, and the tender way Aoneth took care to see her served with tea and fruit.

After a companionable silence had melted into the heavy golden light of late afternoon, Rablorn stirred, turning toward Theomanus. Those who had drifted into naps awoke to his question.

"Theo, what were you and Elrad Kythos discussing so solemnly last evening? Is there trouble? Here?"

Theomanus sat up, shaking his sable head and stretching. Idly, he began picking broken fronds of fern from Elwyn's long, gilt hair.

"No, no trouble, Rab. We were just having another try at interpreting the purpose of Marliondolen."

"Purpose?" interjected Laslorn, surprised. "I thought its purpose was to be a shelter and home for us when the Humans took over the Land."

Theo nodded, his golden eyes holding a brighter light than Las remembered.

"That is certainly its function," the Master of Marliondolen confirmed. "But we were wondering why we are here; what we are to learn; in what ways we are to grow."

"Where else should we be?" asked Davin, his open face drawn in a puzzled frown.

"Actually, I have been wondering something of that sort too," Lucina's crisp voice contributed. "Are we dead? After all, when we arrived, we found here before us those we had thought dead. And if we are dead, like Humans die, why are we not permitted to be in the Presence of the

Creator once again, as in the days of old?" The companions gazed at her with respect. Lucina was known for her twin credos of duty and honor, but few suspected the deep thoughtfulness of her quiet nature. Theo answered her smoothly, as one who had wrestled with these very questions and arrived at answers that brought at least a measure of peace.

"Elrad and I have discussed these very ideas," he replied. "We both believe that our Kindred left behind in the Land would likely think us dead, for we are simply no longer there. But, although our friends who awaited us here claimed to have only just arrived before we did, we also know that time flows differently here in Marliondolen than it did in the Land. Certainly, the Creator may arrange time as He desires to accomplish His plans. Elrad believes, as do I, that the reason we were not ushered directly into the Presence of the Creator, but rather were brought to this delightful place, is because we still have growing, learning, and becoming to accomplish. We feel strongly that the Creator desires us to continue to mature through our experiences, not the least of which is experiencing the many evidences of His great love for us."

The others nodded feelingly. Marliondolen was beautiful beyond what they could have imagined in the Land, and even they themselves had been transformed upon entering the magic realm. Many had thought, when they beheld their own transformations, that they had at last come home to a place their souls had longed for time out of mind: the Presence of their Maker. There had been some disappointment when persistent searching had not found the Person of Aematlon in their midst, but it was impossible to remain downcast in the face of the beauty and bounty He had lovingly prepared for them. Theo watched the faces of his friends and saw the combinations of understanding and confusion in their eyes.

"What we don't have yet are the answers to the question *how*? We're not sure in what ways the Creator wants us to grow and change, only that He does and that He will surely show us His desire in His timing. Last night," he remarked with a mischievous gleam to Rablorn, "Elrad was counseling me *again* to wait upon the Lord and rest assured that He would show me what to do when the time is right." The friends all chuckled at this,

Laslorn going so far as to throw a stray grape at his adopted brother, for they all knew how Theo tended to think *he* had to accomplish the will of the Creator instead of allowing the Lord to work through him.

Into the pleasant banter came a shimmering that raised the hairs along their napes. As the almost-perceived rainbow solidified above the river, they gathered to watch whatever it would show them. The sense of expectation increased, for the Creator's windows onto the Earth gave them clues to what He wanted of them.

The scene within the window clarified into a celebration of some sort, on the deck of one of the three Elven ships. Laslorn thought it was the *Cethastea* by the colors. As they watched, the sounds began to come to them too; songs and the flying music of the fiddles, clapping and the rhythmic drumming of dancing feet. The watchers perceived that the ships were in a still place upon the ocean and that they had linked themselves by means of slender, swaying rope bridges, reminiscent of the tree homes of the Land. There was a brisk traffic upon those bridges, as busy, happy folk, dressed in their finest, gathered to celebrate a wedding.

Theo felt a tightness in his spirit begin to relax as he watched and realized that a part of his heart had been stiff with worry over the grim fate of his Kin and the terrible weight of their grief. Observing this rich festivity, his heart eased some. They were finding occasion to take joy. They were healing, though it would be a long, slow process. Even the faint air of determination he sensed in their laughter didn't dissuade him, for he knew how painful and difficult it could be to allow oneself to take joy while still grieving. He was inexpressibly grateful for the feel of his wife's hand nestling into his as they watched, for he knew she understood and shared all his heart was too full to speak.

They watched in healing content, sharing the joy of their distant Kin, until the window faded into shades of twilight, both there and about them.

Chapter Twenty-Two

Midmorning the next day found Theo in a broad green meadow, several miles from their usual haunts. He was searching for a particular flower he knew Elwyn loved, for he felt a pressing need to bring her a gift to show her something of the depth of his love for her. He knew she understood his heart, for they had had many comfortable hours of sweet converse on the subject since arriving in Marliondolen, but he couldn't escape the fact that they hadn't had time for a courtship before their hasty state wedding. Though he had lost no time beginning a belated courtship once they had arrived in this sanctuary, a state of affairs that delighted his young bride, he found himself wanting to give her the special moments she had been denied by their whirlwind marriage and subsequent flight from the Land.

He gazed around the field, hoping to see the distinctive blue he sought and suddenly felt the flower was a foolish idea. It was silly to think a single blossom, however rare and beautiful, could begin to symbolize the many things he wanted to say to her heart. Feeling somewhat at a loss and knowing he could have no better confidant or guide in matters of the heart, Theo turned his soul to the Creator.

After a time, peace descended on him and he lifted his head. His mind's eye was flooded with the images of the wedding they'd been permitted to watch yesterday. Though the friends had discussed the vision and were pretty sure the purpose had been to show them the progress of their Kin in overcoming their grief, Theo found himself searching on a more personal level. He had not been intimately acquainted with either bride or groom, though seeing Aelric and Caerdrys play their parts had given rise to friendly laughter, mixed with pangs of nostalgia. He found himself awash in memories of their years together in the Court of the Elven King, Beregos. The bittersweet memories merged into a contrast between the Elven wedding and the Faerie ceremony he had attended. The Faeries had the same rituals and grand, solemn, joyful words, but their celebrations were slightly different, with special dances and songs and foods.

At their own wedding, which had been modified for many reasons, not the least of which were their desperate circumstances, Theo had regretted that Elwyn's transparently fragile health and his own lack of wings had required the omission of so many symbolic acts. He recalled one that had stuck in his mind, for he had hoped it would not be perceived by the crowds as a sign of weakness in their union or their future.

The dance central to the festivities following a Faerie wedding involved concentric rings of dancers who passed one another in different directions and interwove with each other in a complex and beautiful pattern intended to symbolize the unity of the people. These tiers of players circled out from the center of the dance, where the newly married couple danced their own steps. The outer ring was composed of single males. Within their ring was the circle of single females. The inner ring, surrounding the newlyweds, was made of married couples, hand in hand, wrists bound with brightly colored ribbons depicting joy, love, and fruitfulness.

As the rings of dancers wove their complicated patterns in and out and around one another, the new husband and wife circled one another, first in one direction, then in the other. They came together, then drew apart, returning together to circle one another again, in a dance that symbolized their courtship and decision to commit to one another. At the climax of the passionate music, all the whirling, stomping bodies stopped, going down on one knee to observe the married couple in the center.

In Elven weddings, the bride would circle her husband as he spun in place for as many revolutions as he could manage before dizziness cast him, laughing and breathless, to the floor in his wife's arms. The duration of his part symbolized his devotion to his bride and his ability to protect her. Her circling of him indicated her desire and intent to surround him in love and comfort. Many goodnatured jests on the stamina of the husband's spinning were expected from the friends and family. It was all part of the camaraderie of such rituals.

In the Faerie dance, however, the husband and wife, as a symbol of their new unity and their ability to work together, were expected to put their arms around one another and to rise upwards in a tight spiral of flight. This was extremely difficult, especially to two unused to each other's movements, for it was easy to foul their wings on one another or to fly at different speeds. It was also difficult to manage a spiral, for that required one of them, usually the husband, due to his larger size, to dominate just slightly, so that his wing strokes propelled them a little faster than hers did. Those couples who could perform this part of the dance with effortless grace were said to be so absorbed in their love for each other that they never noticed those around them. In truth, they were mostly desperately counting together, so as not to falter in mid-air. Many couples practiced the maneuver for weeks before their wedding, hoping not to embarrass themselves.

At their wedding, Theo recalled, Elwyn had been so fragile, she had been unable to rise from her throne to join the dance at all. Though he needed to conserve his own strength for the ordeal that lay ahead the next day, Theo had wanted to show her something of his earnest desire and intent to protect her and her people to the best of his abilities.

Knowing she was watching, hoping she was understanding something of his silent pledge, he had danced alone in the center of their circle. When the time came for all to kneel and watch him, he had flung himself into a tight spin, calling upon all the supple training of swordfights and the endurance of long hours of prayer to force his body to obey him in these moments. He had fastened his gaze on his beloved, whipping his head around to her again and again, so fast that it seemed to him their gazes never broke. Each revolution, his right leg touched down and sprang off again while his left stayed in place; heel and toe, heel and toe.

As the spinning had continued, awed murmurs had provided a quiet backdrop to the singing fiddle and the wailing pipes. If he could have broken into exultant flight he would have done so. He'd felt the depth and power of his love for her filling him with a light he almost couldn't bear. Finally, not knowing what else to do, the musicians had wound up the music with a resounding crash, and Theo had brought both feet down in a defiant, ringing, wide-legged stamp that had left him motionless, staring into her eyes.

There had been no question of the power he was willing to use to protect her and, symbolically through her, her people.

But now, all this time later, in the gentle fields of Marliondolen, when she was safe and strong and he wanted to show her his love, he was at a loss. Remembering the Elven wedding glimpsed yesterday, and feeling a desire to make up to her something of what they'd never had, Theo wished he could fly. If, like his wife, like the rest of his Faerie Kin, he could rise off the ground when his spirit felt light with love, he knew they could fly a beautiful spiral dance. Hadn't they found how well they worked together? Hadn't they continued to become more attuned to one another over the months they had reveled in each other's company here in this green sanctuary? If they could dance this flight together, Theo felt sure it would be the most stunning marriage flight ever made.

An urgent desire welled up in him to fling himself into the sky and feel it receive him gently and bid him stay aloft, above the world his feet sought to escape. Beautiful as the world was, much as he loved and cherished it, suddenly Theomanus resented being chained to its surface, unable to experience the heady joys of tumbling, suspended, in the envelope above.

He closed his eyes and allowed himself to imagine, just for a moment, the joy of playing tag with his wife among the clouds, of darting into a rainbow and through the spray of a waterfall, of swooping and diving in an exhilarating dance that could not be recaptured on solid ground. He gloried in the sensation of weightlessness and laughed as he felt the wind stream over him like dry water and pull his hair back from his face. It was the sound of his own laughter, unexpectedly dragged from his mouth to disappear in the wind, that caused Theo to open his eyes to reality again.

The sight of the field far below his feet shocked him to silence.

Nausika and Laslorn strolled hand in hand along an avenue of white birch trees. Heads tipped back, they drank in the lovely sight of the bright sunlight drenching through the delicate, translucent lime green leaves. The incredible peace and beauty charged Laslorn's senses to a tingling awareness he found almost unbearable. Unable to find words profound enough to express his feelings, he resorted to playfulness, sneaking his arm around and dancing his fingers into his wife's ribs.

With a yelp of startled laughter, Nausika darted out of reach, springing into the air to flee him. Laughing, teasing, he pursued her till a lucky, long-armed grab caught her by a slim ankle. He hauled her down to him and she willingly paid her forfeit in a kiss. As they broke apart, Nausika noted the dreamy look in Laslorn's dark green eyes. Quick as a flash, she reached up and tugged his dapper cap down over his eyes, fleeing ahead, knowing he would follow. His shout of outrage was drowned in laughter as he caught up to her and they burst from the shelter of the trees into a broad, sunny meadow.

Nausika stopped a step ahead of him and Laslorn skidded to a halt between her wings, following her line of sight. A shocked gasp escaped him as he beheld Theo and Elwyn clasped in one another's arms.

This wasn't at all unusual. It was the fact that they were fifty feet off the ground, rotating in a gentle spiral, that took his breath away.

That evening, the garden, bridge, and stream bank behind the clustered homes of Elrad, Beregos and Ashwyn, Riende and Elamani, Aelwyn and Gael, and Iridrys and Thalleam was crowded with those gathered at Theomanus's request. The older couples sat in chairs or on benches scattered about the grassy hollow near the stream. Elrad stood, leaning against a tree near the curved stone bridge that spanned the gurgling cataract. Nausika perched on the curve of the bridge above the water, Laslorn unusually still and watchful between her wings.

Lucina and Davin stood near the opposite edge of the little bridge, their stance reminiscent of their time as Border Guards. By contrast, Kier, Michal, Cador, Aoneth, Rablorn, and the twins rested in easy attitudes in the grass at their feet. Elwyn sat upon a pale boulder, Theo standing between her wings. There was a charged energy between them that intrigued the others, and they waited to hear what Theo would say.

As Theomanus began to speak, the light in his eyes became brighter, though the sky was darkening and the light grew dim about them. Elrad was reminded of the glorious light that had poured through Theomanus when he had been transformed into the doorway between the worlds, and he leaned forward slightly, in anticipation of what Theo would share. He had no hint of what it would be, but his own eyes were keen to note the evidence of the Creator at work in his young friend's life.

Nausika, taut with amazement at the implications of what she and Las had learned from their conversation with Theo and Elwyn, leaned back against the strength of her beloved. They alone of the company had witnessed what Theo would share. She felt the fine hairs along her arms lift.

"This morning I discovered one of the things we are to experience in this wonderful place. I do not know *why* it works, but I have my suspicions. First, allow me to demonstrate." While the company watched, open-mouthed, Theo leapt lightly into the air, plucked a blossom from the mimosa above him, and drifted gently down to present it to his stunned mother with a slight bow. Iridrys took the flower in fingers that trembled slightly. Theo lifted into the air and returned to Elwyn. His eyes turned to meet the waiting turquoise of the Seer and found them bright with excitement and something like glee. The elder's voice was deceptively calm as he responded.

"How did you come to learn this lesson, Theomanus?"

Theo's eyes crinkled merrily as the approval in Elrad's deep voice warmed him.

"I just wished for it. Very hard. But I do not think flight is the lesson learned, so much as it is the gift given with the lesson."

"For an Elf to join his Kindred in flight is truly a marvelous gift!" exclaimed Aoneth. "But what is this lesson it brings?"

"Yes, Theo." Geltheon laughed indulgently. "We followed you for decades until you brought us here. Now, you have learned something new. Come, Master of Marliondolen: lead us again!"

Theo joined the gentle laughter, but his eyes sought Elrad's again and found reassuring confidence there.

"Well then, I will tell you, of course! Be patient!" he teased his merry friends. "I believe the lesson in this phenomenon is that in this place, beyond the veil of sin, yet not quite in the very Presence of the Creator, we *cannot* wish for things that are displeasing to Him. I think we all got some hint of this when we first arrived and found, among other things, that we couldn't feel fear about our new circumstances if we tried. But this is bigger. I believe He is giving us the chance to join Him in exploring our deepest desires. It seems He is even giving us the ability to effect certain changes by wishing for them. Now, I do not suggest that we can cause just anything to come about, for we have not the powers of our Creator."

"Thankfully," put in Laslorn in an undertone. "For neither do we have His wisdom!"

"True, my friend! And that is why I also believe He is giving us a chance to think carefully upon what we would wish for before He grants it. As a case in point, I believe each of us would wish in our uttermost hearts that we could be in the Presence of our Creator right now, but He knows we still have much growing and learning to do before we are ready for that, and so the time is not yet right."

"A good analogy, my son," came the quiet affirmation from Thalleam, whose golden eyes rested proudly upon Theo. "I believe this idea calls for deep and searching prayer. I, for one, would like to understand my deepest wishes better and not continue as I have always done, accepting the vague desires that flit across my mind, according to my circumstances."

"Yes, Thalleam, you have an excellent point," responded Elrad, nodding his dark head. "Such a search may be an important key for all of us. After all, as Theomanus has suggested and we have discussed before, we believe we are here to grow and to mature in a manner pleasing to our Lord. Surely, a careful, honest searching of our dreams and desires may be the first step to deepening our faith."

Laslorn stood on the edge of a green field that stretched as far as his long eyes could see. He had never been this far from their settlement before, but the urge to dig deeply into his own heart had prompted him to remove himself far from distractions.

Several deep breaths calmed him, but he still felt a tingle of nervous excitement. He had never been one to search too deeply, to bare his soul. Las had left that sort of thing to Theo, deflecting the serious moments with his signature humor. He had earned the nickname Laslorn of the Merry Heart, for he was uniformly goodnatured and easygoing, and was famous for the timely jests that relieved tension. But now, he felt a pressing need to explore the depths of his heart, to search out his cherished dreams and buried wishes. He felt an urging to be serious, for once, about what was really important.

He asked the Lord to quiet his heart and to show him what was truly important to him. He asked for wisdom—in the old tongue, *eliom*: to see through the Maker's eyes. As difficult as it was for him, he forced himself to wait, to be patient, to round up his fragmented thoughts time and again and bring them back to the subject of his focus, positive that the Creator would reveal what He wanted to him.

Finally, slowly, a sense of peace descended on him, like a warm cloak. His breathing slowed and he began to pay attention to the images that formed in his mind. With a rush of warmth came the faces of Riende, Theo, his companions. Then, with special gratitude for being with her again after all these years, he saw his mother's face. Robse's familiar features swam before his inner gaze, and his deep affection was colored with faint anxiety as he watched the beloved features change with grief and sorrow.

Unbidden to his mind came images of their home in the foothills of the mountains, where Elamani, and sometimes Riende, would take Las and Theo to get away from the bustle of the City. He remembered the peace and freedom there, the clean smells of unlimited trees and grassy slopes covered in wildflowers. He sucked in a deep breath, remembering.

His love for his family had been fulfilled in Marliondolen by the presence of his parents, brother, friends, and dear wife. He still missed Robse keenly, but he at least had some assurance that in the fullness of time, the Creator would bring the remaining Faeltheon to Marliondolen, too, and they would be together again. Growing up, his father had always taught him that their family would one day live in peace together, and he still believed it. His need for the peace and solace to be found at that mountain house had been more than provided by the lush beauty of Marliondolen. No place in all the Land could rival the beauty found here. The tranquility and utter stability of his surroundings resonated within Laslorn with profound certainty.

He returned to the dreams of his heart, to find if any were yet unfulfilled. He was sure there were more, but he was equally sure that he wasn't very good at this sort of thing and would probably have to do it several times before a deep exploration was accomplished. He closed his eyes, to help him concentrate, and found his other senses heightened. The sound of the gentle breeze hissing through the tall grass that surrounded him evoked memories of the exhilaration he had always felt when he gazed upon the sea. Because Theomanus had lost his parents to the sea, Laslorn had always respected Theo's preference for solid ground. Through the years, Las had ignored his own desire to venture out upon that fascinating, undulating surface, but now, in the honesty of his new explorations, Laslorn was surprised to find within himself a deep yearning for the sea. Deep within his heart, he discovered an affinity for the sea, for its power and its majesty, its proclamation of the Creator's glory, for its colors, its scent, its ever-changing aspect, its eternal, vast presence. Into his mind swelled the rightness of the very word for sea: *gael*—the Creator's power.

He hadn't realized what he had hidden so deeply or what he had been missing all these years, but now that the floodgates were opened, it seemed to Laslorn that he could taste the salt spray on his lips and hear the breakers rumbling against the patient shore, as he had experienced for the first century of his life. With a deep sigh, he opened his eyes, just as a foam-tipped wave curled gently around his feet, soaking his shoes.

Startled, he jumped back with a shout, then turned his slow, incredulous gaze upon the wonder spread before him. Instead of a vast meadow, his vision now struggled to span the edges of the horizon, where his wide eyes found the brightest, clearest blue he'd ever seen meeting the rim of the noon sky. The gentle rhythm of the waves murmured a greeting to the starved places within him, like the welcome of an old friend. He felt a great power swelling inside him. He did not know what it was, but when he thought he would explode with it, it burst out of him in a mighty shout and he discovered it was a wild, exultant, grateful excitement.

Dancing, leaping, shouting, crying, even occasionally airborne, Laslorn cavorted madly upon the newly made shore, worshipping the Creator to a wild music only he could hear. After a time, he dropped, exhausted, triumphant, upon the fine, golden sand and sent up a prayer of praise and thanksgiving. When his wild breathing had slowed and the tempo of his heart subsided to match the waves upon the shore, he became still with the wonder of what had happened, and that he had been permitted to participate. He had always thought that this type of participation in the Maker's plan was for those like Theo and Elrad, and that his duty was simply to support them. He found a surprising joy in knowing that he had been allowed to work so closely with the Creator. The unfamiliar stillness sat comfortably upon his soul, like an old friend he'd just met. The Presence of the Lord came near as Laslorn knelt in reverent quietude, and they communed together for a sweet time.

When he finally arose, Laslorn saw that the sun had descended toward the horizon. There was perhaps an hour of daylight left. Suddenly, he realized that he could not bear to be apart from Nausika. She must know the great and wonderful thing that had happened to him! Without a second thought, Laslorn took to the air, as though flying were natural to him.

A short time later, he tumbled down out of the trees into the green grotto captured between their home and those of their friends clustered nearby. His landing had not been nearly as graceful as he had hoped, and he found himself on all fours in front of Nausika, who was kneeling upon the rich loam, humming to herself as she patted fresh earth about the tender seedlings she'd just planted. Breathless with his pace and exuberance, and in attempt to make it look like he had meant to land that way, he rolled over on to his side, lounging next to her. Nausika's copper curls shook as she giggled and raised an eyebrow at her husband.

"Let's go for a walk," he prompted.

"Is it still called a walk if you're flying?" she teased. Laslorn stood up and started to raise her from the ground. Nausika gave him a startled look.

"Now?"

"Yes."

"Where shall we go?"

Eager to share his new secret with her and bursting with excitement, Laslorn caught her up off the ground into a fierce hug that took them soaring into the sky. Nausika's startled exclamation was cut off by his kiss. She quickly sensed his ebullient mood and demanded an explanation when he let her up for air. His attempts to explain what had happened disintegrated into inarticulation, so he simply grabbed her wrist and flew back toward the waiting, newborn sea. Darting through the trees, they flew at top speed until he abruptly stopped Nausika at the edge of the woods, landing in a small clearing. The space ahead was still shrouded by the dense foliage.

"Now, close your eyes," he urged, a mischievous smile on his face.

Nausika's leaf-green eyes widened slightly. She was suspicious of his suppressed excitement, and suspected a grand joke.

"Laslorn, what is going on? First, you want to go on a walk for no reason at all, then you drag me down here at a reckless speed, and now you're telling me to close my eyes before I approach a spot I've seen before—"

"Please, just close your eyes. Trust me."

Nausika smiled. The excited anticipation on Laslorn's face combined with the pleading look in his eyes made it impossible for her to deny him the joy of his surprise.

"All right: they're closed."

Laslorn took both her hands in his and led her out several paces until she felt the terrain under her feet change dramatically. She almost opened her eyes to see her way but resolutely kept them closed and trusted her husband. His warm voice sounded just above her left ear as he drew her to a halt on the oddly shifting ground.

"Open your eyes."

Nausika obeyed and let out a gasp. She looked down to see that the new substance she stood on was pale sand. Raising her wondering eyes, she looked around her and could see nothing but a clear blue ocean that stretched out for miles.

"It's so beautiful! How is this possible? I was out here just the other day and I think I would have noticed an ocean then! Laslorn, how did you find this?"

"Well... I wished for it."

"You wished an entire ocean into existence?"

"I did," he answered, looking quite pleased with himself.

"This is so amazing! I've never seen the ocean with my own eyes before. It's even more beautiful than I imagined!" She gazed around, wide-eyed, and her silvery laughter rippled out like the waves before her.

Laslorn, in his sheer delight at both the ocean and how happy he had made his wife, scooped her up and ran with her into the sea. She shrieked as he put her down in the water.

"Laslorn Lyserea, do you have any idea how long it's going to take my wings to dry?" she cried, playfully slapping a handful of water at him. A brightly colored school of fish darted around their ankles.

"My goodness," Laslorn remarked. "This water is a lot colder than it looks!" Nevertheless, they swam until their fingertips began to wrinkle, Laslorn sharing the story of his amazing day.

"We should probably tell Theo about this," Laslorn declared as they waded up out of the water.

"Yes, I think the Master of Marliondolen might just be interested to hear that a gigantic ocean has sprung up in the middle of his land!" Nausika replied as she settled herself onto a large, sun-baked rock to wait for her wings to dry. Laslorn laughed tiredly at her teasing and settled beside her, relishing the warmth of the rock beneath his cooled skin.

They stayed, as the sun went down in a blaze of glory, and spent the night on the sands.

As morning coated the slumbering sky with the nacre of the dawn, Nausika awoke to the unfamiliar sounds and scents of the sea. Glancing at her sleeping husband, she felt her heart squeeze with love as the early light caressed the planes of his face and sparked golden gleams off his tousled hair. She wished she could merge with him somehow, to be a part of him on a deeper level than they had yet established. But they had known one another such a short time that, while affection had certainly rooted into a firm love, they hadn't yet built up the layers of shared memories and experiences that brought the comfortable closeness she sought. She desired to be able to sink into him somehow, to be so much a part of him that she could tell him how much she loved him with an eloquent look, in ways that words could never express. She wanted to share with him that deep oneness she saw in many of the older couples. She wished that she could say she knew her husband's soul better than any other Faeltheon did, but that time had not yet come.

Eyes devouring the beauty laid before her, Nausika prayed to the

Creator that He would bless their union and deepen it into a love that reflected His love for them. She asked Him to show her what to do, how to be the perfect helpmeet for her beloved, how to become an essential part of his dreams, as he was of hers. In the stillness and murmuring of the morning, she felt a peace come upon her, as though it were an answer, and she knew that the Lord would make her dreams come true.

At that moment, the sun spilled over the horizon, transforming the multihued grays into flames and flashes of opal and amethyst, sapphire and amber. She became aware of Laslorn sitting up behind her just as a shining silver back broke the sea. She cried aloud, echoing Laslorn's exclamation, and the sleek creature reappeared. This time, it reared right out of the water, balancing for a moment upon its tail, calling aloud to them before turning to splash back into the sea. Within seconds, six or seven curved backs rose in dancing arcs, scattering flashing rainbows in their wake as they hastened to follow their leader.

Eyes shining with excitement, Nausika turned to Laslorn. His merry eyes were alight with the joy of the morning and the beautiful creatures.

"What were they?" she asked him eagerly. He shook his head.

"I don't know. There weren't any creatures like that near home. They look like those ship fish that have been following the others though."

"You're right, they do. I expect that's what they are. How wonderful that we get to experience them too!" *I wonder if I wished them here, or if You just gave them to us. Either way, thank You for the confirmation that You will knit me into Laslorn's most cherished dreams!*

"Why do you suppose all this has given us so much joy?" she asked Laslorn. He put his arm around her, hauling her close to his side as he gazed out over the water. His green eyes darkened as he gave serious thought to her question.

"I suppose because Marliondolen is a place where we can enjoy the same things that we used to, but now we can enjoy them more fully since we are closer to the Creator and farther from the effects of sin." He turned his forest eyes to her lighter ones. "So wouldn't it make sense that our desire for the sea would be fulfilled here?"

"Yes. But I can only imagine what more the Creator has in store for us that He has yet to reveal," Nausika replied, nestling her head into his chest.

Chapter Twenty-Three

The stars glittered in the dark blue sky, as though a great fisher had spangled his net with jewels and cast it across the heavens. Caerdrys, taking her turn at night watch, stood braced in her favorite place in the triangle of the forward rail. Focusing upward, she picked out the constellations she had learned to love: the familiar three sisters, the dipper, the smaller spoon, the unicorn. Far to the south, she could just make out the disappearing edge of the Pyxes, the cross-shaped flower in the center of the larger cross pattern. That one had been new to them when they reached the southern regions but had become familiar over the weeks they had spent becalmed.

It had been bittersweet having to leave that peaceful time and place, but the weather had begun to change and they'd had to unlink the ships and move on. They all acknowledged that they were stronger for their time linked together and filled with renewed hope for their search. Min had suggested that they continue to gather on the decks in the evenings to talk and sing and preserve the sense of community. This had become a favored tradition, so her suggestion was gladly accepted.

As the mariners had predicted at their last stop months before, with the coming of the end of the year and the cold months on land, the winds had picked up again, moving their ships sluggishly out of the grip of that quiet place and back into brisk and active ocean depths. Within ten days of this change, the watch up in the aeries had warned of a landmass ahead. Soon they had found themselves facing a huge expanse of solid land that stretched as far to the north and south as they could see. Small islands and riffs of jagged, half-submerged rocks had menaced the edges of this land, like unfriendly teeth, and the captains of the vessels had been concerned for their safety.

Just before it seemed they would be dashed to death upon those unfriendly outriders, the great currents beneath their hulls had shifted and the force of their impetus had swept the three ships northward along the coast. From time to time over the next few weeks, when large river mouths had been seen to empty into the sea from the land, they had dropped anchor in still evenings and ventured by ship's boat to row up those rivers until they reached clear, sweet water. There they had refilled their water casks and explored a bit, investigating the mainland. So far, though they had found a fertile wilderness, they had found no signs of people.

On the last such venture, one of their party had been bitten by a brightly colored water snake. Though they had done all they could for the poor Elf, his wound had swelled terribly and he had burned with restless fever and pain for two days before dying. After that, there had been no more trips ashore, and all attempts to get fresh water had been made with all eyes carefully alert.

A splash below alerted Caerdrys to the presence of a *delphys*, something they had not enjoyed since their escorting pod had left them when they struck the faster currents nearly a month before. She searched for the flashing figure, but it was still too dark to see, even for Elven eyes. The horizon promised the false dawn soon, so she could be patient.

When at last the pale gray light crept near enough for Caerdrys to make out the sea below her perch, she was delighted to note the shining body still leaping beside them, like a silver needle flashing in and out of a blue and silver cloth. She called out to him and was further overjoyed when the high-pitched response was clearly understandable. With a huge smile, Caerdrys realized their escort was the bachelor male Qualneth.

After happy greetings, he delivered the message he had come to bring them.

"*Swee wys we'ekk'ah e'ah wen'ee*!" Qualneth squealed from the waves below her. Caerdrys had to think for a moment to remember how to translate the *delphys's* accent. *Swy wys weheregan emon wenne. Swift water will carry you to your goal.* Excited at his message, Caerdrys encouraged him to tell all he knew. Qualneth, seemingly inexhaustible in his joy at having found them, was more than willing to comply.

He had come to warn them that the whales claimed that the vast landmass that now rode their port side was in fact all one huge land, as they had suspected. The great whales insisted that the main sea gyres would turn away from that land and push them eastward soon, and that they should follow that eastward current. A flip of his sleek head to starboard caused her to notice the breaching blowhole of a large creature keeping pace beside the three ships but several bowshots away.

The arrival of another Elf to assume the forward watch caused Caerdrys to realize that day had indeed arrived while she and Qualneth were exchanging news. Leaning over the rail, she motioned to the young *delphys* to wait for her and turned to run down the ship's length to the stern cabin. She knew the others should hear Qualneth's news and perhaps meet the whale that accompanied them.

Arriving at the common room, she found all the Companions assembled at breakfast. Unceremoniously, she filled them in on her news, pulling a protesting Cerlim, who was closest to the door, away from his seat. They all rose and followed her, Cerlim carrying his bread and cheese. When they got to the starboard rail, Caerdrys began to climb down it, to be nearer the leaping *delphys*.

Qualneth, humorously full of his own importance, introduced them to their guide, a male humpback whale. The large creature drew near to the side of the *Cethastea* and greeted them in passable, if archaic, Common Speech, his basso voice echoing under the water and tickling Qualneth, to judge by the youngster's squeals. The whale confirmed the course of the sea gyres that would turn them eastward. He reported that while there were islands to the north, they were frozen lands where no one dwelt beyond a few birds and animals.

In his ponderous, nearly unintelligible speech, he shared with them that the old songs of his people spoke of the Faeltheon departing from their island long ago to sail north. Gaelcar, excited to the point of dishevelment, burned to know if the old whale songs could tell them

where the isle lay. Aelric shouted the query for him, as the Seneschal was fumbling to fold open the ever-present Scrolls. The whale replied that the old songs did not specify where the isle was, only that it was east of here rather than due north.

After more general conversation, they all thanked the whale, who was impressed at their courtesy. Before he left them, he tipped his broad snout downward and, turning upside-down, sang them a farewell song. Qualneth volunteered the information that this song would also serve to relate to all his people the story of their meeting. When the whale surfaced again sometime later, Caerdrys conveyed to him that they had given him an honorary name: Geliennos, *Great Singer* in the Common Tongue. Geliennos was very pleased with his name, despite his inability to pronounce it, and flipped his flukes to them several times while departing.

Chattering excitedly and consulting the Scrolls, most of the companions left the rail to return to their interrupted breakfast. Caerdrys remained to thank Qualneth for finding them with this news to guide their quest. As Qualneth then departed to find his breakfast, Caerdrys did the same.

Entering the common room, she found an animated discussion taking place. Gesturing with the Scrolls, Gaelcar was explaining that they had traveled in a great circle because of following the sea gyres. Now that they knew they were headed in the right direction, no one really cared that they had gone so far out of their way. After confirming Geliennos's advice with the Scrolls and the star charts, they determined they would indeed turn east when the great current took them.

Five days later, with small yet distinct ceremony, the Companions watched as Lysion and his fellow captains gave the order for the course correction that turned them eastward, away from the faint shadow of the land that had been on their port side for weeks, and into the rising sun. Much to Caerdrys's joy, Qualneth continued to escort them, and she formed the habit of joining him at the rail in the mornings and between her chores.

They stood, silently, waiting in the approaching dusk.

Elrad, tall and still on Elwyn's left, had summoned them from their dinner a few minutes before. His air of certainty had caused them to obey his odd request unquestioningly.

Now, as the twilight deepened in the wake of the setting sun, Elwyn began to feel a little foolish, standing out in a field, bracketed between two tall, dark Elves, like a pale moth between two glossy starlings. She shifted slightly and tucked one hand into Theo's left elbow, wondering what they were waiting for. Theo, sensing her movement, and perhaps something of her disquiet, hugged her slender hand against his ribs and smiled down on her. She laid her golden head against his broad shoulder, washed suddenly in contentment.

For what mystery do we wait this time? Theo wondered. *So much of what we have known in this new world has been a mystery and a delight—everything from the extraordinary forests and streams of our new homes, to the enhanced senses we enjoy and the wonder of helping to make our own dreams come true. Surely the Creator is good to us.* He paused his pondering in the dusk and looked over toward the still figure of the Seer, standing beyond Elwyn. *He seemed so insistent we must come now to this place and wait—but for what? And why only the two of us? He said he had no clear word, merely a strong urging to bring us to this spot and wait for whatever the Lord would send.*

The cool evening air coalesced into mist at the feet of the great trees not far ahead. In a moment more, Elwyn drew in her breath and Theo strained to peer through the deepening dusk. Surely that was a movement at the edge of the forest. Another moment and they could both hear the sigh of breath released by the Seer as a dim figure emerged from the gloaming and advanced toward them.

When it had progressed a few steps nearer, they could perceive the form of a tall, graceful Faerie woman, clad in flowing garments that melted in and out of the mist. At first, Elwyn thought it was a trick of the clouded moonlight that made the woman appear to be surrounded by a nimbus of light, but as she drew closer, it became clear that she was indeed emanating a gentle, visible radiance. Her wings shimmered faintly in this light, an ethereal backdrop to her beauty. She came on steadily, until she joined them, her elegance and cool luminosity awing the younger ones.

Elrad stepped forth and bowed to her. This mark of reverence from the one they held in highest respect seemed fitting to Elwyn. The newcomer accepted his hand and, with old-world courtesy, curtsied gracefully to all three. Her voice, when she spoke, was low and rich and steady.

"You three are known to all, so I need not ask your names. I am honored to meet you, for the Creator has used you to great purpose in His plans for His Fair Folk."

The dusk had faded into the deeper tones of velvet night now, and the light of the stars seemed to gather in her nimbus. Her hair was a fall of palest silver, nearly white in the intermittent moonlight. Her eyes were shadowed in the starlight but seemed to be dark. Her garments were richly embroidered about the neck and hems with gold and silver thread and many small, glowing gemstones.

And yet, for all the loving respect paid to her by the labor that had created her lovely raiment, there was a sense that she herself was a rare jewel and the garments were merely meant to be a fit setting for her. Her face shone with a serene beauty that Elwyn knew came from deep within. All that this Faerie had learned in her many years of living and communing with the Creator was there in her aspect: dignity, humility, high exaltation, and comforting warmth. With their enhanced sight, the others had no trouble perceiving every detail of their meeting. Elrad bowed his head to her, the starlight catching on the strands of silver in his dark hair.

"May we know your name, Lady?" he asked with his customary grave courtesy. The woman smiled and answered almost merrily.

"But of course you may! Is that not why we were drawn to meet one another? I am Athalenael. I have no Family name, for I lived upon the Earth before the time of the First Families."

This explained the gentle light that came from the Faerie herself, for she had once walked and talked with the Creator, and those who beheld Him face-to-face were said to have such a light of reflected glory about them that one could not look upon their faces easily. Elwyn and Theo saw Elrad's eyes widen, and it did not seem at all awkward to them that he bowed deeply to her once more and raised her hand to his lips. Turning to them, still holding her hand, he made her known to them.

"Lady Elwyn, Master Theomanus, may I have the honor of presenting to you Athalenael, the first Kytha our people ever knew. It was she to whom the revelation of Humans and sin and the twisting of the world was given." While their eyes widened in turn, the Lady Athalenael pulled her hand from Elrad's gentle grasp and spoke with a hint of tartness in her low voice.

"Yes, it was to me He chose to reveal those dark and evil things, but not because of any merit which I possessed! For all the honor given me, I am no different than any other Faeltheon."

Theo chuckled, and the sense of heavy dignity dissolved suddenly into equality and sharing. Elwyn settled beside the Kytha on the cloak that Theo spread over a large fallen branch.

"Will you tell us how it was, this receiving of the knowledge of the twisting of creation?"

The Kytha leaned back, clasping her hands loosely about her knees.

"Confusing, mostly," she began, her eyes taking on a distant look, her mouth drooping slightly. "None of us had ever had a revelation before, of course, so it was hard to tell others what I saw and heard. We were all accustomed to walking and talking with Him, but it had been so long since He had been found among us, we all longed to hear His voice again." She paused, which was just as well, for her hearers wanted time to dwell on the thought that this woman had been one of the Blessed who had known that sacred communion. When she resumed her tale, the regret in her voice made Elwyn's heart tighten in sympathy.

"I recognized His voice in my dream at once. It's not a voice you forget," she said wryly. "He spoke of the other children He had created and the choice they had made, the path they had taken. He showed me more than I could then comprehend: a mass of pain, sickness, evil, and death, a changed Earth, a twisted creation. When I shared it with my people, none of us could comprehend it at all, for none of those things had yet come into our experience."

She paused, and Elrad handed her a mug of steaming tea, which he had poured from the wrapped pouch at his side. Theo handed a similar one to Elwyn. With hearts more moved than ever, they gave quiet thanks for the gifts the Creator provided and drank their tea. Refreshed and warmed, Athalenael resumed her tale.

"Then came the cold.

"At first, we did not understand it, for until that time there had been no seasonal changes more extreme than a slight shift in temperature and rainfall. But first the nights became cold, then even the day was not warmed, as though the sun itself had lost the power to heat the world.

"Still He was not found among us, and a few began to feel a deep sense of loss and sorrow, a thing we had not experienced before. Soon, we were all uneasy, as well as uncomfortable. We began to look for ways to make warmer garments and cloaks, to seal our homes against chilly winds. Then the animals and small birds began to die. At first, we did not understand what was happening, for neither had we known death.

"Another vision was given me, in which much of the same information was shared again, but this time, to the bitterness of our hearts, we understood a great deal more of what was given. We grieved, longing for His Presence among us, but He did not come there again.

"Those of us remaining from those days began to feel our strength sapped by grief. Our infants, always few and precious, began to sicken with a fever and to die, as the animals had. This was the most frightening thing yet. We knew He had not abandoned us, but the loneliness and grief were nearly mortal wounds to our souls." Athalenael paused again, hiding her face in her mug. Her hands, like her voice, were trembling with emotion. The others looked away to give her time to regain her composure.

"Finally came the vision of the ships He had taught us to make and what we were to do with them. When He had first given us this knowledge, it had not been frightening, for He was still with us then, but now.... The knowledge that we were building these floating homes in order to leave our island was at first given only to a few. In time, when the world had changed so much that we could scarcely remember what it had been before, we told the others what we must do. There was a great outcry and protest—not against the Will of the Creator of course, merely a voicing of the fear of the unknown. It seemed to some of us that the world had become so unstable that perhaps we should never again know the peace we had known in our people's infancy. Sadly, that premonition proved true.

"We boarded the ships, taking with us all we could contrive to bring of the lives and world we had known, for we knew not to what end we sailed. Of that venture, I shall speak little, except to say that it was a very difficult journey, made by brave but unskilled people. Many of us did not survive the voyage, myself included, though I had been comforted in my last cogency by a vision of a happy, prosperous Faeltheon living in a green new Land."

She paused, still enmeshed in the past, dappled with moonshadows. They respected her silence. After a moment, she shook her pale head slightly and looked up at them, starlight flashing off the white teeth of her genuine smile.

"When next I awoke, it was to this fair place and these happy folk. It was a little time before I understood that this was not the Land to which my people were sent, but the refuge from the destruction of that Land. So you see, my dears..." She turned her luminous gaze upon Theo and Elwyn sitting hand in hand beside her. "I, too, understand what it is to lose a beloved Land and way of life. And I, too, have known the overwhelming grace of the Creator's provision. Is this world more beautiful than the one I once knew? Assuredly, but for one thing. The most important and beautiful thing about our world, before the advent of sin and death, was the Presence of its Creator. As long as this realm lacks that shaping, enfolding, enlivening Presence, it shall ever be but a shadow of its intended self."

Elrad, sitting at her feet, nodded his dark head.

"And yet, His Presence is not wholly absent from this place," he stated. "True, He does not walk and talk among us ... yet!" he amended, causing Theo to close his mouth upon his ever-hopeful qualification. Elrad smiled the rich smile that had so comforted Elwyn's youth. "But He is among us. When we lived in a fallen world, we came to depend upon the sense of His Spirit drawing near us when we sought Him. We came to know a relationship that was as rich as we could make it in our circumstances. His occasional visions, too, were a great blessing, even when they warned of something unpleasant. We came to learn that He would tell us only what was needful for us to know, and only when He thought we should know it, lest it be too much to bear, and we should be unable to do what He required of us."

"Yes," Elwyn chimed in. "These "windows" He gives us are like visions in some ways. He shows us what He wants us to know—not too much, and never too soon, but just enough to cause us to focus on what He wishes us to see and to be ready to follow where He will lead us."

The Kytha nodded, having shared a few of those "windows." Both women turned back to Elrad, who smiled at them with deep affection. His penetrating teal gaze then sought Theo's golden eyes and found them waiting, as though Theo anticipated his next words.

"And in this place, where the veil of sin no longer prevents us from knowing our Maker, what new revelations may we hope for? Surely He will reveal Himself to us once more! It is our hope, as it ever has been, to be restored to His Presence. We believe that we are to mature and grow in this safe, encouraging place, until His time shall have been fulfilled. Then, when He is ready to reunite us to Himself, shall our hearts finally be healed of the wound they have borne since your day, Lady."

Athalenael nodded her pale head in acknowledgment of his wisdom and hopes. She responded in her resonant voice.

"*Elanímon! Na'cyb!*"

Theo and Elwyn echoed her words in a sudden prickle of gooseflesh, repeating the formal chant that dated from before their knowledge.

God with us! May it be again!

Chapter Twenty-Four

In the cold, dim pre-dawn light, Minlienda curled her stiff fingers deeper into the sleeves of her fleece robe. Shivering slightly as she tied the sash about her waist, she absently picked up Caerdrys's robe from the floor and folded it over her chair. The night had been restless for them both. In the wakeful watches between disturbing dreams, Min had heard her *amia* sister moving about in her hammock overhead. Finally conceding defeat, Caerdrys had risen as quietly as possible and had left their small chamber a few minutes before. Unable to sleep herself, and unwilling to lie in bed any longer without rest, Min had rolled out, too, her bare toes curling at the chill of the floorboards.

Quickly she had donned her dainty fur-lined slippers and the fleece robe she had dyed the colors of peacock feathers. Methodically, Min straightened their small cabin, setting the rumpled covers to rights in their hammocks, splashing water in her face from the pitcher in the bathing room. She paused to look out the large double doors that led to the balcony, but the view was uniformly gray before the appearance of the sun to light the day. Perhaps today would bring the clearing of the dense fog that had obscured their view for the better part of three days. The sea was a bit choppy, but her body adjusted automatically to the pitch and roll of the decks, and she didn't notice. Knowing her sister would be brooding somewhere cold, Min retrieved Caerdrys's maroon robe and left the room to search for her.

As she stepped down the passageway, she paused to poke her head into the common room. The room was empty, with a hapless, abandoned look, the chairs standing at random angles to the table, where they had been left when the Companions had finally sought their beds in the wee hours of the morning. The restlessness that had been plaguing them all for the past few days was growing more pronounced, invading their dreams and haunting their waking hours like an itch in the mind. Min closed the door again and moved to the end of the passageway.

As she exited the door that led to the main deck, she heard quiet voices above her. Turning and looking up to the quarterdeck, she saw Caerdrys, Myrandella, and Robse leaning on the starboard rail. Robse, Min noted, was fully dressed, as if he had never gone to bed. Randa was clutching a forest green quilt about her shoulders against the brisk sea wind. Caerdrys, of course, was standing boldly in the wind, her heavy nightshirt whipping about her, as was her hair. At least she had donned her half boots, Min thought resignedly as she climbed the companionway ladder to join them. She laid the dark robe about Caerdrys's shoulders and received a brief, fierce hug in return. Robse made room for her in their huddle by the rail, and she welcomed the heat of his body as he took his place behind her.

On the eastern horizon, ahead as they watched off the starboard rail, the sky was lightening into the pearl of sunrise. They drew relieved breaths as the increasing light showed them a horizon clear of the insidious mist. As the first streaks of light spangled the wave tips, gleaming silver backs broke the water just ahead of the *Cethastea's* prow. It appeared their lone escort had been joined by a pod of *delphyson*. As the pod gamboled and played ahead of the great ship, Min sensed Caerdrys's attention sharpen.

Min recognized the familiar determination in the firm set of her sister's mouth and so was unsurprised when Caerdrys cinched her belt tightly about her waist and strode down the ladder steps to the main deck. Undismayed, she watched as Caerdrys began to descend the starboard boarding ladder at the ship's waist. A movement of the night watch in the aerie aloft caused Min to look up, catching the expression of consternation on Domel's face. She stifled a giggle at how odd it must look to see someone descending the ladder when there was no boat waiting below. She wondered if poor Domel was grappling with whether to sound the *overboard* alert. She waved reassuringly to him.

Robse and Randa were looking to her with varying degrees of concern and question in their eyes, so she moved to descend the companionway ladder. They followed in strained silence. By the time Caerdrys had reached the lower edge of the boarding ladder, the *delphyson* had dropped back and moved closer to the *Cethastea's* side, and the three companions had reached the starboard rail above them. Caerdrys turned her head back up to Min, shouting against the wind.

"It's Ghaerwe! She has followed us after all! I wonder if this has something to do with Qualneth's warning when the current turned east!" Caerdrys turned her dark head and her attention back to the flashing silver forms swarming beside her in the morning light. There arose a great clacking, squealing chatter, as Ghaerwe and her pod vied to speak to Caerdrys. Min and her companions strained to pick out the message but caught only fleeting images.

Min, surveying the situation with a practical eye, decided that she could be more useful elsewhere. Judging from the wind and the waves, Caerdrys was going to be soaking wet when this conference had finished, and they would all be chilled. As Min knew she couldn't translate the *delphyson's* high-pitched speech any more efficiently than Caerdrys was doing, she determined to do what she could in other areas.

Moving briskly, she left the rail and headed for the galley to put on water for hot tea and to set blankets hanging before the stove to warm while she fixed breakfast. She figured she had just about enough time before Caerdrys came aboard with her message and the king and the other Companions were roused to hear it. Thoughtfully, she added more eggs to the mix.

Gaelcar joined the other Companions in their common room, tired from yet another sleepless night. In his arms, he carried a load of the Ancient

Scrolls, marked at the entries concerning the island where the Elves had originated. In the past few days, many Elves had reported strikingly similar dreams in which they were in their old homes, in the Land, occupying themselves with their typical tasks and activities. In their dreams, they would leave their homes, on simple errands, only to discover their homes to be in a Land radically different from what it had once been. It was obvious to them all that the Creator was telling them something regarding their new home, if only they could undertand His message.

Though the dreams had been gentle and unthreatening, many reported feeling lost and apprehensive when they awoke. Myrandella, in her capacity as Seer as well as assistant, had tried to help Gaelcar to determine the effects of these mass dreams, but the best they had been able to report to the Companions last night had been a general uneasiness and a sense of something important approaching. This, as Caerdrys had pointed out, was no more than confirmation of their own feelings.

It seemed significant to them all that these dreams had begun the same night the lookouts had sighted that string of islands that lay directly in the ships' path. For the next few days, great walls of mist had made it nearly impossible to catch more than fleeting glimpses of the cluster of volcanic islands that had so excited the watch. Although they did not say it aloud, lest they be disappointed were they proven incorrect, many of the Elves guarded a secret inner hope that they might soon be building their new homes on the island of their origins.

Gaelcar passed around the Scrolls, and the group of Elves began to pore over them, hungrily devouring the familiar words that would tell them about what might possibly be their new home.

At Min's insistence, they had paused to eat, consuming the nourishing fare with nearly mindless intensity. Now, they were leaning back in their chairs, pulling their second, or third, cups of tea toward them, the strain around their eyes somewhat eased. Quietly, Min collected the dishes from the table and passed them to Domel, who stacked them in the sturdy basket she had brought for the purpose. Randelos refilled the teapot with hot water.

As she seated herself and stirred lavender honey into her tea, Min took stock of her companions. Aelric was looking worn, with dark smudges around his eyes from the restless dreams that had denied him sleep the past few nights. His mouth was relaxed from the grim line it had become, but he sat forward in his chair, hands cupping the warmth of his mug, as though needing the comfort it provided. Cerlim, though he affected a relaxed attitude, leaning back casually in his chair with one ankle propped on the opposite knee, was strung as tightly as his namesake bow. Min saw the telltale jiggling of his foot and the crease between his fair brows. Randelos slumped into his chair, his dark head bowed over his mug as he inhaled the steam from his fourth cup of tea. Min noticed he had eaten lightly, and his normally candid eyes were dark and didn't meet hers. She wondered what dreams plagued his sleep. While her own had been disturbing, she hadn't been able to remember much about them when she awoke. They had left her feeling vaguely unsettled, as though there was something important she was forgetting to do. Obviously, Randelos's dreams were less passive.

Randa exchanged wary glances with her, having noted the same thing. The Seer's brilliant green eyes were unclouded, if weary. She, too, had been feeling the insistent pressing in her spirit and felt also the nagging sensation that she was missing something significant, but no visions had presented themselves to clarify the general searching.

Min watched as Domel returned to his place at the table, his quiet face retaining its customary look of peace. The creases around his eyes were more pronounced, and his eyes were red from lack of sleep, as he'd just pulled the night watch, but he looked as if his soul were untroubled. Min suspected he had been praying during the long dark hours of his watch. Robse passed him the honey with a quiet smile, but Min noted the heavy eyes and the pronounced downward droop to the young

Champion's mouth, indicators that the general atmosphere was affecting him, too, though he was unwilling to show it.

Min's eyes swept to the door, as Gaelcar returned from his office, arms full of more Scrolls. The Seneschal betrayed his agitation in the slightly disordered waves of his pale hair and the exaggerated stiffness with which he seated himself. When Min's eyes turned to her sister, she almost laughed aloud. She could not contain the smile of amusement that curved the corners of her generous mouth. Several of the others, noticing, followed her line of sight. Aelric indulged in a chuckle that softened the general, weary tension.

Caerdrys was aflame with excitement, the energy fairly streaming off her. The blanket around her shoulders couldn't disguise the windswept snarls of her hair. The hem of her robe was soaking and bedraggled from her knees down, and her lips were only now losing the bluish cast they'd had when she'd come up the ladder. She looked quite unlike the neat, poised Elf she usually appeared, yet her excitement was such that a few expected to see the moisture steaming off her! Her rain-colored eyes were alight and the tired lines around her mouth went unnoticed in her vibrant attitude. She leaned forward, elbows braced on the edge of the table, poised like a racehorse awaiting the signal to leap into action. Taking their attention as a signal to speak, she began to share what she had learned from Ghaerwe and her pod.

"Ghaerwe brought the pod up to find and join us because they heard from other *delphys* pods of whale songs being sung about us! It seems that Geliennos's song telling his people about meeting us has made quite a few whales remember snippets of ancient songs that mention our people. Ghaerwe found out all she could and then came to find us to tell us that we are very close to the place the whales first remember meeting us ages ago!

"According to them, we are nearly home!"

The window shimmered into existence with an arresting shifting and streaming of colors that immediately drew the collective attention of the whole gathering. The eclectic group was comprised of the core of young friends of Theo and Elwyn, the slightly larger group of their parents and elders, and as many again of the newer and widely varied acquaintances met here in Marliondolen. There were close to one hundred of them seated and reclining at their ease on bright blankets spread upon the broad expanse of golden beach before the ocean Laslorn had dreamed into being. Of the twenty or so small fires cheerily crackling in their stone circles, nearly all sported small cauldrons of steaming water for tea. The remains of a merry and hearty repast were still scattered about, but only the younger males were still eating.

At the appearance of this window over the sea, they all sat up alertly and ceased their conversations. The pull of the Creator's Spirit was strong, and many there had been anticipating this event for some weeks, as they knew their Kin on Earth were approaching what might well be their sought-for haven. As the swirled haze of colors cleared, it was at first difficult to distinguish what they saw, for the window, perched above their own ocean, showed them a vision of the open sea of Earth. Soon they discerned the heavier atmosphere and dimmer colors of the Earth seascape and were able to orient themselves. It seemed they were being shown what their Kin were seeing off their own bows.

As they leaned forward, straining as eagerly as their seabound Kin for the first glimpse of some sort of land formation, the hazy mists obscuring their sight began to clear away, like fingers of fog, swept away by the sea breeze. Before them, still some distance away, lay three dark spots in a cluster.

They stared intently for a long, silent moment, analyzing, hoping, praying. Then came a cry of recognition from a throat strained by tears of joy.

"There, the left-most isle! It is the northernmost of them, and see—there at the peak is the crest of the caldera! It is our lost home!" Others of the company now chimed in their own cries, many of their voices thick with tears at this sight they thought never to see again.

"It is!"

"Oh look, see the southern coastline! That's where we brought the sheep down to water!"

"And, look ye, the waves still batter the western cliffs! I wonder, do the great sea eagles still nest there?"

As these joyful cries pierced the soft shore breeze, the teal eyes of Elrad the Seer scanned the crowd unerringly until they met the violet ones of Kytha Athalenael, and they shared a warm communion of hope and the knowledge of promises fulfilled.

Across the small fire from Elrad, Theo's warm hand enfolded his wife's, and Elwyn hid her happy tears in his shoulder. Characteristically, Laslorn was whooping with joy and twirling Nausika about in his strong arms, to the indulgent amusement of their neighbors. Kier, Davin, Lucina, and Michal were rising into the air to get a better perspective on the visionary islands. Amadthalos and Ethalion, arms slung across one another's shoulders, had begun to sing a song of praise to the Creator, their deep voices cutting through the higher cries of the others.

Soon, all had landed, or settled, and the entire company was singing, standing upon that golden beach, in the sunset of their day, watching the future of their Kin through the window awash in the bright sunlight of the Earthly sea.

Later that day, the same group of Companions was still spending large chunks of time reading the Scrolls, familiarizing themselves with the songs, prophecies, and stories of old that spoke of their home island. Aelric, one Scroll in hand, walked grimly to the cabin's wide, bubbled windows, looking from the ancient parchment to the island chain that was once again visible off the starboard bow. They were still several days out, but these were the first islands they had sighted in many weeks.

Their quest had drawn them in a great circle, and they were now closer to their lost Land than they had been since leaving it nearly a year before. With great gravity, Aelric examined the islands, then the passage marked in the Scroll he held, glancing from one to the other several times. The bright afternoon sunlight slanting through the window bathed him in an almost unearthly radiance. He then selected another Scroll from Gaelcar's waiting hands and did the same.

When he had finished his perusal, he returned to the table and sat down in his chair. His eyes were distant, seeing something beyond his tense Companions. They respected his silence, and Aelric appeared to be in deep thought for a while. Finally, he shook his head briskly and looked up, his golden eyes bright but wary. He faced his waiting Companions, praying that the Creator would guide him in his task of determining whether or not they could call one of these islands 'home.'

Aelric cleared his throat and gestured toward the northernmost one of the chain, nodding to Myrandella. "As we have all seen in our restless dreams these past weeks, this group of islands mirrors the descriptions and memories of our ancestors as much as is possible considering we are approaching them from a direction not noted in their descriptions." He shook the Scroll in his hand for emphasis. "Although these records omit far too much, what they do say is matched in the northerly isle of this chain. This island has every feature of the island mentioned by the old prophets and historians, and there is nothing we can see that contradicts what the legends say."

Aelric stopped speaking, gazing at the solemn, wary, taut expressions on the faces of those he had come to love and trust in the past year. He allowed his passion for his father's dream to thaw his own features and watched the rising hope mirrored in their eyes.

"My friends," he said in a voice tight with emotion, "I believe we are finally home."

Part III

Sanctuary

Chapter Twenty-Five

What had been an ordinary morning was radically changed. The herald of the turmoil was the staccato tattoo of running feet along the boardwalk leading to the Office of the Dockmaster. Peering through the open window in the wall his private office shared with the larger general workspace, Dockmaster Strahng beheld young Bran bursting through the wide double doors. The child negotiated a scrabbling curve without losing his footing and hurtled toward the dockmaster's office alcove.

As the boy seemed intent on maintaining his speed, Strahng arose from behind his desk and hastily pulled open the carved wooden door, bracing himself as the boy crashed into his chest. They both staggered back a few steps, fetching up painfully against the great wooden desk that took up most of the tiny office. Even as he plucked the boy out of his shirtfront and set him upon his own feet, Strahng was wondering what catastrophe had occurred to send him at such a pace, and how many were dead or injured. From the crowd of clerks gathering outside his office door, he wasn't the only one entertaining thoughts of disaster.

The boy, redfaced, was gulping great gasps of air and babbling something about Strahng being needed at the dock. The big man shook the boy slightly to make him calm down.

"What's the trouble, Bran? How many are hurt?" he barked as he shrugged into the embroidered yellow vest his wife had made for him. Bran shook his head, flinging drops of sweat from his hair.

"None hurt, sir. But Mister Temple said to fetch you on the run, sir, so I have!"

"On the run, eh?" *What's got Temple's tiller in a twist? It's not like him to call for me if there's no emergency. The weather's perfect, so it's not like there's storm damage coming. I wonder if he's sighted pirates. We don't hardly ever see them around here.* Even as these thoughts stung Strahng's mind, his burly form was striding down the walkway from his quarters to the main dock. His keen eyes picked out the identifying yellow vest on his tall, thin lieutenant.

Temple was standing with the Watch atop the tallest structure on the dock, the sea breeze whipping his bright vest behind him. Strahng could see the slender shape of the spyglass held to his assistant's eye. Pausing, he squinted out into the sunlit sea but could only see the dark spots of a cluster of approaching ships. He judged them to be less than half an hour out. It was unusual for them to be approaching from the southwest, but pirates bent on a sneak attack would have hugged the coast to avoid being seen until the last moment. Hastening his steps, he took the ladder two rungs at a time and arrived puffing at the lookout perch.

"What's all this about, Temple?" he asked with some asperity. The reed-thin man turned to face him, holding out the spyglass.

"Ships," he said with his customary taciturnity. Strahng sighed and slapped the instrument to his right eye, scouting for the dark shapes on the horizon.

"I can see they're ships, Temple!" he began with some exasperation. "But why do you need me to—" He broke off suddenly, as the spyglass brought the vessels into stunning clarity. With a shock, he felt as if he had witnessed a sea serpent rise up out of the calm waters of their bay. Those ships, unique of design, surprisingly larger in real life than he had expected, were chillingly familiar. They were no pirate ships. In fact, they were a wonder, a legend come to life, the breathtaking embodiment of all his childhood fantasies. They could also be a knell of doom.

Handing the spyglass back to his assistant, Strahng reached over to the logbook and tore out a blank page. Grabbing up the quill tethered to its wooden stand, he scrawled a hasty message. Folding it over, he thrust it at the waiting boy.

"To the king, Bran. On the run!"

Robse shook his head irritably, wishing they had not had to don once more their disgusting disguises. The strain of the past week of high-strung nerves, lack of sleep, and general excitement was now further exacerbated by the addition of a general outrage at the presence of Humans on their island and the indignity of having to stain and stink and wear dirty clothes that chafed rudely when they first reached their ancient home!

Caerdrys's outrage had been the most extreme, for the unexpected presence of Humans on their island had forced her to be caged below decks again, and she would not be among the first to set foot upon the legendary isle! Robse recognized the welling resentment in himself and paused to ask help of the Creator to flush it out of his spirit. Certainly resentment would only poison his own heart and would not help their current situation. Also, he was perceptive enough to note, the presence of resentment indicated that he had somehow come to feel the island they hoped would be their sanctuary actually belonged to him. This was sheerest folly, of course, as all places belonged to the Creator, not the creatures who inhabited them. Still, it was hard to think, after all their desperate searching, that they had at last reached their goal, only to find it already claimed by their enemies!

Still, Robse sighed to himself, straightening the filthy hat that covered both ear tips and eyebrows, the Creator knew what He was doing. If He wanted them to make their home upon this island, there would be a way, as impossible as it seemed at present. Ready at last, he quickly searched for Aelric.

He found the king, attired in his role of rich, yet shabby Human, standing near enough to the starboard rail to see the docks but not be seen. Robse unobtrusively took up his place at the king's back. What he saw increased his unease. This dock did not resemble most of the ones they had visited previously. For one thing, it was remarkably clean. For another, the busy, bustling crowd, in which they'd planned to lose themselves, was standing about idly, watching them arrive. Worse yet, there was a brightly dressed handful of Men waiting to greet them as they docked! The big one in the yellow vest had to be the dockmaster, the person whose attention they least desired! How were they going to play their roles and discover what they needed to know if they were singled out and noticed in such a fashion?

Robse turned his attention to Aelric and saw that he was earnestly discussing this very problem with Gaelcar, even as Cerlim, Randelos, and Domel waited nearby. In a very few minutes, it became apparent that there was nothing they could do at this point but go on with their original plan and hope for the best. Perhaps there would be some way of avoiding too much close scrutiny.

As they prepared to descend the gangplank to the scrubbed planks of the dock, Robse found his mind worrying at one question above the others: *why* was the dockmaster waiting to greet them personally, and what were the implications for their quest?

Strahng straightened the bright medals pinned over his heart and tugged his yellow vest down over his stomach. Nervously, he ran his hands over his windblown hair, smoothing down the rough, graying locks at his temples and combing his fingers through his streaked beard. It was an unconscious gesture, but it alerted those around him to the fact that their formidable dockmaster was unsettled—a rare occurrence. The blue and green cords, braided with the gold thread of a Master, were looped around his left shoulder, proclaiming his rank. It was rarely worn, and he had had to send an apprentice to his home to ask his flustered wife to find it for him.

Beside him, Temple was similarly attired. His vest boasted fewer medals, of course, and his shoulder braid bore the silver of a djournee, one who had displayed enough skill to be paid a daily wage but had not yet attained his mastery. Like his master, he held himself proudly, arrayed in his best to honor their guests. The dockmaster's burly form made two of skinny Temple, and the younger man was only half the age of the elder, but they were obviously a welcoming committee.

The leader of the three beautiful ships was warping into the docks now, turning her carved and painted flank broadside to the quay. The docks were lined with gaping spectators, and even the busy dockhands, waiting to catch the snubbing lines and make them fast to the cleats on the quay, were standing slack-jawed at the magnificent sight. The strange ships were half again as large as most merchant vessels, more streamlined and graceful in the water as well. The carved and painted figurehead on the lead ship depicted a man of kingly countenance, crowned with stars. It was fashioned and painted with such skill that it looked as if the man might speak at any moment and tell them of the wonders his eyes beheld on the far horizons. The elaborate carvings and decorations on the cerdems and balconies, and the beautiful colors they were painted, drew gasps and murmurs of wonder from the watching crowd. They had never seen such fine vessels, nor so large.

A few of the older watchers exchanged guarded glances with Strahng. The longer, smoother lines of these ships were hauntingly familiar to a handful of them, who, as intrepid boys, had braved the journey into the rainforest to see the ancient carvings for themselves. The clearest remaining pictures of those etched long years before into the living rock of the old volcano's interior had been of graceful ships such as these.

Strahng surreptitiously wiped his damp palms on his vest. Not normally a man given to uncertainty, he found the present situation highly uncomfortable. Men had first come to settle this island six generations before. Like all the other inhabitants, Strahng was familiar with the tales of their quest to find a safe harbor, where they could pursue their beliefs and found their culture in peace. He knew the history of the building of the City on the Hill, of the labors of the citizens to make this place what they wanted it to be.

He knew, as did all those raised here, the stories of the discovery of the remains of a previous people, an ancient culture who had inhabited the island long before them. The carvings on the cliff faces within the ancient caldera in the center of the island had been a subject of wonder and conjecture for as long as his people had been here. Who were the people who had lived here before? What had they believed? How had they lived? Why had they left? Would they ever return?

The question that rang silently in the ears of every person who had seen those carvings and now watched the three ships moving gracefully to the quay held them all tense with concern.

Had the Ancient Lords returned today to reclaim their island?

Finally, the first ship, glorious in royal purple and gold and emerald, was made fast to the quay. Her graceful balconies over the sterncastle were cunningly carved to resemble trees. Her main and lesser cerdems were carved, painted, and gilded with figures of flowers, trees, and woodland creatures, as well as birds, butterflies, fish, waves, and dolphins. Up close, it could be discerned that she had suffered some damages, likely from storms, but had been repaired with skill. The gangplank was run out and braced against the smooth planks of the quay. Strahng raised his chin a bit higher, preparing himself for his first glimpse of the legendary Ancient Lords, if indeed these were they.

Tall figures appeared at the top of the gangplank. As they began to descend, Strahng was a bit disappointed to note that while they were tall and their figures well formed, they were dirty and swarthy, like most of the ordinary sailors they traded with from the lands to the south and east. As their leader stepped down to the quay, Strahng moved forward to greet him. He was further disappointed to note that the finery at the man's cuffs and throat was soiled and shabby, and, it could not be denied, he stank strongly, though the odor was more that of goat than of man, which further puzzled the dockmaster. It saddened him somehow to think that the Ancient Lords were no greater than this. Still, it was no part of his plan to have the hospitality of the island fail just because their visitors didn't meet the standards of his childhood fantasies.

He held out his hand in welcome, trying not to flinch when the leader's strong grip left something slightly sticky on his palm. He looked into the tall man's eyes, and suddenly his speech of welcome dried up in his mouth. In those burning, golden eyes he found all the mystery and glory of his valiant boyhood dreams. He felt himself drowning in them, unable to speak or to protest. There was something not quite right about their shape, but that flicker of thought was swamped in the force of this unique man's personality. In his bearing, under his dirt and stink, was the air of one who was accustomed to command, of a high lord. Recognizing that, Strahng strove to find his voice and his manners.

"Welcome to Egauswas, my lord," he finally managed, his voice coming out a trifle higher than its usual deep baritone. He cleared his throat and tried again, with better success. "I am Dockmaster Strahng, and this is my djourneeman, Temple." He waited politely for the newcomers to respond. There were six of them now standing upon the quay, all tall and fair beneath their dirt and ragged clothing. Strahng was not the only one to notice their wariness, as though the welcome provided to honor them was perceived as a threat. The leader nodded briefly, as though wishing to dismiss any further formality or notice.

"I am Aelric, owner of these vessels. This is Gaelcar, captain of the *Cethastea*." His voice, with its rich, fluid accent, was all Strahng could have wished in an Ancient King. As much to hear it again as to conduct his business and to buy time, Strahng asked another question.

"Your ships are unusual and beautiful, lord. We have not seen their like in these docks. From whence do you hail?" The question, though mild and courteous enough, seemed to provoke greater agitation among the party. The tall, fair-haired captain to the leader's left bent and said something swift and fluid in the dark man's ear. The liquid syllables of his speech were similar to the Common Speech, but more beautiful and flowing. Strahng could not catch what he had said, but he would bet the gist of it was, "Let's get out of here!" The leader shook his dark head sharply.

"No! We shall not leave thus, when we have just found what we so desperately sought. We must know more!" He seemed unaware of speaking in the Common Speech, but the one who had advised him bowed his fair head in submission. The gray eyes of the one to the leader's right flashed defiantly about the crowded dock.

Strahng noticed the leader had made no effort to answer his question concerning their origins. Just then, a movement in the crowd attracted all eyes. A moment later, a tall herald from the king's Great Hall pushed his way through the people, followed by young Bran, whose eyes widened at the sight of the magnificent ships up close. The messenger handed a folded parchment to Strahng with a slight bow.

"A message from the king, Master," he murmured courteously, his eyes riveted on the six newcomers. Strahng unfolded the king's hasty missive and read it with some relief. The monarch had taken his meaning and acted as Strahng had hoped. He turned to the tall leader.

"This is a summons from our king, my lord. He asks that you and your party be escorted to his Great Hall that he may welcome you personally." At the news of this singular honor, a look of dismay spread across the faces of the young man's companions, but Aelric quickly hid his own reaction behind a mask of polite acceptance and nodded his dark head. Strahng gestured for them to follow the messenger, and they quietly filed away through the curious crowd.

As he watched them climb the paved street toward the hill's summit, tall and proud of bearing beneath their dirty coverings, they seemed to Strahng like confident yet wary kings walking among potential enemies. *Indeed*, he thought to himself as he watched them out of sight, *the Ancient Lords* have *returned to us.*

Sagiro waited, sitting still on his throne by an act of sheer will. The hastily scrawled missive from Strahng was crumpled in his pocket, but the words were burned into his mind's eye.

The ships of the Ancient Lords have returned.

He had never expected to read those words in his lifetime. It was incredible. It was exhilarating. It was terrifying. His blood ran cold and then hot at the implications in those eight words. His people had been on this island for six generations. His ancestor had been the leader of the small band of outcasts who had fled their country seeking a haven where they could worship in peace as they chose. When they had found this beautiful island, with its lovely conical mountain and the wonderful natural harbor in the bay, they had rejoiced and had quickly settled.

The labor of building their terraced City down the slope of the lesser hill to the sea had moved apace with the constructing of the Temple at the summit. All the people had shared in the work of the Temple to honor the Creator. As the City and the docks and the fields and farms had been built, each generation had added to the adornment of the Temple. As their understanding of the goodness and mercy of the Creator increased, so did the desire to praise and honor Him.

They had early discovered the remains of a prior civilization, which they called simply the Ancients. The carvings were exquisitely beautiful, even the ones that had worn away almost to naught. That those mysterious people had been talented had been apparent, if they knew nothing else of them. That the carvings on the rock walls of the caldera were old beyond imagining was obvious, but how long the Ancients had been gone was anybody's guess.

And now, it seemed, they had returned.

Sagiro shifted slightly in his seat. Would the Ancient Lords return to claim their island? Would they claim it with violence and try to oust the newcomers? Sagiro prayed desperately that they could reach some agreeable compromise. His people had prospered here. They had made a home, a place away from those who refused to honor the Creator. He did not want them to be forced to leave and search for a new haven. And, surely, after all these years, a claim could be contested. His people had lived here in peace for so long. Over two hundred years surely gave them some claim. Perhaps, he thought suddenly, the Ancients would want only the interior of the island for their home. After all, the carvings had been found there, deep in the caldera's rain forest. That would be a good solution. Or perhaps they weren't really the descendants of the Ancient Lords at all! Maybe Strahng had been mistaken and the ships merely resembled the unique carvings on the cliff walls.

Either way he'd best be prepared for the worst, or he would be in no way able to work for the good of his people. Once again, Sagiro bowed his head in fervent prayer. As he raised his face from his sheltering hand, he heard footsteps approaching through the tiled entryway. The quiet murmur of conversation in the throne room ceased abruptly, as if he had just ducked under water in the baths. The doors at the end of the long room were opened to admit the party, and Sagiro stood to welcome them, eager for his first glimpse of legend.

Gaelcar, together with Aelric and those of his Companions ashore, walked up the steep hill to the Court of the island nation. He looked about him as they went, noting the carefully shaped and smoothly laid paving stones of the road, the trimmed grass and cultivated trees that lined the way. He saw curved streets of workplaces and shops, many with snug homes built above them and neat gardens behind and before. There was a sense of prosperity and pride in these structures that had more to do with care and cleanliness and beauty of line than any outward adornment.

As they followed the messenger higher up the hill, he saw that they passed great, sturdy walls that separated and supported the terraced levels. Each wall was pierced by the wide road and crowned with a graceful stone archway. Gaelcar saw that they were carved with figures, but their party did not pass slowly enough for him to study them.

About halfway to the summit, Gaelcar noticed the sound of running water. Closer to the docks, it had been masked by the ceaseless sound of the sea, but here where the main noises were birdsongs, it was clearly audible. Scanning for the source, he caught Robse's alert gaze. The young

Champion gestured with his dirty head to Gaelcar's left. There, not far from the path, was a deep stream, its bed lined with smooth stones, or perhaps fashioned tiles. It flowed down from higher up on the hill, and Gaelcar could see that it disappeared under the foundations of an attractive stone building, which was surrounded by flowering trees and a lush garden with smooth lawns. A fountain played on the slope below the building, and the water that spilled from its broad rim flowed back into the lined trough of the stream farther down. Fascinated and curious, Gaelcar slowed to watch it, causing Cerlim to step on his heels.

As they continued upwards, nearly all the buildings on the gently curved side roads were homes; snug and cozy, not very large, most with gardens of vegetables and flowers nestled behind low stone or wooden fences. Though it was early morning and the shadows lay sharply across the landscape, there were no children to be seen, and only a few women sweeping their doorways, colorful kerchiefs bound about their heads. It was orderly, clean, and altogether pleasing, and Gaelcar was amazed to find it so.

In all honesty, he admitted he was greatly shaken at discovering that the island was already inhabited by mortals. Now, it seemed that the island was not really theirs to claim. At the very least it appeared they would have to find a way to coexist with *Humans.* A tingle of fear went through Gaelcar as he recalled how ill Minlienda and Caerdrys had fallen when their party had encountered the disbelief of Men at that first port where they had landed to trade. If the disbelief of Humans had made healthy, grown Elves so ill, the fragile Elven children would surely not last in the presence of their foes. And certainly, they would not be able to continue with their charade of being Humans themselves for longer than it took to trade and take on water.

Yet now, when they had finally reached the island they'd sought, it seemed the dark and dirty world of the Human docks that they had encountered previously was nonexistent here! These Humans seemed very different from those he had seen so far on their journey. These people were almost Faeltheon, he admitted wryly to himself. He did not mean to disparage Human achievements, but they typically did not equal the beauty and serenity of the Faeltheon places, nor did they appear to want to. But here, the architecture, the softly playing music he heard, the care taken to nurture tree and garden; they all struck a homesick chord in him. There was no doubt in his mind that this island was his home, yet his logic chided him, saying that the Creator certainly would not have been so careless as to put Humans, even these Faeltheon-like Humans, on the Elven home.

Would He?

Their climb had now brought them to the end of the road. As it passed through a last graceful arch, the road widened into a great paved courtyard. The stones were a harmonious blend of golden, white, black, and red and were set in various pleasing patterns, radiating out from a huge fountain in the center. Courteously, the messenger allowed them to pause and catch their breaths after the climb up from the docks. As they gazed about them, they were amazed anew at the beauty the Humans of Egauswas had wrought.

The white stone fountain was carved to resemble a large clamshell with exaggerated ridges. It was fashioned thus so that the water that cascaded from its lip was channeled in four separate streams, each one falling like a small waterfall through a cunningly wrought copper grate set into the paving stones. It was obvious that the streams were channeled away under the courtyard, to reappear later in lined troughs, like the one they had passed, and carried away in separate directions down the hillside. The sound of the water gurgling beneath their feet, as it went on its merry way to water the City, seemed an omen of peace and prosperity Gaelcar longed to trust.

Ahead, dominating the landscape, was the distant higher peak of the island's central mountain cone. Closer, the apex of the hill they had climbed rose above them, slightly to the left of the central cone's peak. Nearby, to the right, was a large, graceful building of several levels, with carved pillars in front and a mosaic floor in the entryway. To the left was an imposing structure of tall towers rising off a slender central building. Gaelcar could see that the tallest tower would provide a spectacular view of the terraced City all the way down to the docks. Both of the structures were fashioned of polished stone and were carved and, in places, inlaid with gems and gold.

But, magnificent as they were, they paled utterly before the building set opposite the roadway. This structure was built on the apex of the hill, a fitting crown for the lovely City. It was fashioned with great skill out of stone that gleamed white in the early light. Its towers yearned toward heaven in slender pinnacles that were covered in precious gold and white silver and a substance that gleamed like red fire in the sun. It was inlaid with cut gems and jewels that sparkled like captive stars. The walls and pillars were adorned with carvings, mosaics, and paintings that were nearly as good as Faeltheon work.

Gaelcar was not the only one of the Companions to feel a tug of familiarity. This place, though a bit overdone for Faeltheon style, was clearly wrought by hands devoted to producing beauty and was obviously a place of worship. It was undoubtedly the work of an entire community and had taken more than one of their fleeting lifetimes to create. Set against the darkly forested backdrop of the greater mountain behind, it shone forth like a bright beacon and could probably be seen for miles. This then was the answer to the mysterious flashing light they had glimpsed in this morning's sunrise. It was clearly meant to be the jewel of their land, their crowning achievement, and the Faeltheon felt its importance and honored it. It seemed significant to Gaelcar, and as he exchanged glances with the others he saw that they noted it too, that the dominant place was given not to their Human ruler, but to their Temple.

The messenger got their attention again and requested that they follow him. He crossed the courtyard to the building on the right, and they passed through the pillars and the broad open doorway into a gracious, wide entryway. The colorful mosaic on the floor depicted happy, domestic scenes of families together, farmers harvesting, herdsmen with their flocks, and fishermen in their ships. From either side rose two curved staircases that met overhead in an arch that supported an upper hallway. The company crossed the open space of the entryway and followed the messenger through a set of carved double doors that opened under the arch of the stairway.

They found themselves in a long, well-appointed room, flanked with broad spaces to the left and right, set off from the central walkway by carved pillars. As they looked ahead, down the floor of inlaid wood, they saw they had entered the king's throne room. The monarch rose from his seat to greet them, a regal manner about him.

As they drew closer, they saw that the king smiled a deep, warm smile that reached his eyes, though it did nothing to diminish the countenance of a wise and strong ruler. He was dressed in a simple, yet becoming tunic of deep blue, and his baggy trousers below were of a contrasting bronze color, edged with bands of brown velvet. He was of middling height and build and was girt about the hips with a broad belt of silver links, from which no weapon hung. It was obvious he felt himself unthreatened and meant to make them welcome. His golden brown hair was beginning to silver, and his beard was streaked with pale gray like twin waterfalls. His receding hairline revealed his lofty brow, and there were lines graven on his face, but more of them were from smiling than from care, Gaelcar thought. The king's voice was surprisingly substantial and laced with good humor, though Gaelcar thought he could detect a note of reserve as well. He caught Robse's eye and saw the Champion was aware of it too.

Chapter Twenty-six

The messenger halted before the throne, bowed, and melted off to the side. Sagiro pasted a smile on his face and tried to mean his welcome. The dark-haired man before him was plainly the leader of the group. He was tall and well favored, though ill dressed and unclean.

Sagiro looked deeper, probing with the clear sight that had given him his name. This one, beneath his flimsy distraction of disguise, was truly a King. In his molten eyes, Sagiro could clearly read a frustration and trouble as great as his own disquiet, yet no sign of it sat upon the still face. His bearing was that of a man accustomed to leadership, yet his body clearly showed the fruit of months of hard labor. He seemed too young for the responsibilities Sagiro sensed he carried, yet he was not in any way bowed by them.

Sagiro experienced a fleeting revelation so piercing, yet so sweet, it made him catch his breath. *I would give much to have this one call me friend.*

He turned his probing gaze upon the stranger's companions and found there men of similar ilk. Tall, fair, troubled, yet of noble bearing, they were all the stuff of imagination. He yearned mightily to know them in all their complexity, to hear their thoughts about the Creator, to spend long ages cementing a deep friendship. The yearning was so strong, he almost questioned its innocence. He mustn't lose sight of the needs of his people, no matter how charismatic these strangers were beneath the veil of their disguises. And there was the thing that troubled him most.

Why the disguises? What were they hiding? Could men who went about disguised be trusted? And why on Earth would they go to so much trouble to try to hide what was obviously great beauty? His mind demanded answers, even as his heart urged him to trust.

"Welcome, strangers, to Egauswas," the monarch was saying. "I sense that you have traveled on a long journey to arrive here. Please, I must exhort you to shed your costumes; we are a peaceful people and are ever fascinated by new wayfarers. After all, our differences only bear testimony to our Creator's limitless imagination and power. Surely you have no need of subterfuge here among friends."

A wave of shock rippled through the Faeltheon. How had this Human seen so quickly and completely through their disguises? Who did he suspect they really were? Gaelcar made no move that might reveal more than an ordinary sailor. He realized that these Humans most likely tried to be receptive toward strange cultures and people; yet he was of an entirely different *species* than they. The king could not suspect that and would doubtless be taken by surprise. Disbelief, no matter how tardy it was in coming, would arrive inevitably.

Even as he hoped that the younger Elves with him would quickly arrive at the same logical conclusion, he sensed movement to his left. His hopes were dashed when Aelric boldly removed his grimy hat, showing clearly his pointed ears, so radically different from a Human's that there was no possible way Aelric could have been one of them. Robse moved closer to Aelric, his hand flashing to the sword fastened at his belt, alert to any hostility or danger that might be directed against his king. Gaelcar cringed, anticipating the sharp, poisoned arrows of disbelief that he was certain were already being aimed at them. Several gasps and murmurs spread throughout the people of the Court.

It was not sounds of disbelief or rejection that reached Gaelcar's sharp ears, however. Rather, he heard the people comment on their exotic beauty, the wonder of their differences. Amazed, he watched as the Human king once again smiled a friendly smile of acceptance, seeming more relaxed now that their disguises were acknowledged and breached.

With a sense of wonder and chagrin, Gaelcar realized that he had been the one to judge and reject, automatically assuming that these Humans were as dangerously driven by doubt as the others he had encountered. Though he dared not simply abandon reason, he could not subdue the rising flicker of hope in his breast. Perhaps the Creator *had* guarded their island home, after all, by allowing these oddly receptive Humans to colonize it. Perhaps it *would* be possible to share this haven.

There was a rustling and a stir behind them, from down the long room by the door. Soft voices were heard, and the attention of all shifted to the interruption. In a swift movement, Robse placed himself between Aelric and any potential threat. His sword appeared in his hand as if it had grown there, held at the ready across his chest. A low rumble from King Sagiro grew into a chuckle, and the clustering courtiers parted to reveal a tiny woman in a long blue dress that swept the floor behind her.

"Gentlemen," said the island's ruler, "may I present my wife, Queen Sophia, a woman aptly named and doubly cherished for it."

The little queen blushed like a girl, her charming smile flickering about her demurely curved lips. She gracefully curtsied to them in spite of their dirt and rough apparel. Her dark hair was pulled smoothly back from an oval face just a shade too round to be called slender. Aelric bowed in response, and his companions belatedly remembered their manners. Robse seemed unsure what to do with his sword now that he had drawn it. Sagiro seemed to sense his discomfort, for he left his throne and went to meet his wife and escort her to them. He nodded to Robse in a friendly way as he passed.

"You need fear no attack here. You have come armed into our presence, yet you have no need of weapons, unless you would offer violence to my people, which, I judge, is not your intent." He took Sophia's arm and turned back toward them, as Robse, flushed with embarrassment, slid his sword back into its sheath at his hip.

"Your pardon, my lady. I meant no insult," he stammered, feeling wretched and hoping he wasn't making Aelric look bad. She smiled graciously upon his confusion and then turned to her husband.

"My dear, I heard we had guests and came as soon as I could. Will you not introduce me properly?" The king laughed in true mirth, the wrinkles at the corners of his eyes almost hiding their merry gleam from view.

"In truth, my dear, we had not got so far yet. I have given my name but have not yet had the honor of receiving theirs, so your timing is excellent, as usual." The tiny queen dimpled and the Court relaxed, eager to hear the strangers' names and tale. Aelric bowed to the queen, as though he were wearing his finest clothes and not a noxious coating of filth and ragged finery.

"I am Aelric Rysaelf, son of Beregos, king of what remains of my people, the Faeltheon. These are some of my Companions, my Council. This is my Seneschal, Gaelcar Talathaem, and my Champion, Robse Lyserea. These others are Domel Minquallen, Cerlim Swyren, and Randelos Ommgeon. We regret having appeared before you in this guise, but our experiences at other Human ports were less than favorable. We have found it prudent to appear as like to Humans as possible when walking among them."

Well, that was stating it baldly, thought Gaelcar, wincing inwardly. He wondered if the repeated inferences to their non-Human state would provoke any further response than the first sight of Aelric's ears had. The tension in the throne room had tightened a bit with Aelric's words, as though they were a challenge to the king to make good on his offer of friendship. The little queen smiled around at them, and her words restored the ease in the chamber.

"How dreadful for you! I am sure you would like to be treated as yourselves for once, and so you shall! I will go and prepare rooms for you, with hot baths and servants to see to your needs. You must be weary, both of travel and of those disguises. Please, King Aelric, summon others of sufficient rank, that we may offer them hospitality as well. Then, when you have rested and donned your own clothing, please join us in breaking the night fast together." She turned her warm brown eyes upon Aelric, and behind their friendliness he saw the expression of a woman who would not easily be denied. He wondered if she had any children. If she did, he knew they never disobeyed that steady gaze. He turned his eyes to Gaelcar, who leaned close, as did Robse.

"It could be a trick meant to lure all our important people into one place and trap us," cautioned the young Champion in Faeltheon, but Aelric sensed his lack of belief in his own theory. Gaelcar's snort was nearly silent but clearly relayed his opinion.

"Their welcome and show of hospitality is consistent with the level of civilization we have witnessed so far, cousin. I am encouraged by these signs. I suggest you send for Caerdrys, Minlienda, the Kytha, and our clothes and let us embark on what promises to be an historic friendship," the Seneschal advised. Aelric nodded, seeing Robse's relieved smile. It was obvious his Champion had felt it his duty to issue his warning but hadn't believed it to be necessary. Aelric bowed to the queen once more.

"We would be glad indeed to accept your generous hospitality. I will send Cerlim to summon the others of my Council." He nodded to Cerlim, who bowed and strode from the chamber, an honor escort scrambling to catch up to him. Domel exchanged grins with Robse, wishing he'd been sent so he could have seen Caerdrys's face when the news was delivered.

"Excellent!" the diminutive monarch exclaimed, turning in a flurry of silken skirts. "How many more shall we expect, my lord?"

"Only three more," Aelric assured her with a smile.

"Good! I shall leave now to see the rooms and baths prepared!" Several ladies departed with the queen, and a spate of urgent, if muted whispering ensued among the courtiers. The king waved them all away and then gestured the Faeltheon toward a smaller door near the thrones.

"Come, my friends, let us walk in the gardens until your companions arrive."

Rapid footfalls and raised voices caused the women and children hiding below decks to raise their heads and look about alertly. Caerdrys moved swiftly to the foot of the main companionway, determined to know what was happening above, even if she wasn't supposed to be seen. She was two steps up when she nearly collided with Cerlim, who was hastening downward, speaking over his shoulder to someone out of Caerdrys's sight. She grabbed the handrail to brace herself as Cerlim cannoned into her, catching himself with his customary grace and apologizing profusely. She waved his apologies aside, demanding to know why he had returned and what news he bore to bring him in such a state.

"Are we under attack? Where are Aelric and the others? I will not sit confined here if we are in danger!"

Cerlim had been shaking his head and waving his hands at her, but she was ready to mount the rest of the stairs to see what was happening for herself. He was forced to grab her arm and pull her back down to the second deck, where he could explain his errand to them all. With a wry look in his eyes, Cerlim considered putting his hand over Caerdrys's mouth to make her listen to him. Another look at her fiery eyes caused him to drop that notion in a hurry though.

"If you will allow me to speak, I will tell you what you wish to know!" he exclaimed with some exasperation, propping his fists on his hips. Caerdrys became silent so quickly it took Cerlim a moment to realize he had the floor. Anticipating their reactions, he kept his eyes on Caerdrys as he delivered his message.

"King Aelric has sent me back to summon you, Minlienda, and Myrandella to join us at the Human King's Great Hall… for breakfast!" The silence that greeted this message was so thunderstruck that Cerlim almost laughed aloud. Caerdrys didn't look shocked enough yet, so he added the rest of his errand.

"You are to dress as befits your station and come without disguises."

This time the wide-eyed looks and startled murmurs did make him laugh. Caerdrys looked almost disappointed that there were no enemies to best or friends to rescue. Min's voice sounded softly from his right.

"Undisguised? *Breakfast*?"

"They know about us? They are not hostile? You felt no weakening? This is not a trap, is it, Cerlim?" came the Kytha's voice from his other side. Smiling, the blond bowman shook his head.

"No, ladies, no trap, and they are quite... friendly and accepting. Oh," he added as an afterthought. "We are to bring with us suitable garments for the other Companions."

Half an hour later, as they departed the *Cethastea* and rejoined their honor guard for the mile-long trek up the hill, the three Elven women were resplendent in their finest garments, and Cerlim, dressed in his typical dapper fashion, was still chuckling to himself.

Sagiro stood in the warm sunlight that filtered through the leaves of the trees in his garden and watched as his visitors were led away into his home, to be bathed and refreshed and revealed in their true forms. Sagiro recognized the rising excitement in himself to see these fair creatures without their filthy disguises, but the discipline of years curbed his impatience and he beckoned to a nearby servant instead.

"Please ask Bintah Auren and Beneval to join me here," he requested, and the servant bowed and swiftly left him. Sagiro paced over to a stone bench in the sun and sat to await his elderly Advisor and his future son-in-law, his mind still preoccupied with the events of the past few minutes. His thoughts dwelt on the newcomers and the implications of their return, even as his fingers absently traced the carved scrollwork of the bench. Nearby, emboldened by his stillness and silence, a chickadee hopped along the edge of the flagstones, searching for breakfast.

Sagiro sat wrapped in wonder, dwelling on the amazing event he had witnessed not half an hour ago in this very spot. He had escorted his guests to the garden and had gestured to them to be seated on the benches that circled the great oak tree at its heart.

When they had come out from the Hall, the birds singing in the morning light had fallen silent at their intrusion. But, as the newcomers seated themselves, there began a rustling in the treetops. Before Sagiro could identify the noise, the rustle had become a rushing, and birds had hopped, flown, fluttered, and flapped to the lower branches above the guests' heads. All had become silent; then one bold fellow had chirped loudly. The blond Champion had trilled a response, and instantly they were deluged with a cacophony of birdsong. Hundreds of birds, of all types, had begun to sing, call, scold, and carry on at the tops of their voices. The air had become dark with new arrivals, all calling excitedly to one another. They had begun dropping from the great oak and the surrounding trees, forming a large, vocal, rippling group on the flagstones at the visitors' feet.

Their king, Aelric, had seemed nonplussed, but the slightly shorter one who looked so much like him had spread out his hands and hushed the flurry. One bold little finch had flown down and landed on one of the outstretched hands. He had flirted his tail, given a little chirp of surprise and quickly hidden himself in the mass of bodies below. A hyacinth macaw, his vivid blue plumage faded to an elderly slate gray, had stepped forward out of the mass. He had spoken to the visitors, the liquid syllables pouring forth oddly from his great curved beak. Sagiro had known many folk who had trained the friendly, colorful birds of the rainforest to repeat words, but he had realized with a shock that this bird was actually speaking to the strangers in his garden. In a frozen awe, he had watched and listened, as the dark-haired king had replied in the same fluid language.

Whatever he had said, it had seemed to satisfy the avian council, for they had all burst into song and flight and quickly cleared the garden, speeding out in all directions over the island. Sagiro, stunned and amazed, had sat silently, unable to think of anything to say that wouldn't sound inane. The visitors had murmured quietly among themselves, tactfully giving him time to recover his poise. Soon after that incident, the servants had arrived to escort them to the chambers Sophia had had prepared.

Sagiro looked down. The busy little chickadee seemed completely unaware that anything unusual had taken place. Sagiro shook his head. For all its unreal quality, that wondrous event had been no dream. His own heart was still pounding strongly from it.

Hearing slow footsteps on the crushed shells that filled the path, Sagiro looked up to greet his oldest friend and trusted advisor. The old man was bent with age and walked stiffly now, but his mind was as sharp as ever and his wisdom had guided Sagiro through many circumstances. Now, more than any other time Sagiro could recall, he needed the counsel of Bintah Auren. He rose to greet his old friend and mentor, taking him gently by the arm and guiding him to the stone seat in the warm sun. The page who had escorted him out skipped away into the Hall, singing a childish rhyme. The old man turned his rheumy eyes in Sagiro's direction, a fond smile playing upon his wrinkled lips.

"What are you up to, Sagiro, to be needing my counsel before breakfast?" he inquired in a voice rusty with age but warmed by depths of good humor. Knowing how the Bintah relished a good tale, Sagiro patiently told the story of the morning's events, leaving out no impression. The old man gasped and chuckled and caught his breath and, in the end, sat with tears glimmering in his blind eyes. Finally, he sighed.

"Oh, Sagiro, today and in the days to come, we shall need every ounce of strength our good names can give us. For such a time as this were you named Shrewd Sight, and your wife called Wise. I, too, shall have need of all the wisdom implied in my title to guide you well, for these strangers are a people beyond our ken."

"I cannot help but feel that we have been blessed in this chance to know them, my friend," replied Sagiro, and the old teacher nodded. "For years you have taught, advised, and guided my family, Bintah. Truly, you have earned the title of 'one who teaches wisely.'" He gently pressed the gnarled hand laid upon his sleeve and the elderly man looked pleased.

Strong footsteps crunched in the shells, heralding the approach of people in some haste. Sagiro was not surprised to see Beneval round the curve of the path, the burly dockmaster a pace behind, a sheaf of papers clenched in his big fist. Beneval greeted Bintah Auren respectfully and seated himself on the adjacent bench. Strahng stopped abruptly before them and sketched a quick bow to his king.

"Greetings to you also, Bintah Auren," he said courteously, beginning to untangle his papers. Bintah laughed quietly. Beneval helpfully held some of the curled sheets, as the dockmaster sorted through them, searching for the ones he had brought to show the king.

"Good day to you, Dockmaster. I expect today has been quite a strain for you, with these marvelous visitors arriving first thing! Are their ships so like the carvings in the caldera?" inquired the Bintah. Strahng looked startled for a moment, then his tense features relaxed into a rueful smile.

"For a blind man, you still see more than most! How did you know I'd brought these renderings along?" He turned to his king and held out three of the curled sheets. Sagiro took them and smoothed them flat on his lap. They were old, very old. The identifications in the corners indicated they were part of the shipping records and documents kept in the storage boxes of the dockmaster. The dates were from before Sagiro's grandfather's time. They were drawings, carefully rendered and notated, of long, graceful ships, and Sagiro recognized them at once. They were copies, faithful in every detail to the carvings from the Interior. He looked up at Strahng.

"Yes, my lord," the dockmaster replied. "Aside from the detail of the carvings and the figureheads, they are nearly identical to the strangers' ships. We didn't have a size scale to go by, and these ships are surprisingly large. Also, their colors are quite brilliant and beautiful. But, in every nautical and structural detail, they are exact."

"Well," creaked the old man, "that confirms the designs are of the Ancients. We still do not know for sure that these people come among us are their descendants, though the evidence points that way. Clearly, they are not like us. What a shame that the other carvings were so weathered as to forbid us more detailed knowledge of the Ancients."

"The question that concerns me," Beneval interjected quietly, "is *why* are they here?"

"If they have returned to claim the island, will they share? Or will they offer violence? And, if they do, what shall we do?" Strahng's voice conveyed his worry. Sagiro did not mention that the visitors had come armed into his presence. He did not see that it would help them to reach a wise conclusion.

"I saw the one come down with the escort to deliver a message to the lead ship. Then I saw him return up the hill with three of their women. They were not disguised but were marvelously fair; so beautiful as to fill the heart to the point of pain. If they are not blood of the Ancient Lords, then they are more even than those Ancients were," remarked Beneval seriously. He was a quiet man, not given to flights of fancy. It was obvious the beautiful strangers had moved him deeply, and the depth of that impression had provoked his natural caution.

"What will we do?" asked the king rhetorically. "We will pray, of course. Surely God did not send these strangers among us for us to act foolishly toward them. We have offered them hospitality and friendship. If they have come seeking to reclaim their island, we will propose sharing it. If they offer violence, we will do what we can to protect our people, but we will not war with them unless they force it upon us. God has a perfect plan. Let us seek Him and ask that He reveal to us what He would have us do in this situation."

The tension in Beneval's shoulders eased and the worry in his eyes cleared. Trained to trust in God's perfect will, he knew that the future could bring sorrow and pain, even perhaps great sacrifice. This did not change the fact that it was their part to pray for guidance and to do His will as it was revealed to them. Whatever the cost, bring it grief or glory, they would submit to God's higher wisdom, and as His will unfolded, they would know that they had done their part in honor.

The four men bowed their heads in the garden; the king's heart firm with resolve, Beneval's peace restored, the dockmaster's fears eased, and the old teacher nodding his gray head and smiling.

Chapter Twenty-Seven

Kyria smoothed her long fingers through her auburn curls, hoping she looked acceptable, as the morning's breeze had disordered her hair on the way in to breakfast. Of course, if she had come straight to the dining hall from her rooms, she would still be neat, but she had felt the need to be outside on such a glorious morning. She had risen with the sun and hastened through her morning ablutions and dressing with a speed that had distressed her maid. Feeling full of energy and a swelling happiness that seemed out of proportion to the typically fine weather, Kyria had laughed at her maid's attempts to subdue her rippling locks and had rushed down the stairs and out into the courtyard.

The sun, still low in the sky, had flooded her eyes with deep golden light. The long shadow of her father's columned porch stretched across the courtyard almost to the feet of the Library. To her right, at the apex of the hill, was the Temple, ablaze in the morning light, its pinnacles like fingers of molten gold, pointing the way to God.

With a laugh of sheer joy, Kyria had spun in a great circle and then taken off running up the brief slope to the Temple. This morning, she was filled with such joy, she thought she could not contain it in the fragile shell of her body, and so she sought the cool shadows and dancing lights of the Temple. She would have a good conversation with God, Who was sure to understand this wild exuberance that filled her like spring water trembling in a shimmering meniscus on the rim of a golden bowl.

Today, the air seemed pregnant with the approach of some great event. She felt as if her soul were swelled up in anticipation of something important and threatened to burst out of her skin. She wished she had her father's gift of clear sight, or her mother's wisdom, but all she felt was a tingling all over, as if a huge storm approached, though the skies were a clear, tropical blue.

Arriving at the entrance to the Temple, Kyria touched the carved, gilded paintings on the pillars with reverent hands. The stories they told never failed to move her and to remind her Whom she was seeking. She walked within the cool, shadowed embrace of the Temple, letting her eyes adjust to the dimmer light. Inside, the smell of sweet incense and the beeswax used to polish the benches and the indefinable, cold ancient smell that was the stone itself combined to deepen her sense of rightness. Peace joined the joy in her heart, and she walked up the center aisle toward the altar, delighting in the many colors that drenched her from the eastern windows.

An hour later, when she emerged from the Temple and headed down the slope to the courtyard, hastening, lest she be late for breakfast, she found a great bustle and furor of servants clustered about the fountain. As she drew near, a small page was accosted by several eager women. Kyria arrived in time to hear his response.

"I don't know what's to do!" he complained, looking pained that they thought he would listen to gossip. "I was told to fetch the Bintah to the king, and so I did. No, there were no strangers in the garden when we arrived, though I passed Lord Beneval and Master Strahng on my way back in. If there are strange guests here today, the place to ask is at the docks!" His tone was so aggrieved that Kyria laughed and rumpled his hair. He glanced up and his frown melted away when he saw her, for she was beloved of all the young pages.

"Come, young scamp, let them while away their time at the fountain! You and I shall return to the Hall and seek some breakfast!" The lad skipped off by her side, and the crowd by the fountain took her hint and hurried back to their duties. Once inside the hall, the boy flashed her a wide grin as he headed for the kitchens.

"Thanks for the rescue, my lady!"

Scamp, Kyria laughed as he disappeared down the corridor. She headed for the dining hall, hoping she wasn't late, especially if there were guests to the meal. Arriving breathless with her haste, she was pleased to find her parents the only ones there before her. Smoothing her windblown locks, she was just wishing for her comb when the sound of footsteps was heard in the passageway. A great smile bloomed on her face as two of her favorite people entered the room.

She ran to greet her old teacher, Bintah Auren, and guide him to his seat of honor at the queen's right hand. When he was seated and had smilingly received her kiss, she turned to the tall, strong man beside him. Her face shone with happiness as she contemplated the man before her. It was wonderful to her that he should be handsome as well as kind and loving and wise. God had truly blessed her by giving Beneval to her. His hazel eyes were warm with affection for her as they exchanged a brief kiss. When she tried to smooth her hair again, he laughed at her and teased her about preening for guests when she never combed her hair for him.

"Oh, you!" she exclaimed. "You don't care if my hair is neat! In fact, you're the one who protests if I put it up!"

"Guilty," he chuckled, admiring the roses in her cheeks.

"And I'm not preening! It's just basic courtesy that I should look my best to honor our guests." Beneval took pity on her earnest attempts to bring order to her wayward locks and motioned for a servant to bring the princess's comb. A few moments later, Kyria's maid arrived with comb and golden circlet to hold the waves back from her face. She set to work briskly and soon had her mistress's hair as subdued as the riotous curls ever were. Satisfied that she was at least neat and presentable, Kyria dismissed the maid with a word of thanks and turned to her family.

"So, who are these mysterious guests?" she asked, plucking a ripe grape from the silver bowl of fruit on the sideboard. Sophia, the top of her burnished head coming only to the level of her daughter's nose, explained the morning's events to a rapt Kyria. Excitement flooded her veins, topping off the morning's unusual enthusiasm.

The Ancients had returned? Who wouldn't be excited at the thought? What island child had not spent long, glorious summers daydreaming and pretending that those wondrous people still walked and lived among them? And now, like a fairy tale come true, she was going to get to meet them.

She cautioned herself to guard her heart, lest she be disappointed when they proved to be less than her active imagination had painted them. A child's notions of perfect beauty and perfect honor were the backbone of her fantasies, but the sad reality was that real people, even good people, fell far short of these exacting standards. It was part of growing up, she reminded herself, but her heart beat high with anticipation nonetheless.

A comfortable rest, followed by the most refreshing bath he had had since before the Goblins had begun to invade his home, had done much to improve Gaelcar's already hopeful disposition. Now, walking beside Aelric and trailed by the other Companions, the Seneschal followed a pair of servants down the halls of the simple, yet pleasant palace of the Human ruler. Just behind him, he heard the quiet murmur of Caerdrys answering a comment from Robse, who was escorting her. As the highest-ranking female among them, courtesy would have had Aelric escorting her, but Aelric had felt more comfortable burying their womenfolk in their midst until they knew more about these strangers. So, since the young Champion refused to be more than a step behind Aelric, Robse was given the honor of Caerdrys's company.

Gaelcar smiled. Clearly, from the strain in his voice, it was an honor Robse would have liked to forgo. Though they had come to have a great respect for one another, true friendship had not yet developed between the fiery Caerdrys and the protective young Champion. Behind them, Randelos escorted Myrandella, and behind them paced Domel with Minlienda on his arm. Cerlim, ever watchful, brought up the rear. The Seneschal suspected Robse would have preferred Domel's duty, as Minlienda was much less intimidating than her *amia* sister.

The aroma of freshly prepared food wafted down the corridor, and

Gaelcar's stomach, suddenly awakened to its emptiness, complained fiercely. The Seneschal cleared his throat in a weak attempt to hide, or at least disguise, the noise, and briefly wondered what sort of food these Humans were accustomed to eating. He'd never imagined that the time would come when he would dine with fallen creatures, and now that he was about to, he had to wonder if the rumors of Human eating habits were true. Would they render true thanks to the Creator and ask His blessing on the food and the community gathered to partake of it? Did they eat the flesh of intelligent creatures? The thought made his stomach turn.

They turned from a dim corridor into a brightly lit open space in front of the doors to the dining chamber, and one of the attendants courteously held the carved and embossed door open so that the tall, graceful guests could pass through. A cluster of Humans awaited them in the bright room.

Gaelcar recognized King Sagiro and his queen, Sophia, who smiled in greeting to them. Beside them stood a young woman who was obviously the daughter of the royal couple. She was tall, for a Human, and slender, as her mother must once have been. Her hair was the rich color of good earth and fell in a cascade of ripples down her back. Her merry eyes were the same warm brown as Sophia's. A handsome young man stood at her side.

Kyria heard footfalls approaching, though it was impossible to tell how many were coming. She didn't realize she was holding her breath until it whooshed out of her in an excited rush as the guests entered the chamber. There were nine of them, though at first they seemed just a crowd. Kyria felt the singing joy rise in her again as she tried to comprehend the incredible fact of them. They really were as beautiful as her childhood fantasies had painted them. From the stunned looks on her parents' and Beneval's faces, they hadn't been expecting this either.

Tall, fair, heart-wrenchingly beautiful, their guests stood bathed in the morning light that slanted through the long, arched windows on the eastern side of the room. Though their clothes were gorgeous, Kyria could not get beyond the fierce, piercing joy of their faces. Three were fair of hair, the rest uniformly dark. There were no mid-tones represented among them. At first glance, their faces were nearly identical, but Kyria quickly saw that the illusion was due to a long, narrow cast of face. Cheekbones and brows slanted upward, drawing the eye to the graceful, pointed ears. These, in turn, had no separate lobe at the bottom, but sloped smoothly into the curve of the jaw. Their noses were straight and slim, if a little long, and their eyes, larger than Kyria was used to, slanted in harmony with the bones of their faces, forming a provocative, haunting, fey beauty.

Even with their general slimness of build and narrow jaws, the males were the most masculine creatures she had ever seen. And their women… *Poets will despair of ever committing their beauty to verse, though they'll probably never give up trying*, Kyria thought ruefully. Stinging and sharp and overwhelming, like the scent of the roses that climbed over the south wall, still their beauty was not the kind to inspire jealousy, Kyria realized. *They are* other. *I cannot be that and would not wish to be. Theirs is not a Human beauty. But, oh, to be in their company…*

Belatedly, she pulled her thoughts back into place as she realized their leader had been presented to her mother and it was her turn. The habit of training allowed her to sink into a graceful curtsey as she heard the word *king*. Her hand was gently grasped in long, strong fingers, and she rose to meet his eyes.

Gold, fiery amber, liquid heat of the sun waited for her. She wondered if her eyesight would be damaged from looking into his eyes, the way she had been cautioned as a child not to look into the sun. The momentous portent of the morning had been poised for this moment, this meeting of eyes, of souls. Kyria felt a shiver begin deep inside her and wondered if her bones would shake apart with it. Something significant was happening between them, but she could not get her mind to grasp it. A current, a connection, a charge leapt between them in that frozen instant, and Kyria knew something important, or perhaps dangerous, had happened, or could happen. She didn't understand it, but somehow their wordless exchange was charged with promise, shock, surprise, and the potential for incredible hope or destruction. She tried to break the contact and sensed that he tried as well, but it wasn't until she heard her father's voice that she was able to wrench her eyes away from the golden ones and try to look as though nothing earthshaking had just happened.

"Lord Aelric." She heard her father's voice, like an echo, as though she had missed the words, but her mind was replaying them for her. "May I present Beneval, my daughter's promised husband. They are to be wed next spring, and we are all looking forward to the celebration."

Chapter Twenty-eight

As they were being seated at the long table in the sunlight, Gaelcar kept an unobtrusive watch on Aelric. The Seneschal had noticed that, after bowing over Kyria's hand, Aelric had seemed a bit dazed. It had concerned him enough that his attention had been distracted from the protocol of remembering names and ranks, a mental game that he had always enjoyed. During that brief introduction, before it was his turn, Gaelcar had swept his gaze across the other Companions and noted that Robse stood protectively close to Aelric, as though he, too, had noticed the king's abstraction and could think of no other way to aid him. Domel and Minlienda had seemed graver than usual, but it could have been simply the tremendously significant events unfolding as they were introduced to a *friendly* group of Humans.

Gaelcar watched Aelric carefully, wondering what was wrong, for the king's behavior still seemed oddly out of character, as though something pressing was disturbing him. This worried Gaelcar: none of the other Companions seemed to be suffering any ill effects from the attentions of the Humans, but if Aelric were to weaken, or, the Lord forbid, fade away, the remnant of the Faeltheon people would be left in a dreadful position.

Hiding his anxious thoughts under an unruffled mask of social grace, Gaelcar smoothly intercepted the burden of the conversation, leaving only the smaller questions for Aelric to address. Finally, after what seemed like ages of protecting his king from any drastic social mistakes, he was thankful when servants entered the room carrying trays laden with delicious-smelling food.

Much to Gaelcar's relief, the meal consisted of fruits, eggs, cheese, and bread, much like an Elven meal. To further his amazed wonder and delight, he found that the Humans did not make any inquiries when the Elves bowed their heads to thank their Creator for providing for their needs; rather, Sagiro spoke the heartfelt blessing for everyone. At once interested in this strange group of Men, who seemed to both strive to reflect the Creator's goodness and to pray to Him, Gaelcar began to investigate the culture in which he found himself.

"How long have your people lived on this island?" Gaelcar inquired, hoping to maneuver the conversation to a point where he would be able to ask deeper questions of the king.

"We came to this island over two hundred years ago," Sagiro replied. "My people were searching for a peaceful place where they could devote their lives to pursuing knowledge of God and to learning more of His wisdom."

"You are devoted to following the Creator?" Caerdrys interjected, surprise robbing her momentarily of her tact. If the Humans noticed this at all, they gave no indication of offense. Smiling willingly, Sagiro replied to her question.

"Yes, we follow the One true Maker of this world and everything in it. Although we ourselves are imperfect and often must be purified through the blood of animals, we strive to follow His commands and to live in a way that would please Him."

"And how do you live?" asked Gaelcar, leaning forward slightly to hear the king's reply. He was a little confused about the reference to the blood of animals but figured he could pursue that point later.

"We are, among other things, historians and lovers of philosophy, so we gather and study the knowledge of many peoples, hoping to gain wisdom from the experience the Human race has compiled over thousands of years," Sagiro began. "Unfortunately, we have found that many of the ancient peoples of our race have mixed wisdom with folly and have not lived in a way that pleases God. In spite of this, our studies have shown that those cultures that seek after and try to follow God undergird their lives with the themes of truth, goodness, and beauty. That is why we came here: so that we could be separate from the rest of a world that increasingly seeks other paths and could be left to practice those themes in our everyday life."

Still somewhat suspicious of this Human culture that seemed to reverence ideals similar to those cherished by the Faeltheon, Caerdrys inquired, in a manner more tactful than before, "Is this true for your entire society? What becomes of those who do not choose to believe as you do?"

The elderly man with the strange, clouded eyes responded, turning toward the sound of Caerdrys's voice.

"In the first few generations after this society was founded, there were those who did not want to follow God, and still, occasionally, someone will object to our faith, but they generally choose to leave our island home, since they do not feel comfortable living among us."

All the Elves were now so intrigued by this unusual nation of Men that they had inclined their bodies toward their hosts, even Aelric, whom Gaelcar was relieved to note seemed to have recovered from his strange indisposition.

"We train our children to cherish beauty and to respect wisdom," the elderly man continued. "Thus, the basic standards of our culture have managed to survive the years and the natural inclination of man to deviate from the ways of God."

"How long has your society lived in this way?" Aelric queried, appearing able to carry on a conversation normally, in spite of whatever was bothering him.

"It is very possible our forefathers began this way of life long before we came to this refuge," Kyria replied, shaking her head. "But not even our Bintah remembers our history before the founding of this City, and he is the oldest living among us." She smiled fondly upon the old man with the clouded eyes. He returned her smile, his face turned unerringly to hers, as though he could see her clearly. Queen Sophia smiled brightly upon her guests and laughed with joy at the beauty before her.

"But enough of ourselves!" she exclaimed. "We are eager to know of you. Where have you come from and why have you taken so long to return? Yours is a tale we have often wondered about."

The Faeltheon exchanged wide-eyed glances at that, and Gaelcar quickly placed a restraining hand over Caerdrys's, causing her to close her hastily opened mouth. In the shock of hearing the queen speak as though they had always belonged here and had merely been away for a time, there was no telling what rash words might pour from Caerdrys's impetuous tongue. Aelric seemed at a loss to reply, and even Gaelcar, in spite of his wide experience at formal social occasions, could not find an intelligent response. The tiny queen sensed their unease immediately and a look of contrition spread over her pretty face.

"I am sorry! I did not mean to pry! It was rude of me to suppose you would wish to share your story with strangers, especially we who have settled here in your absence. Please forgive my impertinence and let us speak of other matters. I assume that you, too, follow our Creator?"

The Faeltheon made a great effort to regain their vanished composure, but the queen's words had opened a floodgate of urgent questions, and their hearts were beating high with a mixture of joy, hope, and anxiety. What could she have meant by her innocent statements? It seemed clear that these Humans somehow knew about the Faeltheon, which implied that they had discovered some clue here on the island to point to their existence. This, in turn, confirmed their own suspicions that this was the island of their origins.

Perhaps, Gaelcar thought in a flash of understanding, *that was why they were so accepting of our differences. Perhaps whatever clues they had discovered forewarned them that other creatures existed, and thus they were able to adjust to the idea over time and come to accept it.* Whatever the reasons, the excitement was running high in the Faeltheon, and Gaelcar thought it prudent to turn the conversation into other channels awhile longer and learn more about these people before they began to confide in them and to seek answers to the riddles raised by Sophia's words.

He nodded gravely to Aelric and was relieved to see understanding in the amber eyes of his king. As Aelric began to respond to the little queen's efforts, Gaelcar noted that he seemed to have recovered from his momentary weakness enough to engage the company in the long tale of the their voyage as befitted a visiting ruler. The other Companions lowered bright eyes and composed flushed faces, taking their cue from Aelric's demeanor.

Gaelcar began to relax, in spite of the burning questions that lay unanswered in his heart. They would discover what they needed to know in the Lord's good time. Meanwhile, it comforted him to no small extent to soak up the realization that these people, unlike the overwhelming majority of their kind, sought goodness rather than evil. Perhaps the unfallen race of Elves and this nation of Humans who proclaimed their devotion to the Creator could share this island peacefully after all. He smiled as he contemplated that hope.

Minlienda sat at the strangers' table, wishing she could indulge in her familiar role of Caerdrys's shadow. As one of only three Faeltheon women present, and as she was not seated next to her *amia* sister, Minlienda was forced to shed her natural shyness and interact with these Humans. In truth, she was distracted and somewhat disturbed. The many conversations around her were fascinating, and she wanted to listen and learn, as was her habit. But intruding into that resolve came a concern for Aelric, not to mention the underlying uncertainty they all felt toward their hosts.

She felt naked sitting in the company of Humans as a Faeltheon. Her nape prickled with the foreboding of disaster, yet the Humans continued to talk with them and to treat them as honored guests, seeming to have no difficulty with their differences. All her life, she had been taught that Humans had such narrow minds that, when confronted with anything that did not fit their limited experience, they reacted with disbelief. Certainly, that deadly weapon had brought about the downfall and destruction of their Faerie Kin in the Great Birch Forest.

Still, a haunting tickle of memory surfaced; hadn't Queen Elwyn's final message mentioned that they were sheltering two Humans at the Faerie palace and had come to no harm through interacting with them? Min pursued the elusive thought through the maze of voices and demands for her attention.

Perhaps some Humans were broad enough of heart and mind to accept those who were different from themselves. It seemed Aelric was willing to risk their survival on that belief. She looked across the table to where Gaelcar was seated, wondering what their wisest and most cautious member thought of this situation.

Gaelcar's face betrayed no concerns, but that was typical, she thought. He was conversing with the Human king, his expression intent. Min scrambled to focus on the conversation. Even as she listened, with some awe, to Sagiro's description of the islanders' way of life, she was aware of Aelric's presence on her left. He was not taking part in the conversation between Gaelcar and Sagiro, nor was he engaged with Princess Kyria and Myrandella, who were discussing, of all things, the flowers native to the island! Still, Min sensed that Aelric's full attention, if not his eyes or face, were still on the russet-haired princess.

Min had seen the stunned look that had frozen the two in their places when they were introduced. Standing behind Aelric, she had been close enough to the current that had leapt between them to feel the hairs on her arms lift. They had remained, gazes locked, for only a fraction longer than was strictly appropriate, but Min had sensed that something deep and disturbing had happened to them. She didn't think Aelric had fully recovered from whatever it had been, though the princess seemed to be a fine and vivacious hostess, like her mother.

Min stole a look down the table and caught a fleeting glimpse of worry on the tiny queen's face as she looked at her daughter. The look was gone so quickly, replaced by friendly charm as Sophia replied to something Domel said, that Min wondered if she had imagined it. She could not see Kyria, or her fiancé, Beneval, as Aelric, Robse, and Randelos were seated between Min and the two Humans.

Quietly, while she ate the excellent meal before her, Minlienda prayed, lifting up Aelric and the young Human princess, asking that Aematlon strengthen in them both the character He had instilled in them, that they would face this challenge with honor and purity. She also lifted up once more the Faeltheon's concerns about staying here on the island. It seemed they were surrounded by troubles, but Min had been alive long enough to know that things were not always as they seemed and that their Creator was faithful to help them through the hard times.

A fragment of the conversation going on around her caught her attention, pulling her back into the interaction at the table. It was the queen's voice she heard, though at first only the words registered.

"Why have you taken so long to return? Yours is a tale we have long wondered about."

Even as Minlienda sat up straighter in her chair, she felt the instant attention of all the Companions focus on the tiny woman at the foot of the table. Even Aelric seemed to be fully concentrating on their hostess. The conversation was soon steered away from this topic of vital importance to the Faeltheon, but Min's mind continued to mull over the queen's words. It was obvious the Humans here suspected the Faeltheon had been here before, and it was equally apparent to her that beneath their genuine friendliness and acceptance was a guarded wariness, but she couldn't understand why.

At the close of the meal, as they were all rising from their seats, Aelric spoke beside her. In his voice was the tone of command his Companions recognized. The Humans seemed to sense it, too, and listened respectfully.

"Sagiro, Sophia, you have offered us gracious hospitality, as befits servants of the Creator, and we thank you for it. Let us be honest in all our dealings together. My people are in a precarious position and have sought out this isle in hopes of finding a refuge of our own. To find you already settled here was a grievous blow, made somewhat lighter by your passion for Aematlon. We sense in you, however, an uneasiness, a holding back, which seems inconsistent with your acceptance of us, and this troubles us. Minlienda possesses the gift of searching the hearts of others. Please allow her to read your heart as you answer our questions, that we may all find peace."

Min was a little startled to hear Aelric's request. Looking about her, she saw the alarm and wariness in the expressions of many of the Humans. This was not a gift natural to them, and Minlienda supposed it must seem threatening. Sophia's brown eyes were wide with apprehension as she crossed to her husband, and Kyria looked upon Aelric with something like betrayal in her eyes and moved closer to Beneval. Bintah Auren, still sitting in his chair, seemed unperturbed. Min wondered if he'd understood the request.

But Sagiro surprised them all by laughing aloud. His goodnatured face showed no alarm or reproach, and his merry eyes disappeared once more into the crinkles at their edges.

"This is a good thing!" he cried. "If this can be done, we can all relax, for it is quite a strain always to be wondering whether your fears are about to be realized. I have no objection at all to this young lady 'reading' my heart, such as it is. I have nothing to hide but the sins that are common to man. I hope that won't offend you, my dear," he said in a gentle aside to her. Min found herself smiling back and took her place before the king as he reseated himself in his chair. Aelric stood beside her, and Gaelcar came to her other side.

"King Sagiro," Aelric began, "will you please explain to us the comments made about our 'return' and your people settling here in our 'absence'?"

Gaelcar nodded, adding, "And what is it you fear from us? We do not understand, and we would like to."

Sagiro smiled again and began to tell them about the carvings on the walls of the caldera.

Absorbed in the fantastic tale, they had all resumed their seats, and Sophia had sent for fresh tea. The dockmaster and his documents had been sent for and had arrived, and Cerlim and Gaelcar were still poring over the renderings of the ships. They had all exchanged wide-eyed glances when the conjectured civilization of the Ancients was explored, and it had humbled Min to see the reverence given to their ancestors by these Humans.

Sagiro had spoken of the hope the very idea of the Ancients had given them; how inspired the Human colony had been by their existence. Yet, there had always been that fear that if the Ancients ever returned, they would be either unworthy of the veneration shown them or unwilling to share the island home or both. Sagiro finished his story, explaining their fears of a hostile retaking of the island and their counterbalancing trust that God would have His perfect way, at whatever cost to Sagiro's people.

When he had finished speaking, the room was silent. The Humans were waiting to hear the Faeltheon response, and the Faeltheon were surprised, awed, and humbled at such a show of faith from Humans.

It will take us a while to get used to this, thought Min ruefully as she looked toward Aelric. *We have never before encountered an enemy who can also be a friend.*

"Minlienda Elashar, what have you seen in the heart of this mortal?" Aelric asked. Min rose, matching his formality, wanting the Humans to sense her respect for the Man before her.

"My king, he has spoken truth from a pure heart," she responded. Broad smiles appeared on faces throughout the room. Aelric stood and gave them back the honesty he had requested from them.

"We have searched for more than a year to find this haven, this home of our ancestors, if indeed this was their home. It was our intent to settle here when we had found it, so to find it already inhabited was, as I mentioned earlier, quite a shock. There are reasons why we would never have believed we could be friends with Humans, but we will not go into that now. You are different from any other Humans we have ever met or heard of. This is because of your faith in the Creator and your desire to follow and obey Him in all things.

"Violence is not our way, unless war is brought to us. We would not have asked you to leave your homes to make room for us. Yet, because of your faith, we would like to stay and... *share* this island with you, if you think there is room for us here." Aelric paused as the smiles turned to relieved laughter. He held out his hand to the seated monarch.

"King Sagiro, shall we be friends?"

Chapter Twenty-Nine

In Marliondolen, the majority of the Faeltheon had gathered, patient, dogged, hopeful. There were so many holding vigil that the meadow where they had met the ancient kings and queens appeared to be a sea of Faeltheon bodies. Ever since that night upon the beach, they had been hoping for another glimpse of the island that had once been their home. The two intervening days had seemed like many to the watchers.

The core of the group was made up of those who had lived on the island at the dawn of time. Their appearance among the other watchers had occasioned no little surprise, for though they had been seen, in ones and twos, quietly going about their lives in Marliondolen, they had seldom joined the other Faeltheon in their "meetings" to get to know one another.

A few of them were known abroad: most notably Athalenael the Kytha; Amadthalos the Elven King; his wife, Hadara; his friend and Champion, Ethalion; Elenfea, the first Queen of Faerie; her consort, Lasnov; and the shipwright Hereneth. A few others from that era were also known to the majority of the Faeltheon, but most of those who had known the Elder days upon the isle kept to themselves.

At first, Theo had been troubled about their withdrawal, for Elwyn had sensed a darkness in their spirits that concerned them both. When they had mentioned it to Elrad, he had cautioned them to wait, explaining that Athalenael knew of it and was watching out for them. The Seer had tried to explain to the young Master and Lady the essence of what troubled the oldest among them.

"It's a bit like a sickness, but one of the heart. They grieve, you understand, for their loss. To have known a time of fellowship with the Living Creator such as you and I can only hope for till our very bones ache with the wanting—then to have lost it!" He had shaken his head, eyes clouded with deep compassion. "It takes some harder than others, of course, for everyone is different. For some, that experience with the Creator was a shaping and defining one, always to be remembered and used as a guide, but a strengthening thing, a staff to lean upon when times turned hard. For others, that fellowship, that companionship, can never be matched; the company of others must be lacking and of a lesser joy and comfort. Its loss became an insurmountable grief when the world shifted and they had to turn to other ways. Their loneliness runs blood-deep and will not be comforted until they are with Him again. They live their lives and are useful within the community, but it is a patient, sad sort of waiting for them."

Theo and Elwyn, saddened in their turn by the deep sorrow of those hardest struck, had tried their best to understand the troubles of those very quiet ones and to respect their desire to remain apart from the more bustling, energetic life of the community activities.

Now that so many were gathering, hoping for a window onto their island home, Elwyn and Theo were happy to see these withdrawn ones in the midst of the patient crowd. Of course, nearly everyone else had gathered too. Very nearly the entire compliment of the Faeltheon in Marliondolen was there upon that meadow. It was a vast company, constantly shifting as various members left to prepare food and drink, or to replenish the cook fires, or to take turns bathing and changing to fresh clothing.

Elwyn, Nausika, Lucina, and Michal wove their way through the mass of bodies toward the cook fire their friends maintained, carrying pouches of freshly baked rolls and berry tarts, as well as fruit, honey, boiled eggs, and cheese. The friends gathered around their fire ceased their earnest converse at the women's appearance, hailing the food with a delight that made the girls laugh.

Theo and Elrad had departed to make the rounds of many fires, stopping for lighthearted chat with some and encouraging comment with others. Their progress through the people was followed approvingly by more than one eye. Eventually, Theo returned to their fire, having left Elrad with

Beregos and their friends. He arrived just in time to appropriate the last roll, to the vocal and amusing dismay of Laslorn. Laughing, Theo settled next to Elwyn and accepted the honey pot from her hand. He was busy for a few moments, putting a wedge of cheese into the roll and honey in his tea, while she peeled an egg for him. Finally, with exaggerated relief, he fell to and polished off his breakfast with evident enjoyment.

It was as Theo was beginning on a ripe peach and a second cup of tea that the characteristic shimmer appeared in the air above them. Those away from the gathering hastened to join them. Food and conversation forgotten, all the assembled Faeltheon focused their attention on the events unfolding before them.

The long line of travelers wound up the steep slope of the volcanic cone above the City, heading for the rim of the central mountain. The day was clear and bright, though still early. The clouds that had colored a breathtaking sunrise had dissipated in the warm spring air. As they climbed higher, many of the Humans grew short of breath, for this historic journey had called to many, and not all were in the flower of their youth. They had been walking for nearly two hours, and many were beginning to want a break and a bit of food. The head of the group consisted of King Sagiro, Beneval, Kyria, various guides, and Aelric and his Companions.

Trailing behind them for nearly a quarter-mile came a great host of Humans and the entire complement of Faeltheon. Even baby Gaelal was there, sleeping securely in a pouch slung across his father's chest. The Elves were a fair and glorious sight in the morning light; their faces animated and interested, their garments both subtle and bright, simple of design, but richly decorated. The Humans were mostly silent, concentrating on keeping their breath and their footing as they climbed. The Elves stepped lightly, almost reverently, over the grasses and through the trees, enchanted to be walking on unspoiled land again. Some were talking quietly among themselves; some were singing softly the ancient songs. Many were silent, thoughts turned inward, wondering about the truths that awaited them at the end of this journey.

There had been much discussion and quite a few thoughtful silences since Aelric's edict had spread throughout the three ships last night, informing them that they would all travel today to see the carvings on the walls of the Interior and, based on what they found there, might well remain on the island with the Humans.

The majority of the Faeltheon had not at that time met any of the Humans, of course. Initially, they were frightened and appalled at the thought of remaining in stinking disguises for the rest of their lives. This foolish thought was soon dismissed, however, as they knew Aelric wouldn't mean that fate for them, and so they reasoned he must know something they did not. For the most part, in spite of a tense day spent waiting in the ships, the Faeltheon had retired confident and hopeful that night.

Aelric had not told them much when he had summoned them together that morning, after ordering that the guards be removed from their posts and that the ships be made fast in the island's harbor. Obedient and wondering, they had assembled in a large, vacant space at the east end of the docks. When he had gathered them all together, Aelric had shared with them what he knew so far and a little of what he hoped would prove true.

They had spent the next hour praying together, lifting up to the Creator their praises for this safe haven, their hopes and concerns about sharing it with Humans, and their desire to be shown His will, that they might do as He wished in this unusual circumstance. Many of the Elves were wary, still hurting, and mistrustful of Humans and all the world outside the Faeltheon community. Gaelcar knew this and kept a watchful eye on those he suspected would have the most trouble adjusting.

When they had finished praying, Aelric had confirmed that King Sagiro would lead the entire community of surviving Elves to an "ancient place" within the old volcano, where they would view carvings left by a former civilization, which might, in fact, be their own Faeltheon ancestors. Immediately after this announcement, excited chatter had erupted as each Elf believed, or at the very least desperately hoped, that this "ancient place" would turn out to be the birthplace of their people.

Now, even as they stepped lightly beside the struggling Humans in their climb up the steep face of the mountain, the imaginations of each wearied survivor in the party drew pictures of their hoped-for future home. Gaelcar, pacing alongside Aelric and the other Companions, was noting distinguishable features on the mountainside, mentally comparing them to various Scrolls he had memorized during the long voyage to the island.

He had just finished a detailed examination of a strange rock formation when Aelric suddenly halted, causing his distracted Seneschal to have to sidestep to avoid crashing into him. Startled, Gaelcar looked ahead to see what had caused his king to end his march so abruptly. Even as he felt his own breath draw in with awe, he heard similar responses from the other Companions coming up beside them.

They had arrived at the summit of the mountain, which, Gaelcar noted, was clearly the rim of an old volcano. In reverent silence, they stood on the edge of the yawning caldera of the volcano's mouth, looking down upon the canopy of the vast rainforest that now thrived in the rich volcanic soil.

Everywhere Gaelcar looked, vividly green plants and trees grew thickly, many bearing brightly colored flowers or fruits. Occasionally, a brightly colored bird would flit from one treetop to another. The music of the birds was wild and sweet, some of the voices calling harshly, some singing as sweetly as Faeltheon music. Small forest creatures rustled through the high canopy periodically, scurrying about as though they had pressing matters to attend to. Though the gazers could glimpse little from that angle, it was clear that many of the caldera's inhabitants were creatures the Faeltheon had never seen before.

Elrad, seated beside Riende and Elamani, was aware of the muted sounds of the folk on every side. Some were silent with wonder, but many gave soft exclamations of awe and joy at the sight of their Kin standing on the rim of the beautiful caldera. He could also hear snatches of whispers from throats too tight for speech.

"We stood just there many a time!"

"Aematlon, my Lord, do You remember? I have not forgotten what You said to me as we walked there!"

"Another hour's walk would take me to my door!"

Behind the soft cries, silent tears spoke for those who could not voice their grief. For many, the sight of their erstwhile home was a time of healing. For some, it was the prick of a fresh grief, but a healthy one, like the lancing of an infected wound, that spurred the injured heart on to healing.

Gaelcar breathed in the moist air that drifted up from the rainforest and treasured the smell of what he hoped would be his new home. He sensed that many Elves had moved up to join them, whispering excitedly to each other about the beauties of the place. Aelric, like his subjects, seemed to be temporarily frozen in place by the glorious aspect of the caldera.

A short time later, after the Humans had refreshed themselves with a bite and a sup from the packs they carried, Sagiro called to them to start downward after the guides, as they would be hard-pressed to reach the ancient site before darkness if they lingered much longer. This suggestion the Elves obeyed happily, comforted by the spectacular images before them, which would go far to easing the longing memories of their lost Land. As they descended the steep slope of the caldera, they entered into the lush forest.

Sparkling streams and rushing waterfalls teased their ears and occasionally flashed before their eager eyes. In the early afternoon, the Human king called a halt for rest and food by a vigorous stream that poured itself into a wide pool. The Elves, too full of hope and joy to feel hunger, declined food and drink, though many cupped handfuls of cold, sparkling water from the stream. They settled by the banks, a little apart from the Humans. To their delight, the water was full of glimmering fish and playful water mammals that thrilled the young children. There were new flora and fauna on all sides to the wonder and joy of more than just the children.

After the brief rest, they pressed farther into the forest until they were surrounded on all sides by dense undergrowth and massive trees, roped with vines. The canopy above was so dense they often could not see the sky and walked for a time in dim green light. The atmosphere was one of great age and fecundity. Their footsteps were muted by years of detritus and decaying humus. The joy of the Elves was not dimmed, for they could clearly sense the bright sun above, but many of the Humans felt oppressed by the looming trees and evening shades at midday.

Though it had been hours, it seemed both more and less to the watchers in the Marliondolen meadow. To some, it seemed the sun stood still in the sky while the revelation unfurled and washed their hearts with painful refreshment. To others, it seemed they had but a fleeting moment to savor the cherished home now lost to them. So crowded with memories were the visions of some of the folk that it seemed the shimmering mirage in the meadow could not hold all their hearts remembered. For those who had never been on that island, the reactions of those who had were as interesting as watching their Kin discover each mile of lush forest.

As the shades of evening began to descend on the meadow, several of the ancient watchers became more excited than they had been yet, calling out words of encouragement to the Elves and Humans in the window, though they knew they could not be heard. More and more voices joined them, as all who had made their homes upon that isle sensed the destination of the party in the vision.

"A little more! Keep on northward!"

"You're nearly there! Don't stop now—you must arrive before dark!"

"Yes, you must see what we left you! Surely it will still be there!"

The babble of instruction grew, rapidly infecting the other watchers. In rising excitement they all watched and waited, some calling out, some holding their breaths.

Chapter Thirty

After a few more hours of walking, the party came to a broad clearing that stretched for acres in every direction. It was bounded on all sides by forest, except for the north edge, which ended abruptly at a stern-looking cliff face. With a sense of rising excitement, the Faeltheon realized they had reached their destination. Answers long sought and often pondered might well be gouged into that wall of rock. A quick glance at the now visible sky told Gaelcar that evening approached, for the sky was beginning to pale from blue to gray, and the bright rays of the sun were growing richer, deeper, and more slanted. Sagiro was instructing his people to begin setting up their camp for the night.

As the Humans began to gather firewood and to prepare for the night, Gaelcar motioned for several of the Faeltheon to help. They had discussed various chores before setting out that morning, so the volunteers quickly organized the children into helpful work teams. Gaelcar turned to Aelric as the young king sought his eyes. The message that flashed between them lit a spark in the eyes of all watching. The Companions led a large group of Faeltheon toward the cliff face. The need to know if this place was theirs by birthright rose in them all like a tide that could no longer be held back. They spread out before the immense rock face and were joined by Sagiro, Beneval, and Strahng, who pointed out the areas where they had seen the carved ships years before. The years and the nature of the sheltered caldera had produced a vigorous growth of leafy vines, which had climbed up to cover even the areas that had been cleared by the Humans.

Aelric and his people fell silent, drifting apart to contemplate various portions of the wall for nearly half an hour, each praying, or savoring the moment, or contemplating their future, until, by unspoken consent, they regathered before the area pointed out by the Humans. There was a deep peace among them now, the fruit of that time spent alone with the Creator. Unafraid of whatever the walls would reveal, they waited patiently for Aelric to lead them. The light was dimming in the approaching sunset, the long golden rays painting the cliff in shades of molten lava, echoing the gold of Aelric's eyes.

Sagiro, though he clearly did not understand their waiting, came to tell them that the night meal was prepared. With a sigh of mingled anguish and relief, the gathered Faeltheon followed Aelric as he turned back toward the camp. Caerdrys had to pull on Gaelcar's arm and urge him to accompany them, for he was absorbed in pondering the wall. She reminded him, gently for Caerdrys, that it would be wise for them to eat and rest before they continued on their explorations, for they had not eaten all day. Reluctantly, Gaelcar agreed, though Aelric noticed that he chose to eat with the group who had decided to camp closest to the cliff face and would occasionally turn to face the rock, staring at it as though he would pierce its leafy veil with his gaze alone and discover its ancient secrets.

Eventually, Gaelcar fell to rummaging through the Scrolls he had carefully wrapped and carried with him from the ship, selecting one and poring over it minutely, as though hoping that it held the key to his mystery. Intrigued, Aelric rose and came to settle beside him, even as Min picked up Gaelcar's discarded meal and placed it in his hand. Absently, the Seneschal chewed and swallowed, unaware of anything beyond the Scrolls and the mysterious cliff face now falling into shadow behind them.

As the sun set, Gaelcar rose with determination and returned to the rock wall. Aelric, grinning, gestured the others to accompany them, and all the Faeltheon, and a good number of the Humans, clustered at the foot of the behemoth. As the shadows fell over the vines, Gaelcar reached up his hand to a spot that had caught his eye and began to pull away the clinging vines. Aelric joined his hands to the process, and Robse's came alongside the slender strength of Caerdrys's. In a few moments, they had stripped a portion of the rock and laid bare its mysteries.

Engraved into the face of the cliff, safely hidden by that curtain of plants nature had woven over many thousands of years, were carvings that told a tale familiar to every one of the Elves. In the dimming light of evening, the eyes of the Humans could barely make out the weather-worn remains of the deepest carvings: the ships they had copied into their records. But the light was sufficient for the eyes of the Faeltheon to see much more. There, spread before them, was a tapestry of carvings, telling so much more than just the fragment the Humans had discovered.

The largest of the pictures depicted the creation story of the Elves and Faeries. This was followed by a series of smaller engravings that depicted the Faeltheon's happy years spent on their island before being called away from it by the Creator. Finally, the story ended with a picture of the Fair Folk boarding ships to search for their new land. The mass of Elves that surrounded Gaelcar and Aelric erupted into joyful clamor. This was their history, their story, the legacy of their ancestors! This island *had* been their homeland! Respectfully, they reached to lay their hands over the marks left by creatures just like them many centuries before.

The watchers in the meadow were nearly aflame with excitement and discovery by this time. The artisans who had carved the cliff face were standing with tears streaming down their faces, or embracing one another, or shouting for sheer joy. Those overwhelmed at the sight of their history unfolding were clinging to one another and trembling with deep emotion. Laslorn, watching Robse with eager eyes, had one arm around his mother and the other around his wife as he cried for very joy.

Suddenly, through all the babble of happy noise, the voice of Athalenael sounded, intense and low, commanding the attention of all.

"There!" she exclaimed. "Just there!"

As if to confirm the rejoicing of his people, Aelric followed a strong prompting and stretched out his hand to remove some vines from above the general area they had cleared. His gesture stilled them all, as it revealed to their sight a single deeply carved word, obviously meant as a declaration to stand for all time.

ATLARTYS.

The place where we became.

"Atlartys," breathed Gaelcar. "We have come home at last."

The hushed silence that had fallen over the company of the Faeltheon was dashed like waves against a rocky shoreline. They began to laugh and to cry, celebrating, at last, the freedom and promise in the meaning of that one word. The discovery of the deeply carved name ATLARTYS had released in them all a floodgate that had held in all their hopes and longings for over a year.

Surrounded by giddy laughter and tears, Robse found himself a little numb. He wished he felt the great elation that gripped the others, but instead, his insides seemed immobilized by ice or stone, held apart from his heart as if fearful of rejoicing. Disgusted with himself, and a bit resentful that his emotions should choose such a momentous time to be out of tune with the rest of his people, Robse turned his attention to those around him.

Not far away, some of the Elves had taken out pipes and other instruments. To a wild, skirling music that expressed their bursting hearts, many of the Elves had begun to dance, leaping and shouting in their joy.

Farther away, but drawing nearer, the Humans had noticed the commotion and were running toward them. King Sagiro, Beneval, and Princess Kyria were standing close to Aelric and Gaelcar, clamoring to know what had befallen the wild company. Aelric, face wet with the strong tears of a king, gestured to the carved word, but his throat was closed and he could not speak.

Gaelcar, his storyteller's voice easily carrying above the swooping and leaping of music and revelers, explained to the enthralled Humans the meaning of the ancient word and the confirmation it had provided to the strained hope of the weary travelers. King Sagiro was sympathetic to the heady emotions of the Fair Folk but wanted to hear more, especially about the mysterious carvings now revealed, which he and his kind could barely make out. Kyria insisted that she wanted to know the stories to take back to Bintah Auren, who would treasure them and order them put into the archives of the Great Library.

After a time, when the first bloom of elation had worn off, and many of the Elves, flushed with tears and dancing, had returned to surround their king, Aelric bade them all sit with their new Human friends and hear again the old tales. Speechless with the fullness of their joy, the Fair Folk came and settled like a wave of cherry blossoms about the feet of the Seneschal. The Humans hurried to join them, and many held Elven children in their laps as they prepared to hear the great stories. The emotions of the Faeltheon were running high, and their joy was magnified by seeing the wonder of their old familiar tales shining new in the eyes of the Humans among them. Robse had a strong sense of the unfolding of an historical moment between the two peoples.

Theo, Elrad, and Beregos tried without success to quiet the tumultuous joy of the Faeltheon so they could hear what was happening in the window still visible above the meadow. Finally, Davin caught up a beautifully etched hunting horn from where it lay on Ethalion's cloak. Launching himself skyward, he sounded the deep sweet notes, and all hushed as the notes rippled through them. Dropping back down to Theo's side, Davin returned the borrowed horn, and Theo waved their attention to the window. When they realized the revelations weren't over, the watchers sat quickly, arming themselves with fresh, hot tea.

Out of habit, Robse placed himself where he could guard the king's back, should the need arise, but his heart knew it was an empty gesture. He took great comfort in the nearness of Minlienda, sitting with Myrandella and Caerdrys on the other side of Gaelcar. The Seneschal sat upon a rocky outcropping, where all could hear and see him but still have a view of the wall behind him. He bowed his fair head, and the Faeltheon followed suit, the Humans catching on a moment later.

"We are met in Thy name," they murmured in one accord. Gaelcar raised his head and, with a fine sense of his audience, began to unfold in the Common Tongue the story never before heard by Human ears.

"Children of Adam, be welcome in the company of the Fair Folk. We invite you into our history." Robse felt the fine hairs along his arms rise in response to Gaelcar's expressive voice. The Elf was a master storyteller and had entertained them many evenings aboard the *Cethastea*, but Robse sensed that tonight he was in his element as never before, that the Presence was within him and was speaking through him. Robse felt the ice around his heart begin to melt and sent up a thankful prayer, even as his vision blurred. All eyes settled upon the slender figure of the Seneschal, bathed in late-lingering sunlight, surrounded by purpling dusk.

"In the beginning of time, the Creator spoke all things into being with the thoughts of His mind and the breath of His mouth. His presence hovered over the newness of His creation like a mother bird broods over her eggs. He took great joy in what He had made and desired to make companions to join Him in His rejoicing. So, the Creator made the Faeltheon, shaping them of the light of the stars, the dew of the grass, and the colors of the rainbow. Some He made with wings and others without. He breathed life into us and we became. When we awoke and saw Him, we cried out 'El!' recognizing in Him a life apart and different from our own. The Creator loved us and taught us about this world He had made to shelter us.

"Hearken and we shall sing for you an ancient song of those times."

The Faeltheon lifted up their voices, even the young children recalling their teaching sagas, and sang of the time of their creation.

Aematlon fyalar Faeltheoni
Lihti astea
Minwys quimlihti
Omayin ciridisi
El ruachar eli ruachai ímoni
An íon atlar

Elanímon
Na'cyb!

El s'ceregar hlalriel ímoni
Íon hleapar
El s'ceregar rysarcaeren ímoni
Íon lysar
El s'ceregar fyllolquen ímoni
Íon quallar

El s'ceregar aemm ímoni
Íon liennar halash theoni

Elanímon
Na'cyb!

El quallar anímon
Íon athalenar
El randar anímon
Íon atlar
El s'ceregar ímon fyalat gaelyeon
Íon fyalar
El randellar ímon Lom
Íon randel

Elanímon
Na'cyb!"

When the last haunting strains died away, Robse found he was not the only one deeply moved. Faces of Human and Elf alike were gleaming with the tracks of tears in the last washes of the sun. The Humans did not understand the words they had heard, but the eloquence of the massed voices and the deep, compelling weaving of the melody had stirred every soul of the company. A few soft sobs were muffled in the approaching darkness. Gaelcar's rich voice picked up the weave of the story and returned them to the ancient sacred time.

"The Faeltheon lived in harmony and lightness of spirit with the Creator on the island where He had placed them, and they knew great richness of joy in His Presence."

The ritual words breathed with fresh life, and their oldest story burned anew as the remnant of the Faeltheon gazed around them at the island of their history. Moved by profound emotion at the significance of the place where they gathered, Aelric and his Companions rose silently and paced over to the wall, laying their hands one by one upon the carved name that proclaimed this their ancient birthplace. As Gaelcar continued speaking, the Humans watched, fascinated and reverent as, one by one, the entire company of the Faeltheon rose to walk past the carved word, pausing to lay their hands upon its truth, before returning to sit again at Gaelcar's feet.

A lump formed in Las's throat as he watched Robse brush his slender fingers over the letters, absorbing the reality of that for which they had searched so long. Laslorn prayed for his brother, that he might finally find stability, love, and peace on the island Aematlon had created for His people in the beginning of their existence. He wondered what was in store for Robse as this new part of their journey began. His young brother had been through so much already, and, though he prayed for peace, Laslorn felt a sense of foreboding that Robse would have to face much more before he found comfort.

Theo placed a strong hand on Laslorn's shoulder. As their eyes met, they found that familiar understanding that often passed between the two brothers.

"Robse will find peace eventually," Theo reassured him. "All we can do right now is pray."

Gaelcar's measured tones continued to speak the ritual words, imbuing them with an intense and living presence.

"We lived here with Him and He walked with us and talked with us, and our life was good and full of blessing. We learned speech and wove songs. We learned the languages of the wind and the rain and the stars. We came to understand the voices of the trees and of the rocks and of the caverns within the bones of the Earth. We learned the songs of the creatures of the sea. We learned the stories of the birds of the air and the speech of the creatures of the fields and forests. We learned the quickening of rising sap as the plants grew and budded, bloomed and fruited. We learned to imitate the beauty of the Creator's work as He blessed us with creativity. We learned to draw and to write, to carve and to weave. He gave unto us children of our own kind, though very few and precious have their numbers ever been. We grew in wisdom and understanding, as children will in the presence of a loving, nurturing parent. We were full of joy and content in His Presence. In those days there was no disease and no death, no grief and no partings.

"Then the Creator came to us and instructed us in the building of vessels to travel far upon the sea. He showed us how to carve the wood and how to fashion it to fit together into great ships. He then instructed us that when the ships were complete, we were to board them, leave the island of our birth, and sail north, following the currents of the sea until we would come to another Land. He bade us nurture the forests there and the living creatures that abode in them, to use all our powers to make the Land and its inhabitants flourish. We did not yet know separation from Him, so we did not know fear, and thus we were not apprehensive about this change in our lives. We followed His instructions and began to build the ships."

Nearly every face of the company of watchers in Marliondolen was wet with tears. The pain of the grief and loss of some was eased and shared by all, and the profound joy that only a few of them had experienced was somehow glimpsed by all. The quiet sobs and deep silence alike reflected their shared experience. The Spirit of the Creator hovered over them like a bird over nestlings, like a caressing wind through their souls.

"There came a time, near the end of the building, when the world grew dark and cold as we had never before known it to be. The Lord was not found among us, and, for the first time, we were introduced to fear. The light and warmth of former days were never restored, and we continued our labors, with dread our constant companion. Finally, in the days when the ships were finished, the Faeltheon gathered together in one place and begged the Creator to come to us again.

"He did not come among us as He once had, openly and walking among us. Instead, He made us to feel His Presence still with us, and our fears were eased. He made one of us to see visions and revealed through that one the things we needed to know. Through this Kytha, the Creator told us that sin had entered the world and had brought with it death and suffering. He instructed us in the ways the world would become different and about the creatures who had Fallen away from Him, but we were most grieved that the veil of sin would forever separate us from Him.

"And so the Creator sent us away from the island of our birth and from the time of fellowship with Him to a new Land and a new service in His Name. *Elanímon. Na'cyb!*"

The choked voices of the Faeltheon in both worlds rose to echo his cry, but the Humans remained silent, sobered and wrenched by guilt that the sin of Adam should have ended the paradise of these beautiful folk, as well as their own Eden. Aelric rose from his place to stand in the moonlight beside Gaelcar.

"*Elanímon. Na'cyb!*" he echoed, raising his hands to dismiss the company to its bedrolls, leaving them with the ancient words of a hope undimmed by centuries of separation.

"God with us. May it be again!"

With the morning light, the mixed company began to stir. Those responsible for firewood and breakfast rose early and washed at the stream before beginning their tasks. The others gradually roused, goaded by the delightful smells issuing from the cook fires. Many were stiff and sluggish, for groups of them had stayed up talking for hours. As they shared breakfast, clustered in informal groups about the fires, some of the Humans began to share their stories with the Faeltheon.

Caerdrys, seated with Min on her right and the Human princess on her left, listened as she ate. Beneval was speaking, in their group, telling in his rich voice the story of how their ancestors, looking for a place where they might seek God in peace, were drawn to settle here.

"They found it a peaceful place, with abundant resources to supply their needs. They named the island Egauswas, Echo of God's Voice, in honor of the gentle wind that flows constantly from the caldera, in which many claimed to hear a beloved voice calling them."

Caerdrys liked that thought; it was something her people would have done, and it made her feel closer to these Humans than she had ever thought she could feel. Not far away, on the other side of the fire, she noticed Aelric, Gaelcar, and the Human king in deep discussion.

Listening, she was encouraged to hear them deciding to form a partnership to share the island. A knot of tension, left over from the long, weary months at sea, seemed to melt inside Caerdrys. With so much space and the friendly attitude of these odd Humans, she felt a great hope for their future rise up in her.

She listened as the Humans willingly ceded the caldera to the Faeltheon. Aelric and Gaelcar immediately agreed to the request that the Humans might trade with them for items from the rain forest, and that the Faeltheon were welcome to live and trade among the Humans, if they so desired. Sagiro offered to share the grazing grounds and to help with seasonal tasks, as much as interaction was desired.

They continued to discuss the broad issues, understanding that the finer points would have to be decided at a later conference that would include the counselors of Sagiro's Court. Caerdrys admired Aelric's and Gaelcar's handling of the negotiations. It seemed they were off to a good start.

A shout alerted all those still lingering by their fires that those who had resumed the explorations of the carvings on the cliff face had found something else. Eager and happy, they all crowded around to peer at the new section of flowing script, barely visible in the eroded face. Caerdrys felt a shock of joy when she recognized it as the text of one of their oldest songs. Further study revealed that its words were set forth exactly as they were written in the ancient Scrolls. Though no one any longer recalled the original tune, a simple, easy-to-follow melody, volunteered by a blushing Netharos, allowed them to sing the words they all knew.

Haliht hleaper abeherwys gaeli
Lihti astea ghyllar las drysoni
Aem cieliht halash
An cielemi íron rea
Íron eli herdel
Aiai hlalrieli

In the meadow, the watchers had regathered in the early light of day, not surprised to find that many of their company, exhausted by the emotional excesses of the night before, had simply rolled themselves in their cloaks and slept where they were. More firewood was hunted out and the fires rekindled. Breakfast was soon prepared and shared out, and sleepy voices were enlivened by discussions of the events of the previous night.

In a lull of conversation, while all were sharing the contentment to be found in the company of close friends after an important experience, the by now familiar shimmer began to coalesce in the air once more.

The finding and singing of *Aiai Hlalrieli* was enthusiastically joined by most of the Faeltheon on the meadow. When the song had faded, along with the window, a time of praise and worship of the Creator followed, refreshing and rejuvenating the meadow's inhabitants. As the vocal worship slowed and finally ceased, Athalenael was heard to speak to an Elf standing near her.

"Liennos, did you not compose this song, which Thallos then carved into the cliff?"

"I did, Kytha," came the response from a deep and resonant voice. Judging from the Elf's face, he was deeply moved that the words of his song had never been forgotten through the long stretch of years.

"Oh!" exclaimed Nausika, who loved knowing things. "Won't you teach us the melody you wrote for it? It has been so long since any sang it that no one in my time remembered the tune, only the words." Several other heads nodded encouragement, and someone passed a gitar forward to the red-faced composer.

"Well, then, if you wish it," he agreed, bending his head unnecessarily to check the tune of the instrument. He played the tune through for them first, but when he began to sing it, those from his time, who knew it well, took it up and sang it with a good will. The tune was simple, as suited the words, but had complex overtones and harmonies that delighted the musical among them.

Within a few minutes, the entire meadow was engaged in singing the lovely lyric to the original melody, and the song was finally heard again after its sleep of aeons.

Epilogue

Feeling a hand close over his left elbow, Theomanus turned from watching his beloved friends react to the wondrous events they had been shown. Strong and silent behind him waited Elrad, his teal eyes as bright as Theo had ever seen them. Elrad gestured with his head that they should draw aside to talk, and Theo willingly followed him, wondering if the Kythos had been given any special insight into the scenes they had witnessed. When the excited voices of the Faeltheon had faded behind them, Elrad and Theo settled comfortably on sun-warmed rocks beneath a giant chestnut.

"So they have found at last our ancient birthplace," mused the older Elf as he arranged the folds of his woven jacket over his shoulders. Theo nodded, not yet ready to commit to words the heady emotions within him. Elrad peered closely into Theo's golden eyes, noting again the strong family resemblance to Aelric, whose mother, Ashwyn, was of House Quaeliom.

Over the time they had been in Marliondolen, Elrad had come to value the counsel and input of Theomanus as much or more than that of his own lifelong friends. Elrad had made the acquaintance of many sages of ages past, and liked many of them quite well, but his heart was fast becoming knit with that of this young Elf. That Theomanus was wise for his years was clear to all. As Master of Marliondolen, he carried burdens the others could not share, though there would be times they would be called upon to help, Elrad was certain. Still, there were few who knew Theomanus well enough to know his doubts, his troubled thoughts.

From their long, candid discussions, Elrad knew that the younger Elf did not doubt the Creator, or His plans for them, but he doubted himself, his perspicacity, his ability to know when and how to act to fulfill Aematlon's will in their lives. Privately, Elrad was glad to see this evidence of humility in their leader, for he knew how subtly pride could sneak its way into the unwary heart.

Patiently, Elrad waited for Theomanus to be ready to talk. At last the dark head lifted and the golden eyes focused on their companion. A rueful smile curved Theo's lips, and he shook his head.

"Sorry, my friend. Once again, you must wait for me to catch up in order to find out how much I didn't understand!"

Elrad chuckled in turn.

"No, my son, the time to process what you have seen and heard, and what has affected you deeply, is a necessary gift if you are to understand any of what occurs. How many times have I told you to take the time to contemplate the things you have seen?"

"Many. And you know I do," Theo responded with a glance full of affection.

"So you do," agreed the Kythos. "So what is on your heart today? We have witnessed an event that is personally fulfilling to all Faeltheon. It was a truly stirring discovery. So, tell me what your heart says to you."

"I am reminded of the day, long ago in the Land, when we discussed the future of the Faeltheon; whether to trust in Marliondolen or to rely on the tales of the past. You said then something that has stayed with me ever since and which I have contemplated on many occasions."

"And what was that?" asked Elrad, though he thought he could guess.

"You said that we could never go back. You said that you believed that King Beregos's plan to search for the Faeltheon home island was a fine adventure but should not be attempted for future security. You said that if what they hoped to find when they found the island was a place where the Creator would once again walk with us and talk with us as in days of old, they would be disappointed, because that time was gone, vanished into the veil of sin. I remember feeling a sinking feeling when you said that, for I had harbored a secret hope that we might come to those days again, but your words rang in my heart with the resonance of truth, and I understood my hope to be in vain."

"No! The hope of having once again intimate fellowship with the Creator is never a vain hope, Theomanus! It is the *only* hope! It is for this hoped-for reward that we continue to breathe, and to wait, and to attend faithfully to the duties He gives us. It is for this hope realized that we wait with longing. Our souls pant for this chance for fellowship, as a deer pants in a time of deep drought. It is very life to us, this hope. Never give up on it, for without it, we are as dust; useless, unfertile, blowing aimlessly in the grip of the wind."

"Then you believe we shall someday have this joy of walking and talking with Him, like the old tales claim?"

"I do not think it will be like those old tales. I think it will be *better*, in ways we cannot now imagine. I believe it will be so in part because we will have grown somewhat in wisdom and in understanding of Him Who calls us to Himself."

"I see. This is part of not going back. Things can never be the way they once were for many reasons, not the least of which is that we ourselves are not who we used to be. And it would be folly to think that what was made for a certain time and a specific people would satisfy the needs of a different relationship."

"You see, you are growing!" remarked Elrad with some satisfaction.

"Which leads us back to what is on my heart today. Though I cannot imagine what will be in store for our Kin upon that island, now that they are bound to these Humans and have found our birthplace, I find my heart wrestling again with a different question." Elrad raised an inquiring brow, so Theo continued. "We cannot go back to achieve our hearts' goal. We know we must press on, to take hold of whatever the Creator sends to us. It is clear we are meant to grow and to mature in wisdom, and possibly other ways, as well. We have a clear desire to do that, so that we may hasten the day when fellowship with Him is once again our portion. Yet, the question remains unanswered: what are we to do? How are we to do it? And, most specifically for me, how am I to lead my people upon the road the Creator would have us walk? These are the questions that return to my heart often, my friend. I try not to entertain them in a spirit of concern, but to wait patiently for their secrets to be revealed. Still, I fear I will miss His quiet voice."

"Theomanus," Elrad said, laying his hand upon the younger Elf's shoulder. "Trust Him. We have spoken of this before, my son. When it is time, He will tell you, or lead you, or prompt your heart, or give me a vision for your guidance. What He will not do, my dear friend, is leave you with no guidance. It is *His* plan, Theo. He will cause it to come to pass. Trust Him."

Theo released a great sigh and leaned back against the old tree.

"I know it's true. I haven't forgotten it. But thank you for reminding me again."

Corot stood on the narrow balustrade of the outer curtain wall, facing the sea. The brisk, salt-laden wind whipped his black garments about him and disordered the oiled locks of his beard, but he ignored it. Beneath his feet was a warren of activity encased in quarried stone. This fortress, built into the side of the rocky bluff that overlooked the turbulent Great Sea, had taken many slaves and many years to construct. On his journey from his desert homeland, a decade before, Corot had taken his time, observing carefully the landscape and settlements along his way. He had chosen several likely locations for outposts of his spreading power and had left in his wake orders, designs, and underlings to carry them out.

Now, with that pleasant business to the northwest concluded, Corot had removed himself to this stronghold on the rocky coast, midway between those cold, Goblin-infested lands to the north and the curving coast where the Great Sea entered the Mediterranean. Already, in the years he had been away, this fortress had been hewn and built, and the seaport below had been established, along with the growing town around it. It was, as he had predicted, a good place to establish a base. From here, information could be gathered and disseminated via sea and land.

His underlings had done well the work he had left them. Upon his arrival and inspection of the fortress that stood brooding above the seaport like a raptor in her eyrie, he had rewarded his faithful with positions of rank in his household. Already, they had begun to adopt his fashion of wearing unrelieved black. Corot smiled grimly: it suited them.

A sigh of satisfaction swelled Corot's chest. His most demanding allies had been pleased with the results of his work in that remote northwestern isle, as he had been sure they would be. The destruction of the Faeltheon had been his greatest work for Lemyuria so far. It had also been a strategic move in his climb to ultimate power. His six-fingered hand in its specially tailored leather glove clenched into a powerful fist and smote the stone balustrade as he remembered the report of the Goblin spies he had sent to the ruined Elven City after that last battle.

He had taken great satisfaction in killing them for their news, of course, but it had been disquieting. Someone, they had declared, must have lived long enough to burn and bury the dead, but there had been no sign of survivors. The hope that the few who had survived had fled into the northern mountains had been carefully omitted from Corot's own account to his dark allies. He had sent many hunters into that region over the intervening time and had received regular reports from the minions he had left to manage his holdings there. That none had been found alive had been a source of comfort and confidence to Corot.

As he turned to go back within, he encountered one of his guardsmen seeking him with a message. The man bowed low before him and waited for Corot's acknowledging gesture before speaking.

"My lord, one of your lieutenants has returned with a prisoner. He says you will want to question the captive."

Corot nodded sharply, as though he had been expecting this word.

"Have them taken to the chamber off my office," he commanded curtly.

"Very good, my lord," responded the man, retreating quickly down the steep stone stairs.

When Corot entered the small, bare stone chamber a few minutes later, it was to find the captain of one of his merchant vessels standing near the small table that held a pitcher and two goblets. He had not served himself, nor had he taken the one chair in the room. Behind the man, in the shadows of the room, stood two burly, greasy seamen, holding between them the sagging and filthy body of a man in chains. The stench of all four was less than pleasant, but Corot made no comment as he crossed to the table, poured himself a goblet of wine, and sat in the chair. When he had seated himself, the captain made bold to pour himself a goblet of wine as well. Corot prudently waited until the captain had quaffed a healthy gulp with no ill effects before sipping himself. At his nod, the captain began to explain the presence of the prisoner.

"We found this man seeking employment at an island dock, my lord. His tale caught my attention, and I knew you would want to hear it for yourself, so I had him brought here." At Corot's further nod, the captain turned to the prisoner and cuffed him sharply. "Tell my lord the tale you told me!" he commanded harshly. The prisoner lifted sunken eyes to stare in Corot's general direction, but he didn't seem to take in anything he saw. His voice was weak, but Corot's bored annoyance vanished as the man's tale unfolded.

"I sailed aboard the *Cutlass*," he began tonelessly. "We were a pirate rig captained by Jed Haggert. We sailed as a threesome and never lost a battle with those odds. Until we met up with *them*. There was three o' them, big ships, and rich looking. They let us get close with never a suspicion of danger. We boarded 'em and fought them. We thought the odds still in our favor, as the ships weren't armed and sat low in the water. But… they was… different. They fought like demons, for all they looked like angels. It was queer, seein' such beautiful folk with teeth bared and swords singin'. A good number of 'em got up into the radlings and fired arrows at us. Deadly aim, they had, like they could see where we couldn't. And with them eyes, I ain't surprised. In the end, they burnt two of our ships, and only half of us made it back to the *Cutlass* and escaped." The ragged little man stopped there, wavering on his feet between the two sailors.

Corot stood slowly, hiding from these scum the flame of white-hot anger that had begun to burn within him. The man's tale had to be false! Or else, he must be exaggerating, as all sailors did. None of the Faeltheon had survived—certainly not three ships full of them! He crossed to the erstwhile pirate and grasped him by the hair, pulling the man's filthy face back until he had to squint up into Corot's forbidding visage. The man, already pale, turned faintly greenish when he met Corot's eyes.

"Tell me about their appearance," Corot commanded insistently. "Leave out nothing."

The captive gulped, his Adam's apple bobbing audibly in his scrawny throat.

"They . . . they was tall, my lord," he stammered, oily sweat beginning to trickle down his temples. "Their eyes were . . . were large and . . . and slanted like. And their ears, my lord!" He hastened to babble as Corot's fist tightened in his hair. Tears of pain leaked down his unshaven face, and he thought desperately to come up with more information for the intimidating man in black. "Their ears was pointy at the tips—I swear they was! And they must've had some sort o' magic, my lord, for they fought most fiercely, even the women and children, when we breached the lower decks! Their clothing, goods, and ships was rich indeed, and beautiful, and we wanted 'em badly, but even we, seasoned pirates as we was, couldn't defeat *them* in battle!" The little man's voice faded as he ran out of things to say. Corot's visage grew grimmer, and his eyes took on the adamant gleam of obsidian. Releasing the captive's filthy hair, he turned to his waiting captain.

"Find all the crew members of this man's vessel. Bring them here. I want them all, you understand? Spread word that I will pay for information of these 'fair folk.'" The captain nodded, plainly uneasy in Corot's presence.

"Go." The man left, his sailors scurrying behind him. An orderly appeared in the doorway, waiting for Corot's commands.

"Take this man to my dungeons. Get all the information he has. Do not let him die until you have it all."

When he was alone, Corot allowed his rage to surface. *How can this be? How can there be Faeltheon survivors upon the sea? Surely it must be they! With that description, it could be no others, and yet… did not they all perish? Incredible! Impossible! Insufferable!*

With an inhuman bellow of rage, Corot picked up the chair and flung it against the far wall, smashing it into splintered fragments. The pitcher followed, shattering, splashing wine over the carnage like a parody of bloodshed. Corot stood, eyes glaring wildly, chest heaving, breath gusting in hissing pants through his clenched teeth. His limbs trembled with the force of his fury.

This cannot happen! I will not allow it! The survival of these creatures could not be permitted to ruin his plans, his glorious future. *I will find them all*, he vowed, spittle foaming at the corners of his snarl.

I will wipe them from the Earth.

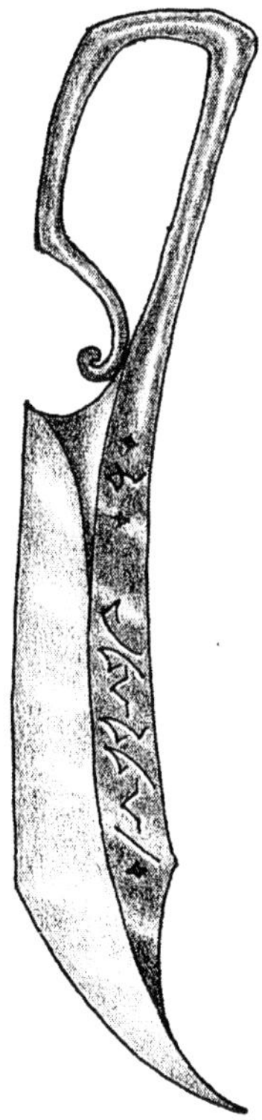

Appendices

Appendix A

A Glossary of Faeltheon Names and Terms

Aelric Rysaelf—(A-el-rick ree-SAY-elf: *Consecrated Leader, High Elf*) an Elf; son of Beregos and Ashwyn, last king of the Elves, leads the remnant of his people on the search for their ancestral home.

Aelwyn Elenthea—(A-el-win el-EN-thee-ah: *Given to God, God's People*) a Faerie, mother of Elwyn, wife of Gael.

Aematlon—(A-em-AT-lon: *Our Creator*) one of the Names of God.

aerie—(A-ree, EYE-ree); an eagle's nest, the lookout's post on the mast of a ship.

Amadthalos Rysaelf—(ah-mahd-THAL-oss: *Land's Guardian*) an Elf, the first Elven king in the Land.

Amiel—(AHM-ee-el: *Faith of God, Daughter of Faith*) an Elf, one of the ancient queens.

Amiela—(AHM-ee-EL-ah: *Faith of God*) a Faerie of the ancient days.

Aoneth of Westlawn—(A-oh-neth ree-SAY-elf: *Richly gifted, High Elf*) an Elf, companion to Theomanus, of the Royal Tribe.

Ashwyn Rysaelf—(ASH-win: *Blessed Maiden*) an Elf, wife of Beregos, mother of Aelric.

Athalenael—(ath-el-EN-ee-el: *Listens to God*) a Faerie of the ancient days, the first Kytha.

Atlartys—(at-LAR-teece: *The Place Where We Became*) the original name of the isle of Elvenhome.

Beneval—(BEN-eh-vahl: *Well-wisher* (City)) a Human, betrothed of Kyria.

Beregos Rysaelf—(BEAR-eh-goss: *Bright*) an Elf, king of the Elven City, husband of Ashwyn, father of Aelric, called Good King Beregos.

Bintah Auren—(BIN-tah ORE-en: *Wise Teacher, Golden One* (City)) a Human, of Egauswas, a teacher, tutor, and advisor to Sagiro and Kyria.

Bran—(BRAN) a Human, an errand boy on the docks of Egauswas.

Bregos—(BREG-oss: *Bright One*) an Elf, one of the ancient kings.

breherege—(breh-HAIR-egg-eh) a braided loaf of sweet egg bread (similar to challah), traditional for weddings, to symbolize the twining of two lives into one.

Cador Elionde—(KAY-dor el-lee-ON-deh: *Shining Home, Holy Haven*) a Faerie, *amios* brother to Davin. A former Border Guard.

Caerbryht—(kay-AIR-breet: *Bright Heart*) an Elf, Champion to King Qualdruth and negotiator with the dragons of the Battle of Fyrenfyld.

Caerdrys Gaelathnalienn—(kay-AIR-dreece gay-EL-lath-NAH-lee-en: *True Heart, Echo of the South Sea*) an Elf, *amia* sister to Minlienda Elashar, one of the Companions, the representative of Tribe Gaelathnalienn.

cathelath—(KATH-eh-lath: *Southern Crown*) a vine with heart-shaped leaves.

cerdem—(KER-dem: *Crown*) the broad wooden beam on the outside of a ship that holds the ribs securely.

Cerlim Swyren—(KER-lim SWEER-en: *Bow, Swift Feet*) an Elf, a noted archer, one of the Companions, the representative of Tribe Ammastea.

Cethastea—(keth-AST-ee-ah: *Crown of Stars*) a gaelyeon, the lead ship of the three that brought the Elven remnant from the Land to Egauswas.

Cethlas—(KETH-lass: *Crown of Leaves*) an Elf aboard the *Cethastea*.

Chassidy Cooper—(*Holy One*) a Human, called *Cielay* (*Sky-Eyes*) by the Faeries, owner of the star necklace, betrothed to Nicholan the cooper and smith.

Chloe Cooper—(*Blooming*) a Human, younger sister of Chassidy; as a toddler she was captured by Goblins in an effort to bring about the doom of the Faeltheon.

Ciella—(kee-EL-lah: *Sky*) an Elf woman.

cinna—(KEEN-nah) cinnamon bark

cinnamaon—(keen-ah-MAY-on) ground cinnamon.

Corot—(ko-ROT: *Corruption* (by power)) a Human, leader of the Lemyurans.

Dahlrys—(DAHL-reece: *Royal Shoot*) an Elf, of the Tribe Rysaelf, next in line to rule after Gaelcar.

Dashiela Hleafa—DAHSH-ee-ELL-ah hlee-AH-fah: *Grace of God, Dance*) a Faerie, second of triplet sisters whose sacrifice gave rise to the legend of the Three Sisters.

Davin Iridistheon—(DAH-vin ear-i-DIS-thay-on: *Beloved, Glory of God*) a Faerie, distant blood relation to the Family Elenthea, former Border Guard, husband of Lucina Brithwyd.

delphyson—(DELL-feece-on: *Beautiful Ones*) the Faeltheon name for dolphins, derived from the word *delphys*, meaning "swelled womb," great with child, one of the highest accolades of beauty among the Faeltheon. Dolphins were thus named, not only for their beauty, but also for being mammals.

djournee—(DJOR-nay: *Day's Worth* (City)) a title, a person who has completed apprentice training and is skilled enough to command a daily wage, but has not yet attained mastery; i.e., journeyman. (This term led to the common usage of diurnal (day-long) and journey (the length of travel usually accomplished in a day's travel (typically ~20 miles.)))

Doma—(DOE-mah: *Gift*) an Elf child aboard the *Cethastea.*

Domel Minquallen—(DOME-el min-KWALL-en: *Gift from God, Gentle Speech*) an Elf, one of the Companions, representing the tribe Rysaelf, cousin to Aelric.

Domiela Lisea—DOM-ee-EL-ah lee-SAY-ah: *God's Gift, Laughter*) a Faerie, youngest of triplet sisters whose sacrifice gave rise to the legend of the Three Sisters.

Domiella—(DOM-ee-EL-ah: *Gift of God*) an Elf, mother of Netharos.

Dremwyn—(DREM-win: *Dream Maiden*) a Faerie, one of the ancient queens.

Dridelphanen—(dree-DELL-fan-en: *The Three Sisters*) a galyeon, one of the three ships to carry the remnant of the Faeltheon to Egauswas.

Drythiela Lienda—(DREE-thee-ELL-ah lee-EN-dah: *God's Truth, Song*) a Faerie, eldest of the triplet sisters whose sacrifice gave rise to the legend of the Three Sisters.

Egauswas—(eh-GOWSS-wahs: *Echo of God's Voice(City)*) the Human name for the isle of Elvenhome, so named because of the eerie, voice-like whispers that came from the caves in the caldera due to wind and the ocean.

Elamani Ammastea Lyserea—(el-ah-MAHN-ee ahm-mah-STAY-ah lee-SEH-ree-ah: *Hope, Lover of Stars, Friend of Laughter*) an Elf, wife of Riende, mother of Laslorn and Robse, foster mother to Theomanus. She died giving birth to Robse.

Elrad Ruachliende—(EL-rahd rue-ACH-lee-END-deh: *God's power, Spirit Song*) an Elf, a prophet who is given dreams and visions. He is sometimes called Elrad Kythos, Elrad the Seer. He has lived many long ages and is a valued friend and advisor, known for his wisdom.

Elrys—(EL-reece: *Joy*) an Elf, a shipwright.

Elwyn Elenthea—(EL-win el-EN-thee-ah: *Hand Maiden of God*) the last Queen of Faerie, daughter of Aelwyn and Gael, wife of Theomanus, *amia* sister of Nausika, now titled the Lady of Marliondolen.

Ergos—(AIR-goss: *Artisan*) an Elf of ancient times, designed the trap in which the dragon was netted and forced to negotiate with Caerbryht.

Ethalion—(eh-THALL-ee-on: *Son of Strength*) an Elf, friend and Champion to Amadthalos.

Ethanos—(eh-THANN-oss: *Strength*) an Elf, husband of Leawyn, father of Gaelal.

Faeltheon—(fay-EL-thay-on: *God's Fair Folk*) the name of the race of Faeries and Elves.

Freos–(FRAY-oss: *Freedom*); an Elf child, one of those orphaned in the last battle.

Fyllys—(FEE-leece: *Full of Laughter*) an Elf woman, wife of Hederos.

Gael Faelionde—(GAY-el fay-EL-lee-ON-deh: *Sea, Fair Haven*) a Faerie, father to Elwyn, Consort to Aelwyn until his death in the Goblin Wars.

Gaelal—(gay-EL-al: *Shining Sea*) an Elf, born at sea, son of Leawyn and Ethanos.

Gaelcar Talathaem—(gay-EL-car ta-LATH-ay-em: *Sea Heart, Steadfast Purpose*) an Elf, of the Tribe Rysaelf, cousin to Aelric, a member of the Council of Beregos, one of the Companions, Seneschal to King Aelric.

gaellea—(gay-EL-lee-ah: *Sheltered Place Upon the Sea*) the galley, or kitchen, of a gaelyeon.

Gaelneth—(gay-EL-neth: *Gift for Sea (faring)*) an Elf, the captain of the *Dridelphanen*.

Gaelrandel—(gay-EL-ran-del: *Sea Quest*) a ship, one of the three gaelyeon that transported the Faeltheon remnant to Elvenhome.

gaelyeon—(gay-EL-yay-on: *Distant Sea*) a ship, the forerunner of the galleon.

Geliennos—(gell-ee-EN-noss: *Great Singer*) a humpback whale who aids the Faeltheon on their sea journey.

Geltheon Quaeliom—(GEL-thay-on kway-EL-ee-om: *God's Heart, One Who Speaks God's Wisdom*) an Elf, twinborn, companion of Theomanus.

Ghaerwe—(gay-AIR-weh: *Silver Arrow*) a dolphin, leader of her pod.

Glimring Quaeliom—(GLIM-ring: *Shining)* an Elf, twinborn, a companion of Theomanus.

Gren—(GREN: *Green*) a Goblin, insanely talkative, lacking in manners and proper protocol, a slave of Corot.

Grimswrath—(GRIMZ-rath: *Rage*) a Goblin commander who desired the triplet sisters but in the end had to sacrifice them.

Hadara—(hah-DAHR-ah: *Beautiful*) an Elf, wife of Amadthalos the First.

Hederos—(HED-er-oss: *Honor)* an Elf, husband to Fyllys.

Hereneth—(HAIR-eh-neth: *Gifted Hands*) an Elf, a shipwright of the ancient days.

Iridrys Quaeliom—(EE-ree-dreece: *Blossoming Tree*) an Elf, wife of Thalleam, mother of Theomanus.

Jed Haggert—Human, pirate, Captain of the *Cutlass*, and leader of three pirate vessels.

Kier Readrys—(KEER re-AHD-dreece: *Set Apart One, Tree Friend*) a Faerie, former Border Guard, *amios* cousin to Lucina Brithwyd.

Killern—a Human, pirate, first mate to Jed Haggert.

Kyria—(KEER-ee-ah: *Ruler(City)*) a Human, called Kyrie, daughter of Sophia and Sagiro.

Kytha, Kythos, Kython—(KYTH-ah, -oss, -on: *Seer*) a title, meaning "one to whom revelation is given," a prophet, a dreamer, and seer of visions. (The verb form is pronounced to rhyme with "tithe," but the pronoun has a soft "th," as in "thin.")

Lashar—(lah-SHAR: *Blessed Leaf*) an Elf, cousin to Domel.

Laslorn Lyserea—(LAS-lorn : *Autumn*) an Elf, friend, and foster brother to Theomanus, brother of Robse, husband of Nausika, a skilled tree-home fashioner, called Laslorn of the Merry Heart.

Lasnov—(LAS-nov: *New Leaf*) a Faerie, Consort to Elenfea, the first Queen of Faerie.

Leawyn—(LAY-ah-win: *Sheltered Maiden*) an Elf, wife of Ethanos, mother of Gaelal.

Lemyuran—(lem-MYUR-an: *One Who Walks in Darkness*) the name of a group of people (Humans, Goblins, and others) who are sworn enemies of God, hating the light, and loving darkness and evil deeds. They are scattered throughout the world and are known by many names, including: Lemurians, Muans, the nation of Mu, and Ur. They translate their name as "Ones Who Walk the Night" and are very proud of it, considering the night and darkness to be their special realm.

Liennos—(lee-EN-oss: *Song*) an Elf of the ancient days, a composer, who wrote the original tune to *Aiai Hlalrieli.*

longeye—a slender refractor telescope, typically used at sea.

Lucina Brithwyd—(loo-SEEN-ah BRITH-wid: *Light, Birchwood*) a Faerie, a former Border Guard, wife of Davin Iridistheon. She is often called Lucina Trueheart and is known for her loyalty and her devotion to duty.

Lysion—(LEE-see-on: *Merry*) an Elf, the captain of the *Cethastea*, master fisherman.

Maegos—(may-EGG-oss: *Mighty*) an Elf, friend of Amadthalos.

Michal Tsippora—(MI-kahl tsip-POR-ah: *Who is Like God?, Little Bird*); a Faerie, *amia* sister to Kier, a former Border Guard trainee, currently being courted by Aoneth.

Minlienda Elashar—(MIN-lee-EN-dah ELL-ash-ar: *Little Song, God's Blessing*) an Elf, *amia* sister to Caerdrys, representative of the Tribe Quaeliom, one of the Companions.

Myrandella Durilyse—(meer-RAN-dell-ah DYUR-ee-leece: *Bitter Quest, Land of Laughter*) an Elf, a Kytha, of the Tribe Ruachliende, later added to the Companions, a trained healer, called Randa.

Nausika Brithoniel—(NAH-sih-ka: *Next in power*) a Faerie, *amia* sister to Elwyn, wife to Laslorn, called Clever Nausika.

Netharos—(neth-ARE-oss: *Gifted*) an Elf boy of musical talent, son of Domiella.

Nicholan Cooper—(NICK-oh-lahn: *Victorious One*) a Human, journeyman cooper and smith, betrothed to Chassidy Cooper.

Pellos—(PELL-loss: *Shield*) an Elf, friend to Amadthalos.

Pyxes—(PIX-eez: *Crosses*) a group of small white or purple star-shaped flowers, or a double cross-stitch, like an asterisk, used for embroidering flowers, also the name given to the cross-shaped constellation later known as the Southern Cross.

Qualdruth—(KWAHL-drooth: *Speaks Truth*) an Elf, one of the ancient kings.

Qualneth—(KWAHL-neth: *Gifted Speaker*) a dolphin, a young male of Ghaerwe's pod who communicates clearly.

Rablorn—(RAB-lorn: *Lost Power*) an Elf, friend, and companion to Theomanus, killed in the Goblin Wars prior to *The Alliance*.

Radlas—(RAD-lass: *Powerful Leaf*) a young Elf aboard the *Cethastea*, known for his far sight.

radlings—(RAD-lings) short for "radiating lines," the ladder-like rigging lines on a ship that radiate from the aerie to the hull and are used to secure the sails and for climbing, later called ratlines.

Randelos Ommgeon—(RAND-el-oss om-GAY-on: *Questor, Sees Far*) an Elf, representative of the Tribe Ruachliende, one of Aelric's Companions.

Rannel—(RAN-nell: *God's Path*) an Elf, first mate aboard the *Cethastea*.

Raros—(RAHR- ross: *Shouter*) an Elf, captain of the *Gaelrandel*, formerly a fisherman under Lysion.

Rearys—(ray-ARE-eece: *Royal Friend*) an Elf, Champion to Beregos.

Riende Lyserea—(ree-END-deh: *Stands Firm*) an Elf, Guardian to Aelric, husband of Elamani, father of Laslorn and Robse, foster father to Theomanus, good friend of Beregos and Elrad, known for his faith and his integrity.

Robse Lyserea—(ROB-see: *Present Power*) an Elf, second son of Elamani and Riende, brother to Laslorn, foster brother to Theomanus, reluctant Champion to Aelric, one of the Companions.

rundine—(RUNE-deen (City)) a utensil, similar to a shallow spoon, with short tines like a fork.

Sagiro—(sah-GEER-ro: *Keen Sight(City)*) a Human, king of Egauswas, husband of Sophia, father of Kyria, known for his openness of heart and his sagacity.

Sophia—(so-FEE-ah: *Lover of Wisdom(City)*) a Human, queen of Egauswas, wife of Sagiro, mother of Kyria, known for her wisdom and serenity.

spyglass—a telescoping tube, with or without a glass lens, used to see distances, usually at sea. Not as effective as a longeye.

Stealiht—(stay-AH-leet: *Starlight*) a Faerie, friend to Amadthalos.

Strahng—(STRONG: *Strong(City)*) a Human, dockmaster of Egauswas.

Talrys—(TALL-reece: *Strong Lift*) an Elf, a cousin to Caerdrys, died in the Last Battle for the Land.

Temple—(TEM-p l) a Human, djournee-man dockmaster, assistant to Strahng, known to be a man of few words.

Thalleam Quaeliom—(THAL-ay-ahm: *Strong Will*) an Elf, husband of Iridrys, father of Theomanus, head of the tribe Quaeliom until his death at sea, friend of Elrad, Riende, and Beregos, called Thal.

Thallos—(THAL-loss: *Guardian*) a Faerie of the ancient days who helped carve the cliffs of the Caldera.

Theomanus Quaeliom—(thee-AHM-ah-nus: *Hand of God*) an Elf, son of Iridrys and Thalleam, heir to the Tribe Quaeliom. A prophecy spoken over his birth claimed that he would one day be used of God to help the Faeltheon, thus he was named "Hand of God." He is husband to Elwyn, Master of Marliondolen, foster brother to Laslorn and Robse, the first Elf to fly, called Theo.

Tiros Talatheon—(TEER-oss tal-ATH-ay-on: *castle, God's Strength*) a Faerie, a renowned jeweler, and master craftsman.

Vyggos—(VEE-goss: *Victory*) an Elf, friend of Amadthalos.

Appendix B

Songs of the Faeltheon

This is a traditional song of the Faeltheon that dates back to the earliest Scrolls.

Agen Randel	**(Life is a Quest)**
Cybel ash eam	(May God bless you)
Cybel thal eam	(May God guard you)
Cyb ear randel	(May your journey)
Reg eam doma	(Lead you home)
Ea randal	(As you wander)
Ai yeonder	(Ever farther)
Cyb ear ren	(May your feet)
Ende yori randia	(Stay on His path)
Agen randel	(Life is a quest)
Anam ear wigos	(With faith your guide)
Ai fy ear geldar	(Always do your best)
Ommat ageni eliom	(To see life through God's eyes)

Cybel fys eam	(May God mature you)
Cybel s'cereg eam	(May God teach you)
Cyb ear caer	(May your heart)
Emhereg drys eliom	(Find true wisdom)

This song is in the Ancient Scrolls, but it was also found in the cliff carvings in the caldera of Atlartys. The original tune is recalled only in Marliondolen.

Aiai Hlalrieli	**(Days of Joy)**
Haliht hleaper abeherwys gaeli	(Sunlight danced upon the waves of the sea)
Lihti astea ghyllar las drysoni	(Starlight gilded the leaves of the trees)
Aem cieliht halash	(Day was for praise)
An cielemi íron rea	(And night was our friend)
Íron eli herdel	(We were in the palm of His hand)
Aiai hlalrieli	(In the days of joy)

This song is said to be the very oldest song. It has survived from before the days the Faeltheon departed Atlartys. It is a teaching song and is typically learned by rote but is often sung in four or more parts at celebrations.

Liende Mianatloni	**(Creation Song)**
Aematlon fyalar Faeltheoni	(The Creator made His Fair Folk of)
Lihti astea	(The light of the stars)
Minwys quimlihti	(The dew of the dawn)
Omayin ciridisi	(The colors of the rainbow)

El ruachar eli ruachai ímoni	(He breathed His breath of life into us)
An íon atlar	(And we became)
Elanímon	(God with us)
Na'cyb!	(May it be again!)
El s'ceregar hlalriel ímoni	(He taught us joy)
Íon hleapar	(We danced)
El s'ceregar rysarcaeren ímoni	(He taught us happiness)
Íon lysar	(We laughed)
El s'ceregar fyllolquen ímoni	(He taught us language)
Íon quallar	(We spoke)
El s'ceregar aemm ímoni	(He taught us love)
Íon liennar halash theoni	(We sang praises to Him)
Elanímon	(God with us)
Na'cyb!	(May it be again!)
El quallar anímon	(He spoke with us)
Íon athalenar	(We listened)
El randar anímon	(He walked with us)
Íon atlar	(We became)
El s'ceregar ímon fyalat gaelyeon	(He taught us to build ships)
Íon fyalar	(We built)
El randellar ímon Lom	(He sent us north)
Íon randel	(We go)
Elanímon	(God with us)
Na'cyb!	(May it be again!)

This song, a haunting, yet hopeful lament, was made by Netharos aboard the ships as the remnant of the Faeltheon sought for their island home (original lyrics and music from "Hymn," by Randy Stonehill, copyright 1985 Stonehillian Music and Word Music, used by permission.)

Rysarliende	**(Hymn)**
Fylarai	(In the end)
Íon nedistale	(We are not forgotten)
Íron randel	(And our journey)
Nean eam	(Is not in vain)
Aematlon	(For the Master)
Brygar ím sia	(Who brought us here)
Yo regan ím	(Will lead us)
Namad	(Home again)

This is the traditional blessing, usually spoken by parents or close friends, at a wedding or upon entering a new home. It symbolizes the blessings wished upon a couple, or siblings, who are beginning a new phase of their lives together. Traditionally, it is spoken, as poetry, but the musically creative often chant or sing it.

Ash Yuani (Nov Doma)	**(Blessing for a Wedding (or New Home))**
Edom yehonímen breherege	(Receive from us bread)
Cyb eon an ernon cenan	(That you and yours may know)
Nae neod	(No want or need)
Edom yehonímen yelfaon	(Receive from us butter)
Cyb eon cenan	(That you both may know)
El faonydeni; aon anfaon	(The rich and abun- dant provision of God)

Edom yehonímen lyssen	(Receive from us sugar)
Eron beheret	(That your life together)
Cyb lyssi	(May be sweet)
Edom yehonímen cinna	(Receive from us spices)
Eron agen	(That your daily life)
Cyb bryhatla yehon hla-lriel anaromen	(May be enlivened by joy and pleasant surprises)

This is the traditional *Welcome Song*, sung to all newborn Faeltheon. This version is for a baby girl.

Liende Agweni Novatla	**(Song of Welcome for a Newborn (Girl))**
Hlalriel aímon earsa, mynova!	(We rejoice in your presence, baby girl!)
Nov aímon don caertheon,	(New to us from God's heart,)
Earsa ash ímon	(Your presence blesses us all)
Gelig lihti astea.	(Like starlight.)
Lulla, nov ayapana, lindea,	(Sleep, new blossom, tender shoot,)
Thallari íron behereti aemm.	(Safe in our weaving of love.)
Gwena íroncaer, íronaemm,	(Welcome to our hearts, our love,)
Íronagen, íronatlan.	(Our lives, our world.)

Appendix G

Notes on the Faeltheon Language

1. As caretakers of the living creation of the Land, the Faeltheon are very aware of the creatures around them. Thus, in their language, all living creatures are gender specific, except in the cases of immature plants or certain sea life, in which cases the "gender unknown" suffix is used. Gender is not used for non-biological creatures.
2. Plurals are indicated on the noun to which they refer.
3. Verbs are conjugated in (at least) the infinitive, present, past, future, and state-of-being tenses. These tenses are indicated by suffixes. Related nouns are usually formed from the root word of the verb and often end in an "e."
4. When the root verb ends in a vowel, a consonant is typically added before the suffix, unless the final vowel is an "i" or a "y." If the root is archaic and ends in a consonant, the consonant is often doubled before the suffix is added.
5. Vowels are a, e, i, o, u, and y. They differ somewhat from English in that the "i" is almost always pronounced "ee." The "y" is usually pronounced "ee" if it is followed by only one consonant. If it is followed by two consonants, it makes the short "i" sound. It typically sounds like a "y" when it falls at the beginning of a word, or immediately following an "n" or an "i." Two vowels

together are generally pronounced separately, except when one is the silent "u" after a "q," and in the case of "ai," which is usually pronounced "eye." For example, *caer* is pronounced kay-*air*, and *ciel* is pronounced kee-*el*. An "e" at the end of a word is seldom silent, but is softly voiced, as in *liende*, pronounced lee-*en*-deh. "I" and "y" are often interchangeable.

6. Consonants and consonant blends sound much as they do in English. "T" and "th" (as in *thin*) are often interchangeable. The voiced "th" (as in *they*) is almost never used. "Ch" is usually the guttural "k" sound at the end of the Scottish word *loch*. The letter "c" is almost always pronounced as a "k," and the letter "k" is almost never used.
7. Family structure has three tiers: the nuclear family of those blood related, the second-level family (parents and siblings-in-love) who share a home and the raising of the children, and the third-level family (aunts, uncles, cousins-in-love) whose homes one visits frequently. The term *amia* is used (with appropriate gender modifications) to refer to these relationships. The literal translation of this term is "in-love."
8. The Faeltheon do not have the verb "to be." Their legends say that when the first Faeltheon opened their eyes and beheld God, they cried out "El!" which translates roughly as "the One who is." Because they recognized from the beginning that their own existence was on a different level than that of God, they substitute the verb "to become" for the verb "to be," or leave it out of their construction entirely. For example, in Human tongue, one might say: "I am home." In the Faeltheon, it would be: "I home," with the construction of the personal pronoun "I"indicating that it is the subject of the sentence. As a sign of respect, reverence, and acknowledgment that God is other than His creation, they do not use the verb of His being in any form other than as his name, El. (When "el" is a part of a word, it almost always exists as a reference to God.) When they first encountered Humans and began to learn their speech, the Faeltheon were horrified and aghast that Men would so equate themselves with their Maker. Some sages among the

Faeltheon have speculated that is may be a very fundamental clue to the heart of sin, a mystery to the Faeltheon.

Gender Suffixes: (points 1 and 2)

Feminine: -a (pronounced ah, not ay), -en (pl.)
Daughter of: -iel
Maiden: -wyn, -wen, -ien
Masculine:-os (pronounced oss, not ohs), -o, -es (pl.)
Son of:-ion
Gender Unknown: -y
Mixed Group (plural): -on

Verb Conjugation: (point 3)

Infinitive:= root + -at
Present:= root
Past:= root + -ar
Future:= root + -an
State-of-Being (-ing):= root + -al
Noun Form:= root + e (or + gender endings, if a person)

Example of a Conjugated Verb: (point 3)

English	Faeltheon
To abide	Amadat
Abide	Amad
Abided	Amadar
Will abide	Amadan
Abiding	Amadal
Abode (dwelling place)	Amad(e)
One who abides	Amad + gen. end.

Appendix D

Selected Faeltheon Vocabulary

A

to abide	=	amadat
abiding place	=	amad(e)
abundance. Abundant	=	fyllare, faon
to act	=	agat
an act	=	aga, agen (pl.)
action (to take)	=	heregat (lit. "to lead (with the) hand")
activities (life)	=	agen
to add	=	andat
add	=	an(d)
added to	=	andar, a(n)-
aerial	=	aeria (in the air)
again	=	na-
against	=	oppyx (set cross-wise), o-, o(b)- o(p)-
age (time period)	=	aetas, aetes (pl.)
to aid	=	yuinasat (to help), faonydat (to fill needs)

aid (help)	=	yuinase (help given)
aid (stuff)	=	(see Provision)
air	=	aer, aer-, (aeria, aerie–in the air, eagle's nest)
alert	=	atale, athale
alive	=	chai
all (of us)	=	-on
all (the whole)	=	ao(n)-
alone	=	yue, dysyue (set apart)
and	=	a(n)
to announce	=	talathqualat (lit. "to say strongly")
apart	=	dis, dys
an apiary or hive	=	cathyscyr (from: cathar + hys + scyr)
arm(s)	=	ceryse(n) (from bend = cer + lift = rys)
arrow	=	aerwe (arcs thru the air)(related to wyf–swift, swoop)
artisan	=	erg + gen. end.
to ask	=	quennat
to assist	=	yuinasat
assistant	=	yuinas + gen. end., quimas + gen. end., nasikas = gen. end.
autumn	=	laslornaia (lit. "lost leaf time"), faonydaia (lit. "provision time")
aware	=	atale, athale
away (far)	=	geon, yeon

B

back	=	na-
to bake	=	breherat

bake	=	breher
a baked morsel	=	brea, breen (pl.)
ballad	=	nycaerliende (lit. "sad song")
band (thin strip)	=	da(m), binda, bindah
barley	=	pellihtsean (lit. "white seeds")
barren	=	neanfys ("without growth")
battle	=	haermatle, chailorn (loss of life)
to bear	=	baherat
bear (a burden)	=	baher → b'her → bear
beautiful	=	hadar
because	=	mianare
to become	=	atlat
a bee	=	pelaer + gen. end.
a swarm of bees	=	ghathal (a surrounding cloud)
before	=	regai (lead time)
to begin	=	quimat
a beginning	=	quime
(in the) beginning	=	quimalai
beloved	=	davin, ammar + gen. end.
below	=	nia ("down(ward) place")
to bend	=	cerat, scerat
bend	=	(s)cer
beside, near	=	saewe
best	=	calhaldar (lit. "great good"), cahal-dar, geldar
between	=	cethardwo (surrounded by two), yisneyit (lit "this not that")
to bind	=	demat, bindat
bind	=	de(m), binden
birch	=	bryth, brith, brycht

bitter	=	myr, mir
to bless	=	ashat
blessed	=	ashar
a blessing	=	ash, ashe
to bloom	=	flaerat (lit.: "to open to the air)
a blossom	=	ayapana, ayinpana (pl.) (lit. "open eye"), flaewyr
blue	=	cinth
body (physical)	=	amadru, amadruen (pl.) (from amad + ruach = spirit dwelling)
born	=	nasci (lit. "next + life")
boulder(s)	=	gelithe(n)
bounty, bountiful	=	fyllare
to bow	=	cyrimat, cerimat
bow (gesture)	=	cyrim, cerim
a bow (weapon)	=	cerlim, cyrlim
a braid	=	beherege
a braided loaf	=	breherege
a branch	=	lim, elim
brand (torch)	=	brynne
bread	=	brea, breen (pl.)
to break	=	dysatlat (to (be)come apart)
breast (full)	=	brysse
breath	=	ruach, russ (soft)
Breath of Life	=	elruachai
breeze	=	russ
bright	=	bryht, brycht, breg, bereg
a bright thing	=	brege, bregen (pl.)
to bring	=	brygat, brigat, (related to lead (regat), guide (wigat))

bring	=	bryg
broken	=	dsyatlar
brother	=	delphanos, delphanes (pl.)
brow	=	bhru, beheru, behru
to burn	=	brynnat
burn	=	bryn (related to bryht = bright, breg = flash)
burning	=	brynnal
but	=	oppe
butter	=	yelfaon (lit. "yellow richness")
by	=	mianare

C

candle(s)	=	flyme(n)
candlelight	=	flymyn (related to hlyfyr + myn = flame + small)
to care for	=	faonydat (lit. "to fill the needs"), see "to provide"
to carry	=	weheregat
carry	=	wehereg
a carry sack (backpack)	=	wehere
castle	=	tiros, tiroth
castellan, chatelaine	=	tiregasa (lit. "head castle worker" (fem.))
to cause	=	mianat
cause	=	mian
to cease	=	neagat (to "not-act")
to change	=	n'endat
to chant	=	betal, bethal (a cross between speech and song)
cheese	=	ghylfaon

to cherish	=	secaerat
child	=	fyllandom + gen. end.
children	=	fyllandomon
to choose	=	yuinandarat ("one among many"), yisneyit (lit "this, not that")
cinnamon	=	cinna(m) (the bark), cinnamaon (ground cinna)
a clearing	=	lea (usu. in woods, used for cooking, shelter) (lit "place of light")
cloud	=	gherys, gherlem (dark cloud), gherliht (white, puffy cloud), ghathal (a cloud or swarm), gherceleth (purple storm cloud)
to cluster	=	angatheregat
a cluster	=	angatherege, angathereg + gen. end.
cold	=	cealdh, ceald, (related to celeth = purple)
color(s)	=	omaya, omayin
to come	=	gwennat
consecrate(d)	=	ael (lit. "to God")
to continue	=	endat
a cover	=	pel, pelle
to cover	=	pellat
to create	=	mianatlat (lit.: to cause to become)
create	=	mianatlan
creation/creature	=	mianatle- + gen. end.
creative	=	geligel- + gen. end. (lit: like God)
creator	=	mianatl- + gen. end.

the Creator	=	Aematlon (lit.: One Who willed all to become)
cross purpose(s)	=	oppyxaeme(n)
crossroads	=	pyxrandia
crown (of a ship)	=	cerdem, cyrdem
crown (diadem, circlet)	=	cether, atarah, (jeweled: cethastea, atarastea)
crown (brow-band)	=	bhrudam, bhrudastea (jeweled)
to cry (weep)	=	saerwysat
to cry out	=	rearat, rarat
a cry	=	rear (implies "cry to someone"–see rea=friend)
curve	=	(s)cer , (s)cyr (related to cyb)
curved	=	cyrrar, cyrar, (s)cyrar
curving	=	cyrral, cyral, (s)cyral, whence; circle

Ð

daddy	=	see Papa
to dance	=	(s)wypat, (s)wyfat (related to swift, swoop, arrow), hlypat, hlyfat, hleapat, hleafat (to dance for joy, to leap for joy)
dance	=	(s)wyp, (s)wif (twist, turn quickly), hlyf, hlyp, hleap, hleaf
a dance	=	(s)wype, (s)wypen (pl.), etc.
dark ones (Goblins)	=	lemyuran (lit. "ones who walk the night")
darkness	=	lem, lam
daughter	=	delphiel, -iel
dawn	=	quimliht (lit. "first light")
day	=	cieliht

dead	=	finnar
death	=	finyas
to decide	=	yuinandarat ("one among many"), yisneyit ("this, not that")
to declare	=	talathqualat (to say strongly)
deer	=	cerven (pl), (lit: "joined curve," for the antlers), cerva (doe), cervos (stag), cermyn (fawn), cerwyn (archaic)
to defend	=	pellhaermat
defender	=	pellhaerm + gen. end.
to depart	=	geat, gehat (related to away (geon))
depart	=	ge(o)
depressed	=	nicaerar
desire	=	wenne
desire (darkly)	=	dyscwenne (from dyscerar wenne = twisted desire)
dew	=	mynwys, minwys
difference	=	nagelic (unlike)
to differentiate	=	cegenagelat (to think on differences), yisneyit ("this, not that")
discernment	=	ruachomma
dissonance, discord	=	snear liende, snehere liende (intentional), (lit.: "tangled song")
distance	=	gelgeon
distant	=	geon, yeon
to divide	=	diat (in two), driat (into thirds)
to do	=	fyat
doing	=	fyal
dolphin	=	delphys + gen. end.(for their beauty and for being mammals)

doom	=	izhodan
down (ward)	=	ni, ny
dragon	=	dragaeron (from ra(myn) +g(hyl) +aer(ys) +on: lit: "tiny precious shining fliers")
dragon silk (raw or woven)	=	dragiriden (from drag(aeron) iridal: lit.: "dragon's shimmerings")
dream(s)	=	dreme(n)
a drinking skin	=	brysse
to dwell	=	amadat
dwelling place, land	=	doma, domea, dur

E

east	=	derre
to echo	=	naliennat (lit. "to sing back")
echo	=	nalienn
Elf	=	aelf
Elven	=	aelfi
to encompass	=	catharat, atarat
to end	=	fylaraiat
end	=	fylarai
(in the) end	=	fylarai (lit.: "fullness of time")
endurance	=	ende
to endure	=	endat
entire	=	ao(n)-
-est	=	gel-, cal- (add prefix of "great)
eternal	=	anel, antheon
ever	=	ai
evil	=	dyscerar, + gen. end. (twisted, from split apart from God)

eye	=	aya, ayin (pl.)

F

to fade	=	finnat
fading	=	finnal
fair (beautiful)	=	fael
faith	=	am
faithful	=	aman
fall (season)	=	–see Autumn
to fall	=	aernat (from aer (air) + ni (down))
falling	=	aernal
fallen, fell	=	aernar
far (away)	=	geon, yeon
farmer	=	saew + gen. end.
family (nuclear)	=	driatle (from driatlat: to become three)
farther	=	geonder, yeonder
father	=	saenos
to favor	=	domashat (lit.: "to give blessing")
favor	=	domashe
fear	=	neam ("no faith")
female, feminine	=	-a
fertile	=	chaiheregal (lit. "holding life"), cheregal (contr.), aon- ("rich")
field (n.)	=	fyld, fylld, fylde, fyldh
to fight (defend)	=	pellhaermat
to fight (destroy, war)	=	haermatlat (to unmake with malicious intent)
to fill	=	fyllanat
fill	=	fyllan

filled, full, fullness = fyllar, fylar
final (last) = naon (lit.: back (of) all)
to find = emheregat
to finish = fylaraiat
finish = fylarai (lit.: fullness of time, or filled with time)
fire! (archery command) = aerweon (lit. "arrows away!")
fire = fyr, fyre, hlyfyre (hot fire)
to set or start a fire = hlyfyrat (to set a fire dancing)
fiery = fyren
first = quim
flame = hlyfyr (leaping fire)
flesh = amadru, amadruen (pl.) (from amad + ruach = spirit dwelling)
flight (aerial) = aerys
flour = brean
to flourish = flaerashat (lit.: "to bloom with blessing")
to flow = russhat, russat
to flower = flaerat
a flower = flaewyr (a flared curve)
flowing = russhal, russal
to fly = aerysat (lit. lift (into the) air)
fly = aerys
to follow = nasigat
follow = nasig
follower = nasig + gen. end.
foot, feet = ran, ren
for = a- (for someone), because (mianare)
to forget = diatalat, diathalat, disthalat (lit: "not mindful")

a forgotten thing	=	diatale, disthale
forfeit	=	dollar ("yielded")
to (be) free	=	freat, friat
to (set) free	=	neademat
free	=	frea, fria (also a little bird)
free (released)	=	neadem
freedom	=	freon
friend	=	rea, reaen (pl.)
from	=	yehon
frost	=	n'ix (from archaic form: napyxes = pattern of repeated stars or Crosses, see: snow, ice)
fruit	=	pellysse, pellyssen (lit. "sweet thing with skin")
full	=	fylar, fyllar
fur	=	pel(t)
future	=	gwennataia, gwenn'aia ("in days to come"), gwennataetas, gwenn'aetas ("in ages to come")

G

galley	=	gaellea (sheltered place to cook at sea)
galleon	=	gaelyeon (a ship to sail far upon the sea)
to gather	=	gatheregat (from catharat = to surround or encompass + heregat = to hold)
gentle	=	min-, minya
gift	=	dom, don, dol, dole, neth (ability)
to gild	=	ghyllat

gild	=	ghyl (shine w/silvery-golden light)
to give	=	domat, dollat (archaic–more at yield))
giver	=	dom + gen. end
gleam	=	glam
glimmer	=	gher (shine w/white or silver light)
glory	=	iridis, iridys
to go	=	geat, gehat (related to far (geon))
go	=	ge(o)
goal	=	wenne, wynne
goat	=	geoat
Goblins	=	lemyuran, lemuran
Goblin territory	=	lemuria, lamyuria
God	=	el, theo
God's	=	eli, -iel (of God)
God the Creator	=	aematlan
God the Father	=	elsaenos
God's Spirit	=	elaem, elruach
gold	=	ghyl
golden	=	ghyllen
good	=	haldar,elder(relatedtohadar=beauty, honor=heder, shine=hal)
grace (favor)	=	dashe (contraction of domashe)
grace of God	=	dashiel
grains	=	ghyllsaen (lit. "golden seeds")
to grasp	=	emheregat (lit.: to take hold)
great	=	gel, gel-, gil, gyl-, cal
greatest (mightiest)	=	meagel, maecal

great with child	=	delphys, delfys (lit. swelled womb) (highest accolade of beauty)
greed	=	dysceregé (from dyscerar heregal = twisted holding)
green	=	gren
greetings (see May God bless you, May God guard you)		
grief	=	saer
grim	=	nicaer
ground (earth)	=	dur
a grove	=	lea
a growing thing	=	growan = gen. end., ghren (plant) + gen. end.
to grow (swell up)	=	physat, fysat
grow (swell, as with child, or a bud)	=	phys, fys (related to fyl = fill, full)
to guard	=	tallat, thallat
Guardian	=	tal-, thal- + gen. end., athal- + gen. end.
guard post	=	talan, thalan
guidance	=	wige
to guide	=	wigat, wygat (related to wehereg = carry)
a guide	=	wige-, wyg- + gen. end.

H

hair	=	pel, pelle
hand	=	her, heren (pl.), man (to give a hand, to aid w/the hand)

handful	=	= herfyl (a unit of measurement ~ ½ Cup)
happy	=	= rysarcaer (lit.: lifted heart)
happiness	=	= rysarcaeren (light heartedness)
to harm	=	= haermat
harm	=	= haer(m)
harmony	=	= beheret liende (lit. woven song)
to harvest	=	catheregat (from catharat = to encompass + herehat = to hold)
a harvest	=	catherege
haven	=	lionde, liande
he	=	yo
to hear	=	atalenat, athalenat (lit: alert to sound)
heart	=	caer, car, careen (pl.), careen (pl.)
to heat	=	hlyat
heat (v.)	=	hlyt (related to halit = sun)
heat (n.)	=	hlyte (also "a hot thing")
heather	=	calleth + gen. ending. (from ca l+ celeth = great (expanse of) purple
heaven	=	aneldom
to help	=	yuinasat (to aid), faonydat (to fill needs)
helper	=	yuinas + gen. end.
her	=	yam (obj.), yar (poss.)
here	=	se (present), sia ("this place")
hers	=	yarn (poss. adj.)
hidden	=	tamar
to hide	=	tamat, tammat
high	=	rab
him	=	yom

hip(s)	=	hlyp(en) (related to curve (s'cer) and dance (hleap))
his	=	yor (poss.), yorn (poss. adj.)
to hold	=	heregat, herecat
holding	=	heregal
a holder	=	herege, heregen (pl.)
holly	=	hallas hallys, from hal+las (or lys) = shining leaf (leaves)
home	=	doma, dor, amad, amar
honey	=	ghylysse (golden sweetness)
honor	=	eder, heder (related to beauty =hadar)
honored (one)	=	hedar + gen. end.
hope	=	elaman
hot	=	hlyten
house	=	dom, amad(e)
housekeeper	=	domasa
however	=	see "but"
to hug	=	cerysatarat (from arms (cerysen) + encompass (atarat))

I

I	=	í
ice	=	h'ix (from hys + pyxes = six-sided stars)
in	=	-i
in order that	=	mianare
inside, inner	=	qwin
to insist	=	talathqualat (to say strongly), qual-laemat (to say one's will)
to instruct	=	(s)ceregat

in the beginning	=	quimalai
in the end	=	fylarai
in-love	=	ami + gen. end.
intent	=	aem
it	=	yu (subj.), yum (obj.)
its	=	yur (poss.), yurn (poss. adj.)

J

to join	=	yuanat (to wed), yuinat (lit. "one-with"), gwennat
joy	=	hlalriel, elrys
to journey (quest)	=	randellat
journey	=	randel, randelen (pl.)
to jump	=	hleapat

K

a kid	=	hleamyn + gen. end. (lit. "little dancer" or "little one who leaps for joy")
kin	=	ammi- + gen. end. (lit. "Loved one(s)")
to knot	=	sneherat (whence snarl, sneer)
a knot	=	snehere, binden (to make secure)
to know	=	cenat, genat
know	=	cen, gen (whence ken)
knowledge	=	cene, gene

L

lamb	=	hleamyn + gen. end. (lit. "little dancer" or "little one who leaps for joy")
land	=	dur, domea

language	=	fylloloquen
to laugh	=	lysat, lisat
laughter	=	lysia, lyse, lise
to lead	=	regat
leader	=	reg + gen. end., -eg + gen. end.
leaf	=	las, lys
to leap	=	hleapat
to learn (skills or methods)	=	nasigat sceregon (lit: "to follow teachers")
to learn (facts or information)	=	braheregenat (lit: "to gather knowledge")
a learner (apprentice, trainee)	=	nasig + gen. end. sceregon
a learner (student)	=	braheregen + gen. end.
learning (v.)	=	nasigal sceregon, braheregenal
learning (n.)	=	erge, braheregene
to leave	=	geat, gehat
leg(s)	=	hleag(en), hleagel (archaic) (from "great dance")
life (daily)	=	agen
life (alive)	=	chai
life (aware)	=	ruachai (lit. breath of life)
to lift	=	rysat, risat
to lift a shout or cry	=	rarysat, rearysat
light (luminescence)	=	liht, leht, lucin (poss. from another language, as the c is soft like an s; generally refers to moonlight, or pale light)
light (pale, white)	=	pelliht (from pelle + liht = luminous skin, like a birch tree)
like (unto)	=	gelig, gelic

to listen	=	atalenat, athalenat (to be mindful of sounds)
lithe	=	hlythe, hlithe (a supple movement)
to live	=	chaiat (to be alive)
long	=	gelgeon (distance), gelaia (time)
to look	=	omnat
Lord	=	rysar + gen. end. (lit. "lifted one")
lost	=	lorn
to love	=	ammat
love (n.)	=	aem, aemm
loved one	=	ammar + gen. end.
lover	=	amm + gen. end.

M

maiden	=	-wyn, -wen, -ien, -iel
to make	=	fyalat (related to fyl and atlan)
male, masculine	=	-os
malice	=	haer(m)
mama	=	amma, affectionate term derived from babytalk
many	=	nandaren (lit. "added again") (pl.)
marriage (the life)	=	yuane
marriage (the ceremony)	=	yuani
to marry	=	yuanat (lit. "to become one")
may (it be that)	=	cyb (lit. inclined toward) (the word "curve" will evolve from this) (Also khib, from which will come "hip")
may God bless you	=	Cybel ash (gender) (traditional greeting)

may God guard you	=	Cybel thal (gender) (traditional parting)
me	=	ím
meadow	=	fyldh, fyld, fylld, fylde (field, fold, wold)
meet	=	yuin (lit. "one with")
meaning	=	aem
merriment	=	lysia, lyse, lise
merry	=	lysi + gen. end.
message (urgent)	=	rare, raren (pl.), rearen (+ gen. end. for urgent messenger)
might (power)	=	maeg, maec
mighty (one)	=	meag + gen. end., maec + gen. end.
to milk	=	bryssat
milk (v.)	=	bryss
milk (n.)	=	faonbrysse (lit. "richness, abundance from the breast")
mindful	=	atale, athale (lit. "on guard")
mine	=	írn
mist	=	ghatharal (lit. "silvery surrounding")
mortal	=	finn + gen. end.
mother	=	delpha, also see "mama"
my	=	ír

N

to name	=	nomat, namat
name	=	nom (personal), nam (impersonal, ungendered)
near	=	saewe
nectar	=	lywys, (from lyssi + wys + "sweet water")

to need	=	nydat, neodat
need	=	nyd, neod
needful (having needs)	=	nydfyl, nydfaon
negation, negative	=	ne-, nea-, nae- (prefix)
new	=	nov, niwe
newborn	=	nasci
a newborn	=	nasci + gen. end.
next	=	nasik, nausik
next to	=	saewe
night	=	cielem, cielam
no	=	ne, nae
none, nothing	=	n'yú (lit. "no thing")
no more, nevermore	=	nanae (lit. "not again")
no one	=	n'yu
north	=	lom
now	=	yisaia (lit. "this time")

O

oats	=	brysaen (lit. "flat seeds")
to obstruct	=	sneherat
of	=	-i
on	=	a-
on guard	=	atale, athale
on the other hand	=	see "but"
one	=	yu (lit. "this one")
open	=	pana
to oppose	=	oppyxat (to set cross-wise), opendat (to resist physically)
or	=	nan

orange (fruit, smell)	=	n'arome(n) (from na + arome = "to smell again," from the way the strong scent lingers on the hands after eating the fruit)
orange (color)	=	narom (adj.), narome(noun), (from the fruit)
our	=	ir + gen. end.
ours	=	irn + gen. end.
out	=	izo(n) (from dys + yeon → exo-)
outward, outside, outer	=	izho(n)
overlooked	=	diathale, disthale

P

pale	=	finnar (lit. "faded"), pelliht (luminous skin, like a birch tree)
palm (hand)	=	herdel (lit. hand-hollow)
papa	=	abbos–an affectionate term derived from babytalk
to part	=	diatlat (lit.: to become two)
a part (of)	=	myne
parting	=	diatlal
parts (of)	=	mynen
past (time)	=	geharaia ("in days gone (by) or "in days departed"), finnaraia ("in days faded")
past (distant)	=	geharaetas ("in ages departed"), finnaraetas ("in ages faded")
path	=	randia
patience	=	ende (endurance), erende (at peace while enduring)

peace	=	eranel (lit. "rest with God"–a physical or emotional state)
peace	=	eriel (lit. "rest in God"–a spiritual state)
people	=	elen, elon
place (where)	=	-tys, -tis, -ia, -ria
plain (field)	=	fyldh, fyld
plan	=	aem
to plan	=	aemat
a plan, plans	=	aeme, aemen
a plant	=	growan, ghren
power	=	rad, rod, rob, maeg (might)
praise	=	halash, hlalash
to pray	=	rysliendat
a prayer	=	rysarliende
precious	=	dra (from dramyn–a tiny precious thing)
a precious thing (s)	=	drae, draen
presence	=	sa, seh
the presence (God)	=	elisa, eliseh
present (here)	=	se
press (v.)	=	bryss
to press	=	bryssat
to promise	=	venat (from wenat = to wish)
a promise	=	vene
to provide	=	faonydat
provider	=	faonyd + gen. end.
provision	=	faonyden
purple	=	celeth
purpose	=	aem

Q

To quest	=	randellat
a quest	=	randel
to question	=	quennat
a question	=	quenna, quennen (pl.)
a questioner	=	quen + gen. end.
a questor	=	randel + gen. end.

R

rain	=	niwys, nywys (lit: downward water)
rainbow	=	ciridis, ceridis
to reason	=	cegenat (whence–cognate)
to receive	=	edomat (related to take = emat + a gift = dom)
to release	=	neademat (to "not-bind")
to remain	=	endat
to repair	=	nademat (lit. "to bind again")
to repeat	=	na'at
repeat	=	na
to rescue	=	yehaermat (lit. "to (make) distant (from) harm")
rescue	=	yehaerm
rescuer	=	yehaerm + gen. end.
to resist	=	oppendat
to rest	=	erat
rest	=	ere
rest (place of)	=	eren, ertys
resting state (peace)	=	eranel, eriel (lit. "rest with God," "rest in God")
resulting in	=	mianare

to reveal	=	kythat
revelation	=	kythe
rich (full, complete)	=	ao(n)
richness	=	faon, aone
right (correct)	=	riht
road	=	randia
rose (flower/color)	=	rosa, rossa
to rotate	=	nascyrat (repeat curve)
round	=	cyr-
rounded	=	cyrar, cyrrar
royal	=	rysar, risar + gen. end.
rye	=	lemsaen (lit. "dark seeds")

S

sad	=	nycaer
sadness	=	nycaere
say, says	=	qual, quall
to scatter	=	dismynat
scatter	=	dismynen ("many pieces apart")
a (pleasant) scent	=	arome, aromen (pl.)
to scent	=	romat
to scent the air	=	aromat (from aer + rom)
scoop (v.)	=	s'cwyp (from s'cer + swyp = rounded swoop)
to scoop	=	s'cwypat
a scoop	=	s'cwype (a ladle made to replace the "handful" measurement)
sea	=	gael
to search	=	omnaemat (to look with purpose)
season	=	-aia, -aien (pl.)

second	=	nasik, nausik- + gen. end.
to see	=	ommat
seed	=	sae, saen (pl.)
to seek	=	omnaemat (to look with purpose)
seer (prophet)	=	kyth + gen. end.
to select	=	yuinandarat ("one among many")
Seneschal	=	tiregasos (lit. "head castle worker" (male))
to share (out)	=	mynat (to split)
to share (in)	=	yuinat (to join with)
a share	=	myne (a portion)
she	=	ya
sheep	=	s'ceap + gen. end.
shield	=	pelle
to shield	=	pellat
to shimmer	=	iridat
shimmering	=	iridal
to shine	=	halat, hlalat, gherat (silvery), ghyllat (golden)
shining	=	halal, glimring (gleaming)
ship(s)	=	gaelyeon
shoot (tender plant)	=	linde+ gen. end, lindy
shoulder(s)	=	nascere(n) (from rotate = nascyr)
to shout	=	rarat, rearat
a shout	=	rar
to show (demonstrate)	=	(s)ceregat
sibling	=	delphan- + gen. end. (lit. "with-womb," shared womb)
side	=	lat(e), laten (sides)
silence	=	nelen (lit. "no sound")

silver	=	gher, ghyr
to sing	=	liennat
singer	=	lienn + gen. end.
sight	=	omma, omme
sister	=	delphana, delphanen (pl.)
six	=	hys
skill	=	erge
skilled worker	=	erg + gen. end.
skin	=	pelle
sky	=	ciel
to sleep	=	lullat
sleep	=	lulla, lullen
small (thing)	=	mynym
small (one)	=	myn- + gen. end.
to smell, sniff	=	romat
snow	=	n'ix (from archaic form: napyxes = pattern of repeated stars or crosses), hysna (from hys + na = repeated hexagons), nahys
soar	=	swyry, swyri (lit. "to swoop upwards")
so that	=	mianare
soft (gentle)	=	min-, minya
son	=	delphion, -ion
song	=	liende, lienden (pl.)
soon	=	swai, (from swift + time)
sorrow (s)	=	saer(en)
sound	=	len, lien (musical sound), lint, lent (sharp sound)
south	=	lath
sow (seed)	=	saew(e)
to sow	=	saewat

sower (farmer)	=	saew+ gen. end.
sower (father)	=	saenos
to speak	=	quallat
speech	=	quallen
a sphere	=	s'phyre (from s'cer + physar = swelled curve)
spherical, spheroid	=	s'phyr
spice(s)	=	arome, aromen
spicy	=	aromyn (lit. "little scent")
spiral	=	s'phyral (from s'cer + phys + al = curve swelling (outward)), nascyre (rotate, repeat curve)
spirit	=	ruach
The Spirit (of God)	=	Ruachos
split	=	(in two parts) - dia, (in three parts)–dria, drya, (into small parts) —mynen
to split (into pieces)	=	mynat
spring (season)	=	ayinpanaia (lit. "blossom time"), dhalaia (lit. "sprouting time"), delaia (lit. "pregnant time, or time of the womb")
to sprout	=	dalat, dhalat
a sprout	=	dal-, dhal- + gen. end.
to squeeze	=	bryssat
squeeze (v.)	=	byrss
to stand (unbending)	=	endat, (endyt; old vers.)
to stand against	=	opendat (to oppose physically)
star	=	stea, astea (pl.)
steadfast	=	talath, thalath

steward	=	tiregasos (lit. "head castle worker" (m.))
still	=	end (yet, even so, continue, remain)
stillness	=	n'agen (lit. "no activity"), n'ceral (lit. "no bending, no turning")
stone(s)	=	lithe(n), lythe(n)
to stop	=	neagat (to "not-act")
storm (rain)	=	gelniwys (lit. "great rain")
storm (violent)	=	maegwys (lit. "mighty water")
storm cloud	=	gherceleth (lit. "purple cloud")
strength	=	ethan, ethal
to stroke	=	bryssat
stroke (v.)	=	bryys
strong	=	talath, thalath
sugar	=	lysse, lyssen (sweet things)
summer	=	aonaia (lit. "rich time"), growenaia (lit. "growing time")
sun	=	haliht
supple	=	hlythe, hlithe
to supply	=	faonydat
to surround	=	catharat, atarat
swarm (of bees)	=	ghathal
sweet	=	lissi, lyssi
to swell	=	physat, fysat
swelled up, puffed out	=	physar
swift	=	swyf, swy-
swollen	=	physar
swoop	=	swyr (related to (s)cyr = curve, bend), swyp (related to (s)wyp = dance)

T

to take	=	emat
to take action	=	heregat (lit. "to lead (with the) hand")
to tangle	=	sneherat (with intent), snearat (accidental)
tangy	=	cytra, cythra, citra
a tangy thing	=	cytre, cythre
a task	=	asa, asen (pl)
to teach	=	(s)ceregat (lit.: to lead (through the) twist or turn)
teacher	=	(s)cereg + gen. end.
tear(s)	=	saerwyse(n)
thank you	=	ea ash ím (lit. "you bless me"), see other gender forms
that	=	yit
the	=	yi
their	=	y'r + gen. end.
theirs	=	yrn + gen. end.
them	=	y'm + gen. end.
then	=	yitaia ("that time")
there	=	yitsia ("that place")
these	=	y'is
they	=	y + gen. end.
to think	=	cegenat
third	=	dri- + gen. end,
this	=	yis
those	=	y'it
a thought	=	cegene, cegenen (pl.)
thread	=	brege, bregen (pl.) (lit. "a bright or flashing thing")

three	=	dri-, drio, dri - + gen. end, if persons
time	=	aia (related to ever (ai), life (chai))
today	=	yiscieliht (lit. "this day")
together	=	gatheregar
tomorrow	=	nasicieliht (lit. "next day")
toward	=	a-
to travel	=	randat
traveler	=	rand + gen. end.
travels	=	rande, randen (pl.)
treasure	=	secar, secaer
tree	=	drys, dris + gen. end.
true (steadfast, unchanging)	=	drys, dris
truth	=	druth, dryth
trust (worthy)	=	dryst, dristhe
to turn (or twist)	=	cerat, scerat
to turn the opposite way (180)	=	cerpyxat (to turn cross-wise)
twisted (evil)	=	dyscerar, dyscerar + gen. end.
two	=	dwo, diwo

U

unchanged	=	n'end
under	=	nia ("down(ward) place")
unhappy	=	nicaer (down-heart)
unique	=	yunagelic ("one unlike others")
unicorn(s)	=	yunarcyr = gen. end, yunarcyron, (lit.: "one repeated curve")
until	=	a'aia (lit. "toward the time")
up (wards)	=	ry, ri
urgent message	=	raren, rearen (+ gen. end. for urgent messenger)

us (all)	=	im + gen. end.

V

valiant	=	caerdrys, caerdris (lit. "tree-heart," "trueheart")
victor	=	vic + gen. end., vyg + gen. end.
vigilant	=	geoat (lit. "far alertness")
violet (the color)	=	vi(o)-
to Vow	=	venat (from wenat = to wish)
a vow	=	vene

W

to wait	=	endat
to wake	=	atalat
wake(ful)	=	atal
to wander, walk	=	randat
to war	=	haermatlat
war	=	haermatle
warrior (defender)	=	pellhaerm + gen. end.
to watch	=	tallat, thallat
watcher	=	tal-, thal- + gen. end.
a watch (one keeps)	=	tale, thale
watchtower	=	talan, thalan
water	=	wys
wave(s)	=	beherwys (lit.: flashing water, or water weaving)
way (path)	=	randia
we	=	í + gen. end.
weak	=	minyethan
weakness	=	minyethal

to weave	=	beherat
a weaver	=	beherec + gen. end.
weaver of Life	=	Beherechai
a weaving (woven thing)	=	beherete
to wed	=	yuanat
wedding (ceremony)	=	yuani
to weep	=	saerwysat
weeping	=	saerwysal
welcome	=	gwen
went	=	gehar (past tense of "to go")
west	=	desse
wheat	=	ghyllsaen (golden seeds)
when	=	aiai (lit. "in the days," or "in time")
where	=	ria?, tys? (lit. "place?")
whisper	=	russ
white	=	pelliht
who, what, which?	=	yù (a question; lit. "one?")
wild (adj.)	=	wyld (usually refers to undergrowth)
wild (n.)	=	wylde
wilderness	=	wylden
will (spirit, purpose, intent)	=	aem
to win (achieve a goal)	=	wynat, wynnat, vicat (to win a contest)
wind	=	ruach, russ (soft, light, or warm)
winter	=	endalaia (lit. "enduring time"), finnalaia (lit. "fading time"), finnaia (lit. "dead time")
wisdom	=	eliom
to wish	=	wenat
a wish (or goal)	=	wenne, wynne

with	=	an, an-
within	=	qwin (from qwennat = to enter + -i = in)
without	=	nean, nean-
wold	=	fyld (field, meadow)
womb	=	del, delle (whence dhel (cavity, hollow), delve, dell, dale)
woods	=	wyd, wydon, (pl.)
wool	=	gherpeliht (lit. "cloud fur")
word	=	loqua, loquen (pl.), bet, beth (more at chant)
work (task)	=	asa, asen (pl.)
work (great, skilled)	=	ergasa, ergasen
work (set by God)	=	asel

Y

yellow	=	ghaliht, ghalle, yelhe, yalhe
yet	=	n'end (unchanged)
to yield	=	dollat
you	=	ea, eo (subj.), eam, eom (obj.)
you (all)	=	e'+gen. end.(subj.) , em+ gen. end. (obj.)
your	=	ear, eor, er-+gen. end. (pl.)
yours	=	earn, eorn , ern + gen. end. (pl.)
young	=	nov
young (one)	=	nov-+ gen. end.

Appendix E

Gallery

The Isle of Egauswas

The Cethastea

Elwyn Elenthea, Lady of Marliondolen

Theomanus Quaeliom, Master of Marliondolen

Nausika Brithoniel, called Clever Nausika

Laslorn Lyserea, called Laslorn of the Merry Heart,
a skilled treehome shaper

Lucina Brithwyd, called Lucina Trueheart

Davin Iridistheon, former Border Guard

Elrad Ruachliende, a wise Seer, called Kythos Elrad

Chassidy Cooper, called Sky-Eyes

Robse Lyserea, Champion to King Aelric

Aelric Rysaelf, King of the Elves

Caerdrys Gaelathnalienn, a Companion of King Aelric

Gaelcar Talathaem, Seneschal to King Aelric

Minlienda Elashar, a Companion of King Aelric

Myrandella Durilyse, a Kytha and healer

Running before the wind with Ghaerwe's pod

Corot of Lemyuria

e|LIVE

---

listen|imagine|view|experience

AUDIO BOOK DOWNLOAD INCLUDED WITH THIS BOOK!

In your hands you hold a complete digital entertainment package. Besides purchasing the paper version of this book, this book includes a free download of the audio version of this book. Simply use the code listed below when visiting our website. Once downloaded to your computer, you can listen to the book through your computer's speakers, burn it to an audio CD or save the file to your portable music device (such as Apple's popular iPod) and listen on the go!

How to get your free audio book digital download:

1. Visit www.tatepublishing.com and click on the e|LIVE logo on the home page.
2. Enter the following coupon code: 0796-529e-c614-0164-fd27-910e-2f9c-1e24
3. Download the audio book from your e|LIVE digital locker and begin enjoying your new digital entertainment package today!